# *Jonathan Dearborn*

# BOOKS BY WILLARD M. WALLACE

## Nonfiction

**APPEAL TO ARMS**
*A Military History of the American Revolution*

**TRAITOROUS HERO**
*The Life and Fortunes of Benedict Arnold*

**SIR WALTER RALEIGH**

**SOUL OF THE LION**
*A Biography of General Joshua L. Chamberlain*

**INTERVIEW IN WEEHAWKEN**
*The Burr-Hamilton Duel as told in the Original Documents*
*(Edited by Harold C. Syrett and Jean G. Cook*
*with an Introduction and Conclusion by Willard M. Wallace)*

## Fiction

**EAST TO BAGADUCE**
**JONATHAN DEARBORN**

## Juvenile

**FRIEND WILLIAM**

# Jonathan Dearborn

## A Novel of the War of 1812

### by WILLARD M. WALLACE

Little, Brown and Company · Boston · Toronto

LIBRARY OF CONGRESS CATALOG CARD NO. 67-11225

*Third Printing*

*Published simultaneously in Canada
by Little, Brown & Company (Canada) Limited*

PRINTED IN THE UNITED STATES OF AMERICA

**To**
my wife
Elizabeth M. Wallace
and
my friend
**Gorham Munson**

# *Acknowledgments*

I WISH to express gratitude and thanks to friends who have listened to the adventures of Jonathan Dearborn and who have made useful suggestions, even to bibliography. I desire to mention in particular my wife, my indebtedness to whom I could not attempt to measure; my good friend Gorham Munson, unfailing source of encouragement and constructive criticism, whose superb book *Penobscot: Down East Paradise* was a proverbial mine of information; my daughter Pamela for her enthusiastic interest and devoted service in transcribing my scrawling handwriting into workable typewritten copy; and Mrs. William Hay for her gracious and expert rendering of the final draft.

# *Contents*

# ONE

## *The European Adventures*
## *of*
## *Privateersman Jonathan Dearborn*
## *of Maine*

[September, 1813–August, 1814]

# I

THE sound of running footsteps on the gravel sidewalk below my window startled me. Perhaps I should say it really woke me up from my dozing over the laws of property as expounded in Blackstone's *Commentaries*, a great but very dull work which Mr. Stephen Longfellow, Jr., had urged me, only that late forenoon, to review. I had listened to a case he was pleading on the second floor of the courthouse down on Congress Street, and I had been so hazy in my knowledge of the principles of property law that he directed me, in a kindly but very firm manner, to remove my deficiencies at once. I fear he found me all too often a delinquent student, though I truly appreciated the privilege of reading law with him.

"Jonathan, they're about to begin!"

I stuck my head out of the window and saw Brad Pettigrew down below, his blue eyes aflame with excitement.

"Who's about to begin what?" I asked sleepily.

"The ships. They're about to start fighting."

"What ships?" For the life of me, I didn't know what he was talking about.

"The *Enterprise* and the *Boxer!* Don't tell me you've forgotten!"

"You're right," I admitted, my sleepiness vanishing. "Can we see them from Munjoy Hill?"

He shook his head. "It's too far away. They're off Monhegan Island. But Captain Lemuel Moody up in the Observatory has the telescope all lined up. He'll make sure we know what's happening. We'd better hurry!"

I leaped down the stairs three at a time, told my mother where I was going, and joined Brad in a rush.

[ 3 ]

As we hurried up to the Observatory on that fifth day of September, 1813, it seemed that all Portland was also streaming toward the east end of the town. It wasn't every day that we were this near to a sea fight. Besides, the English brig *Boxer*, fourteen guns, under Captain Samuel Blythe had made her presence felt along our coast and Captain William Burrows of the *Enterprise*, sixteen guns, had promised to bring home the *Boxer*'s colors.

"If you ask me, it'll be anyone's battle," Brad said.

"Not the way I see it."

"You think the *Boxer* will win?"

"I do not!"

"But Burrows is new. Besides, the *Enterprise* is an old ship and slow. You know she's slow, Jonathan."

"Yes," I said, "but she handles well, she's got a good crew, and Burrows is a real seaman even if he's had her only a month. And don't forget, Brad, she has one more gun in each broadside than the *Boxer*. I'll bet you the *Enterprise* wins in less than an hour, maybe even thirty minutes, after they start pounding each other."

"I hope you're right, but just to make it a little interesting, I'll stake you to a glass of rum."

"On the *Boxer*?"

"Hell, no!" and Brad shook his head as if trying to ward off an attack of midges. "D'you think me a Federalist or a traitor? I'll bet you're wrong on the time — I say it will take at least an hour."

"Done!" I exclaimed, and we shook hands on the rum. "But I'll have to drink it at your house or down at the Eagle Tavern," I added quickly. "You know what my parents think of spirits, except for medicinal purposes."

"Better make it the tavern," he laughed. "My mother can't stand the smell of rum, though she likes a glass of wine."

Reaching the Observatory, we still found ourselves some distance from it because of the crowd. We could see Captain Moody on the platform staring through the telescope. Several men were with him, and, after conferring, one of them, a little man in a bluebottle coat with brass buttons, would come out on the balcony and announce to us what was happening. He had a voice that boomed over our heads like a conch shell on a fog-bound sloop. I could hardly believe that a

[4]

man of his size could have such a monstrous voice. Presently he remained on the balcony as Captain Moody passed on to him what he saw.

"Who is he?" I asked Brad.

As Brad shook his head and stepped forward to ask the information from a man in front of us, a voice behind me said suavely, "His name is Benjamin Vail, Dearborn."

I turned around, and recognized Warren Bierce, one of the principal merchants in our town of Portland. Bierce was at least ten years older than myself, and I had been born in 1789, the year the Constitution was adopted. He was a lean but powerful man, skillful with sword and pistol and a good hunter and yachtsman. He was also a successful businessman who had moved to Portland from Boston just before President Jefferson's Embargo and had no sooner arrived than he became an outspoken critic of Jefferson and the Republicans. After the lifting of the Embargo he had evidently done very well for himself, and was thriving during the war. Apart from his politely patronizing manner particularly towards his juniors and his less successful rivals, I think what annoyed me most about him was that shortly after war with England broke out in 1812, he had published a letter in the *Portland Gazette* criticizing my father's reluctance to speak on political issues from the pulpit. My father had ignored the letter, but I had had sharp words with Bierce in his office which thereafter kept us on practically a nonspeaking basis.

"Thanks," I said curtly at his explanation, and glanced, then stared, at the young woman with him.

Though our town had only about eight thousand people, a young lawyer-hopeful like myself, busy with his reading, doesn't make everyone's acquaintance, especially since I had spent the three years between 1805 and 1808 at sea, most of the time on two of my Uncle Tom Dearborn's ships, and from 1808 to 1812 at Harvard College. I would have preferred going to sea again after my graduation, but, out of respect for my parents, I agreed to study law. I had thus had little time for socializing. Certainly I had never met the girl whose Celtic blue eyes looked so arresting in a face tinted ever so slightly golden by the sun and surrounded by a straw bonnet beneath whose wide brim peeped tendrils of thick black hair.

Still, I knew of this girl, as who did not in Portland? She was India Mitchell, niece and ward of that formidable old grampus, Judge Jason Kent. The Judge had lost his seat when the Federalists went down in the election of 1800, and had never since failed to allude to a Republican as "a damned Jeffersonian" or "a democratic jackass," or some such appellation. He divided his life between the bar and the sea but reportedly made no financial success of either, though he antagonized many a jury by his gruffness, in which there was both ill will and contempt.

India had been his ward for at least ten years. She was the daughter of a sister whose marriage to Captain Vernon Mitchell of Cape Elizabeth he had vigorously opposed as beneath the Kents. The Mitchells gave their child the name India because she was born while their ship was lying in Bombay Harbor. Years later, when Captain Mitchell and his wife died of yellow fever in Jamaica and a friendly sea captain brought India home, the Judge and his wife took charge of the girl. She had tutors and trips and clothes, but when she was old enough to receive gentlemen callers, the Judge became practically a jailer. Neighbors and workmen said there were some rip-roaring arguments between the Judge and India until India succeeded in getting the Judge to agree to callers if his wife was in the room. The Judge, though usually contemptuous of his wife, had reluctantly consented. Lately, after an appropriate time of mourning following Mrs. Kent's sudden death from a heart attack, India had been seen increasingly at what our newspapers referred to as "gala events," particularly in the company of Warren Bierce.

Though Bierce did not introduce us, I bowed to India and looked up toward the Observatory telescope again, but not before I observed a man push through the crowd, nod to Bierce, and take a position on the other side of the girl. He was big and burly with a nose that had been broken once upon a time, a wide mouth and heavy jowls that gave him the appearance of an ugly frog, and black eyes, slightly popping, that stared unblinkingly at me from under massive black eyebrows falling back onto a low, receding forehead. I wondered if he could be one of Bierce's captains or the Judge's. India evidently knew him for she gave him a slight smile that had little warmth in it as he ranged up on her other side. There was something almost

[ 6 ]

malevolent in the man's presence, yet he appeared to acknowledge an even more intimidating authority in Bierce. He reminded me of a bosun on one of Uncle Tom's ships who had a reputation for brutality. At Le Havre, where we were loading, there had been a great brawl in a local wine shop one night between rival American crews, and the bosun had died of a half-dozen knife thrusts, inflicted, so our officers were pretty certain, by our own crewmen. The French police had made a perfunctory investigation, then ordered both ships to leave port. If a Frenchman had been killed, there would have been a different ending.

Brad seemed not to have heard Bierce's mention of Vail, so jabbing my elbow surreptitiously into his ribs, I said, while staring up at the tower, "Look behind you."

Brad turned at once and, after exchanging greetings with India and Bierce, who now introduced the man with him as Captain Jake Rudd, he grimaced to me, and his eyebrows arched questioningly. Though I shrugged, I could only pretend indifference. I liked neither Bierce nor the looks of Rudd, and I felt uneasy to have both men in back of me. This was silly, of course, since India was with them and Bierce was a man I rarely saw and had nothing to do with.

"The brigs are still becalmed!" Mr. Vail shouted from the Observatory. "Been this way for nigh six hours. Thought the breeze was coming up awhile ago, but it's died. What's that?"

As he looked around to Captain Moody, I could imagine how impatient the crews of both ships must be after all this time of watching each other.

"They're movin'!" Vail yelled. "*Enterprise* has the weather gauge. Burrows has just squared his yards and is bearing downwind."

The boom of a distant, very distant gun came faintly to our ears followed by silence.

"That's *Enterprise* answerin' *Boxer*'s challenges of this mornin'," Vail yelled.

Then white smoke laced with black started to roll skyward, and long seconds after we spotted the smoke came the ripping crash of many guns. Sometimes we heard the volley-like firing of a broadside; at other times guns fired singly. But at no time did the firing cease,

[ 7 ]

and the smoke cloud towered higher than ever over the distant horizon. Meanwhile the birds never ceased to scold in a tree below us, and the crowd preserved a kind of apprehensive silence.

As Vail relayed Moody's account, we could see in our mind's eye the *Enterprise* and *Boxer* approach side by side, the American brig in the windward position. Gradually Burrows drew ahead of the *Boxer*, raking her with a gun in the stern. With superb timing the *Enterprise*, though a slow craft, then rounded to on the starboard tack and pounded the *Boxer* from a raking position off the Englishman's port bow.

"There goes the *Boxer*'s main-topmast!" Vail yelled.

A roar went up from the crowd, and all of us stared across island-studded Casco Bay toward the smoke.

"Her foretops'l yard has gone, too!" Vail called out almost at once; and another roar went up from the crowd.

"We've got her!" Brad shouted with an exuberance unusual for him, and clapped me on the shoulder.

"And you're going to lose a glass of rum!" I laughed. "The *Enterprise* took just forty minutes from the first broadside."

"With pleasure, sir, I lose, with pleasure," he said, bowing elaborately.

But it was at least another ten minutes before the guns ceased. Then Vail, his feet capering as if in a dance, raised his hands for silence.

"Ladies and gentlemen," he boomed out, "the *Boxer* has surrendered."

The pandemonium that ensued was something I had never witnessed before. Men pummeled one another in their delight, pounded shoulders, shook hands; ladies shrieked, waved handkerchiefs, and even wept. I saw small boys on the fringes turning handsprings, and, of course, everyone shouted.

My own shoulders were sore from Brad's fists and I'm sure his were from mine when he said hoarsely, "Come on down to the Eagle and let's start on that rum I owe you!"

Hundreds must have had the same idea, judging from the rush down the hill. There is a lot of feeling in Maine against excessive drinking but little was evident that late afternoon and evening.

As we left quickly, I noticed India Mitchell, Bierce, and Rudd walking slowly behind us. India looked pleased as she spoke to Bierce. The merchant smiled back, but his face had little of the joy that was so evident everywhere. Surely, I thought, he could not be sorry the *Enterprise* had won. I had seen several people I knew to be Federalist in their sympathies looking as happy as the most ardent Republican supporter of President Madison. Of course Bierce was a Federalist of the Federalists, as strong in his convictions as Judge Kent, if less vociferous. Besides, he was known as "a deep 'un." Perhaps he had reasons, whatever they were, for not revealing how he truly felt. As for Rudd, he looked as fierce as the first time I had seen him, as unsmiling and formidable.

Sometimes, my mother tells me, I am given to flights of fancy like my father, probably a truthful criticism of both of us from one who, while knowing our faults, yet loves us. It might have been a flight of fancy now, but I was certain that Bierce and Rudd would have been happier if the *Boxer* had won.

As we hurried ahead, however, it wasn't fancy when I heard Bierce amusedly relating how I had objected to his criticism of my father in the newspaper.

"I'd have kicked the bastard out of my office if I'd been you," Rudd growled.

Bierce laughed, and the sound infuriated me. "Oh, I could have done so with ease, but, frankly, I didn't have the heart to destroy the young man's confidence in himself."

"But how can you be so sure you would have won, Warren?" India asked in a low-pitched, somewhat husky-throated voice with just a hint of mockery in it. "He looks like a strong man."

"Bless you, India!" I heard Brad whisper. And as I glanced at him, he said, "Now don't let them get under your skin, Jonathan. Bierce would probably like nothing better than to provoke you."

"Oh, I assure you I'd have had no difficulty with him," Bierce said to India. "I'd have taught the minister's son a lesson he would never have forgotten."

"Brad," I said, "I can't let him get away with this. I'll give him a chance to teach the minister's son a lesson!"

"No, you won't!" Brad said, taking me by the arm. "We'll go on to

[ 9 ]

the Eagle as if we'd never heard them. Don't you realize that he's speaking for India's benefit? He's showing off before her."

"But why?"

"He would like to marry her, and, so far, she has resisted him. It's common knowledge around town."

"I didn't know it."

"You wouldn't! Now I make a point of learning about such things. You see, this is one way of trying to convince her what a fine, virile fellow he is. What he's finding out is that India has a mind of her own."

Brad, as a handsome, promising young lawyer, whose father was also a lawyer and whose mother was related to William King of Bath, one of the greatest merchants and Republican powers in Maine, was welcomed in the best social circles of Portland. He knew India well and Bierce "better than I'd like to," as he expressed it.

"India has too much common sense to marry someone like Bierce," Brad said, "though there's some talk that Judge Kent favors him as a son-in-law. Now let's forget about Bierce and Rudd and even India and get to that rum."

But I couldn't forget them. In fact, it was a long time before the Eagle's rum and the good humor all around me dispelled the anger that had gripped me as we left Munjoy Hill. And I never did lose a sense of uneasiness at Bierce's odd conduct and the glowering, forbidding presence of Jake Rudd.

# II

ON THE morning of the seventh, the *Enterprise* brought the *Boxer* into Portland. In no time at all crowds gathered as the two battered brigs tied up at the end of Union Wharf. Word that both commanders had lost their lives in the battle shocked everyone. Furthermore, Midshipman Kerwin-Waters of the *Enterprise* was so seriously wounded that his life was despaired of. Commodore Isaac Hull, who had commanded our frigate *Constitution* in her victory over the British frigate *Guerrière* early in the war, had arrived the day after the battle from his post at Portsmouth to take charge of the two ships. He now found he had also to arrange for a double funeral.

I was itching to get away from Mr. Longfellow's side, but it was noon before he finally let me go with a weary smile. Brad Pettigrew joined me after he finished a case at court, and the two of us hurried to the waterfront. The smell of fish frying in a sailors' tavern set my mouth to watering, but we resolved to look at the men-of-war before eating.

Actually we couldn't approach the ships closely because of the marine guard. We were near enough, however, to see how badly cut up the *Boxer* was in both hull and rigging while the *Enterprise*, though her bulwarks were splintered here and there, showed comparatively few other effects of the battle. Some of her crew were mending sail, while the carpenters were busy repairing the superficial damage to her hull. We saw less activity aboard the *Boxer*. A few of her crew stared over her high bulwarks at us, but they appeared apathetic, as, indeed, who could blame them — now that they were prisoners under the alert eyes of American marines aboard? Several Britishers, commissioned and noncommissioned officers, seemed to be on parole since they were down on the wharf and marching to the nearest tavern with an equal number of men from the *Enterprise*. As the party passed, people stared curiously at the Englishmen but with no show of feeling except compassion, so far as I could see. Nor did anyone speak to them. Though most of the Englishmen looked straight ahead, I could have sworn one of them, a bosun's mate, nodded ever so slightly to someone in the crowd. Following the direction of his nod, I saw the "Frog," as Brad and I called Jake Rudd. Yet I couldn't be sure he was the one among the watchers the bosun's mate had in mind. Rudd's face was stony, almost hostile, and he gave no sign of recognition.

"Did you see that?" I muttered to Brad.

"See what?" he asked. Then as I explained, he shrugged his shoulders in his expressive, almost Frenchified way. "Your imagination perhaps, Jonathan. And what would it mean anyway, if one seaman recognized another? Ships and men get around in this world, you know."

His slightly patronizing air was a mannerism I had long ago become used to, as far back indeed as when he, newly graduated from Harvard and starting to read law with Mr. Longfellow, had persuaded me to go to Harvard. Though I understood how his manner could antagonize someone who didn't know him, I ignored it and said, "I don't like the looks of the Frog, and I don't like Bierce. If you ask me, Bierce is making an uncommon lot of money, judging by the new house he's putting up and the new pair of grays he's bought and that new sloop he races around the harbor."

"Maybe he's made some good privateering investments," Brad said, glancing uneasily about as my voice rose.

"He's a good Federalist," I scoffed, "and Federalists are against the War!"

"Are you implying there are other ways of making money nowadays, my friend?"

"We know there are a lot of people trading downeast directly with the British," I said bitterly.

Brad took me by the elbow and pushed me along up the street. "You should know better than to talk like that in public," he said at last, and his voice was sharp with reproof. "You know nothing for sure about Bierce or Rudd. Now, in the name of common sense, drop this kind of talk or you'll make real trouble for yourself."

Of course he spoke wisely — he often does — and I had been foolish. When I admitted as much, he shrugged and suggested we get something to eat while they were still serving at the Eagle. I hastily agreed, but the fish chowder we ordered tasted flat to me, although Brad praised it to Mrs. Casey.

When I reached home to study during the afternoon, I was unprepared for the horse and carriage outside the door. I recognized the rig as belonging to one of our local politicians, Robert Ilsley, postmaster and son of our late Congressman, Daniel Ilsley. Walking into our front hall, I heard the rumble of several voices and, curious, glanced into the front room where my father had his study; the front room on the other side was our parlor where no one went unless my mother was receiving the ladies from the church.

Tiptoeing out to the kitchen, I found my mother peeling apples for a pie and staring out at our little orchard of three apple trees beginning to look heavy with fruit. I had already propped up the lower branches of one of them.

"Who's seeing Father?" I asked, slumping into a chair opposite her at the table and loosening my stock.

Even as I spoke I thought of how many of my friends called their parents Mama or Dad or some such affectionate appellation, whereas I had been brought up to say Mother and Father and would have regarded myself as being overfamiliar had I done differently.

"They are Dr. Deane, Commodore Hull, and Mr. Ilsley," she said in her precise way.

It was so like my beloved but correct mother to name Dr. Samuel Deane first. I am sure she thought the elderly minister of the first parish deserved such precedence in view of his being a clergyman and having served Portland so many years; Commodore Hull might be a national hero because of his great victory over the *Guerrière*, but he was not a servant in the Lord's vineyard.

"But what do they want of Father?" I persisted.

"Jonathan, if your father chooses to tell us, he will do so, but he has had no time as yet. They came only a few minutes ago."

"Yes, Mother," I said with a slight bow.

She smiled faintly at my raillery, and her face lost something of its weariness. My mother had long been unwell, and with reason, considering that she had buried four children, nearly died herself two years ago of pneumonia, and suffered with my father over the many criticisms of his ministry. "Really, Jonathan, I don't know why they are here," she said. "Perhaps it has something to do with the funeral of those poor officers tomorrow."

"You don't mean they want him to give the funeral oration?"

"Could they ask a better man? Could they make a more appropriate choice?"

My mother's rhetorical questions came so convincingly, admitting of no other answer, that I wondered if it was from her that I acquired my interest in the examination of witnesses in court. The trouble was, my mother could ask the most pointed question in a cool, detached sort of voice, while I usually had to fight to keep eagerness or anger from showing in my tone.

That I shared her view about the Reverend Gerald Dearborn goes without saying. My father had tried for years to keep politics out of the pulpit. This was difficult enough during the years of the Embargo and the Nonintercourse Act when under President Jefferson and then President Madison American ships were forbidden to trade with England and France. Such action had been prompted by Napoleon's Continental System, which closed Europe to British goods, and by Britain's blockade of Continental Europe. Specifically the action had been the Republican answer to the British policy, on the one hand, of stopping and searching our ships on the high seas and often bringing them into British ports, and to Napoleon's policy, on the other hand, of confiscating any neutral vessels so treated if they subsequently touched at a French port. Despite the fact that by 1807 Republicanism had risen to a position of dominance in Maine, claiming sixty per cent of the electorate, the Embargo was not popular. Republican strength was based on a combination of squatters looking for support of their rights against the great landholders, a locust horde of office-seekers, people dissenting from the Congregational Church, and a number of merchants. The last in particular disliked the Embargo about as fiercely as the Federalists, who represented the landed, financial, and most of the mercantile interests. In fact, hardly anyone in Maine who was connected with sea-trading approved the administration's action, and denunciations were sharp in the taverns where the shipowners and merchants gathered, in the press, and in the pulpit.

My father privately supported the Republican policy as a noble effort for peace but he refused to use his pulpit as a means of rallying public opinion to the government. For this refusal Republicans impugned his patriotism. When war broke out, much to the wrath of Federalists, who, because of trade, were eager for appeasement of England, my father persisted in remaining nonpolitical while preaching; and the Federalists, whose party now controlled the legislature in Boston as well as the governor's chair, scored him as bitterly as the Republicans had earlier. As a consequence our family was treated somewhat as social pariahs.

I suppose our reputation suffered even more among local Federalists because of me. Having grown up in a household that usually admired Mr. Jefferson and Mr. Madison, I felt that since we were committed to a war, we should fight it for all we were worth. For that matter, my view not only differed from that of most people in New England but also from that of my father and mother. They felt that no war was just and, though Republican politically, they condemned both Jefferson and Madison for not continuing the nonintercourse policy rather than submitting, first, to the Federalists and repealing their policy and, later, to the war hawks in the South and the West and taking the nation into war. Personally I had been for war ever since the British man-of-war *Leopard* had halted our unprepared frigate *Chesapeake* off the Virginia Capes in 1807, fired on her, and taken seamen off her decks on the grounds that they were British deserters. The Embargo which eventually followed seemed an act of cowardice. My father attributed my position to the fevers of youth. Though he may have been right, I soon learned that, to keep peace in the family and present a united front to the outside, there were times when I must button my lip.

At the sudden sound of voices in the hall, my mother and I looked at each other. Then the door opened, and my father stepped inside. "Alice, and you, too, Jonathan, won't you please come and meet our visitors?"

We rose at once and went with him. White-haired Dr. Deane was a beloved minister in our town who had practically retired. Mr. Ilsley I also recognized at once, a broad-shouldered man, whose slight stoop often deceived men as to both his age and energy. He was a shrewd, ambitious politician. The other caller I knew only from the accounts of people who had seen him. A fat man, taller than his fleshiness led one to believe, Commodore Isaac Hull had a face that looked like a cherub's. Yet when he turned to me from bowing and smiling affably to my mother, his eyes measured me with a cool, steely appraisal that seemed to have nothing to do with the heartiness of his greeting. Was it true that his tight pants had split when he leaned over and gave the order for our frigate *Constitution* to open fire on the British man-of-war *Guerrière*? I had heard nothing about anyone aboard the *Constitution* laughing over the incident. I'll bet no one dared. Still, his handclasp was firm and his manner more brisk than unfriendly. After an exchange of greetings, our callers left promptly, Mr. Ilsley driving the carriage.

[ 15 ]

My father then put an arm around each of us and led us into his study, with its walls of books; and I couldn't help thinking how much of a poor minister's salary goes into books if he has any love at all for learning. "Well, I am the recipient of a very singular honor," he said in his quiet, mellow voice.

I was bursting to ask him what it was all about, but a warning glance from my mother kept me silent. Instead I looked sideways at my father's thin, deeply lined face which was saved from appearing fragile by its firm chin. His hair was iron gray in color and stood out in sharp contrast to the black of his eyebrows. Though he seemed older than his years, there was an air of quiet strength about him that was very reassuring; he would never let criticism defeat him.

"The deputation has asked me to preach the funeral sermon tomorrow," he said with just enough of a twinkle in his eye for me to realize that he was touched by the honor and the irony of the request.

"I am so pleased for you, dear," my mother said, resting her head lightly on his shoulder.

I grasped his hand. "It's an honor, Father, and it's due you!"

He shook his head as if to ward off my praise. "The situation can be explained very simply. The town authorities did not dare ask a Federalist minister for fear he would say something derogatory about the administration, and the navy people wouldn't like that at all. By the same token, an outspoken Republican minister would offend too many of the good Federalist folk here in Portland. I am a safe choice, you see. I may be a Republican, but since I am also a minister who has chosen not to identify his pulpit with political factions, they know I will say nothing to offend either party. I am simply against war itself!"

At the dry tone in his voice I couldn't help smiling. "That makes you the least safe choice of all, Father."

"Well, I surely hope you will point out the folly and cruelty of war," my mother said firmly.

But my father shook his head again. "No, Alice, I'm afraid I shan't, much as I should like to. After all, these men died for a cause greater than themselves, and there are griefs to assuage and hearts to strengthen. Though I deplore the occasion of their passing, there are

[ 16 ]

worse things than to serve one's country — and there are less honorable ways to die," he added softly.

My mother and I stared at him. He hated war for its inhumanity its surrender to irrationality, its essentially unchristian character. Now was the moment of his life when he could denounce it before the largest congregation he would probably ever confront, yet he chose to let the opportunity pass in order not to belittle in the minds of mourners the deaths of those they mourned. In his place I wonder whether I could have been so considerate.

My mother looked at him half angrily, I thought. Then her face softened. "Very well, Gerald, if that is the way you feel, that is the way it will be," she said, but with just a touch of asperity struggling with resignation.

I shook his hand again and did not trust myself to speak.

The funeral procession the next day was impressive. At nine o'clock in the morning the procession formed at the courthouse under the direction of Robert Ilsley and Levi Cutler, another of our politicians, assisted by a dozen marshals. The procession then marched to Union Wharf and waited for the coffins. It would have been an easy matter to bring them directly up the wharf but hardly dignified. Instead the crew of each ship lowered the coffin containing its captain into a ten-oared barge. The barges, rowing with minute strokes which were synchronized with minute guns fired by our two militia artillery companies in town, brought the coffins to land. Once they were ashore and mounted on caissons, the procession moved solemnly up Fore and Pleasant streets to High Street, then down Main and Middle streets to Father's meetinghouse. Behind mourners like Commodore Hull and Lieutenant Edward McCall, who had assumed command of the *Enterprise* when Captain Burrows fell, came the entire crew of the *Enterprise*. Likewise behind the coffin of Captain Blythe marched the crew of the *Boxer* on parole. Many dignitaries from Portland, military companies, and hundreds of citizens, among whom were Brad and myself, brought up the rear. When the procession reached the meetinghouse, the guns ceased firing, the drummers abruptly halted that deathly slow cadence, and the principal mourners, select details from the *Enterprise* and the *Boxer*, and numerous distinguished citizens filed into the meeting-

[ 17 ]

house until it could hold no more. Thanks to the sexton, Brad and I found seats in Mother's pew.

My father's funeral oration was brief. It was really a kind of eloquent testimony for nobly dying as a fulfilment of nobly living. He alluded to war as a calamity attributable neither to God nor to Satan but to man's own lack of forbearance, understanding, and right reason. And the tragic irony, he pointed out, is that good men on both sides are equally convinced their own cause is right. Then he spoke of death and how, as Thucydides, the great Athenian historian, wrote, "The whole earth is a sepulchre for famous men." Death itself was not so much to be feared as a shameful death, and these two captains had died honorable deaths, a fate infinitely to be preferred to a dishonorable life. He mentioned their youthfulness — Burrows, twenty-eight, Blythe, twenty-nine — and their promise. But he bade his hearers learn from their courage, their readiness to sacrifice their lives for the cause they believed in, and the humanity that overlooks political differences and inters two such enemies in life side by side as comrades in death while friend and foe alike grieve together as willful children of the Heavenly Father.

He spoke simply and sincerely, and when he finished, there was a great blowing of noses from the men, and an occasional sob from a woman. I was proud of him, and stood up uncommonly straight as he moved past us up the aisle and joined the procession for its final march to Eastern Cemetery. It distressed me as I watched him that, believing in the war as I did, contrary to the Federalists, I was doing nothing in support of my belief.

Soon the drums began to beat, the minute guns started firing again, and the procession moved slowly toward the cemetery.

Although I thought I'd leave my mother at the parsonage, she insisted on going to the cemetery, too. With a young man on either side of her, she said, she had no fear of the crowd. Certainly she didn't find the procession difficult to follow in view of its slow pace, and Brad and I were there to assist her if necessary.

At the cemetery, services were brief, consisting of prayers by my father and the Episcopal clergyman, the firing of muskets, and the filing of mourners past the two coffins, each draped with the flag of the respective captain's nation.

[ 18 ]

This last took a long time, and as we slowly walked away afterward and waited for Father to join us, Stephen Longfellow and his wife came up to us and congratulated Mother on the oration. Their two older children, another Stephen and young Henry, were shy but polite, and were already more interested in the fifers and drummers marching away than in any of us. Mrs. Longfellow — she was "Zilpah" to Mother — was a tall, slender woman, greatly talented but with nerves so finely strung she couldn't ever seem to stand still. Often she was even less well than my mother; in fact, I sometimes thought it was their poor health that drew them together.

While we were all chatting, I saw Mr. Longfellow stiffen. A moment later, he bowed over India Mitchell's hand, but was less affable to the Judge, her uncle, was just this side of hostile to Warren Bierce, and remained utterly frigid toward Jake Rudd.

"Mrs. Dearborn," India said warmly, "I wish you to know how wonderful your husband's sermon was. I cried."

"Yes, it was excellent, just what one would expect of him," the Judge said, a shade pompously.

"Ah, yes, very appropriate," Bierce added; and his voice sounded so false I bristled.

"Thank you," my mother said simply but graciously.

Then as she looked at Rudd, he snapped his head forward in a crude bow. "I wasn't in the church," he muttered, staring at her as if defying her to criticize.

"I'm afraid, sir, that I do not know your name," Mother said coolly.

"Forgive me, Mrs. Dearborn," Bierce said. "This is Captain Jake Rudd."

"Captain Rudd is a friend of Mr. Bierce," India explained. "He has come from New York to arrange to get supplies through the British blockade."

"Oh, a smuggler," I said.

"You don't call anything like that smuggling if it's for a patriotic purpose," Brad added, with the suggestion of a wink at me. "Isn't that so, Captain?"

"I wouldn't know," Rudd growled.

[ 19 ]

"Oh, all this talk of smuggling when we have just buried those two young men," Mother said with a shudder.

"Very true, Mrs. Dearborn," Bierce said. "It is like a sacrilege."

"And yet I have heard," Longfellow said, "that the *Boxer* was actually escorting a smuggling schooner down the coast when several of our fishermen saw her and reported her presence to the *Enterprise*."

"That's the story going around town," Bierce said, "but who's to know for sure that it is true?"

"But you can't deny there is a good deal of trading being done with the British!" I said.

"I can't admit to something I know nothing about," Bierce laughed. Then, turning to Rudd, he said, "It's lucky you were seen here on the day of the sea fight, Jake, else someone might accuse you of running contraband down along the coast."

He slapped Rudd on the shoulder as he spoke, but Rudd merely grunted and stared — rather, glared — at us.

"Uncle Jason, don't you think we had better go home now?" India flashed an appealing look at the Judge.

"Yes, the crowd seems to have thinned out so that we needn't rub shoulders with too many of the rabble," the Judge rumbled. "Your servant, ladies." He bowed to Mother and the Longfellows, nodded to Brad and me, and left with India.

Bierce and Rudd — I still thought of him as the Frog — followed, and Mr. Longfellow's eyes narrowed as he watched them go down the hill. "A strange man, Warren Bierce," he said.

"And he keeps strange company when he mixes with a man like Rudd," I added.

"Rudd's a fellow to look out for, if you should ask me," Brad said.

"But no one is asking you, Bradford Pettigrew," Zilpah Longfellow said with a nervous laugh, "and I think it's time we, too, left, Stephen. The boys are restless now that the soldiers have gone, and I have such a headache."

"Oh, you poor dear!" my mother was instantly sympathetic. "Yes, Mr. Longfellow, do take Zilpah home at once."

That night, the funeral of the captains still vivid in my mind, I decided I could no longer continue my legal studies until I had done something in my own way about the war. I needed advice, and I realized my father, with his hatred of war, was the last one to turn to. I knew only one man I could talk with about the matter who would at least understand, even if he disapproved. That was my Uncle Tom. I made up my mind, therefore, to go to Cape Elizabeth in the morning.

On that resolution I fell asleep, though it was a repose broken by several moments of consciousness when I felt guilty about leaving my parents for such a reason and quitting my studies with Mr. Longfellow, for whom I had the greatest esteem and whom I wished to think well of me.

---

# III

My Uncle Tom Dearborn had made a success of seafaring and farming. Not that he splashed his affluence about for all to see like a number of people in Portland who were either building or planning to build mansions for themselves. Uncle Tom had a broad, low-beamed, clapboarded farmhouse raised on the foundations of a house destroyed by a sea raider during the Revolution, but greatly enlarged. It was shaped like a square 'U' with a large barn away from the main house. Uncle Tom said that because of the fire menace it was folly to tack the barn onto the sheds attached to the house as a number of our neighbors did. He had broad fields, orchards, a good tract of woodland. Down on the shore a brig was taking form in his shipyard under the direction of an old friend of his, Joab Cummings, whose children seemed to vie with the Jordans' in populating all this part of Cape Elizabeth. Inside the house were tapestries from the Levant, a Chinese fire screen, a Persian carpet, Spode chinaware from England and Sèvres from France, a few paintings from somewhere in Europe — in short, Uncle Tom and Aunt Betsy, who had occasionally sailed with him, had brought home many treasures. These, however, were all so much a part of their house with its lived-in look that a visitor didn't feel he was in a museum or a rich man's abode.

It was late forenoon when I arrived hot and sweaty from the long walk from the Pooduck ferry to the Cape. Though there was a slight breeze off the water, even here the air was sweltering. Turning from the road into the house path, I saw my Aunt Betsy in her garden snipping off some late blooms. In spite of the heat, she looked cool in her crisp, blue dress and white-lace bonnet. From the kitchen came the clatter of pans and the wonderful fragrance of baked fish as black Sapphira prepared dinner.

Quickly I put my jacket back on and called out, "Good morning, Aunt Betsy!"

She straightened up and looked at me. "Why, Jonathan, how nice to see you!" She spoke in a high, rather sweet voice, though it had a cool, measured quality about it, like her manner, which kept most people at arm's length. In fact, few people got "close" to Aunt Betsy. Some said she had ice water in her veins, but they didn't really know her. They should have heard her heat up on the subject of the war and the politely worded but incisive way she cut the Madison administration to slivers. She managed her house expertly, assisted my uncle with his accounts, and acted as a superb hostess at the parties she and my uncle gave. Her son Paul, married and a merchant in Boston, adored her, I knew full well, but stood in awe of her, too. Her daughter Eliza, who resembled my uncle with his brown hair and eyes, loved her but stood up to her and often caused her to laugh. As for myself, I admired her enormously as a great lady but never dared open my mouth to her on the subject of politics. In her view Alexander Hamilton had been the greatest man America had produced, and the only man living more perfidious and loathsome than his political opposite, Thomas Jefferson, was his murderer, Aaron Burr, who deserved every iota of the unhappiness that had come to him with his treason trial, his exile, and the misfortunes of his family.

She presented me her cheek to kiss, and I smelled the delicate scent of the jasmine powder she used. "Aunt Betsy, you're like a lovely flower yourself," I said, and meant it.

She stared at me, then the blue eyes crinkled and her face lighted up in one of her rare warm smiles. She was still a handsome woman despite the gray in her hair and I understood how appealing she must have been to my uncle when he courted her. "Why, Jonathan Dearborn," she exclaimed, giving me a slight tap on the wrist, "what a flatterer you're becoming! Is it the influence of your friend Pettigrew?"

My face grew warm. "You know I'm forthright, Aunt Betsy. I usually mean what I say, and it often gets me into trouble."

"Well, my dear, this isn't one of those times. Just continue saying nice things like that and meaning them. Now go into the house and tell Sapphira to set a place for you at the table. She's about to ring the bell for dinner."

"Yes, ma'am," I said, and went in to greet the fat colored cook and my cousin Eliza.

Eliza was no sylph like her mother, but no plump pigeon, either. Let it be said that she had a generous figure and a real sense of humor. Although she had had several proposals, she had rejected all of them. At the present, she seemed to favor Brad Pettigrew, but whenever he tried to warm up to putting the fateful question to her, she shied away, so he told me.

"Did you come alone?" she asked.

"This time," I said. "Brad would have sent his best, I'm sure, if he'd known I was coming."

"Ah, my dear young friend," she said pompously, "this visit must be of the utmost importance — and veddy secret," she added in a whisper.

"I'd hardly say that," I laughed.

"Well, whatever it is, you'd better wash up before the men come in. We're having baked haddock with cream sauce, mashed potatoes, biscuits with lots of butter, and blueberry pie — think of it, Sapphira's blueberry pie!"

"If only I were hungry," I groaned in mock anguish.

"You'd better be, cousin, you'd better be."

At the moment Uncle Tom had four men helping him in the fields and the shipyard. He worked with them himself from time to time, but after a slight case of sunstroke this past summer he had done very little except supervise. A carry-over from the custom of the sea was the family's dining apart from the workers. These men might live near him or be the sons of neighbors, but at home, as at sea, he was "Cap'n Tom" and the captain dined apart from the crew. So after

Sapphira and Eliza had carried heaping dishes out to the men beneath an old crab apple tree, the family sat down at the damask-covered mahogany table in the dining room and had dinner "in state" as Brad once described the custom.

During the meal, I told them about the sea fight as seen, or rather heard, from Munjoy Hill and the burial of the captains in Eastern Cemetery.

"We could hear the guns from this very house," Eliza said, "and we went up on the rocks and saw the *Enterprise* bring the *Boxer* into the harbor."

"It must have been a good scrap," Uncle Tom said. "They were pretty evenly matched."

"Why Tom," my aunt exclaimed, "how can you say that? The *Enterprise* was larger, had two more guns, and carried more men."

"Yes, Betsy, that's true but the brigs didn't come close enough for the *Enterprise* to make use of her manpower, and she mounted only one more gun to the broadside. Besides, the *Enterprise* is about as fast as molasses in January. I'd say they were a match."

My uncle's voice was unruffled, but obviously he wasn't conceding to the sympathies of his wife. Aunt Betsy had been a Tory and the daughter of a Tory during the Revolution and still took the English point of view on many issues, while Uncle Tom had fought with Arnold at Valcour Island and Bemis Heights, with Paul Revere at Bagaduce, and on the high seas as captain of a privateer. My aunt and uncle must have shared a deep and abiding love not to have let their different opinions divide them over the years. Even my mother, who liked Aunt Betsy as little as my aunt liked her, admitted that there was no doubt Aunt Betsy loved Uncle Tom. Now, though I half waited for a sharp reply from her, she merely tossed her head and said, "So they were even. But I still am glad we did not go to Portland for the funeral ceremonies."

"Why on earth not, Mother?" Eliza asked. "I'd like to have heard Uncle Gerald."

And have seen Brad Pettigrew, I thought. But I looked attentively at Aunt Betsy as she said, "The funeral would merely have under-scored the folly of Mr. Madison's war, and we need no more reminders of it — that is why I am glad we stayed here. I hope your father came down out of the clouds for once, Jonathan, and denounced what he hates so much."

"You sound like Mother," I said; then gave them a brief account of Father's funeral sermon.

"Good for Gerald," Uncle Tom said.

"I'm not so sure, Tom," his wife replied. "It is my opinion that men will always fight and Gerald is hopelessly idealistic to think otherwise. But here was an opportunity to make his stand public knowledge before the largest group of people he had ever spoken to, and he faltered. Believe me, Alice was right."

I thought I could not be hearing aright — that she should ever agree with my mother! Usually Aunt Betsy regarded my mother as a mousy little creature, though she had been heard to say that anyone less self-effacing than Alice Dearborn would have been driven mad by her husband's impossible idealism and the criticism it evoked. Not that she disliked my father — though deploring his views as half daft, she admired his courage and had said that when she died she wanted him and no other minister near her in her last moments. Personally, I was convinced she grossly underestimated my mother.

Dinner over, Uncle Tom took me outdoors. After giving the men their instructions for the afternoon, he strolled with me down past the brig rising in its cradle, spoke briefly with gaunt, old Joab Cummings, whose hand nearly crushed mine in its grip, then climbed to a hillock crowned with a little grove of pine trees. Uncle Tom loved this spot, and often came here, Father said, to smoke his pipe, listen to the breakers foaming over the reefs below, and dream or think. So now we sat down with our backs against a tree, and I watched him in silence as he filled his pipe from a deerskin pouch tied with a thong and worn almost a chocolate color from handling.

"Well, Jonathan," he began in his deep voice, "you didn't walk so far on this hot day for even one of Sapphira's dinners. What's troubling you?"

Mother said I had inherited Uncle Tom's forthrightness and that this was one of the reasons my Aunt Betsy liked me. Whether this was so or not, I came directly to the point. I told him I must do something about the war, and I realized how any such decision would affect my family. I said that I realized he and Aunt Betsy, being

Federalists, would not approve. Still, this was my feeling, and I felt I should stand by it.

He smiled as I finished. "You've evidently made up your mind already, so what do you expect from an old Federalist like myself?"

"Two things," I said. "In the first place, I had to tell someone in the family first who might understand, and since you've been a fighting man in your time, you were the obvious one. Besides, you and I seem to get along pretty well. In the second place, I wanted to ask your advice as to how I might serve most effectively."

"Everything stated in good lawyer fashion," and Uncle Tom grinned as if what I had said had pleased or amused him — maybe both. "What have you thought you might do, Jonathan?"

"I thought I might enlist."

"In the army?" Uncle Tom nearly choked on his pipe.

"Is it as bad as that?" I laughed.

He cleared his throat. "I think a lot of those in land service. I saw a good deal of it myself during the Revolution, but I guess I was born to do my fighting on a deck. I think you were, too."

"Well, to tell the truth, I had thought of enlisting in the navy."

Though he nodded, his face looked doubtful. "Yes," he finally conceded. "You could do worse than enlist in the navy — "

" — but not much worse!" he added sharply as I opened my mouth to reply.

Mother often said that when I became stubborn or defiant or angry I lowered my head like a bull getting ready to charge. She said it looked most inelegant and I should break myself of the habit. Sometime, perhaps, I shall succeed. Just now, I caught myself lowering my head as I demanded, "What do you mean, 'not much worse!'?"

He sighed, and taking his pipe from his mouth, turned to me. "Jonathan, we had a wonderful little navy until Jefferson decided to concentrate on puny, little gunboats that won't stop anything British that floats, instead of continuing to build those splendid frigates of ours and brigs and sloops and maybe even some ships-of-the-line. So where does our navy find itself? Blockaded. Oh, yes, occasionally we get a ship to sea, but it's rare, and it'll get rarer when Napoleon is beaten. Why, the British can then send their ships over in droves and seal up our coast. They won't care about placating New England any longer at that point. You'll see nothing but the British ensign along the whole Atlantic seaboard. No, if you join the navy, you'll spend the war scrubbing decks down in Portsmouth, and that won't help the country much. Now you're not cut out to be a fancy diplomat, and I can't see you as a spy, so that leaves only one thing."

"What's that?"

"Privateering," he growled. "Damn this war, Jonathan. I don't believe in it, and, believing as I do, I share enough of your conscience not to send out a privateer or invest in any. Paul doesn't agree with me, I realize. He's a Federalist, too, but he's got stakes in several privateers out of Boston. Well, that's up to him. Now if I were in your shoes, son, I'd sign articles for a privateering cruise. A privateer can roam at will and give the British hell. I'd head straight for the British Isles, too. There's less danger there from cruisers than over here, and better pickings, too."

"I hadn't any idea of getting rich off the war," I said.

"Hell, boy, don't talk like a fool. Even the men on a navy ship get prize money when they make a capture. 'Course you're not thinking of getting rich, and you won't, but you might at least save enough to help your parents in their old age."

The last point hadn't occurred to me, and it registered at once. "I'll go down to the waterfront tomorrow and make inquiries," I said.

"Now look here, Jonathan," and Uncle Tom pointed his pipe at me, "don't you go signing on as an able seaman. You're young, but you were even younger when you served as third mate on my brig. You go on the roll as third mate now, and don't forget it. In fact, there's an old friend of mine from down in Castine who's fitting out a privateer in Portland, and I'll write you a letter of recommendation to give to him. His name is Benjamin Vail."

"Why, he's the one who told us all about the sea fight!" I exclaimed. Quickly I explained how Vail had announced to the crowd on Munjoy Hill the account of the battle as Captain Moody had watched it through the telescope.

"Shouldn't wonder if everyone in the crowd heard every word," Uncle Tom laughed.

[ 27 ]

"Well, he surely has a carrying voice," I said.

"That he has. If he has a place aboard his ship, I think 'Little Ben' will take you. I've known him since the war with France back in '98 when our two brigs fought off a sloop-of-war. He owes me a few favors."

"But I don't want him to take me as a favor," I protested.

"Hell, be reasonable, son. Once you're aboard, you're on your own, of course, but it's getting aboard that often requires help."

He was right, of course, so swallowing my pride, I thanked him and said I'd see Captain Vail the first thing in the morning.

"Good lad," he said, then added, "but I don't envy you telling your mother and father."

We soon went back to the house, and while I visited with Eliza, Uncle Tom wrote the letter to Vail. Aunt Betsy was taking a nap, which seemed to relieve my uncle greatly. After he sanded the letter and sealed it, he told me to put it in my jacket pocket. When Eliza asked what was going on, Uncle Tom said, somewhat gruffly, that he and I had been talking business.

"You mean I should mind my own?" she countered.

"Now that you put it that way, yes," her father said with a grin. "And don't you go telling your mother anything."

"I won't promise unless you tell me the secret," she laughed.

He nodded. "Oh, all right, but not for a day or two at least, Liza. Is that fair enough?"

She agreed, looking triumphant if anyone ever did.

The next morning I headed for the wharves right after breakfast, and soon found Captain Vail's brig, the *Argus*, and Vail himself aboard in his shirt sleeves booming orders in a voice I had heard up on Fore Street.

"Well, what do you want?" he asked when I climbed aboard.

He looked harassed and irritable, and as I glanced across the *Argus*'s deck littered with gear, I sympathized with him. Riggers were at work aloft, a gang of men were lowering a gun to its carriage amidships, and painters hung in bosun's chairs over the side daubing on an eggshell blue. Vail seemed about the only man around giving orders, so while I felt a little guilty to take up his time, I grew hopeful, too.

"Looks as if you could use some help here," I volunteered.

"Help? What kind of help?" And the rasp of his voice made me want to clap my hands over my ears.

"Perhaps you'd better read this first, sir." I handed him Uncle Tom's letter.

Glancing at the handwriting and then at me, he said, "Let's go below a moment. Not that it'll be cool down there but at least we'll have quiet."

Annoyed at his irascible manner, I wanted to tell him that he was making a lot of the noise himself, but I overcame the temptation.

His cabin was small but a model of housekeeping with his bunk neatly made up, clothes on hangers, a rug on the floor, and a square-cornered stack of papers and letters under weights on the table. I noted that chintz curtains hung at the open stern windows and that in a sling from the deck above swung a pot of red geraniums. It was this last touch that really surprised me. While he sat down at the table to read, I seated myself in a chair near the bunk and wondered about this little gamecock of a captain who was evidently a good fighter from Uncle Tom's account and yet who kept flowers in his cabin. Uncle Tom wouldn't have flowers in the house if he could help it — which he couldn't since Aunt Betsy loved them. My uncle protested that flowers in the house always reminded him of funerals. Aunt Betsy retorted that he had a morbid mind.

Suddenly I observed Captain Vail studying me. "So you're Tom Dearborn's nephew. Well, that don't mean a thing to me, not a thing. But he says you sailed third mate with him on the *Betsy*, and that does. Still, you've not been to sea for four years?"

"That's right, sir." I told him about my going to college and now studying law.

He nodded, but frowned, too. "Don't suppose you know how the British sail their convoys, do you?"

I thought of what I had read and heard since the war began but also how the British used to manage the operations near hostile French waters when I had been with Uncle Tom in the Mediterranean. "Yes, sir, I think I do," I replied. "A warship takes the lead — she's the commodore's flagship. No one goes ahead of her, and everyone watches for her signals. There's a fast frigate in the rear of the convoy like a sheepdog to keep the stragglers in line. And on each flank the British have a sloop-of-war or a brig."

"What do they do at night?"

"The whole convoy closes in tight and huddles under the stern of the van ship."

"Very good," he said, just like a schoolmaster. Then he leaned forward and barked, "You're a privateer's master. What do you do about that convoy?"

"Well, sir, it's best for two privateers to team together. Then while one diverts the enemy's attention, the other watches his chance, dashes into the convoy, and captures what he can."

"Come, come," Vail roared, his voice filling the little cabin with noise and disappointment, "that's a dodge. Oh, it's true, of course, but you're acting alone, Dearborn, not in company."

"Then I'd try to cut out stragglers in the daytime, put prize crews aboard them, and while the enemy chased me, the prizes could escape — I hope."

"But if the weather's fine, you might never have an opportunity to take prizes. What then?"

"That's so, sir," I conceded. "And in that case I'd try to hang on to the convoy at a distance until thick weather set in or a strong wind blew up. There'd be stragglers for sure under such conditions."

"Uh-huh. But what would you do, just cut out as many ships as you could and send them into port?" His voice was surprisingly quiet.

"No, sir," I said. "I'd take aboard my ship whatever specie I found and the most valuable goods in case any of the prizes were recaptured. I'd then put aboard the worthwhile prizes what men I could spare and destroy the others."

"Not bad, not bad at all," he mused.

Just as I thought the inquisition over, he shot questions at me for maybe fifteen or twenty minutes on navigation, sailing measures, management of the crew, trimming ship, and armament. "What caliber of guns would you mount on this brig?" he asked.

I thought of Uncle Tom's opinions on this subject and of what I had heard and read on the subject. "Sir, I would have a Long Tom amidships — an eighteen- or a twenty-four-pounder, and for broadside guns I'd have long twelve-pounders — say four to a side and one carronade to a side — a thirty-two-pounder."

Vail vigorously waved my words aside. "Carronades are a waste, Dearborn. They throw a heavy shot but have so limited a range you have to come right up alongside the ship you're after. I'd rather stand off and pound him with long guns. He can't hurt my ship or my crew that way — remember, most merchantmen carry few guns themselves. With Long Tom and stern chaser the *Argus* carries fourteen."

"I understand," I replied in a conciliatory manner, "but if there should ever be a time when we'd have to close, or if an enemy as strong or stronger attacked us, I'd feel safer with at least two carronades aboard."

He stared at me. "Why do you say 'we' and 'us'? You're not a member of this ship's crew."

"No, sir," I gulped. "It was just a manner of speaking."

He was right, of course, but I had become so carried away by the conversation that I had already identified myself with the *Argus*. If there was no place aboard her for me, I'd try somewhere else, possibly that big schooner lying next door at Bierce's wharf. I had heard gossip in the ship chandleries that she, too, was fitting out for a cruise.

"Dearborn!"

The ear-shattering blast of his voice startled me into almost as loud a "Yes, sir!"

"Dreaming, weren't you, Dearborn?" he asked with a sly grin.

"Planning, sir," I replied.

"Dearborn" — his voice was quiet now, and as he stood up, I rose, too — "I need a second mate — more to the point, I need a responsible man I can really trust. You're rusty from being on land so long, but I'll take you."

He brushed aside my thanks and shook my hand warmly. Though I was no giant, I towered over him, yet I had the feeling that "Little Ben" Vail, as Uncle Tom had alluded to him, was himself of no small stature as a man.

As we went on deck, he explained that he would give me the next day to break off my studies and make my arrangements to come on board. He'd expect me to report the day following, but I could stay at home on alternate nights until we sailed. When I asked him when that would be, he shrugged.

"Maybe a week, maybe two," he said. "It'll take at least a week to complete signing on a good crew. That old lady over there" — and he pointed to the big gray schooner — "is skimming the cream off the waterfront. She's the *Ghost*, and well named by her looks."

"Whom does she belong to?" I asked.

As he didn't answer at once, I glanced around the *Argus*'s cluttered deck again, being far more proprietary than when I'd come on board. I could see that it would certainly take a lot of hustle to get the brig ready for sea in a few days. Then Vail's low, heavy whisper startled me.

"Reports have it, Dearborn, that Warren Bierce heads up a syndicate that owns her."

"I didn't know Bierce had anything to do with privateers," I said. "He's a hot Federalist, and against the war."

Vail laughed scornfully. "That don't stop a man from wanting to make a little money off the war."

I thought of Paul, my cousin, and agreed. Then I asked, "Who's taking the *Ghost* to sea?"

"New man in these parts — course I'm from out of town but at least I'm from Maine. His name's Jake Rudd."

"But I thought he was here to work out some new way to get supplies through the blockade at New York!" As he looked puzzled, I explained what India Mitchell had said.

"Well, it's still possible," Vail said thoughtfully.

He clutched my arm. "That the girl you mentioned?"

I stared at the *Ghost* and at the woman in green being helped aboard by Warren Bierce himself. I also recognized the Judge and Rudd. Several men behind them carried trunks and valises.

"That's India and her uncle," I said in astonishment, "and it looks as though someone's going off on a voyage."

Vail shrugged his shoulders and, turning away, said, "Well, it's done, you know. Look here, I've got to get to work, and I suggest you go break the news that you're now with me to Stephen Longfellow and your parents."

"Yes, sir," I said, but left the rail myself only when the group disappeared into the schooner's cabin.

Now where could India be sailing to, I wondered. I wasn't sure that I really liked her, but she had a directness and a vibrant quality, as well as an undeniable allure as a woman, that fascinated me. I found myself envying Rudd and whoever was sailing with her. In fact, I was not only envious and wished she were sailing with the *Argus* instead, I also began to feel some apprehension. Without knowing anything about the Frog, I neither liked nor trusted him. If I'd been the Judge and India were my ward, I'd be wary too about committing ourselves to Rudd's charge. It was a pity the Judge's wife was no longer alive to protest, though the Judge was reputed to have rarely heeded her advice or paid her much attention. I realized, of course, that none of this was my business, and amazed myself by suddenly wishing it were.

---

# IV

I TOLD my parents of my intentions late that forenoon in my father's study. It was about the hardest task I had ever set myself, and the half hour that ensued was one of the longest passages of time I can remember. Actually my father took the news with a forbearance that I deeply admired, though I was inwardly sick at how pale his face became. My mother's lips drew together in a tight line of repressed anger, hardly the mark of the spiritless person Aunt Betsy considered her. "How can you do this to your father?" she cried. Then she broke down and wept so hard I was appalled. When I put my arm around her to comfort her, she shrugged away from me and went to my father. This was certainly understandable, but for a few moments I felt more alone than at any time since I was a child. I could only stand there, feeling clumsy and cruel, while Father gradually calmed her. "Come, come, my dear," he said repeatedly, almost like a litany, but with a compassion in his voice that made me feel worse than ever.

Eventually she got control of herself, and the three of us sat down and talked over the matter. I am sure they understood how I felt. In fact, my father said that though my decision came as a shock to him, he had recently sensed from my opinions and my restlessness with my legal studies that I might enlist. He had hoped that the war would be over by the time I had made up my mind. At his statement my mother looked at him in surprise, but said nothing. Later she announced that she would collect my clothes and pack my old sea chest at once, and when I said I would do this myself, she hushed me down.

Telling Stephen Longfellow of my plans was not easy, either. To my surprise, however, where I had expected a sharp reprimand, he became philosophical about the whole question. In fact, I felt somewhat let down at first.

"Jonathan," he said, as we sat in the front room of the brick house that General Wadsworth had given to him and Zilpah, "your mind hasn't been on your work for months. Isn't that right?"

"Yes, sir, that is correct," I replied.

"You really believe in this silly war, don't you?"

I bristled a little at his use of words. "I don't think it's a silly war, sir, and I do believe in it."

"Very well, Jonathan." He crossed his leg, and the strap of his dove-gray pantaloons coming under his instep grew so taut I thought it might snap. "You know my opinion of this administration and of this conflict Mr. Madison has got us into. I hate to see you jeopardize your life so unnecessarily. At the same time I respect your right to your own opinion, and feel that, believing as strongly as you do, you should do your part."

"Thank you, sir," I said humbly. I hadn't expected such understanding from a Federalist of his commitment.

"When you've had enough of fighting and are ready to take your place in a peaceful society again, we'll talk more about the law — provided you wish to continue studying it. You still wish to become a lawyer, don't you?"

"That is my family's dearest wish for me," I replied.

"I asked if that was your wish, Jonathan."

"I think so, sir," I said slowly.

He nodded. "Well, you will have plenty of time at sea to do a great deal of thinking on the subject. When you're finally home, come around and we'll have another chat on the matter."

I don't know what I had expected — perhaps some expression that he would miss me, and certainly a word or two of reproof. Instead, he seemed to take the whole thing quite casually indeed. It was only later that afternoon when I looked up Brad to tell him the news that he took me up to his room, with its numerous books, eighteenth-century French paintings, and boxes of thin, pale Havana cigars, and told me how I had upset Mr. Longfellow.

"Of course he knew better than to ask me to persuade you to change your mind," Brad said. Drawing a silver cigar holder from his pocket, he offered me one of his slender beauties and took one for himself. Then he carefully ignited both with his new equipment. He was very proud of this Instantaneous Light Box, as it was called, which had been invented in France only eight years before. Actually it was a bottle that had some sort of fabric inside soaked in sulphuric acid. A chemically treated flint — there were fifty flints to a box — when rubbed on the fabric and withdrawn, burst into flame.

"As a matter of fact," Brad continued, "though I didn't say anything to him since he looked as if he'd just buried someone, I found myself envying you."

"You — envying me?" I scarcely believed him. Surely the elegant, accomplished Brad Pettigrew, just starting an independent law practice and already well regarded, could not envy a restless, disgruntled law student like myself.

"Ah, come now, old boy," he laughed, blowing gigantic smoke rings. "It must be something to go to sea as second officer of a privateer in support of a cause you believe in."

"But you believe in it, too," I said.

"Yes, but not enough to break with what I've been doing."

"Then you don't believe in it strongly enough," I said bluntly, and probably a little self-righteously.

He flushed as I spoke, but the slight smile never left his face. "There is such a course as jeopardizing one's career in what is, for the time being, a Federalist town," he said.

"Don't you think that hasn't crossed my mind, too?" I asked. Actually I realized that I was still only a student, whereas Brad, a full-

[ 35 ]

fledged member of the bar, had much more to lose and would indeed be putting his career on the line. "Besides," I added, "this war isn't going to last forever, and when it's over, people will still want legal competence in their lawyers before political opinions.

"Perhaps," he said, "but just remember this: people in Maine have long memories. Most of them don't approve of the war and distrust people who do."

"Brad," I replied with an impatience in my voice that I regretted the instant I was aware of it, "it comes down to a matter of conscience."

He looked at me. "Are you sure it was just conscience and not also a discontent with the law as a lifework that swayed you?"

He was right of course, and I admitted it. "On the other hand," I added, "I really believe in this war."

"Of course you do," he said. Then, spiraling his finger through one of his smoke rings, he said, "Tell me, Jonathan, what does a man do to get himself aboard a privateer?"

"As an officer? Oh, he knows someone who knows someone connected with the owner or the master," I said, thinking of what my Uncle Tom had told me. "Are you serious?"

He laughed. "Let's say I'm interested."

The possibility that Brad might go to sea on the *Argus* delighted me, but I wondered what he could do. Though he was a militia lieutenant, he knew little or nothing about ships and sea duty. He was a good shot with a musket and a pistol, but I doubted that he had ever had a cutlass in his hand. To be sure, he could quickly learn anything that was necessary. But what captain would sign on anyone so green when hundreds of experienced seamen were available? Still, there were two possibilities. Some privateers carried supercargoes, though these were usually men who were engaged in mercantile business. Others carried a detail aboard that corresponded to marines in the regular navy. Captain Vail had said that he had arranged for ten of these, but he did not say whether the complement had been filled. If it had not, Brad might be able to sign on in such a capacity. When I now mentioned it to him, he agreed to go with me to sound out Captain Vail.

We went late that very afternoon to see Vail. He boomed a tired welcome to us, brought out rum from his cabinet, and expressed his satisfaction when I told him that I had cleared matters with my parents and Mr. Longfellow. Then I came to the point about Brad.

"So you've never been to sea, Pettigrew," Vail barked.

"No, sir."

"But you've been a militia officer. Ever see any action?"

"No, sir."

"How do I know you wouldn't run below when the fighting starts?"

"You don't," Brad replied with a smile. "But I don't think you need to worry about that."

Vail looked at him, then grunted and said, "Maybe so, but we can't be sure what you'll do when you hear bullets whizzin' by you. You a follower of Harrison Gray Otis?"

The change of subject came so suddenly that Brad, rarely at a loss for words, was silent for a moment. "Do you mean to inquire if I'm a Federalist?" he finally asked.

"There are Federalists and Federalists," Vail said testily. "But up in Boston Otis is the high priest for all New England, and all acknowledge him as that, don't they? I hear he wants New England to secede from the Union."

"I am not a follower of Otis or a Federalist of any sort," Brad said calmly, "but I think you're a little harsh on Otis. I've never heard that he believes in secession any more than Stephen Longfellow does."

"Well, Otis and Governor Strong and those other Federalist leaders in Boston act as though they're speaking for all New England. I tell you they're not. Caleb Strong don't give a hoot about us down here in Maine. He hasn't done a thing to help us build defences. As soon as this war's over, the best Maine can do is to separate from Massachusetts."

"That may be true, Captain, and I for one agree with you, but you may recall that back in 1807, Portland voted against separation 392 to 73," Brad said.

"And a damn fool decision it was," Vail muttered. "It'll be different after the war."

"But, meanwhile, Captain," I cut in, "can't we find a place for Brad Pettigrew here in the *Argus*'s marines?"

"You related to the shipbuilder in Portsmouth?" Vail asked Brad, apparently ignoring my question.

"He's my father's cousin — 'Uncle' to me," Brad replied.

"Well, I suppose that gives you some connection with the sea," Vail grunted. Then, turning to me, he said, "I take it you can vouch for Mr. Bradford Pettigrew."

"Yes, sir, he'd make a fine marine officer."

"I didn't say a word about making him a marine, let alone an officer," Vail protested, holding up his hands.

"He'd still make a good officer."

"Maybe he would," Vail conceded. "It so happens I've got two places left, but not one for an officer."

"I accept," Brad said.

Captain Vail squinted up at him from deep-set eyes. "I ain't offered it to you yet, Pettigrew."

"Well, if you do, then I accept."

Vail laughed his great, bold laugh and thrust out his hand. "Glad to have you aboard, Pettigrew. Sign on now and report tomorrow noon. If you need a little more time to settle your affairs, let me know then."

I was surprised to see my friend's hand tremble as he took up the quill. I hadn't realized how eagerly he had wanted to go with us.

As we went on deck, I glanced across the dock. "I see the *Ghost* is still with us."

"Missed the tide this morning, so she sails this evening, I've heard," Vail said. "The passengers went back to their homes. Seems the Judge and Bierce have some kind of mission in France."

"And India Mitchell is obviously sailing with them," I added.

"It looks that way."

The Captain's tone was so dry I glanced up just in time to catch a sly wink from him to Brad. Surprised, Vail coughed violently and reached for his handkerchief.

"We'd better go now," I said to Brad. "You've got business to clear up and farewells to make."

That evening I was so restless I strolled down to the waterfront to see the *Ghost* depart. A violent shower in the afternoon had muddied the streets, but already quite a crowd had gathered on the wharf as the crew worked under extra lanterns to clear the decks of the big schooner. A light breeze and a favorable tide should see her free of land. No raiders had been reported off the harbor recently, so she should be able to make the open sea. Once she was beyond Cape Elizabeth, it would take something faster than anything the British possessed on this coast to overhaul her. Though no racer like the Baltimore clipper types, she was still very fast and powerfully armed.

I was standing alone when someone suddenly gripped both my upper arms and hurled me to one side. "Out of the way, bully boy!" a harsh voice snarled.

The man's sheer strength dropped me to one knee, and as I rose, hot with gusty anger, Jake Rudd strode to the gangway. Behind him came Bierce, India Mitchell, and Judge Kent. India's curious glance embarrassed me as deeply as Bierce's sneering smile infuriated me, but the group swept by me so quickly there was no time to do anything but stare, burn inside, and swear that some day I would wipe Bierce's smile off his face and give Rudd cause to regret his rudeness. Never had I felt so humiliated. For a moment I even contemplated going after them. In fact, I must have made some move toward them, for a hand plucked at my elbow and a strange voice whispered with respectful firmness, "I wouldn't do that, seh. It would not be wise."

Whirling about, I looked into the broad face of the biggest and blackest Negro I had ever seen. He was a sailor for sure by his dress, but he spoke like no Negro I had ever heard. "Who are you?" I demanded. "And why did you prevent me from going after them?"

"I'm Philip Adair, seh. I come from the Bahamas, but I'm a free man."

"All right, Adair, tell me — "

"Philip, seh," he said gently.

"Philip, then! Now, tell me why you held me back."

"What could you have done against Cap'n Rudd? Pardon me, seh, but he is stronger than you, and he has his whole crew to call on. You would have been hurt, and Cap'n Vail needs you."

I was more astonished now than annoyed. "How do you know?"

"I saw you come on board this morning, and again this afternoon. I am the chief gunner of the *Argus*."

"Then why are you here?"

His teeth shone whitely as he grinned. "There's a ship sailing, and that does not happen often these days. Isn't that why you are here, too, seh?"

It was, and yet there were other reasons. I wondered why India Mitchell and her uncle and Warren Bierce should be going to France. I wondered, too, about Rudd. Why were they sailing in his schooner? And I had hoped that somehow I might contrive to see India for a few minutes alone. Then I wondered about this Negro. A chief gunner talking better than most Harvard graduates! And with an English accent, too! He had had no trouble recognizing Rudd, either. Not that this necessarily meant anything. "Are you sure it was just the excitement that brought you here?" I asked.

"Oh, yes, seh."

"You recognized Captain Rudd, Philip. Do you know him well?"

"Yes, *seh!*" And at the wild, thick sound in his voice I decided not to press him further at this time.

Besides, the shouts that now rose indicated the *Ghost* was about to cast off her lines. Her sails began to rise, and, laying hold of a hawser, men started walking her down the wharf, helping her move into open water. I saw India standing with Bierce and waving her scarf. Suddenly the breeze whipped it out of her hand, or she let go of it in her enthusiasm. At any rate, it flew crazily over the heads of the crowd. Several men lunged for it, and on an impulse I leaped high in the air and pulled it down. I think she recognized who caught it, for she pressed her hands to her lips as if in surprise or even dismay. Then she waved, but whether at me or at the crowd, which broke into a cheer as the *Ghost* slipped clear of the dock, I could not be sure. I only know that I waved back wildly, and all at once felt a strange sense of loss as India became indistinct with distance. The sails of the *Ghost* soon filled, sending the schooner swiftly through the dark waters of the harbor.

When the *Argus* followed the *Ghost* to sea nine days later, also at night, the scarf, smelling of verbena, was stored deep in my sea chest. It was one item my mother had not packed, and Chief Gunner Philip Adair was too much of a gentleman, or too discreet, ever to ask what I had done with that square of white silk.

[ 40 ]

# V

"Nothing in sight, sir," I said, and handed the glass to the *Argus's* first lieutenant, Lester Jordan of Cape Elizabeth.

My watch over, I went to the galley, scrounged a cup of hot coffee from the cook, then returned to the main deck to watch the marines drill. Many privateer captains dressed their marines in gaudy uniforms; others let them wear their own clothes. Captain Vail, himself a trim little man, issued his marines white-duck pantaloons, dark green jackets and high, hard, black caps. Lanky John Cutter of Portland was the marine captain, and he put his detail through the manual of arms with expert precision. He always acted a little embarrassed when he was alone with Brad, for he had been a militia sergeant while Brad was a lieutenant. Actually both had had to do some tall talking to free themselves of militia duty in order to go privateering. Brad tried to put Cutter at his ease, but time and again Cutter would drawl that Brad should be captain of the detail instead of himself.

Captain Vail ran a fairly "taut" ship, as they say in the regular navy. He was a bear for discipline and neatness. Not that he tried to imitate the navy; he was simply that kind of skipper. He insisted on a considerable degree of punctilio from his officers. Jordan and I had little difficulty with this, but the third officer, Oliver Jones of Brunswick, loathed all formality as much as he loved food. Jones just missed being enormously fat, but, like so may fat people, he was catlike on his feet, and he knew ships and fighting; I suppose these were the reasons Vail signed him on. Vail exercised the men daily at the guns, and here I learned how proficient Philip Adair was at his work. Though he was colored, the men respected him for his competence. Probably his size had something to do with their attitude, too; he was easily the biggest man aboard and could practically handle the Long Tom, our large pivot gun, by himself. Because I seemed to "take" to gunnery and got along so well with Philip, Captain Vail let me assume principal charge of the cannon.

[ 41 ]

Though the *Argus* was a privateer, the group that owned her didn't want her to miss an opportunity to make money for them by more peaceful means. Accordingly we headed down the coast to Charleston, South Carolina, where we were to take on a cargo of cotton and run it into Bordeaux or any French port. Personally I thought we took an unnecessary risk of capture by this detour southward since British cruisers were numerous along the coast. Captain Vail, however, pooh-poohed me when I once mentioned this opinion, but I noticed that he doubled our lookouts whenever we approached any port and that, on sighting a cluster of sails or any large sails, denoting a man-of-war, he took the *Argus* farther out to sea. We were now near Cape Roman, which is about four to five hours of fast sailing from Charleston, and the prospect of having to slip through a cordon of blockade ships and pick our way through the tricky shoals just to load a measly cargo of cotton didn't please any of the officers.

As the marines ended their drill, I motioned to Brad. I couldn't help thinking, as he approached, how my cousin Eliza's eyes had opened wide in admiration when she saw him in his uniform, which was gorgeous compared with what he had worn in the militia. We had gone out to Cape Elizabeth to say good-bye. Uncle Tom affected to be surprised, as did Eliza, that we were going to sea. This was for Aunt Betsy's benefit, of course. Aunt Betsy herself became tight-lipped and distant to both of us. Yet as I kissed her before I left, she clasped both my hands in hers, a most unusual show of feeling for her, and bade me do nothing foolish to endanger my life. She said much the same to Brad, too, and he gallantly kissed her hand, which brought a blush of pleasure to her cheek. After first asking permission of my aunt and uncle, Brad said his farewells to Eliza privately. I don't know what he said, but Eliza's brown eyes, when she emerged from the garden, were like stars moistened with tears. Brad would be a real catch for her, but he would be lucky to get someone as fine as Eliza.

"Private Pettigrew reporting," Brad said, drawing himself up to attention and saluting.

I grinned and, returning the salute, said, "Private Pettigrew may stand 'at ease.'" Then I asked, "Ever been to Charleston before?"

"Never, and I understand I've really missed something."

"It's a pretty city," I said, "though it's best in the spring when the flowers are out. At any rate, we'll be there before long, so you can see for yourself."

The words were hardly out of my mouth when the cry of "Sail ho!" burst from up in the maintop.

Jones, who had taken over the deck from me, began to question the lookout. It was a heavy brig — a man-of-war and British — on the weather quarter. Notified at once, Captain Vail came on deck with his telescope, and, after verifying the vessel's nationality, ordered the *Argus* cleared for action and all sails set.

The brig, aware of us even before we were of her, was already in chase. Since the wind was blowing off the land to the north-north-east, the enemy stuck like a leech to windward even if this meant sailing close to shore.

"I know what she's up to, but it won't work," Vail grunted. "There are other ships waiting just out of sight of Charleston bar, so she wants to push me toward them. I'm going to hug the wind and head for the channel at the bar. If she gets near us, you and Philip go to work on her with the Long Tom, Dearborn."

The chase went on for four hours, and we drew away from her hardly at all. She had speed to burn. Every now and then she'd let fly with a bowchaser, but the ball fell so short that it was clear the gun was a carronade. We therefore concluded that if the bow gun was a carronade, the brig was probably armed with carronades in her broadside, too. This meant we could pound her safely at a distance but must not let her get close to us; carronades at short range were murderous to any ship and crew.

The brig, however, was so fast despite her heavy armament and carried the wind so favorably that Captain Vail finally turned to me and growled, "You and Philip get to work with the Long Tom, Dearborn. Try for her rigging but hit something, even if it's her hull."

The Long Tom had a crew of eight and these leaped to their station. Bags of powder, a ball, and wadding were rammed down the throat of the twenty-four-pounder. Then Philip sighted and clucked his teeth at what he found. Slowly the elevator screw raised the long black barrel. Again he sighted, tinkered again with the screw, and stepped aside for me to check the aim. When it looked accurate to me and I stepped back, Philip picked up the lanyard and waited for me to give the order to fire.

The first shot, a ranging shot, was close enough to splash water aboard the brig. The second and third were near but not as good as the first one. As we loaded for the fourth, I heard Philip muttering to himself and patting the big gun. "Tom will do it this time," Philip said softly.

"Let's hope so," I said with some impatience. "But how do you know?"

Philip smiled in a mysterious, knowing way and tapped his temple. "I know, Mr. Dearborn. Just you watch."

The gun bellowed again, and this time the foretopmast came tumbling down, snarling the brig in a flurry of canvas, ropes, and spars. She lost headway immediately.

As our crew broke into cheers, I ordered the Long Tom loaded again and fired. This time we must have hulled her badly, though high up, for we saw a small mushroom of splinters blossom from her main deck.

"That's enough for now," Captain Vail roared. "Good work! But stay by your gun, Dearborn."

I soon saw why he said this. Evidently alerted by the firing, two other brigs were trying to beat to windward to intercept our passage into the channel. For a few minutes it looked as if they might succeed, but we had the weather gauge and presently went flying over the bar and up to Charleston.

We stayed in this southern port only long enough to load our cargo and wait for a favorable departure. The cargo was a small one, about three hundred and thirty bales of cotton at twenty-six cents a pound, with five per cent primage. The gross freight and primage amounted to $23,000 which, for sea-island cotton, is no small potatoes, as we would say in Maine, when cotton could be bought for twelve or thirteen cents a pound. Still I suppose the freight wasn't excessive when one considers the cost of operating a privateer with insurance running from fifteen to twenty per cent and a seaman's wage at thirty dollars a month. War runs all commodities wastefully high.

While in this lovely, little port, the trees and gardens of which looked green even in late fall, I made the acquaintance of the dashing Dominique Diron, one of our great privateering captains. Only a few weeks before his schooner, the *Decatur,* had taken His Majesty's schooner *Dominica* in a terrible combat lasting more than an hour during which the Englishman lost two-thirds of his crew killed or wounded. On the very next day Diron also captured the valuable merchantman *London Trader,* which he sent into Savannah. He was refitting now and preparing to leave again.

It was in Charleston that I sensed for the first time a strong feeling of support for the war. Though there was criticism of the administration, it was criticism directed at the management of the war rather than at the war itself. Charleston's privateers, though not numerous, were more than three times Portland's number, and were active all over the Atlantic, bringing the war to the enemy. I heard great admiration for the Baltimore privateers, above all, and envy expressed for the clipper-built schooners of the whole Chesapeake area. More privateers were running out of Baltimore than any port in the Union. Though New York was pressing closely, Boston had only half as many registered as Baltimore. Of all the Baltimore captains the name of Thomas Boyle stood out, first in the *Comet* and then in his magnificent schooner, the *Chasseur,* which was forcing up insurance rates at Lloyds in London because of its amazing number of captures. Privateering wasn't winning the war for us, but it was one sure way we could make the war expensive for the British. Unfortunately, a great many of our people in Maine hated the conflict so intensely they had disavowed any connection with it, even privateering.

The weather presently turned dark and rainy with a wind blowing into the harbor so that it was impossible to leave. With Congress soon to assemble, Captain Vail feared that an embargo would be laid, so he was especially anxious to depart. The loading of the cargo completed, he therefore dropped down the harbor as near the bar as he could and waited for a favorable turn in the weather. After several days the clouds broke, the wind shifted, and we slid easily across the bar at night. Vail ordered an extra ration of rum for everyone to celebrate our departure.

Within a week we ran from three frigates and took two prizes, a brig bound for Jamaica to Halifax and a ship from London to

Jamaica. After that we didn't sight a sail for four days, and Brad said that he had about decided that monotony was the worst thing in a sailor's life.

Then in the late afternoon that very day, the cry of "Sail ho!" brought us all on deck with a rush. We soon identified the craft as a brig, British by rig, and chased her almost until darkness set in before a shot across her bow brought her to. To our disappointment she proved to be under an American prize crew. Then we discovered she had been captured by Jake Rudd's *Ghost*.

Captain Vail invited the officer in charge to supper that evening, while the two brigs rode the Atlantic swell in company. The officer in charge, a James Creighton from New York, told us news that interested all of our officers aboard the *Argus*. The *Ghost* had captured the brig *Petrel* weeks before and sent her to a French port. Storms, however, had blown the *Petrel* so far off course that Creighton decided to head for the American coast. Then, Captain Vail's wine loosening his tongue, Creighton, a slovenly looking person with a wild shock of sandy hair and a heavy jaw, told of a quarrel between Bierce and Judge Kent.

"Were you a witness to it?" Captain Vail asked.

"Hell, no. But it was my watch and I could hear them shoutin' at each other."

"What was it all about?" I asked.

"Don't know," Creighton said thickly.

"But you've got to have some idea," Lester Jordan said.

"What do all you want to know for?" Creighton asked.

"We don't, not really," Captain Vail said, holding his glass of ruby-red wine to the lantern light. "It's just that all of us here know both Mr. Bierce and Judge Kent and are curious. It's actually none of our business."

"Well, wish I knew more about it myself," said Creighton, evidently mollified. "I gathered Bierce wanted the Judge to do something, an' the Judge refused. That made Bierce mad, an' before you could look, he an' Jake Rudd were givin' the Judge a rough go."

"You mean they were actually fighting?" Lester asked.

"No, nothin' like that," Creighton mumbled. "Just yellin', especially Rudd an' the Judge."

[ 46 ]

"What was Miss Mitchell doing while all this was going on?" I asked.

"India?" Creighton leered. "Now there's a lively piece I'd like to — "

"That's enough, Mr. Creighton!" Captain Vail said. "Just tell us if Miss Mitchell had any part in this altercation."

"What's that? Oh, you mean while they were yellin'?"

At Vail's nod, Creighton said, "Miz Mitchell wasn't around. Well, I didn't see her, anyway, an' everyone aboard had his eye on her most of the time. Know I did. She didn't get on well with Bierce, though. Treated him pretty cold most of the time. But was she ever scared to death of Rudd! Not that I blame her."

"Why do you say that?" I asked.

"She must have looked down her nose at Rudd sometime to get him so mad at her. Jake don't take that from anyone, man or woman. But it looks like Bierce cracks the whip where Jake's concerned, so as long as Bierce stays soft on India — I mean Miz Mitchell — she's safe. 'Sides, Jake must've landed 'em all in France long ago."

"I suppose they had some pretty important business in France," Captain Vail said so casually that I grew alert as if an alarm bell had begun to ring. Why should Vail be interested in the *Ghost's* mission to France?

"Hell, I don't know why they were all goin' to France," Creighton said. It was clear from his tone of voice that he was now resenting our questions. "All I know is there was talk of fixin' up some deal in business. Now if you gen'lemen have any more questions, you'd better save 'em till next time. An' that'll be months from now." He cackled and, gripping the cabin table, rose unsteadily to his feet. "Good to meet you, Cap'n," he said to Vail. "Good meat, good wine."

"Here, take a bottle with you," Vail said, and pressed an unopened bottle on him.

Creighton grinned and, cradling the wine bottle like a baby, nodded to us and left.

We soon parted company with the *Petrel*, but it was long before I could dispose of the apprehensions created by the encounter with Creighton. Talking it over with Brad later helped clarify the situation even if it didn't make me feel easier. We both agreed that what Creighton had said, had really added little to what we had already suspected might happen. India was a strong-minded girl who would not easily knuckle under to threats or blandishments. Rudd we knew from the start was dangerous. Bierce was equally dangerous, in fact probably more so, though in a more subtle way. Judge Kent we had both known to be something of a blowhard. What the issue was between him and the two other men remained a mystery — likewise India's relation to it. On the other hand, as Creighton said, they were in France now, so the potentially explosive group was scattered. We were left, said Brad as he finished his analysis, as if he were summing up a case in court, only with a confirmation of our earlier suspicions. Nothing vitally new had been added except, he said with a sly grin, "the obviously increasing interest of the *Argus*'s second lieutenant in the destiny of Miss India Mitchell."

"All right, I admit the increasing interest in India," I said. "But there is one more addition. Why should Vail show such interest in the reason for those people going to France? I got the impression, despite his casualness, that he was more than just curious."

Brad shrugged. "Who can tell? It is possible you were mistaken — I myself didn't feel there was anything really significant in what he said. But what does it matter, one way or another? Besides, we'll touch at Bordeaux pretty soon, and we can make some inquiries there if you're still interested."

It was evident that I was unusually perceptive for once, a capacity my parents would probably not have conceded me, or else I was being unduly suspicious, which was more likely. Before going on watch, I walked through the berth deck with its rows of hammocks and stopped to listen at the companionway. It was dim in here with only a few lanterns lighted and those masked. But it was surprisingly noisy, too, with the moans and sighs of sleeping men and the never-ending creaking and groaning of the timbers as the brig pitched in the rising sea. All was well, so I went on deck. Only the binnacle light showed, and I checked our course with the man at the helm. Overhead the canvas cracked in the wind with an occasional clap like thunder. The *Argus* was digging deep into each sea, and I noted that soon I must shorten sail. A twelve-pounder nearby showed a little motion; I must get its lashings secured at once.

Suspicious? Of course I was. A sailor lives on suspicion day and night, lest some hurt come to his ship, some hazard to his own life and the lives entrusted to him. He develops a kind of sixth sense, anticipating what might happen. Perhaps there is a carryover of this attitude into his everyday life. At any rate, to my admittedly suspicious mind, the *Ghost's* mission to France looked stranger than ever and the purpose of our trim little captain with the cannonading voice something more than that of a mere privateersman.

---

# VI

WE captured two more prizes on our way to Europe. One was the ship *James* from Demerara to Liverpool with a mixed cargo of cotton, sugar, coffee, and rum, worth nearly two hundred thousand dollars. The other was the ship *Elizabeth*, of four hundred tons, Jamaica to Plymouth. She was larger than the *James* but carried much the same cargo, with the addition of logwood, ebony, and a quantity of hides and spars. We valued her at three hundred thousand dollars, and sent both ships into Portland. Though both were armed, they put up scarcely a fight. This was owing to Philip Adair's marksmanship with the Long Tom. Captain Vail refrained from coming sufficiently close to either ship for her guns to be effective. Instead, we stood off and let Philip drop a few twenty-four-pound shots near or aboard the vessels.

From the time the *Elizabeth* squared away for Portland under its prize crew we did not sight another sail until we entered the Bay of Biscay. All of us had speculated at what port, if the British were tightly blockading Bordeaux, we would try to land our cargo of cotton, which had now become extremely valuable because of the additional bales we had removed from the two prizes. Finally Captain Vail called his officers together in his cabin and announced his plan.

After tots of rum all around, he rumbled in that tremendous voice of his, "If this was a town meeting like we have in Castine, I'd give each of you a chance to tell us where I ought to try to make port."

He paused, and we looked expectantly at him. He had created an effect — there was no doubt about it. But the effect was somewhat spoiled when fat Oliver Jones, the third officer, shoved his empty glass toward the rum pitcher. "Mind fillin' my glass again, Lester?" he asked Lester Jordan. Lester, as the first lieutenant of the *Argus*, gave him a hard look and hesitated.

"Fill it, Mr. Jordan," Vail growled. In a council and at many other times, Captain Vail was very formal, "mistering" all of us.

We waited while Jordan poured Oliver's glass. The pitcher had a wide spout, and Lester had to be careful not to let any drops fall on the table. Jones slurped from his glass and sighed gustily. "That's good rum, Cap'n, mighty good rum. Out of Demerara?"

"Yes, from a puncheon off the *James*. Now are you ready to listen, Mr. Jones?"

"Course I am. Sorry, Cap'n." But it was plain that Oliver, who gave me a sly wink, was by no means sorry. I'd heard him say before this that he always needed a drink or two to help him listen to speeches.

"I learned a good deal of information down in Charleston from other captains," Captain Vail said briskly. "Some of it confirmed what I already knew. Most French ports are covered by British cruisers, particularly those near England itself. I want to get as close to Bordeaux as possible, though that's guarded, too. The British keep frigates and brigs off Cordouan Light, so I don't like the idea of entering the Garonne River."

"I don't understand, Cap'n," Jones interrupted. "You want to go to Bordeaux, but it's on the Garonne an' the British are blockadin' the mouth. How the hell are you goin' to get to Bordeaux, and how's Bordeaux any safer to get into than Cherbourg or Havre or some other place?"

Vail's little eyes narrowed to blue pinpoints. "I'll thank you to keep from interrupting me, Mr. Jones!" he roared.

Jones ducked his head and spun the rum glass in his big hands. Actually he had raised the very question that had been in my mind, too, though I had hoped Vail would go on before I asked him to explain.

"Did you ever hear of La Teste?" Captain Vail asked us. Then before any of us could reply, he said, "It's a port about thirty miles overland from Bordeaux. Dominique Diron said it's so little used the British don't pay much attention to it. I'll aim for there, then find a horse or mule and get to Bordeaux where my consignees, Messrs. Brun Frères, will advise me as to the disposition of the cargo."

"Do you mean that we might have to ship that cotton overland to Bordeaux, sir?" Lester Jordan asked. "Isn't that pretty risky?"

"It may be downright dangerous," Vail admitted. "Everything depends on how the war is going. The last we heard there was a big battle shaping up around Leipzig. If Boney won, there'll be no danger. If the Allies won, then they may be in France by now from the east, with Wellington also coming up from Spain. In that case, authority may have broken down and we'd be fair game for bandits. We'll have to wait until we get to La Teste to learn what the situation is."

But everyone knows what can happen to man's well laid plans. In the Bay of Biscay a gale blew up from the westward. Although we shortened sail and made the brig as snug as possible, a tremendous sea struck us just aft of the starboard foreshrouds, broke one of the top timbers, and split open the plank-sheer so that I could see directly into the hold. Not only that, but the volume of water drove the brig practically on her beam-ends. Fortunately Captain Vail had ordered everyone below except those seamen necessary to work ship. As it was, two men were washed, screaming, overboard into the wild tumble of water. I held onto a stay for dear life and knew this was the end. To my surprise I didn't have any final lofty thoughts or even think of my parents. I simply regretted that I'd never find out whether India Mitchell had deliberately let go of her scarf so that I might catch it.

Then, with a rumble and a great wrenching of wood, our bulwarks gave way under the weight of water, and two of our guns crashed overboard. Relieved of the water and lightened by the loss of the cannon, the *Argus* righted. Oliver Jones and I with four seamen nailed canvas over the broken plank-sheer, while Captain Vail veered the brig, being mortally afraid that the injury would endanger the foremast. For a while, running before the wind, we leaped from sea to sea, and the effect was like running over a washboard. Finally, however, Vail brought the *Argus* up into the wind, and under a mere patch of canvas, the brig lay to.

I was just finishing covering the split deck with tarred canvas when I heard Vail roar something through the speaking trumpet. The wind whipped even his voice away, however, so that it was impossible to make out what he was saying. Cautiously we crept aft, where Lester Jordan met us and, by yelling into my ears and by pantomiming, told me what Vail wanted. He intended to have us ride out the storm by means of a sea anchor. We got hold of a square sail yard, spanned it at the ends with a new four-ply rope, and, making the bower cable fast to the bight of the span and the other end fast to the foremast, we threw the spar overboard. We payed out more than sixty fathoms of cable, but the device did the trick. The spar broke the sea and held the brig's head to the wind through the rest of the gale. Though I have seen seamanship in stress, Captain Vail displayed a skill I have rarely seen matched, and never exceeded, in that terrible storm in the Bay of Biscay.

One result of the storm was that the English blockading ships were so scattered — in fact, several went down or were blown ashore — that we limped unmolested, not into La Teste as we had planned, but into the Garonne itself and up past lush farming country to Bordeaux.

Those were busy days. We got rid of our cotton for a booming price, worked around the clock repairing the *Argus*, and, watching our chance, slipped to sea on a starless night. A British frigate finally spotted us and threw a broadside at us, then lost us in the darkness.

We had learned while in Bordeaux that the *Ghost* had also been there. She had landed the Judge and India, who had set out in a diligence for Paris. Then the privateer, with Warren Bierce aboard, departed almost at once on a raid into the waters off the British Isles. Brad and I both wondered why, if Bierce had business in France, he had not lingered longer. Of course he may have completed whatever he came for. We knew, too, that few Americans were remaining longer than necessary in France since Bonaparte's armies were everywhere being defeated. The Austrians, Prussians, and Russians were pushing toward Paris, while the British were smashing up from the south. American privateersmen were therefore trying to take as many prizes as possible before the Emperor's government fell. A monarchy restored by the Allies might not offer a friendly haven to privateers of a power hostile to one of them. I suspected that was one of the reasons Captain Vail wanted to be at sea as quickly as possible. And indeed we considered ourselves lucky to make it to open water as soon as we did.

Once clear of the land, we raced toward British waters, keeping well off the French coast and cruising between Penzance and the Isle of Wight. Between Start Point and Portland Bill we took three prizes in as many days. Two we sent to the United States with prize crews, hoping they would find their way through the British blockade of our coast. The third, a brig of no great value, we released after first putting all the prisoners aboard her. Vail treated prisoners well, and when he let them go, they actually cheered him. I noticed that he was especially cordial to the English captains and invariably liquored them so thoroughly in his cabin that they were more than a little high when they came out on deck.

I thought, with word reaching Britain of the *Argus*'s presence off the south coast, Vail would surely take the brig around into the Irish Channel, a choice area for American privateers to operate. For that matter Captain Boyd with his lovely schooner *Chasseur* out of Baltimore had laid the entire British Isles under blockade according to a broadside sheet he sent into England. Rates at Lloyds shot up wildly. The *Argus* was no *Chasseur*, but within a fortnight more we took twelve additional prizes and therefore must have had some effect on the transactions at Lloyds. Certainly the British knew of us, for we had been chased three times, the last occasion being a near capture by a 38-gun frigate. Only our superior sailing qualities and skillful handling by Captain Vail saved us from Dartmoor, that dreadful gray prison where so many thousands of American and French seamen were rotting through the war. Notwithstanding the pressure on us, Vail stayed in those dangerous waters off the south coast. Even more puzzling and hazardous, he now worked his way closer to the coast and to Beachy Head.

But it wasn't until after we took a ten-gun brig of the Royal Navy, HMS *Alert*, thinking her a merchantman because of her rig, that the grumbling started. Our casualties would have been heavy without the superb gunnery of Philip Adair, who almost alone was responsible for reducing the *Alert* to a dismasted hulk rolling in a heavy swell. As it was, we had suffered five deaths and double that number of wounded before we were able to pull out of range of the brig's heavy carronades and cut her to pieces at long distance. A converted merchantman, she had given us a genuine fright. After she surrendered, we scuttled her and buried our dead. Then Captain Vail broke out his Madeira and toasted the British captain for his gallant fight until the Englishman had to be carried to his cabin. Though Vail himself must have been almost awash with wine, none would have suspected it from the crisp, almost joyfully efficient way he took charge of the *Argus*. With the prisoners clapped in the hold, repairs under way and blessed darkness enveloping us, Vail directed us, not south toward the French coast or west down the Channel, but up toward the Straits of Calais where the waters were narrow and the English cruisers numerous and watchful.

"Mr. Dearborn!" Adair whispered to me as I stood by the larboard rail peering at the coast of England. It wasn't my watch, but I felt uneasy so near enemy country and couldn't sleep. I turned a little stiffly because of a splinter wound in my left thigh, and saw the big Negro almost behind me.

"Yes, what is it, Philip?" I asked, a bit sharply, I'm afraid, because he had startled me; I hadn't heard him approach.

"May I speak with you, seh?"

"Of course. Is anything the matter?"

"Well, seh," he began awkwardly, "it's the crew. They don't like our being so close to England."

"Well, who does?" I retorted.

"But we're really a privateer and not expected to take the risks of a government ship. The men see us ending up in Dartmoor."

"Look here, Philip," and I tried to control my annoyance, "I won't argue the point. But hasn't Captain Vail done right well by all of us? This is a remarkable cruise. How many privateers have taken as many prizes in so short a time since leaving France?"

"Not many, seh."

"And nothing serious has happened to us yet, has it?"

"No, seh."

"Then I think the men should continue to trust Captain Vail. He knows what he's doing, and I'm sure he doesn't like the prospect of a stretch in Dartmoor any more than you or I or anyone else."

"Yes, seh. But you must admit it is dangerous here in the Channel."

"Yes, of course it's dangerous," I said. "But it's no worse here than off our own Atlantic coast, probably not so bad. Now you'd better tell your friends to keep trusting Captain Vail."

"Very good, seh."

But our course was peculiar, despite my assurance to Adair. Was it because the English cruisers were searching for us back the way we had come? Did Vail intend to slip through the Calais Straits and up into the North Sea? Though he kept his own counsel, he doubled the lookouts, ordered all lights doused, and insisted that one section sleep near the guns.

Toward midnight, we edged near Eastbourne when a warning whisper passed along the decks. Though the advance streamers of a fog bank were wiping out the stars, we could dimly see a solid mass of darkness that denoted a craft of some kind moving toward us from land. Orders flew in whispers and the sleepy crew pattered swiftly on bare feet to their stations.

"What's it all about?" Brad asked as the marines filed by me.

"You know as well as I do," I muttered. But he was gone so quickly I doubt if he heard me.

Soon Captain Vail grunted an order to Lester Jordan and the helmsman, and we started to come about slowly, moving to parallel the course of the approaching vessel.

Then the fog shut in, bitterly cold and impenetrable. For a while Vail kept all the men at the guns, but presently ordered half of them dismissed. Still, though he was clearly resigned to remaining in the fog, he refused to alter the new course of the *Argus*, which, if maintained with a wind, would eventually have brought us onto the French coast near Boulogne. Not that we now made any headway in the fog; our progress was more a drift sideways because of the tide.

Nor did Vail permit any talking; we could only whisper. He seemed convinced the other ship had not seen us. At the same time, he wouldn't tell any of us the reason for our strange behavior.

Seeing Jordan glance at our canvas as a block squeaked, I went up to him and asked him if he knew what all this was about. He shrugged. "Don't know more'n you do, Jonathan," he said gruffly. And knowing that he used words the way a Scotsman spends dollars, I didn't press him further.

With daylight we continued to drift, and the fog was so dense that we could not see the length of the ship. There is something about fog under any circumstances that subdues one. Voices instinctively hush; one even starts walking more quietly. Aboard the *Argus*, not knowing just what to expect, we scarcely dared whisper at this point. Certainly Captain Vail expected something to happen, though he didn't tell us what. The fact that he wanted fresh men at the guns every two hours and new lookouts posted every half hour was ominous.

Sometime before midmorning a puff of air caught us. Instantly Vail passed the word for the officers to assemble on the afterdeck. When we reached there on the run, he handed telescopes to Oliver Jones and myself and said, "I want you officers to go aloft and tell us what you see. The fog should be clearing to larboard. Mr. Jordan, I want you to see that, if possible, we remain in this fog bank. If there's not enough breeze, get the longboat ready to pull us, and mind you muffle the oars. This ship must not be seen."

For a moment we stared at him, then darted for the masts, Oliver for the foremast, I for the main. Brad, crouched against the cabin house with the marines, raised an inquiring eyebrow, but I merely shrugged. I felt like Aladdin with Vail rubbing the lamp. What genie was about to appear was a mystery, but I was certainly curious.

Yet up in the maintop with the two lookouts already there and my back firmly against the mast I could see nothing at first. The sun, a lemon disk, was trying to break through. Here and there, patches of filmy blue sky were visible. Otherwise, it was a white, half-luminous world I looked out upon, a mass of unsubstantial, feathery down.

Then another light puff of wind, and I saw them. Protruding above the fog, though still partially enshrouded, drooped the topsails of a schooner, perhaps a thousand yards away. Yet even as I brought the

[ 56 ]

glass up to my eye, fog shut out the view. I was just about to report my discovery to the deck when again the schooner appeared. This time the rising breeze rolled more of the fog away from her, and for a moment I studied her. Then, even as I reached for a rope, I heard Oliver whistle softly. He, too, had seen her.

"Keep your eye on her, Oliver," I called softly to him, and slid to the deck, burning my hands on the rope in my speed.

"Larboard about two points, sir, and a thousand yards away, a big schooner heading east-southeast," I said to Captain Vail.

"Let's take no chances, then," Vail growled. "Get the boat out, Mr. Jordan."

"Aye, aye, sir," Lester said crisply.

I thought he was a little annoyed that either Oliver or I had not been given the longboat duty, but surely he could see that "Little Ben" had assigned it to him as the most experienced and reliable of the officers.

"Now, Mr. Dearborn, is she flying any colors?" Captain Vail asked.

"The fog was too thick for me to see."

Vail cupped his hands and, keeping his voice down, called up the same question to Oliver Jones.

"Can't see, sir," Jones replied. "Wait a minute, fog's clearin' a little. Yes, sir, she's flyin' a British ensign."

"Break out the same," Vail said to me.

It was a strange morning. We stayed under the fog cover as long as there was any density to it and kept relieving the men in the long-boat. Just before concealment was no longer possible, we picked up the longboat, and, continued to steer the same course as the powerful-looking British schooner, though by this time we were far astern of her and at least two miles laterally distant. I don't think she had observed us until the fog lifted; certainly thereafter she paid no attention to us. She was a vessel of great speed, for she drew away from us with ease. Why she didn't challenge us puzzled me unless she judged us to be one of His Majesty's war brigs.

Just exactly who she was likewise puzzled me until Philip Adair confirmed a nagging suspicion growing on me for hours. We were making the Long Tom secure when he said, out of a tired silence as I dismissed the gun crews, "Mr. Dearborn, in case you don't know by now, seh, that schooner was the *Ghost*."

"The *Ghost*, of course!" I exclaimed. "I thought she looked familiar. But how did you know, Philip?"

He softly caressed the polished barrel. "I sailed on her for two years under Captain Rudd. 'Tisn't likely I'd forget her."

"Or him?"

"Or him," he added softly.

I had no need to ask where he had acquired the great welts on his body. Rudd, it appeared, was quick to use the cat-o'-nine-tails. Stripped and spread-eagled to a grating, a seaman was punished for the slightest offense aboard his ship. He ruled his crew through fear, and colored men, in particular, he treated badly. "He likes dogs better than my people," Philip explained.

"Was he a slaver, Philip?"

"A slaver and a very cruel one," the big Negro nodded. "Very cruel, seh."

In the late forenoon, Captain Vail summoned us again to a conference in his cabin. This time he served us hot coffee heavily laced with rum, and God knows we needed it. Our eyes were bloodshot, and my head roared from strain and loss of sleep. Of all of us Captain Vail alone looked alert and tireless as he perched on the edge of his chair. The only aspect out of keeping with his neat appearance was that he needed a shave. There was silence for a few moments as we sipped the steaming drink; then Vail's stern, little face began to crack in a grin, though his deep-set eyes remained serious.

"I guess it's time to explain about this cruise," he said. "First, you know, I'm sure, that the schooner was the *Ghost*."

It seems that others besides Philip had recognized her, including Lester Jordan, and the *Argus* had hummed with speculation as to how she had managed to get in so close to the English coast and out again without being molested. It was generally held that Captain Vail had really thought her an Englishman until the fog blew clear, and this appeared a plausible explanation for our conduct since first spotting her the previous night.

As we remained silent, merely nodding at his remark, Vail flexed his fingers, cracking the knuckles, then folded his hands. "I want to swear each of you to secrecy as long as we are on this cruise," he said in a voice so low it was like a rumbling whisper.

With that he literally had each of us swear on his Bible not to divulge what was said. Then, still keeping his voice down, he said, "I have reason to believe that Bierce and Rudd were in communication with the British authorities. What their business was with the British I don't know for sure, but I'm certain it boded no good for our country."

"Why, those bastards!" And Oliver Jones belched in his disgust, then wiped his mouth with the back of his hand.

"You know now why we've hung on in these waters," Vail continued. "I asked the captain of every ship we've taken if he'd seen the *Ghost* or a schooner like her. It wasn't until just before we met the *Alert* that I learned from a captain that a schooner he believed to be an American had sailed by him without stopping him. This surprised him. Then the captain of the *Alert* spilled the information I was looking for — with the help of my Madeira," Vail added with a wry grin.

"You might've got more out of him with rum," Oliver put it boldly.

Vail looked for an instant as if he would blast the fat man, then shook his head and said with great self-control, "The Madeira was adequate. The *Alert* stopped the *Ghost*, but Rudd showed the officer who boarded her a certificate signed by the British consul at Fayal — Rudd had stopped at the Azores on his way to Europe. The certificate requested a safe passage for the *Ghost* to and from England because of business of state. The *Alert* actually escorted her into Eastbourne where Bierce went ashore and hired a carriage to London."

Lester Jordan's lips formed a soundless whistle, which was going far for him.

"Well, even the Britisher thought it strange conduct," Vail said. "Which reminds me," he added, "he must have slept off his drunk by this time. I'd better have a look at him soon."

"But where does this leave us, sir?" I asked. "I mean, what do we do now?"

Vail sat so far forward his chair actually tipped. "It means this, Mr. Dearborn, it means that we'll put into the nearest French port that isn't blockaded and send you and your lawyer friend Pettigrew to Paris with dispatches for the United States representative to France, Mr. William Crawford."

"Paris!"

"Did I mention some other city?" Vail growled.

"No, sir, but — well, I'm trying to get used to the idea."

"Then get used to it and be quick about it. You're going to Paris, Jonathan. Understand? Tell Pettigrew, and you won't wear your uniforms, either. You speak French?"

"Not well," I admitted, sorry now that I never applied myself to the language when my father had tried to teach it to me. "But Brad does," I said quickly.

"Good. If I can't find any port open by tomorrow, I'll land you and Pettigrew on the French coast tomorrow night. You've got to get to Paris as fast as you can. Then come back and join us at Bordeaux — if we're there."

"And if you're not?"

He shrugged. "Wait for us awhile — a couple of weeks, at least, maybe a month, then get back home as best you can. I'll see that you have funds. There'll be plenty of privateers leaving with the Allies closing in on the ports. Now, back to your duties, gentlemen. I'll have more specific instructions for you later, Mr. Dearborn," he said as we rose to our feet.

Paris, the most exciting city in Europe! And India Mitchell was there. I had difficulty maintaining my composure as second officer of the *Argus* but succeeded in walking with unhurried deliberation to the marines' quarters to inform Brad of our assignment to the French capital.

---

# VII

THE next night, Captain Vail set Brad and me ashore on the French coast just above Dieppe. Having extracted the British signal code from the *Alert*, he appeared confident that he could disguise the *Argus* as that brig and answer any signal directed to him. I considered it our good fortune, however, that we were not challenged, though we saw a cluster of sails off Dieppe indicating the presence of blockaders.

As we were closing in on the coast, Vail summoned both of us to his cabin. Handing me a sealed packet, he said, "See that this gets into Mr. Crawford's own hands. Don't give it to one of his secretaries. I don't think you'll have any trouble with the French, but if the Empire falls before you can deliver it, be careful. A new government would be friendly to Britain. You may even have to destroy the packet."

"But what should we tell Mr. Crawford in that case?" I asked, looking first at him, then at the thin brown packet, sealed with red wax.

Captain Vail strode across the deck and looked out of the cabin windows. Then he spun around. "Tell him exactly what you have observed," he said roughly. "Tell him I represent a group in Portland that thinks Bierce more Federalist than the Federalists — however our people may differ about the war, with some of them even trading with the British, they're not traitors. I'm not so sure about Bierce, and my associates in Portland share my doubt."

"But what could he possibly do to hurt us, sir?" Brad asked.

Vail stared at him. "What could he do? Young man, if Boney goes under and the Allies put one of Louis XVI's brothers back on the French throne, the whole British fleet can take off for America. You know the British haven't cracked down on us in New England as hard as they have on the rest of the seaboard. But, with Boney gone, they'd be off our coast thicker'n clams in a pie. I think Mr. Warren Bierce might have told those highups in London how they could end the war quickly."

"How could they?" Brad pressed him.

"How could they! They could land a force somewhere on the Maine coast and build up a base of operations nearer than Halifax or St. John in New Brunswick. They could play on our differences about the war and invite our merchants to trade with them. That's what they could do, and it wouldn't help the United States one particle. 'Course Mr. Warren Bierce would see that he didn't lose in any arrangement that was made."

"What can Mr. Crawford do with this information?" I asked.

"He can send it to the administration in Washington by the fastest ship. The administration will do a better job of alerting our people than we can. Besides, coming from Crawford, the information would be official and would carry more weight than anything we could say."

"Can't we carry back this information in the *Argus* if he endorses it?" I asked.

Vail nodded. "Yes, if we happen to be around. And I'll try to stay somewhere near Bordeaux in case you bring that letter back with you."

Later, dressed in our civilian clothes and with francs in our purses provided by Vail, we waded through icy water and, quickly taking shelter in bushes growing near the shore, watched the four-oared boat pull quietly back to the brig. I won't deny feeling, momentarily, somewhat bewildered and lost. Then we put on our stockings and shoes, picked up the valise each of us carried, and headed up the bank toward a road that wound near the shore. Our fear was that some French customs or revenue agent might think we were English spies despite the identifying papers we carried, including a letter of introduction from Captain Vail to Mr. Crawford which we were to show to any official who stopped us.

Walking along that empty road at night didn't seem the wisest course if a patrol should come along, so when we drew near a clump of trees, we snugged down as best we could and dozed and shivered the rest of the night with our backs up against a tree trunk. With morning we started out again and soon got a ride into Dieppe with a farmer taking eggs and cheese to market. At first he was so suspicious and afraid I thought he'd refuse us. Fortunately Brad's French was easily equal to explaining that we were Americans who were trying to get to Paris. Certainly there appeared to be no reason for not telling the truth. Despite Brad's fluency, I think it was the francs I suddenly showed in my hand that persuaded him. He grinned under his heavy mustache and invited us to join him on the seat of his cart.

Once in Dieppe we went to the inn from which, so the farmer said, a coach left for Paris. At the inn we were told a coach would not leave until the following morning. There was nothing to be done, therefore, but to register at the inn for the night and book seats on the coach.

The day seemed endless. I fully expected a police officer would call at the inn and demand to see our papers, but nothing of the sort occurred. Instead, the innkeeper told us he would make a routine report of our presence as lodgers. There seemed to be a looseness of procedure on the part of officials, which may have come with the severe French defeats and the subsequent breakdown of morale. People thought the war about over and were fearful that the Allied armies might sweep to the coast before it ended. They were especially worried that the Russian Cossacks would appear. It was as if no one cared whether two foreigners landed on the coast so long as they weren't Cossacks. The innkeeper's wife, a burly woman whose powerful arms and raucous voice would have intimidated most men, said she prayed the English would arrive before the Cossacks, who had a dreadful reputation for maltreating women. I think she was a little disappointed that we were Americans and not the advance agents of an invading English army.

The coach to Paris took aboard only two people besides ourselves — a well-dressed, middle-aged couple who soon explained that they were going to the capital to bring their daughter and their new grandson back to Dieppe. "It will be dangerous for them in Paris with the war coming so close," the woman said nervously, looking to her husband as if for confirmation. All he did, however, was to grunt, his numerous chins quivering.

Cutting down through Rouen, where two more couples, elderly people, climbed aboard, the coach swung along the Seine Valley. One thing we could not help noticing was that while the spring plowing was everywhere in progress, nowhere did we see young men. This seemed to bear out a rumor we had heard in Dieppe that the peasants were hiding their sons lest they be caught up in the Emperor's latest draft. Regardless of the absence of young men and the fact that it was still only early April, the countryside had a trim, well-cared-for appearance, reminding me of a park.

As we approached Paris on a fine graveled road, we began to encounter people streaming towards us, driving carts or carriages piled high with goods, or walking bowed over from the packs on their backs. Our driver with much cursing and cracking of his whip kept a way open for the coach, though at times we made little progress.

"Oh, these refugees!" the Dieppe woman moaned in exasperation, while her husband again grunted and buried his chin in its folds.

Evidently the fear of the Cossacks was all-pervasive. Leaning out the windows, we chatted with some of these people. They said that Napoleon was beaten and would probably abdicate. They urged us, if we valued our lives, not to continue to Paris since the Allies must surely have occupied it by this time. We wondered for a while whether our coachman would keep on, but at one rest stop he stuck his hatchet face into the coach and said that he'd been hired to do a job and he proposed to do it, war or no war. This was cheering news.

As we approached Paris, the stream of refugees fell off to a trickle, then stopped altogether. The answer came when we were halted by a patrol just outside the city: the patrol consisted not of French troops but of a detail of stolid Austrians in dirty white coats. The young lieutenant who examined our papers was spruce and friendly enough, however, and, in French with a Germanic accent, informed us that on March 31 the Allies had entered the city, which officially surrendered on April 2 and was now under Allied control. A curfew was imposed from nightfall to sunrise; otherwise, people might come and go as they wished. Once our coach lumbered into the city it was clear that the occupation was orderly and peaceful. Certainly there were no signs that Paris had risen in a deadly street-to-street fight in behalf of Napoleon. Evidently even the capital had wearied of the little Corsican, who, so the garrulous lieutenant said, had just abdicated at Fontainebleau, and the French Senate, under the direction of Talleyrand, endorsed the restoration of the Bourbons in the person of Louix XVIII.

Where to stay presented no difficulty. Captain Vail had strongly recommended the Hotel Strasbourg in the Rue Notre Dame des Victoires. The hotel, if not elegant, was at least comfortable, and we were glad to settle down for the night. Then, the urgency of the situation goading our consciences, we headed in the early morning for the United States Legation. Half expecting not to find the minister in his office, we were pleased to be told by the young Frenchman who was his secretary that Mr. Crawford would see us, though we should have to wait our turn.

At least a half-dozen Americans sat on the benches. From their conversation two were privateering captains; the others, merchants. All seemed desperately concerned about their status in this conquered country, though the privateersmen said they thought they would have to get their ships out of French ports quickly.

When we finally were admitted to Crawford's office, he stood up — he was an extremely tall, broad-shouldered man — and greeted us. "We've heard of the *Argus* here in Paris," he said in his affable Southern manner. "You people have done excellent work. Now, how can I help you?"

Crawford had replaced Joel Barlow when Barlow went to meet Napoleon in Russia and died in the disastrous retreat from Moscow. A Georgian in his early forties, Crawford held his left arm close to his body. His wrist had been crippled ever since a duel in 1806, while four years before that, he had fought a duel in which he killed his opponent. He had served in the United States Senate, declined when Madison offered to make him Secretary of War, but accepted the Paris post in 1813. Frankly I was impressed with this big, handsome man, and, hoping he might understand, I briefly summed up the situation with respect to Bierce and the *Ghost*, and handed him Captain Vail's letter.

"This is very interesting, gentlemen, very interesting indeed," he said, leaning back in his chair and gazing at each of us. "Look here, let me read Captain Vail's letter tonight, then you two come back tomorrow about this time. Can you arrange to do so?"

"Yes, sir," I said. "And that'll give us at least this afternoon to look around Paris."

He smiled broadly. "Good. See what you can, and don't get into any trouble with the Allied soldiers. Some of them are feeling their oats. In fact, I'd advise you to stay off the streets after dark. Good day, gentlemen."

It was not until we were out on the street that I remembered we had forgotten to ask Crawford if he knew where Judge Kent and India Mitchell were staying.

"Cheer up," Brad laughed when I lamented my sievelike memory, "we'll ask Crawford tomorrow. Besides, maybe someone at the Strasbourg will know."

But unfortunately no one at the hotel had heard of them, which surprised me a little since the Strasbourg seemed quite a gathering place for Americans. In fact, I think I heard as much English as French spoken there.

Accordingly we spent the day wandering over the city admiring the gilded dome of the Hotel des Invalides and especially the view from Montmartre. Yet it was down in the twisting, narrow streets that we caught the flavor of the Paris of the moment. People hung in groups outside the stores talking at furious speed. Whenever foreign soldiers passed, they would hush or simply mutter and give the men dirty looks. There was one element in the populace, however, that was certainly an exception: the whores. Standing at the doorways or leaning out of windows, they called out a chorus of invitations that reminded me of the raucous bluejays in my father's yard when they spied Nelly, my mother's cat. Some of these were girls who looked attractive in a brazen way, while others were mottle-faced, straggly haired harridans that made my flesh crawl. A man would have had to have been at sea for a long time or involved in an extended land campaign to turn in at these doorways. Yet I saw a number of soldiers do so, especially brawny Cossacks and men wearing the scarlet of King George. Brad and I were invited, too, but whereas I looked stonily ahead, feeling embarrassed and annoyed, Brad raised his hat to the girls and gaily assured them he would be back another time. This never failed to touch off a storm of pleading and whistling which made Brad laugh and even amused me.

In Paris, the palaces, the avenues, the historic places were truly impressive, but it was the people that fascinated me even while I often struggled with my disapproval. They were so colorful, so noisy, so excitable compared to our more somber, Puritanical people at home. I can't say I'd like to have made my permanent residence in Paris, but I had to admit it was alive as no city I had ever seen, not even London with its boisterousness or Naples where it seemed that every third day was a holiday and knives flashed at the slightest, most fanciful affront to honor.

It was late when we returned to the Strasbourg, to clean up after a dusty day and dine. We had scarcely entered our room when the proprietor's apprentice knocked at our door and handed me a note that had arrived, he said, in late afternoon.

It was from Mr. Crawford; he hoped we would find it possible to come to his office without fail at nine in the morning. This struck Brad and me as curious since we had already agreed to be there about that time anyway. We decided this must be Mr. Crawford's way of reminding us to be prompt.

The next morning found us waiting in the dingy little waiting room, its once light-green walls streaked with brown stains where the rain had leaked through the mansard roof. As soon as the French secretary announced us, Mr. Crawford invited us inside his office.

"Gentlemen," he said, leaning forward on his desk and looking like a mastiff about to jump at us, "the letter you gave me yesterday went off to Washington last evening in the diplomatic pouch with an endorsement from me. Captain Yardley of the privateer *Good Hope* will try to slip out of La Rochelle. He has a fast ship and has disguised her as a Spaniard. He speaks Spanish himself."

"He'll have to be lucky to get through the blockade on both sides of the Atlantic," I said.

"Of course. But just in case he doesn't get through I had copies made of everything and wish you to carry a set to Captain Vail. As soon as you make your rendezvous with him, he should sail at once for America and get this information to Washington. I am so instructing him in a letter."

"You certainly haven't wasted any time, Mr. Crawford," Brad said with obvious admiration.

"Frankly, I haven't," Crawford admitted. "I cannot testify as to whether Captain Vail's suspicions have been confirmed, but intelligence I have just received from London does indicate that Warren Bierce was closeted with Lord Liverpool, the Prime Minister, and Earl St. Vincent, head of the Admiralty. We know, too, that Bierce was given certification of safe passage for his ship."

"Do you suppose Bierce has landed in France, sir?" Brad asked.

"Why, yes," Crawford said quietly. "He's here in Paris now. He arrived the day before you did. In fact, he called on me yesterday to pay his respects just about an hour after you left. You may know that he has had an agent here in Paris for at least a fortnight setting up contacts with various French merchants. An irascible man, this Judge Kent, as Bierce calls him. Do you know him?"

"Yes, sir," Brad and I said together, then looked at each other and laughed.

"Is he loyal to our country?"

Again we looked at each other, but this time in silence. "He is not a friend of the administration," I said, "but I know of nothing against his loyalty to the country."

"I agree," Brad said.

"Do you know his ward, Miss Mitchell?"

I nodded. "Yes, sir."

"Is she loyal?"

"Absolutely!" And I'm afraid I was suddenly so angry at the question that my tone was harsh. At any rate, Crawford's large eyes became even larger.

"It's like this, sir," Brad said with his ready smile. "My friend here has a certain attachment to Miss Mitchell that hardly qualifies him to be objective. I, on the other hand, have no such attachment. Miss Mitchell is loyal despite her uncle's association with Warren Bierce and Captain Rudd. And, of course, neither of these had been proved disloyal."

"Rudd!" Crawford stood up. "Do you gentlemen know anything about Jake Rudd?"

"Nothing to his credit," I said, thinking of Philip Adair.

"I should think not, I should think not!"

A certain quality in the man's voice put me suddenly on guard. Having been brought up in a ministerial family and having heard many ministers speak from the pulpit, I was aware of oratorical techniques. Moreover, as a boy I had occasionally slipped off, unbeknownst to my parents, to hear the theatrical company down at Union Hall on Free Street. Unfortunately, in 1806 the people in a town meeting not only expressed their opposition to the proposed erection of a theater as such but also to the continuance of further stage plays. I had heard enough actors, however, to detect the significance of intonations, so that now I had the feeling that Crawford, an orator of long training on the stump and in the Senate, was putting on something of an act. Resolving to draw him out, I asked, with seeming innocence, "What's wrong about Rudd?"

"Young man, what is wrong with a rattlesnake? Down in my part of the country we're quick to avenge our honor, maybe too quick," he added, gently massaging his left forearm. "Rudd has been a slaver for years, and though we own slaves in the South, that doesn't mean we agree with all aspects of slavery, especially the cruelty of those who bring the slaves to our shores. Rudd had a good record for getting his ship over without too many dying, but I think he must have got it by treating those about to die so meanly he frightened the rest into living. Anyway, I met him through a planter friend of mine. I didn't like him, but my friend owed him a lot of money, so I was polite to him, or tried to be. Next thing we knew, my friend provoked Rudd into fighting a duel, and Rudd shot him dead. It seems that Rudd was paying mighty close attention to my friend's wife. When my friend told him off, Rudd threatened to sue for what was owed him. My friend challenged and died. Later on, Rudd ran off with the daughter of a family down in Savannah. Got her with child and deserted her; then, when her father caught up with him, Rudd gunned him down. Rudd claimed it was self-defense. Maybe it was, and maybe it wasn't. The man is rotten. He finally found it too risky for him in Georgia, so he drifted north. He knows the sea, and I'll wager he's made a lot of money off the war."

"So have a lot of people," Brad said.

Crawford shrugged his shoulders. "Of course, of course. But I'm telling you young men to watch out for Rudd. Now this Bierce is too smooth and shifty to be healthy. Maybe he's a traitor, or maybe he's just a merchant interested in making money regardless of the political issues or the means — I suspect he's that rather than a traitor as such, though, in effect, it boils down to the same thing. At any rate, he's obviously a man of few scruples, and he has associated himself with a man who has no scruples."

Captain Vail had mentioned that Crawford liked to talk and was a gifted raconteur. I could agree that he had no regard for the virtues of brevity. At the same time, much of what he said rang true.

"Mr. Crawford," I asked, "do you know where India Mitchell and her uncle are staying?"

Crawford's eyes twinkled. "Mr. Dearborn, are you a card player?"

I shook my head, all too aware of my bringing-up in a minister's household and wishing I had been interested enough to learn to play while at sea with Uncle Tom. He and Aunt Betsy had often played, but I never accepted their invitation to teach me, not even when Aunt Betsy teased me for being uncivilized. In fact, I think it was lack of interest rather than any sense of sin carrying over from parental influence that had kept me in ignorance.

Crawford's eyes opened wide. "I forgot," he said apologetically, though his tone was faintly mocking. "You Yankees up in New England don't approve of card playing, do you? Why, down in our part of the country our youngsters grow up with a bottle of whiskey in one hand and a pack of cards in the other." He laughed uproariously at his own remark, and even harder, I think, as I began to flush with embarrassment. It didn't help my composure to see Brad smile, too.

Then Brad drew out his silver cigar case and offered a cigar to Crawford, who accepted and stared in amazement as Brad lighted both cigars with a match from his combustion box.

"Why, I never saw one of those contraptions before," Crawford said with almost childish interest.

"Very neat, Senator, don't you think?"

"Beats flint and steel!"

"It surely does. Now, sir, if I understand correctly, you were about to say something to my friend here concerning the advantage of retaining trumps until last. Is that correct?"

How I envied Brad's smooth manner and deftness in shutting off the Georgian's laughter and bringing him back to whatever he was going to say.

Crawford drew deeply on his cigar and exhaled the smoke with a long, audible sigh. "Splendid cigar, Mr. Pettigrew, splendid. And you, I see, are not ignorant of those wicked, little pasteboards. Now, Mr. Dearborn," he said, his voice suddenly becoming very businesslike, "forgive my little humor at your expense, but a politician is a little like our Lord at the wedding at Cana who was congratulated by the governor of the ceremony for saving the good wine until last. Yesterday afternoon, Miss Mitchell came to see me."

"India, here?" I half rose to my feet. Was this how Crawford had learned about Rudd's being with Bierce?

"Now, now, relax, young man," and he gestured me back into my chair.

"Miss Mitchell is a charming young woman," he went on. "She seems to think well of you and Mr. Pettigrew, though I was not aware from her conversation that any kind of attachment such as Mr. Pettigrew mentioned exists between you and her."

At his sudden, sharp look, I swallowed hard. "I think my friend exaggerated a little," I said.

"In fact, I gathered you are only an acquaintance."

I nodded. "That is right, sir," but I felt silly and angry at having to admit it.

"Very good. I am glad to understand this point." He tapped a small bell, and when his secretary entered, he excused himself and conferred briefly with the man.

Meanwhile Brad and I glanced at each other, and I had no feeling of reassurance as Brad shrugged eloquently in an ignorance as deep as mine.

"Now, gentlemen," Crawford said, as his secretary left, "I think both of you should make your arrangements for leaving Paris tomorrow. I shall have the documents ready for you late this afternoon and will have them delivered personally to you, Mr. Dearborn, at your hotel. You said that Captain Vail would be waiting somewhere in the vicinity of Bordeaux?"

"Yes, sir," I said.

"It will take you four to five days to reach Bordeaux. You must then find Vail and get home as fast as you can. And always keep the packet I will send you on your person, Mr. Dearborn."

He rose, came around from his desk to shake hands with us, and wished us Godspeed. But as we started for the door, he suddenly cleared his throat, then tapping his fingers on the desk as if trying to recall some final thought, he struck the bell.

Instantly the door opened, and his secretary reappeared, only to step aside, and I looked into the amused gray-green eyes of India Mitchell.

[ 71 ]

# VIII

"INDIA!"

Her name leaped out, and only afterward did the thought strike me that I had never before called her by her first name.

As Brad bowed and Crawford held a chair for her, she curtsied briefly, and sat down, smoothing her dark blue dress.

"Won't you join us, Mr. Dearborn?" Crawford asked.

I then saw to my discomfort that both he and Brad had seated themselves, and that Brad seemed greatly amused. I suppose it did look funny to see me standing there all by myself staring at India. Talk about country bumpkins! Hastily I thanked Crawford and sat down.

"Mr. Dearborn seems surprised to see you, Miss Mitchell," Crawford said dryly.

"There is really no reason why he shouldn't be," she said — and her voice with its throaty huskiness held a note of laughter.

"Well, India," said Brad, "you and Mr. Crawford have evidently played a little game on us."

"Mr. Crawford is responsible for that," India laughed. "He knew you and Jonathan were returning this morning, so he had me time my arrival accordingly. I think he should manage a company of actors as well as the affairs of the United States in France."

"Believe me, Miss Mitchell," Crawford said, "that is what I believe I am doing when I consider the problems and temperament of some of the people who come to my office. Seriously, gentlemen, I thought it would be advisable for Miss Mitchell to come here today and explain her situation. Miss Mitchell?"

She looked at both of us, and as she moved her head, the white ostrich feather on her saucy blue hat waved jauntily. "I have known neither of you really well — you fairly well, to be sure, Brad, but you only by name and face, Jonathan. Still, both of you come from Maine, and I feel you are the only people in Paris I can trust right now — except, of course, Mr. Crawford."

Crawford bowed like a courtier, while my mind was a tumult of admiration and curiosity, which included my wondering whether she had deliberately or accidentally omitted the name of Warren Bierce.

"Both of you know that Jason Kent is my uncle," India said, and her voice became oddly flat. "The Judge was to become Warren Bierce's business agent here in Paris — that was our reason for leaving Portland. Unfortunately, Uncle Jason has become ill and now wants to go home."

"Is Bierce about to go home, too?" I asked, and startled myself with the harshness of my voice.

"Yes, Warren — Mr. Bierce is about to leave for Portland, too."

"On the *Ghost?*"

"I really don't know, but I presume so."

"Then why aren't you and your uncle going on the *Ghost*, too?"

She clasped her gloved hands together, then as quickly unclasped them and held them closely again in her lap. "That is exactly why I have come here to see you and Brad."

"Any reason will do so long as we can see you, India," my friend said.

She gave him a quick, nervous smile in return, then looked back at my sober face. Whatever she had to say I was evidently the one she felt she had to convince.

"As I explained to Mr. Crawford," she went on, "in his illness Uncle Jason has formed a dislike for Mr. Bierce."

Crawford cleared his throat. "If I understood you aright, Miss Mitchell, your uncle and Mr. Bierce quarreled before he became ill."

She nodded. "Yes, they quarreled several times on the way over to France, but I was not aware of how my uncle felt until he was sick. He developed a cough and has intermittent spells of fever. But the most disturbing thing is the hatred he bears for Warren Bierce."

"Why does he hate Bierce?" Brad asked.

"I'm not sure," she said. "It may be because Mr. Bierce has asked me to marry him and he disapproves."

I looked at her face, suddenly pale, and could not speak for a moment. My throat was dry, and momentarily I felt dizzy. Then, after an eon of silence, my head cleared, the sounds of a dray creaking over the cobblestones of the street no longer seemed shattering, and a certain cold clarity possessed me. Though I longed to ask her if she had accepted Bierce, I asked, instead, "Are you sure the Judge's feeling has nothing to do with the question of Bierce's loyalty?"

"My uncle is sometimes — well, fanciful. I am sure there is no question of Warren's loyalty," she said. "Moreover, they did have hard words on two occasions over business."

I saw the exchange of glances between Brad and Crawford and Brad's slight shrug. If India only knew what we suspected about Bierce!

"What is it you want of us, India?" I asked.

"As soon as I learned that you and Brad were in Paris and mentioned the fact to Uncle Jason, he insisted that I ask if you would kindly see that he got back to Maine. I had come to Mr. Crawford, and he suggested that you would be willing to help me."

"Are you going back with the Judge?" Brad asked.

"I'll have to. He needs someone to look after him. And I may as well be frank with you: there are times when Uncle Jason doesn't know or doesn't care what he says. I think you two gentlemen will understand and make allowances."

I stared at her. She had practically told us that Judge Kent was hurling accusations right and left about Bierce that wouldn't sound good in the ears of strangers. But she herself, it also seemed clear, didn't believe them.

"Look here, India," I said. "We're going to Bordeaux on the coach tomorrow morning. Captain Vail may not be there or even near the port when we arrive. As you know, the *Argus* is a privateer, and Brad and I have been in Paris to see about — well, business connected with our cruise. Captain Vail will put in at Bordeaux, but we may have to wait for him."

"We'll be willing to wait," she said, "though I hope it won't be for long."

"Besides," I added, "Captain Vail may encounter an enemy warship after he picks us up, and it's possible he'll object to taking you and your uncle aboard because of the danger."

"We'll take our chances on the danger, and I'll rely on you and Brad to overcome Captain Vail's objections."

[ 74 ]

She smiled at me, but, though my heart did a crazy flip-flop, I continued to look at her soberly. "Does Warren Bierce know what you are planning?"

"That was one of my questions yesterday to Miss Mitchell," Crawford said.

She turned to him. "And I said then that he did not, and he still doesn't know unless Uncle Jason has said something to him."

"Which he might have," Brad said. "You must know, India, the Judge doesn't have a reputation for keeping a secret."

She flushed and her toe began to tap the floor. "But that is only when he has had too much to drink. He's not supposed to touch spirits now because of his condition."

"Well, what if Bierce does know?" I asked. "It could be embarrassing for India and awkward for us, perhaps, but what more?"

"Probably nothing," Brad admitted, though the reservation in his voice was not lost on me.

I studied India. No longer did she look amused or calm or vehement. She was downright anxious, and I began to realize how much what I had to say would mean to her.

"India," I said, "if you wish to take a chance on a wait and on our not being able to persuade Captain Vail to carry you and the Judge back to Maine, we'll gladly have you come to Bordeaux with us."

Her relief was so obvious that she looked at her gloves as if trying to conceal how she felt. "Thank you, Jonathan, and you, Brad — and you, too, Mr. Crawford, for your kindness. Uncle Jason and I will be on the Bordeaux coach tomorrow morning."

And so they were when the big coach clattered over the cobblestone streets of Paris and finally picked up the fine-graveled road that led through Orleans, along the banks of the Loire to Blois, and hence through Tours, Poitiers, and Angoulême to Bordeaux.

The coach held eight passengers, but the four of us were the only ones going through to Bordeaux. Others got in and out at the post stops along the way and often eyed us in an unfriendly manner as we talked in English. And talk we did. There was a certain stiffness at first, particularly on the part of the Judge, who, despite his pallor and clearly weakened condition, was inclined to huff and puff and bluff his way. In fact, he acted so superior and domineering at times that I half regretted having consented to the travel arrangement. For example, he started in on the subject of Caleb Strong, the Federalist governor of Massachusetts, the very first day. I had never seen Governor Strong, but I had no regard for him, and when the Judge started to extol his virtues, I grew angry.

"What has he ever done for Maine?" I demanded. "He's left us to build and man our own defenses and has kept so tight a hold on the public purse we haven't the money to afford either the material or the men required. All he thinks about is his own power and glory. The District of Maine and the United States can shift for themselves."

"Now, now, young man," the Judge said in a pompous, patronizing manner that infuriated me. "Governor Strong is concerned, as are all citizens who have the welfare of the states at heart, with the growth of power in Washington. Mr. Madison has flagrantly disregarded the rights of New England. He has sacrificed us to the South and the West. I tell you the power of the federal government must be diminished."

Brad cut in smoothly before I could retort, "Odd, isn't it, that only a few short years ago, Federalists were demanding a strong central government. Alexander Hamilton, if I recall, wanted such a government. Now they favor the opposite."

"Ah, yes, young man, but Hamilton has been long dead, and the Republicans, under Jefferson and Madison, have created a government that makes a mock of Jefferson's claims to respect the rights of the states. He and Madison would support the farmers, but they hate the mercantile and financial and industrial interests in New England. New England cannot stand by and submit to such treatment."

"But we are at war, Judge Kent!" I said.

"War or no war, the New England states must prevent the encroachment of the national government on their sacred rights. Governor Strong knows this, and I honor him for his opposition."

"His refusal to meet the troop quotas requested by the administration comes pretty close to treason," I said.

"Treason!" The Judge's face became livid. "You dare insinuate . . ."

"Now, now, Uncle Jason, if you can't talk with our friends without getting excited, we had better change the subject." India's voice was soothing and her pat on the Judge's wrist gentle.

"But he called Governor Strong a traitor, my dear!"

"No, he didn't, not exactly. Besides, you yourself said only day before yesterday that the Governor had left Maine practically defenseless and you didn't like it one bit. Nor do I."

The Judge stared at her, the dewlaps of his jowls quivering. His eyes were yellow and rheumy, and he looked genuinely miserable. I began to feel a little sorry for him.

On the whole, we got along rather more easily than I expected. India loved plays and had seen *Tartuffe* by Molière and a Racine tragedy, *Phaedra*. She said she preferred French drama to English because of its greater naturalness. At this, Brad challenged her. He insisted that French classical drama was far more stylized than Shakespeare, of which he quoted yards.

Finding much of this conversation beyond my competence or interest, I often followed the Judge's example and dozed. At other times I stared at the countryside and admired its beauty and orderliness while missing the shagginess of our own. Occasionally, however, we would climb a wooded hill or pass through a rocky defile that was rugged enough to appeal even to my unsophisticated taste.

I began also to notice something else on the third day out of Paris, and when the coachman gave the horses a breather at the top of a hill and we stepped down from the coach to stretch our legs, I nodded to Brad and went up to the driver. He was a big-bellied man, as sociable and friendly as his assistant on the box with him was silent and distant. At the moment, the coachman was examining the hoof of one of the horses. When he straightened up, I complimented him, in my creaking French, on the quality of his driving. He looked surprised but thanked me, while his assistant stared at me as if he thought I was crazy.

"But tell me, m'sieu," I went on, "do we have a postrider?"

He gave me an odd look. "No, we have no postrider. Why do you ask?"

"All day long a rider has been following us."

"Any one may ride along the road — after all, this is a public highway. But how do you know he is following us?"

By this time the four of us were staring back the way we had come. And sure enough, up the long hill, raising little puffs of dust, came a rider on a dun-colored horse.

"I'll admit I can't prove he's following us," I said, "but why doesn't he catch up with us and pass us? He could do so easily."

The rider, however, chose not to do so. Evidently noticing us, he drew off into the shelter of a scrubby growth of trees.

"I wonder what he would do if we spread out and went back for him," I said.

"Let us leave him alone as long as he leaves us alone, m'sieu," the coachman said. Then he looked keenly at me. "Do you know any reason why a man should follow us?"

I shook my head. At the same time, I decided that if Warren Bierce felt it urgent enough to pursue the coach or waylay it, perhaps relations between him and Judge Kent were even worse than I thought. Frankly I hoped that they had broken wide open between him and India at least, but I could not recall a single word of criticism from India; in fact, she had been explicit that any altercation was between Bierce and the Judge.

Later that afternoon, a sudden spring squall swept across the hilly countryside. The rain fell in such torrents that the coachman drew off to one side and waited for the storm to pass. It was so dark that inside the coach we could scarcely make out the faces of the people opposite. Actually, there were but two passengers besides ourselves, a stout, pleasant-faced woman and her son, a lad in his late teens who looked as shy as any girl but who was yet bold enough to give India many an admiring glance. Not that I blamed him. The downpour on the roof of the coach, piled high with trunks with a tarpaulin lashed down over them, was so loud that speaking was too great an effort. We simply sat and waited and pitied the coachman and his assistant who must be getting soaked despite the piece of canvas they had drawn over their heads.

Suddenly jagged lightning struck a tree nearby, and tumbling thunder crashed with deafening impact. The coach jerked forward as the horses reared. Both India and the other woman screamed briefly with fright, and I must confess I was pretty shaken myself. We could hear the coachman shouting to his horses as he fought to control them. Then, above the shouting and the roar of the rain, came a fierce drumming of hoofs, and a riderless horse pounded by us, neighing in terror.

Brad and I glanced at each other at the same moment. Whoever had been the rider behind us was no longer a menace. Had he dismounted to take refuge under the trees and the horse then broken away from him? Had he been thrown, and, if so, was he hurt? Would it be safe to go back looking for him? I was sure the same questions were troubling Brad. Personally I felt the rider must have been thrown and that we should go searching for him.

Leaning out of the window, I told the coachman what I intended to do. By now he had the horses under control. He said I was crazy but that if I wanted to take a chance on getting shot, it was my life to risk, not his. Besides, didn't I realize I'd get soaked?

"No more so than you probably are now," I said.

He laughed and told me he would wait a few minutes more but only a few minutes.

I now explained to the others in the coach about our having been followed. "My friend, Monsieur Pettigrew, and I did not want to alarm you," I said, addressing myself to the Frenchwoman, "so we said nothing except to the driver and his man. I think the horse that just passed us was the rider's and that he may be lying injured back in the road."

"How long has he been trailing us?" India asked.

I shrugged. "Who knows? I first noticed him in midmorning. Probably he's just another traveler like ourselves."

"But perhaps he is not, perhaps he is a brigand, and if he is that, we should leave him alone and let him die," the Frenchwoman said in such rapid French I was words behind her in translating it in my mind. I could now see how right Brad was when he once said that a person really hasn't mastery of a language until he thinks in it.

"Oh, we couldn't leave him!" India exclaimed.

"No, we couldn't," I said, and buttoning my coat and pulling up my collar, I stepped down from the coach, followed by Brad.

"D'you think India suspects anything?" I yelled as we hunched our way through the rain.

"If she doesn't now, she soon will," he replied.

[ 79 ]

Our search presently began to strike me as silly as the French-woman and the coachman thought it — depend on the French for being realistic! Here Brad and I were unarmed, our pistols in our valises. Even if we had stuck the cumbersome things in our belts, we couldn't have used them because the rain would have soaked their priming. Though the brigand, if he was that, might have the same difficulty, he would surely carry a knife, and we had none. Of course, if he was hurt, that was another thing altogether. But if he was unharmed, and we surprised him, we might find ourselves in real difficulty, particularly if he was not the only rider trailing us. On the other hand, I felt as certain as one can be, without actually knowing, that our pursuer was either Warren Bierce himself or someone hired by him, which, I suppose, really didn't make our task the less dangerous.

Then we saw the rider in the strange, premature darkness, which was neither true darkness nor light but a kind of greenish-gray twilight in midafternoon made more somber by the rain and the black clumps of trees irregularly bordering the hilly road. It was Warren Bierce, as I had suspected. He was sprawled on his back. His head lay to one side and was badly gashed on the forehead, and half immersed in a puddle of blood and water which bounced in miniature pink splashes as the raindrops landed in it.

As I knelt beside him, I could have sworn he was dead. Then, my fingers on his wrist, I caught a slight pulse beat. A further inspection revealed no bones broken so far as I could tell.

"Brad," I said, "if you'll take his legs, I'll get him by the shoulders."

Brad nodded. "Another minute and he'll literally start drowning in that puddle."

With considerable straining we raised him on our knees; then, with a good carrying hold, we started for the coach, a hundred yards or so away. He was a big man, dead-weight, so we had to rest once on the way. For the last few yards the driver and his assistant joined us.

"Do you know him?" the driver asked.

"We know him," I said, and let it go at that.

As the assistant opened the coach door and I climbed inside to draw Bierce in, I saw India's face. There was no need to tell her the

[ 80 ]

rider was Bierce. She looked horrified. When we had placed Bierce on the seat, his legs stretching into the aisle, she gently dabbed his forehead with her handkerchief.

"Oh, Warren, poor Warren!" she exclaimed, oblivious of us, and her voice warm with such concern that I felt a little sick and hopeless.

"We must go on now," the coachman said, his face sympathetic but his tone impatient. "I'm far behind schedule already."

"Drive on, m'sieu," Brad told him. "We'll take care of this gentleman."

A moment later the coach lurched forward, nearly sending me to the floor as I tried to steady Bierce opposite me. From my awkward position I looked up at the Judge, the first time, in fact, that I had noticed him since we had brought Bierce aboard the coach. If ever I saw an agonized expression of hatred and fear, it was on the face of Jason Kent.

---

# IX

THAT night we put up at an inn in a little French village not far from Poitiers. Despite our delay, we might still have reached the town had the storm not washed out part of the road. Fortunately the inn was large enough to accommodate us, and, of course, the porky innkeeper was quick to insist that his beds were as comfortable as those in the best hotels in Paris. After a night in one, I could only conclude that he had obviously never visited Paris. He was a man who was also quick to shift with the political winds, for a freshly painted sign announced that his inn was the Bourbon Lily; formerly, the coachman growled over a glass of red wine, it had been the Austerlitz Inn, in honor of Napoleon's greatest victory.

I had reason to remember the Bourbon Lily for other than its miserable beds or its weathervane innkeeper, for it was there that I had a sharp argument with India. Brad and I had put Bierce to bed and India demanded that the innkeeper, whose name was Jules Poisson, summon a physician. Rubbing his pudgy hands and bowing with every rub, Poisson soon sent a kitchen boy racing down the street. When the doctor arrived, a stubby little man with garlicky breath, he examined Bierce with less care than I had done during the storm, told us to leave him alone until he became conscious, then to feed him warm soup. Bierce had had a bad fall, but nothing more; and a little bleeding would remove the pressure from his brain.

India's relief was clear to all, and when Bierce presently regained consciousness and she told him what had happened, he smiled at her in a way that as plainly pleased her as it annoyed me because of its intimacy. The man, moreover, had a rugged constitution because almost at once he demanded something to eat. India kept him to the clear soup with a slice of bread dipped in it which the doctor said he might have. He showed such pleasure having her feed him that I left the room disgusted. Jealous I certainly was. At the same time I was sure he was strong enough to feed himself.

Later that evening he was so far recovered that he asked India to summon the Judge, Brad, and me to his bedroom. And when we had gathered, Brad and I standing by the mantel, India and the Judge seated by the bed, he apologized for causing us so much trouble.

"You see it was like this," he explained in a calm, steady voice. "I was stunned to find India and Judge Kent gone from Paris. There were points of business to clear up and arrangements to make for the disposal of the *Ghost*'s prizes. I knew you were ill, Judge, but I had no idea you and India would return so soon to America. And why you should not go back on the *Ghost* still puzzles me. In fact, I do not understand why you should choose to return with Dearborn and Pettigrew of all people. Why, Judge, I've heard you denounce Dearborn as a thoughtless fire-eater and Pettigrew as a know-it-all legal upstart. I've been your friend, Judge, and I wish to continue to be, if you'll permit me. But I do think some sort of explanation is in order."

It was a long speech for a man who had been knocked unconscious that afternoon, which led me to believe that he was more than feeling fine again. And as I looked at the Judge puff out his cheeks and suck them in while he shaped a reply, I could not help being impressed by Bierce's tactic in trying to drive a wedge between the Judge, on the one hand, and Brad and me, on the other. Actually no warmth of feeling other than a casual sympathy had developed on our part toward the Judge. So Bierce missed on this move.

Finally the Judge cleared his throat in a series of little rattling coughs. "Warren, if you don't mind, I don't think I'm up to a lengthy explanation. Suffice it to say that I'm a sick, old man who wants to see my native land before I die. When India told me these young men were leaving Paris at once, I welcomed and embraced the opportunity to accompany them."

I had trouble keeping a straight face as I listened to the sepulchral voice and the ornate manner of expression. The man who had argued with me about states' rights the first day out of Paris had hardly been anticipating his deathbed. Nor was he now, I could have sworn; he simply would not be drawn into arguing with Bierce, who evidently knew something Jason Kent didn't wish to talk about.

As Bierce lay back on his pillow, looking scornfully at the Judge, India said, "What Uncle Jason says is true, Warren. And it was I who got in touch with Jonathan and Brad."

"I'm sure it's true, my dear," he said gently, "so far as it goes."

At this point I decided to ask the question that had been on my mind for hours, and I know my voice was accusing. "Mr. Bierce, why were you following the coach?"

He smiled contemptuously. "I wasn't aware there was any law in France or anywhere against riding along a road a few yards behind a public vehicle."

"That's hardly an answer to my friend's question," Brad said.

"I'm not sure that it deserves an answer, but I will give you one. Until today I rode hard to overtake the coach, and I had planned to get rid of my horse tonight and accompany India and Judge Kent the rest of the way to Bordeaux."

"But why?"

"Pettigrew, you are presumptuous."

"Perhaps I am," Brad conceded in his unruffled, courteous manner. "Perhaps I am being very personal. But it seems to me that you behaved strangely in your pursuit of us. When we stopped to rest the horses at the crest of the hill before the storm struck us, you made no effort to overtake us. You drew your horse off the road."

"And why shouldn't I have rested him at that point?"

Brad shrugged. "You were pretty heavily armed for even a lone traveler, Mr. Bierce: two pistols, a shotgun, and a knife."

"These are unsettled times and places, Pettigrew. Now I think it's high time this ludicrous inquisition ended."

As his voice rose and he raised himself off the pillow, India gently pressed him back. "Warren, don't excite yourself. You have had a bad fall and must rest. Now please leave him alone, gentlemen, I beg of you."

"India, we didn't invite ourselves here," I said. "He was responsible, and he still hasn't told us why he should want to go to Bordeaux with you and the Judge."

I half expected an angry reply, but instead he smiled, rather triumphantly, too. "Dearborn, this is really none of your business, but the reason I wanted to board that coach tomorrow concerns India and the esteem in which I hold her."

At that, we left the room, leaving India, her face aflame, smoothing out his pillow and drawing the coverlet around him.

"God damn him, God damn him, God damn him," the Judge said, after we closed the door.

He clumped to his room with his cane, and only Brad's strong arm kept him from falling when he slipped on a scatter rug. "Thanks," he muttered, then swung toward us, clutching my waistcoat. "D'you know what that bastard's done? He's sold us out to the British. I may be a Federalist, but I'm no Benedict Arnold whatever he may say. If India marries him, it'll be to save my life. And even then he'd probably get rid of me."

"Aren't you a little excited, Judge?" Brad asked gently.

The Judge stared at him; then the dewlaps began to quiver. "You're damn right I'm excited and with reason! He wants India and me aboard the *Ghost* with that murderer Rudd. And if Bierce gets us there, my life won't be worth a snap of your fingers whatever he may promise India, and India will end up as the wife of a scoundrel. A scoundrel, d'you hear? A cold, greedy, traitorous scoundrel!"

"I think you have said enough, Uncle Jason."

We turned, completely surprised, to see India standing in the room, her eyes blazing. I didn't know how much she had heard, but she could not have missed the Judge's final eloquent expression of opinion.

"Enough?" the Judge growled. "I haven't said half enough."

"You have for tonight," India said. "I think it's time you went to bed."

"You know I have only your welfare at heart, child." But the Judge's voice had lost its defiance and was now scarcely more than a pleading whine.

"I'm quite capable of looking out for my own welfare," she retorted, "and without help from these gentlemen."

"Then why did you ask to come to Bordeaux with Brad and me?" I'm afraid I pleaded like the Judge.

"To humor my uncle, as I thought I made clear in Paris."

"Then you have no reason to fear Bierce?" Brad asked.

"Fear Warren Bierce? Of course not. He wants me to marry him."

"But you can't do that!" I cried. "You can't marry a man like Bierce, India!"

"Oh, can't I? Who are you to say I can't, Jonathan Dearborn?"

I looked at her standing there in that wretched, little room, hands on her hips and defiance raging in her eyes, and loved her fiercely. How could I tell her, with Brad and her uncle present and our mood one of unreasoning anger, that I loved her? I simply couldn't. I could only say, and very lamely, after a gulping pause, "Because you can't, India. You're too good for a man like Bierce."

"Now let me tell both of you," she said less hotly, but with a sincerity that cut deeply, "Warren Bierce is a fine man and a true gentleman. You may have heard the opposite from my uncle, but he neither understands nor likes Warren. I think I understand him, and I know I like and respect him. Is there anything more I need say?"

I suppose there really wasn't. Had I given her any reason over a longer period of time to think well of me, there would have been more she would need to say, but not as things were. I could only stare at her, amazed at her trustfulness, and feel despair gnawing at me.

"Are you and the Judge going back to America with Rudd or Captain Vail?" I asked.

She looked at the Judge sitting on the side of his bed, his head bent over his cane, and shrugged. "I don't know, I honestly don't know."

"We're sailing with Vail," the Judge said in his pontifical way.

"Well, I hope you make up your minds by the time we reach Bordeaux," I said harshly. "If the *Argus* is there, Captain Vail won't want to delay sailing much longer."

Brad and I went to our room, but sleep was long in coming. I began to regret having returned to find Bierce. Had he remained in the deep puddle of the road, he would surely have drowned or at least become so ill as not to trouble us now with his presence. At the same time, I realized I could not have lived with my conscience not to try to find him. Oddly enough, he had thanked neither Brad nor me for having brought him to safety. Or perhaps it wasn't so odd; as Brad said, he was just that kind of bastard.

The next two days were miserable. The Judge, for once, rarely opened his month during the ride to Bordeaux. Brad would occasionally small-talk with India, which was more than I could do, while we both avoided conversing with Bierce. True, India would chat with Bierce, but even she talked with constraint. The French contingent, consisting of the mother and her son and a linen merchant who boarded the coach at Angoulême, kept to itself.

The only one who appeared comparatively at ease was Bierce, whose health improved rapidly. To Brad and me, especially me, he was like a burr under a horse's tail. He asked how I expected to become a lawyer by serving as a privateersman. He wondered how my warlike spirit could possibly be acceptable to my pacifist father. He jested about the patriotism of all Maine privateersmen who obviously would not help their country unless there was a dollar-and-cents profit to them in fighting, and he frankly admitted that patriotism which paid off appealed to him as a man of business. He said much in the same vein to Brad but in a manner less pointed and on a level less personal. Of course he antagonized both of us. In fact, he infuriated me so greatly that I gave up arguing with him and wished more strongly than ever that I'd left him in the road.

What he had to gain by provoking us puzzled me until I realized that it was a game with him. By remaining calm himself, but baiting me into a rage, he could demonstrate to India his superiority in dialectical skill and maturity in emotional control; by the same token, he could try to expose me as naïvely young and inexperienced. My refusal henceforth to rise to his baiting clearly amused him but must also have disappointed him. An argument requires at least two participants.

I wondered what effect his tactics had on India. She kept still when the three of us were going at it, but I could see her studying each of us with those gray-green eyes. Nor did she smile, nor register any kind of feeling other than curiosity, so far as I could tell, except when Bierce said that as a businessman he appreciated the mercenary value of patriotism; then she gave him a long, slow look that I could have sworn was either incredulity or disapproval — I couldn't be sure which. I wasn't certain Bierce noticed that look, and probably it wouldn't have made much difference to him if he had.

As for myself, the look was the only bright moment of the ride. Not that there was much to hope for from it, certainly nothing that would improve relations between India and me. She treated me like a complete stranger, an unfriendly one at that. And I suppose that was just about what I deserved. Her attitude that night had so astonished and antagonized — and disheartened — me that I could respond civilly but with no cordiality to anything she said. As a matter of fact, I was tired of all of them — even Brad with his chitchat occasionally annoyed me. I half hoped that India and Judge Kent would sail on the *Ghost* with Bierce and Rudd. That way we'd all be spared further trouble. At the same time, the very thought that India might accept Bierce to save her uncle made me almost literally sick. So from wishing Brad and I were again with Captain Vail on the *Argus* in pursuit of British ships, and unvexed by emotional involvements, I came, full circle, to wondering what could be done to persuade India to sail on the *Argus* if she should now favor the *Ghost* and what measures to take if she stuck to her original decision to sail with us and Bierce and Rudd should try to prevent her.

We drove into Bordeaux the next evening too late to check on whether the *Argus* was in port. For that matter, Bierce couldn't have known whether the *Ghost* was in either, but the possibility that she wasn't didn't appear to bother him. He was cheerful and assured as if

[ 87 ]

there were no doubt that India and Judge Kent would return with him.

That night Brad and I discussed what to do. We agreed that if India insisted on going home on the *Ghost*, we had no right to prevent her, though if the Judge definitely proposed that we take him aboard the *Argus*, Captain Vail approving, we ought to do so. If Bierce and Rudd should try to prevent us, we knew, of course, that there could be real trouble. How we should deal with it depended on what form it would take.

In the morning, as soon as it was light, Brad and I were down on the waterfront. But as we anxiously scanned the shipping moored at the long line of wharves or lying in the Garonne, we saw nothing of the *Argus*. We were not surprised in view of the time schedule Captain Vail had given us, but we were disappointed to say the least. The only consolation, though a real one, was that the *Ghost* wasn't in port, either. We therefore returned to the hotel, feeling somewhat relieved.

Several times that day we kept watch on the river. In fact we visited the establishment of Brun Frères on the chance that they might have heard something of Vail and the *Argus*. We found they had heard nothing that we didn't already know of either ship's movements. Like it or not, I saw we were probably in for a real wait and that, depending on how the Judge felt, the first of the two privateers to make the harbor would bring the suspense to an end.

That evening Brad and I went to a café. We dressed in clean linen, though the rest of us was pretty mussed and wrinkled from traveling. Before leaving the hotel, I made sure the packet Crawford had given me in Paris was pinned securely in my inside coat pocket. The café was filled largely with elegantly dressed middle-class people who seemed so affected in manner that until we had rather more than sampled a fine white wine we half wished ourselves in a hole-in-the-wall café down on the waterfront. There was also a sprinkling of British officers from Wellington's army that had taken over the city. A pianoforte and a violin played throughout the evening, although at times the conversation became so loud that one could scarcely hear the music. Our waitress was a girl with a pair of roguish black eyes, built as she should have been fore and aft, who walked with a provocative switching that would have fetched audible approval on the waterfront but which only brought forth sly looks here. She said her name was Jeanne, and when she learned we were Americans, she brought us the cheese omelet, chicken livers, puffy rolls, and white wine we ordered with remarkable promptness.

"I love Americans," she gushed in French.

"But why?" Brad asked with that friendly yet challenging smile that so few girls seemed able to resist.

"Because they are like children, and who does not love children, m'sieu?"

"Pretty big children," I said, and stared hard at a British officer who looked our way.

She tossed her head. "Big, yes, m'sieu, big and strong, but boastful like children, and so generous with their money as if they do not know its value."

"You French are too practical," Brad protested. "Don't you ever think of anything but money?"

She raised her hands and rolled her eyes. "M'sieu would be surprised what else we think of."

I don't think either of us would have been surprised, but, even as we laughed, she said, "We like money because it buys us bread and clothes and a place to stay the night, and if it does not buy love, real love I mean, still it is a great comfort to have. So we do not throw it away like you Americans."

Though she gave Brad back smile for smile as she spoke, I sensed she was really serious. Besides, there was some truth in what she said: privateersmen had a reputation even among themselves of being great spenders, particularly on drink and women. Bordeaux swarmed with wine shops and brothels. Quite by contrast, La Rochelle, not far up the coast, was as clean a port as one could ever hope to find, and probably a little dull for Jack ashore after a cruise.

Just what little exchanges like this would have led to between the girl and Brad I don't know — or perhaps I do — but a curfew at eleven drove us out before Brad could make any arrangements to see her again. If he hadn't already been staggering, yet sober enough to realize it, I doubt that he'd have let a curfew restrain him. As it was, both of us stumbled along the dark streets to our hotel, talking much

[ 89 ]

too loudly I fear, singing off key I'm certain, and in general behaving in a way that the growing body of prohibitionists in Portland would have deplored with much shaking of heads and clicking of tongues against teeth. I could just hear some of them say of me, "And a minister's son at that!"

At one of those times between songs when we gasped to catch our breath, I thought I heard the clip-clop of hoofs behind us. I thought nothing of it since we were already aware that British cavalry patrols regularly rode through the city, thus supporting the local police in assuring peace and order. At the same time I had no desire to be stopped by a Britisher. We were silent for a moment; then as we no longer heard anything, we started to sing again. The narrow streets were dark, but here and there a lantern burned over a doorway, as did one, we noticed, over the entrance to our hotel. It cast a weak and wavery sheen over the cobblestones, still damp from a light shower in midevening.

Then once more both of us heard the sound of hoofs, this time moving rapidly behind us. I don't know how we managed it, but we broke into a ragged run for the hotel door at the same time without saying a word to each other. Brad was on the inside and steadied himself on the hotel wall.

We almost made the entrance, but only almost. A hackney coach suddenly jammed us against the wall, the horses rearing at the sudden stop. Three men jumped out. While two grappled with me as nearest the coach, another tangled with Brad. It was a short but vicious scrap, for surprised though we were, and in hardly the best of condition for such an affair, both of us fought furiously. In fact, Brad knocked his man down and, shouting for help, plunged in to help me. I was doing pretty well myself until one of the men got his arm around my throat from the rear and applied such pressure I felt the blood tighten in my ears. Desperate for breath, I kicked backward but to no avail. My brain swimming, I saw lights appearing in doorways.

"Get him in here," a voice called from the coach. "There's a patrol coming!"

I struggled harder than ever, particularly as Brad's assailant recovered and knocked him against the wall.

Then whoever was in the coach leaned out and brought something hard down over my skull. At once everything whirled in a pinwheel of sparks. Though still resisting, I felt myself sliding over the rim of consciousness into oblivion — but not before I had identified the voice as that of Warren Bierce.

# X

A PERSISTENT wrenching and groaning in slow, regular rhythm was the first sound I heard. I thought at first that it must be my throbbing head, then decided it existed as something separate. Presently a stench like the essence of swamp pollution became so strong that I shrank back. At once I felt constricted in both arms and legs; and sudden panic, more than any other factor, brought me back to consciousness. It took me but a moment or so to realize that I was bound hand and foot in the hold of a ship with a dreadful-smelling bilge and that the ship was under way.

Working like a creaking windlass, my mind reconstructed what had happened. Bierce had tried to kidnap Brad and myself on the way back to the hotel. But why? And had he captured Brad, too? I had a feeling that, being farther from the carriage, Brad might have escaped, especially as a patrol had been approaching. But even if he had got away, what could he do to help me now that this ship was at sea, if it was at sea; I doubted that I had been unconscious long enough for whatever vessel I was on to clear the mouth of the Garonne. I wondered if this could be the *Ghost*. Though I listened carefully, I could hear little overhead: a shout or two, the sound of a rapid footstep, nothing more. The *Ghost* was too heavily manned to be so quiet. I sniffed as if to tell what the vessel was from the cargo she carried, but the bilge stink drowned out all other odors. Nor could I see anything down here. I tried to sit up, but my hands had been knotted securely behind me, and sitting up was not easy. A scurrying near me as I moved brought the goose flesh out on me: rats! Again pure panic gripped me. I shouted and wrenched at my bonds. If anything, they seemed tighter for my struggles. Then I realized my jacket was gone and with that, of course, the packet from Crawford and my money. Wet with sweat, yet shivering in the stifling hold, I fought to control myself. My father, I suspect, would have prayed to the Deity and asked a blessing on his enemies. As for myself, I was momentarily the prey to unreasoning terror and consuming rage. I knew now I should have let Bierce die in the storm as the French-woman had urged. And someday, I vowed, he would have cause to regret the night's business.

Sometime later I fell asleep, though for how long I had no idea. I was awakened by the rays of a lantern shining in my face and some-one roughly shaking my shoulder.

"Get up!" a voice rasped.

For a moment I stared stupidly at a black-bearded man, then said, "I can't."

"Oh, hell, them!" and he nodded to the knots at my ankles. "Here, Ed, hold that lantern closer."

As a tall, gangling sailor stooped over with the lantern, Blackbeard reached into his belt and, drawing a knife from its sheath, cut me loose. "Now up on your feet, you!"

I stumbled to my feet, my legs feeling as if they were being stuck with a thousand pins and needles, and teetered my way up to the deck. It was night outside, and we were still in the river, which was wide at this point. But I had little time to look around me other than to note that this was a small two-masted schooner.

Once inside the captain's cabin I had no doubt of the ship's na-tionality. A broad, squat figure stared at me from his chair, where he sat nursing a mug of rum in his hands. His face, badly needing a shave, was darkly mottled and his eyes were small and beady and bright with malevolence.

"So you're still alive," he growled in a voice that came straight out of Boston.

"Evidently no thanks to you and your men," I said.

"You hear that, Ben?" he asked Blackbeard. "You hear that, Ed?"

As the men behind me grunted, the captain suddenly burst into a wild laugh. "So you got beaten up. Now ain't that too bad, just too bad! Think my boys are pretty rough?"

[ 92 ]

I shrugged and stared at him. Then to my surprise, he snapped, "Take that rope off his hands, Ed."

"Thanks," I said coldly, and flexed my wrists and rubbed them to restore the circulation.

"Now look here," he said, coming around his table to stand in front of me, his hands grasping his belt. "You got a surprise comin'. It wasn't any of my boys who did you in. It was lads from the *Ghost*, that's who it was. I happened to be leavin' port at just the right time, an' you got slung aboard my *Ginny*."

"For a consideration, no doubt," I said. Still I was surprised, especially that I wasn't aboard the *Ghost*. But when he ignored my remark and I asked him directly why I was on the *Ginny*, he hunched his chin and stared hard at me over his big belly.

"I can always use an extra hand, especially when we're waitin' off the African coast for ships comin' round the Cape. Fever thins out a crew when a ship's lyin' in one of them lagoons."

"Are you a privateer or a pirate?" I asked.

Again he laughed, a huge, short laugh almost like a bark; and glancing around, I saw the two men behind me grinning.

"Why, a privateer, of course, my friend," he said. "I have papers to prove it. Ed, you an' Ben go on out now. I'll call you later."

When his two bulldogs were gone, he sat down again and gulped more rum.

"Where's my jacket and my money?" I demanded.

He shook his head. "You never had either when I got hold of you."

"I don't believe you!" I shouted.

"You'd better, 'cause it's the truth. Now, look here," he said, "you're alive because you may be useful to me. As far as your friends and your enemies know, you're a dead man. At least you're supposed to be dead, dropped in the Garonne in a canvas shroud with a few twelve-pound shots to weigh you down."

"So you were hired to kill me after all."

He grinned. "Well, let's say I was supposed to get rid of you. Jake Rudd's an old friend of mine. He's done me favors before, so I agreed to do him one. Now I don't know what you did to make him mad, an' I don't care."

[ 93 ]

"He sails for Warren Bierce, and Bierce hates me."

"Never heard of Bierce. All I know is that the *Ghost* got into port in the evening, and later on Rudd dumped you on my deck. Now what I want you to get through your head is that you're dead. By the way, what's your name? Mine's Black."

"What does it matter if I'm dead? But if you want to know —"

He quickly raised his hand. "Don't tell me. I changed my mind. Let's call you Smith."

"John Smith?"

"Hell, no," he laughed. "We got two of those already. You're Adam Smith."

"You *must* be a pirate," I said.

This time he did not laugh. Instead he looked at me with such malevolence that I was startled. "Smith, you use that word again an' I'll throw you overboard. Now if you're willin' to sign on, you'll be treated like one of the crew. If you're not, you haven't got long to live."

I was certain he meant what he said. "Can I have a while to think it over?" Anything to play for time. He was nothing but a pirate, and the last thing I wanted was to join his crew.

After a hard stare at me, he nodded. "Ben! Ed!" When the two appeared, he said, "Ben, see that Smith here gets something to eat, then tie him up again an' heave him back into the hold. He wants to do some thinkin'. Maybe the rats'll help him."

Back in the hold I was chained now by a leg ring to one of the deck supports rather than bound. Though I appreciated the additional room for movement, I was as deeply resentful of my condition, and puzzled as to how to prevent myself from signing on. This ship was a pirate masquerading as a privateer, no doubt about it, and short-handed, too.

Meanwhile the *Ginny* slipped into the Bay of Biscay at night without even being challenged and whirled southwestward toward Cape Ortegal at the northwestern tip of Spain. I knew that long before we reached the cape I'd have to sign on unless Vail had learned what had happened and intercepted us. But such an occurrence depended on Brad's having escaped. And what of India? Had Bierce forced her and the Judge to go back to America on the *Ghost?*

After a while I slept. How long I don't know, but I awoke to a heavy pounding of seas against the hull. Before I had dropped off to sleep, I had noticed that we had begun to roll in a rising sea, but the steepness of the angle as we now plunged downward and then came up in a rolling twist made me uneasy. This was a major storm.

For the hours that the *Ginny* battled high winds and roaring seas, I sweated and stewed in that suffocating hold. Then, just when I thought I had been forgotten, a lantern showed at the stern of the hold, which could be entered either fore or aft as well as through the hatchways. It was Ben, his wet clothes clinging to his skin like a sheath and trailing water at every step he took. Without a word he bent and unlocked my leg ring.

"Lost two men overboard," he growled. "We can use you."

I nodded. This was obviously no time to insist that I would not sign the roster of the *Ginny*. After the storm would be soon enough.

The next four days were one long fight to stay afloat. A number of times the entire deck was underwater as seas billowed over us. The rag of canvas we tried to keep on the schooner for headway blew to shreds twice. The main-topmast went by the board in a tangle of rigging and threatened to drag us onto our beam-ends until we could hack our way through the mess. The longboat was swept away, the live chickens kept there for fresh meat scattering feathers over the deck and squawking wildly before they drowned. Spume hurled at us by the gale stung like hail when it hit.

I wondered if Captain Vail was at sea in this blow and hoped he wasn't. Frankly I considered our chances of survival pretty slim. Yet I must admit that even Vail could have done no better than Black. He was constantly on deck and alert to every threat that developed. He acknowledged my presence with a nod, but we exchanged no words — they wouldn't have been heard anyway.

Then on the sixth day the storm broke up almost as suddenly as it had appeared, and if ever the sun shone on a bedraggled, bearded, haggard lot of wretches, it did now. We had had scarcely any food and certainly nothing hot since the storm began. Rum, more than anything else, had kept us going. Without exception we looked villainous, and I suppose that's exactly what most of us were. Two men had been lost overboard, four had been sick ever since we left Bordeaux, and one had been injured when the topmast went by the board. Ten remained, not including myself — hardly a sufficient number to continue a piratical cruise.

But continue the cruise we did, though it took us long to get back on course. I helped work ship, and Black said nothing about my signing on. I was determined, however, not to take part in any piratical venture.

My resolution was put to the test when we sighted a big, lumbering brig flying the Spanish flag, and, despite our missing topmast, overhauled her rapidly. As soon as I saw that Black had made up his mind to take her, using his pivot gun to pound her, I went to him and told him I'd have nothing to do with his action.

He turned quickly from speaking to the helmsman. "By God, Smith, you'll do as I say. We'll have no mutiny here."

"I don't give a damn," I said. "I won't raise a finger to help you."

Those were my last words for quite a while. Someone had raised more than a finger behind me, and I came to, eventually, to find myself chained in the hold again. What brought me back to consciousness was the crash of a big gun overhead and a fierce shouting. From near at hand came the thunderous reply of a heavy broadside, another blast of the Long Tom, and still another broadside close at hand. To my dismay, two shots ripped into the hold, not twenty feet from me and the water gushed inside like a millrace. From up forward came a violent explosion as something, perhaps loose powder, blew up. The *Ginny* staggered as a succession of blows struck her like giant hammers. A few minutes more, and I was thrown to the limit of my chain as the two ships crunched together. Instantly a deep-throated cheer broke out, and the deck above echoed to the racing thud of boarders' feet.

It took no genius to figure out what was happening. Black had caught himself a Tartar. Instead of giving in to the threat of the heavy long gun, the brig had boarded the *Ginny*. She obviously had many men aboard, too, and had fired so effectively that I began to wonder if she wasn't a man-of-war.

Presently the small arms firing ceased, and a half-dozen men poured into the hold. My relief that at least I wouldn't drown was tempered somewhat by the fact that they were bluejackets led by a young lieutenant in the uniform of the British Navy.

"And who the hell are you?" he demanded. "Another bloody American?"

"Yes," I said as calmly as I could. "I'm an American citizen who was kidnapped aboard this schooner at Bordeaux."

"A likely story! Well, we'll just kidnap you aboard the *Beagle* and you can lie to Captain Sage if you dare."

At my suggestion they soon located the key in Ben's pocket. Ben had died from a terrible pike thrust, I discovered, when I came on deck, blinking in the strong sunlight. In fact, so far as I could see, the only survivor of the *Ginny's* crew, apart from two men who died the next day of their wounds, was Captain Black himself. The crew had fought savagely, killing four Englishmen and wounding as many more, but the *Beagle's* solid shot had made kindling wood of the schooner, and her grapeshot had swept the *Ginny's* decks clean. A small powder magazine had blown up, the mainmast had gone by the board, and the *Ginny* looked like a wreck. Black, I found out, had run afoul of one of the formidable sixteen-gun brigs in the British Navy. The bait — her flying the Spanish flag — he had swallowed completely.

I have no love for the British, and British naval captains rank especially low in my estimation. It makes my blood hot when I think of how a man like Carden of the *Macedonian* compelled our citizens, whom he had pressed, to serve against the frigate *United States,* and I rejoice that he lost the battle; of Hillyar commanding the *Phoebe* which, with the *Cherub,* attacked and captured David Porter and the *Essex* when our frigate, having lost her main-topmast, took refuge well within the neutral waters of Chile; of Cochrane and, above all, Cockburn who ravaged our Chesapeake towns without mercy. There were many others, too, whose conduct was ruthless beyond the point of need, perhaps because our war effort was generally so feeble they had nothing but contempt for us. On the other hand, there were notable exceptions. For instance, Hardy, Nelson's flag captain at Trafalgar, hated having to blockade the southern New England coast and deplored his own bombardment of Stonington, which, fortunately, was so ineffective it killed but a chicken. Another exception was W. F. Wise, whose frigate *Granicus* captured George Coggeshall's privateer *Leo* off the mouth of the Tagus; Wise treated Coggeshall with the greatest courtesy and consideration.

In my own case I hardly knew what to expect when Black and I were brought before Captain Robert Sage of the *Beagle*. Actually Sage was only a lieutenant in rank, as were so many of these British brig and sloop commanders, but he had sufficient seniority and the *Beagle* such a good record that he was already due to be posted for captain. He was a tall, young man, about thirty, with the fresh coloring so prevalent among the northern Europeans, and eyes of almost a glittering blue. It was a hard, competent-looking face and his manner brimmed with confidence.

As we were brought before him on the quarterdeck, flames were shooting up from the *Ginny* and the *Beagle* was getting under way. A bulwark splintered in one place and several holes in the sails were all the damage visible. I did notice, however, that in several locations along the deck details were busy removing bloodstains.

When the haughty officer who had released me introduced us, Sage looked at both of us with curiosity, then ordered us brought to his cabin after the ship's surgeon had examined Black's arm and dressed his wound.

Admitted to Sage's tiny cabin with a marine sentry just outside the door, we took chairs as he directed, and submitted this time to more than curiosity. After establishing Black's identity as a native of Boston and the *Ginny* as a privateer of that port, Sage turned to me, crossing his long legs with difficulty under his little table.

"Now, Mr. Dearborn, what is this story about your being kidnapped and found by Lieutenant Eustis chained in the hold?"

"It's true, sir," I said. I wanted to be careful not to reveal that I was an officer of the privateer *Argus* which was charged with the duty of reporting the suspicious operations of an American believed to be working with the British. At the same time I saw no point in denouncing Black as a pirate unless I was forced to do so by whatever Black himself might say; piracy was punishable by death and, after all, he had not dropped me overboard as he had been directed to. I therefore told Captain Sage that I had American enemies in France who had paid Black to get rid of me.

"Why did you change your mind?" Sage asked Black.

The privateersman scratched his head. "Well, sir, I ain't a murderer."

"But you did take the money offered you."

"Yes, but I figured that if I kept Dearborn here out of sight for a while, it would accomplish their purpose and it wouldn't hurt him."

"But to keep him chained like a slave!"

"Well, I suppose it wasn't comfortable, but I intended to set him free once we got really out into the Atlantic. Then that storm broke, and I forgot about him."

"But the storm had been over for some time, Black."

Black looked uneasily at me, then said, "I gave him a chance to sign on, but when we sighted your ship flying the Spanish flag, he refused to fight. Said we'd be pirates if we attacked you. So I chained him up again where he would be out of the way."

"Is that right, Mr. Dearborn?"

Black had left a lot unexplained, but I let it go. "That's correct," I admitted.

Captain Sage nodded, then looked at Black. "Why did you attack us, Captain Black? You saw we were under Spanish colors."

"I figured you might be a British merchantman tryin' to protect yourself with a neutral flag."

Black was quick and unabashed, and Sage nodded again. "Sounds natural," he said, then snapped, "but if we had really been Spanish, Mr. Dearborn would have been quite right, man. You would have been a pirate."

"I suppose so."

"Suppose! You damn well would have been. Surely you know that."

"Yes, sir."

"And if I'd been the Spanish captain and had beaten your *Ginny*, I might not even bother to take you to port for trial. I might hang you at the masthead at once."

Sage's voice was so sharp and his eyes so fierce that Black seemed to shrink into his chair. "Yes, sir," he said meekly. And I was sure that he, like myself, believed Sage half suspected that all was not as it appeared here.

In the succeeding days, Captain Sage treated Black decently, but he went out of his way to be kind to me, inviting me to dine with him almost daily. Even young Eustis, untamed cub that he was, was reasonably agreeable once he saw his captain was friendly to me. "Don't feel depressed," Sage urged me. "Try to forget you're a prisoner, and imagine you're only a passenger. Besides, when we arrive at Gibraltar, the Governor may rule that since you were not taken in arms against us, you should go free."

We learned a little about each other. I told him that I came from Portland and was a minister's son, while he informed me that his father was a country squire in Devon, and that he himself had been years at sea, but a prisoner of the French for two years. He seemed to feel that had it not been for those two years, he would now have been a captain of a frigate.

Sage admired the way Americans built and sailed ships. "Dearborn," he said one evening over walnuts and port, with Lieutenant Eustis present, "in England we can't build such vessels as your Baltimore clippers, and whenever one of our fast frigates has caught one under its lee in a heavy wind or taken one with boats, we don't know how to sail them. We're afraid of their long masts and heavy spars, so we cut both down to our standard and thereby sacrifice their sailing qualities."

"Oh, come now, sir," Eustis protested, "what about the *True Blooded Yankee*? Granted that she's now an American privateer, worse luck, but wasn't she ours originally?"

"Sorry, Eustis," Sage said, shaking his head. "She was originally French, we took her, the French recaptured her, and now the Americans have her. No, both the Americans and the French build better ships than we do."

"I don't know too much about the *True Blooded Yankee*," I said, "but I've met Dominique Diron; and, of course, at home we're all great admirers of Captain Boyle and his *Chasseur*."

Both officers groaned at my mention of Boyle. "He's more valuable to you people than most of your navy," Sage said. "I chased him once, but he rides his ship like a racehorse. We lost him in a fog."

"Well, Boyle isn't the only slippery devil," Eustis said, cracking a walnut viciously in his hands. "There's that new privateer, the *Argus*. What's her captain's name?"

"Vail, Benjamin Vail," Sage said quietly. "He and Boyle have practically had our coast under blockade. Did you ever hear of him, Mr. Dearborn?"

I was now very wary. As an American supposedly on business in France, I could not have helped hearing of Vail. "Yes," I said, bidding myself be calm, "I've heard of him."

"Where does he come from? What's he like?" Eustis was intensely curious.

"I understand he's a little man," I said cautiously, "and he comes from the District of Maine where I live."

"Is Portland his town, too?" Sage asked.

"I believe he hails from Castine."

"Vail hails! I say, that's good," laughed Eustis. Then he stopped. "Castine! Why, where's that? I don't think I ever heard of it."

"Did you ever hear of Bagaduce, Lieutenant Eustis?" I asked.

"Baga — what? No, can't say I ever did. You bloody Americans have the oddest names for places."

"That's enough, Eustis," Captain Sage said with cold crispness. "If you've never heard of Bagaduce, you should have. That's where Sir George Collier won a crushing victory over the Americans in 1779. You've dropped the Indian name, Mr. Dearborn."

I nodded. "Yes, sir. The town is now Castine after the Frenchman Baron Castin, who was something of a devil in the old days. The new name has pleasanter associations for us, I guess."

"Did you have any relative in the Bagaduce affair?" Sage asked.

"My uncle, sir, Captain Thomas Dearborn. He commanded a ten-gun sloop. When your people came up Penobscot Bay, he moored it across the river channel, fought it as long as he could, then set it afire. He saved several troop transports from being sunk with all aboard."

"Good man," said Sage. "Is he at sea these days?"

"No, he and his wife don't believe in the war. My aunt was a Tory in our Revolution, and she has never quite approved of the separation of our two countries."

"But what about you, yourself, Mr. Dearborn?" Eustis asked in his arrogant way. "Don't you believe in supporting your government even if you disagree with it?"

"I didn't say I disagreed with my government," I replied, trying to conceal my irritation.

"Then why aren't you helping it? If you're not a soldier or a seaman, why aren't you out privateering with someone like Boyle or Diron or Vail?"

"Come, come, Eustis, this isn't the Spanish Inquisition," Sage said, to my great relief.

"Sorry, Dearborn," Eustis said curtly. "But it still strikes me as odd that I should find you chained like a mutineer or a slave in the hold of that schooner. You must have done something pretty drastic for your business enemies in Bordeaux to send you out with Black. He may call himself a privateersman and have papers to prove it, but I think he's a damned old pirate."

I shrugged, and said nothing. Any reply I might make could lead to a revelation of my true identity as one of the *Argus*'s officers, and this would mean, for a certainty, a stretch in Dartmoor Prison, where I could not possibly warn the Madison administration of Bierce's negotiations with the British, if Mr. Crawford's other messenger was lost at sea or failed to get through the blockade. Even if Crawford's letter was in Bierce's hands, I could still give an oral report.

It was Sage himself who came to my rescue by drawing out his fobbed watch. "Gentlemen, it is getting late, and since we put into Gibraltar early tomorrow, I bid you good night."

"What did he say about what's goin' to happen to us?" Black whispered when I returned to our tiny stateroom.

"He didn't," I replied. The man often played stupid, but he was so foxy I was wary of him.

"Think we'll go to Dartmoor?"

I stared almost with hatred at his heavy bewhiskered face, sagging at the jowls. "I suppose they'll send you to Dartmoor, but God knows what they'll do with me — release me, I hope."

"Well, thanks to me, you're alive, so put in a good word for me," he whined.

"And thanks to me you won't hang for piracy!"

[ 102 ]

"I dunno if you did me a favor or not," he grumbled. "If Jake Rudd ever finds out I didn't get rid of you, he'll kill me."

"To hell with Rudd! He'll soon forget all about both of us."

"Jake Rudd ain't a forgettin' man." Black shook his head, then leaned forward so that his beady, little eyes were hardly six inches from mine. "I should've dropped you overboard, Dearborn — I should've killed you. If Rudd finds out you're still alive, he'll kill both of us. And don't you forget it!"

The terror of Rudd's vengeance clearly weighed the man down. His face was sweating, and his breath came quickly. In all honesty, however, I can't say the thought of either Rudd or Bierce raised so much as a single goosebump on me. Rather, what concerned me was what might be happening to India aboard the *Ghost*, where Brad was, and what judgment the Governor at Gibraltar would render in my case. The first two I knew I could do nothing about. The last prompted me to a resolution I was determined to carry out: I would not be sent to that great stone prison on dreary, dangerous Dartmoor, a prison where hundreds of American and French seamen suffered, and many died of mistreatment.

---

# XI

THE *Beagle* put in to Gibraltar by nine o'clock the next morning. I had been there once before when Uncle Tom stopped on his way to Naples. At that time, with the Barbary Coast pirates recovering from the fright our country had given Tripoli only a few years before, we kept a sharp eye open toward the African coast for armed feluccas with their lateen sails and were glad to take refuge under the great bulk of the Rock. Now, with Britain and the United States at war and my status unclarified, I felt apprehension instead of relief as the *Beagle* approached her moorings.

Captain Sage went ashore at once, and, as I watched his boat move among the line of battleships with their towering sides and massive guns, the swift frigates, and the numerous little sloops-of-war and brigs, I wondered what possible chance our country stood against

Great Britain now that the full power of its one-thousand-ship navy could be turned against us. I was convinced that despite British sea power we could prevent them from winning any decisive victory on land provided the individual states would furnish their troop quotas for the main army and train their militia to stand fast. Surely with a larger population and a wealthier economy than in 1775 we could do as well or better than our fathers did in the struggle for independence. Up to this point, however, our performance had been worse, despite our occasional victories at sea and on the lakes and the superb work of our privateers. Now, looking at the powerful British squadron in Gibraltar, I felt nothing but discouragement.

When Captain Sage returned, he summoned both of us to his cabin. Though it was stifling inside and sweat stains darkened his uniform, he kept his jacket on and looked severely at us from behind his table. "Captain Black and Mr. Dearborn," he said crisply, "it is necessary that you go to the Admiralty Office to be examined concerning your late cruise. I am afraid those people will want to send you to England, Captain Black. As for you, Mr. Dearborn, I pled that you be released on the basis of your status on the *Ginny*, that you were aboard her involuntarily and took up no arms against us. They declined to accept my plea. Instead, they wish to question you as to the circumstances, first, of your being in France and, second, of your alleged kidnapping. The court of inquiry will convene tomorrow morning at ten o'clock."

"Well, now, Dearborn," Black laughed harshly when we went back to our cabin, "I may be going to Dartmoor, but it looks like you may be in for real trouble. I never did ask why you were in France or why Rudd had a grudge against you, but you can bet the court will."

"I'll tell them when the time comes," I said.

"Sure you wasn't doin' a bit of spyin'?"

"No, damn you, I wasn't doing any spying!"

He ran his hand over his bearded face. "Then you must have done something pretty bad to get Rudd down on you. Course it don't take much to make Rudd mad."

"How did you get to know him?" I kept my voice casual, though I was deeply curious.

Black stripped to his waist and plunged his head into a basin of water. "Jesus, it's hot here!" he gasped. Then toweling his chest and fat belly, which drooped over his waistband, he said, "Jake an' I ran slaves. He was master an' I was mate of the schooner *Ghost*. We used to run 'em into Savannah an' Charleston on a regular schedule, an' sometimes into Cuba. We lost some blacks — Jake packed 'em in pretty tight, but the *Ghost* was fast, so they weren't in misery too long. We made a lot of money, but the time came when I wanted to be a master, too. Jake didn't mind — fact is, he helped me get hold of the *Ginny*. Took me quite a while, but I finally owned that schooner, Mister, lock, stock, and barrel. An' sometime I'll collect on her insurance, if I live to get out of Dartmoor."

"You're a tough bird, Black," I said. "I'm sure you'll live to collect. But tell me, were you a pirate long?"

His face turned an angry red. "Now I ain't never said I was a pirate. Remember, a privateersman ain't a pirate."

"Some act like pirates, and you're one who did," I insisted. "But I didn't denounce you, I couldn't prove it anyway, and I'm not going to try — you saved my life. But you were a damned pirate all the same."

He grunted and sat down on his bunk.

"Look here," I said, trying to draw him out and therefore asking a question I knew was not the truth, "did Rudd own the *Ghost* the way you owned the *Ginny*?"

"Hell, no," Black said. "Rudd was a gambler an' whenever he had any money, he'd blow it on women an' cards. Matter of fact, he got a bad reputation in the South for killin' husbands."

"Then who does own the *Ghost*, a syndicate?"

Black's beady, little eyes narrowed to mere slits. "You know him," he grunted.

"Warren Bierce? All by himself!" That Bierce and not a syndicate he headed owned the *Ghost* was indeed news, and I couldn't keep the excitement out of my voice. "But you said you'd never heard of him."

"Why should I have told you I knew about him? I had to find out more about you before I'd admit to anything like that." Then he snorted. "I guess you've found out Bierce ain't a man to fool around with any more than Rudd is. Fact is, Bierce is the one man Rudd's afraid of. Well, maybe 'afraid' is too strong, but Rudd takes his orders from Bierce."

"Then I was put aboard the *Ginny* because of Bierce?"

"Ain't I been practically tellin' you that?"

"I just wanted to hear you say so. I really didn't have any doubts about it."

"But it ain't just Bierce," said Black, thoughtfully stroking his scraggly beard. "Rudd don't like you on his own."

This didn't surprise me, but his bringing in Rudd's name again made me curious about something else. "Black," I said, stretching back in my bunk and folding my arms behind my head, "since you sailed with Rudd, maybe you know of a Negro gunner named Philip Adair."

Black whistled softly. "So you know Adair."

"I've met him," I said. "I don't think he and Rudd get along well, do they?"

"Dearborn," Black turned on his side and looked up at me, "if you know that much, you've more than met Adair. By God, Dearborn, are you a privateersman?"

"I know Philip hates Rudd, and I know he's got welts on his back."

He grunted, looked at me suspiciously, and lay back again. "It ain't just the beatings Adair got from Rudd, Dearborn. That Adair earned his freedom. Saved his master's life in Jamaica, so his master let him buy his freedom for a song. But he come from Africa in the beginnin'. Fact is, Rudd brought him over an' sold him in Jamaica. Adair was a chief or something an' he an' some of his tribe were sold by Arab slave traders. His favorite wife — Seba was her name — was captured with him an' sold to Rudd. Well, sir, Rudd threw her overboard long before we got to Jamaica."

I sat up in my bunk and stared at him.

"Yeah, she got sick. You know we used to bring those slaves up on deck once a day so we could exercise 'em, an' of course, while they were on deck, we'd slosh out below with sea water an' vinegar. Jesus, what a stink! Rudd kept a clean ship as slavers go, but you can never really get the smell out. A stable smells clean alongside a slaver."

"But what about Philip's wife?"

"She got sick, I told you. No one knew just what it was. You can never tell about niggers. They wanta die, they die. They wanta get well, maybe they can do that, too. Anyway, Seba got sick for some reason — maybe for Adair — an' Rudd decided he didn't want to take a chance of her infectin' the others. So he had her heaved overboard, an' by God, she'd hardly hit the water when a shark got her."

"Good God!"

Black got up and soaked his head again. "Yeah," he said, "sharks follow slave ships. Sick niggers are always bein' tossed overboard. Rudd wasn't no worse than any other slaver that way."

"What happened when Philip heard about it?"

"I'm tellin' you that nigger went wild. He tried to get at Rudd when we brought him an' some others up on deck. Rudd had him whipped then, and Adair didn't get on deck again till Rudd put the slaves on the auction block in Kingston. By that time, he was a mighty sick nigger, an' his wrists and ankles were like raw meat from the chains. A man named Adair finally bought him, and Philip later took his name. Funny sort of planter — liked books better than sugar, I guess. Well, he took a fancy to that nigger, treated him well, and taught him to read an' write. Taught him to speak good English, too — fact, he speaks almost as good as I do."

He looked at me as if he thought I might scoff, but I said nothing.

"Well, after Philip won his freedom, he sailed on several English ships, an' got to be a gunner — a good one, too. Then he come to America lookin' for Rudd, an' when he found him in Charleston, he signed up on the *Ghost*."

"Did Rudd recognize him?"

"Nope. But I did after we were at sea headin' for Africa, an' I can tell you I was mighty uneasy. When I told Rudd, he thought it was a great joke. I didn't. But, a funny thing, Dearborn, that Adair was meek an' mild. Did everything he was told. Rudd whipped him hard once for something, I forget what — wasn't important, anyway. That nigger actually begged his pardon when they cut him down, so Rudd got mad an' had him whipped again for back talk. I left the *Ghost* before Adair did. 'Tween you an' me, I didn't think it was goin' to be healthy for anyone aboard whenever he decided to have it out with

Rudd, an' I was glad to leave. You ought've seen the broody way Adair looked at Rudd."

"Did Rudd suspect that Philip would try to get him someday?"

"Maybe — I don't know, Dearborn. Jake Rudd's a hard man to scare. I guess he ain't afraid of any nigger. But, once or twice, I saw him lookin' at Adair, an' I swear he didn't seem very happy. Got to wonderin', myself, if Adair wasn't tryin' to put him under a spell."

The rest of the day and the next morning, Black was surly again and hardly civil. I think he regretted that he had told me so much the previous day. He was still sullen when we were summoned again to Captain Sage's cabin right after breakfast.

"Gentlemen," Sage said when we were alone, "if you will pledge your honor not to try to escape, you may go on shore without a guard; otherwise, I shall be obliged to send a guard with you."

Black looked at me and I at him. Neither of us had discussed the possibility of escape, though I had thought about it, believe me. Now, playing for time, I said, "Captain Sage, I'm surprised you should think it possible anyone could escape from Gibraltar."

"Come, come, Mr. Dearborn," he said pleasantly but with a hint of impatience, "that won't do. You must pledge your honor not to try to escape, or I will send a guard with you."

Again I glanced at Black, who stared at Captain Sage without expression. "As far as I'm concerned, sir, you had better send a guard," I said.

"And you, Captain Black?"

"I ain't askin' to go to Dartmoor, Cap'n. Send your guard."

"Very well. Good luck, gentlemen."

True to his word, Captain Sage ordered a detail consisting of a sergeant and four marines under Lieutenant Eustis to conduct us to the Admiralty Office. Eustis disliked me; he had never made any bones about it; and I think it afforded him no small satisfaction to have an enemy national, to whom his captain had shown favor, called up for questioning by the Admiralty Office. Certainly, while sailors from the *Beagle* rowed us ashore, we were made to feel that we were prisoners.

I should have liked to have presented more of a civilian appearance. The civilian clothes that I had worn to Paris had deteriorated so badly aboard the *Ginny* that Sage outfitted me from the *Beagle's* slopchest and pressed a much mended and shiny, old coat of his own on me, though it was a trifle long in the skirt and narrow in the shoulders. From somewhere, too, he had also found an old hat with a black cockade. If no one took time to examine me, he might have guessed that I was some kind of British officer. This was exactly the impression I did not wish to convey since it might give my inquisitors ideas when they interrogated me about my business in France.

The cases were so numerous that it was late afternoon before ours was heard. The courtroom itself was small, and proceedings in the cases were remarkably informal, with officers entering and leaving during the interrogation. Even the captains and merchants being questioned came and went freely. When the Board summoned Black and began to drone on with questions that already appeared on a printed form, I glanced behind me. Eustis had disappeared, probably hunting for a drink to relieve his boredom, but the sergeant and his marines were there on duty. Suddenly I decided that if I was to make a break for freedom, now was the time; I had no confidence that I could deceive the judges for long about the nature of my business in France.

Trying to show in my face and manner none of the feeling of near panic at being trapped, I got up and walked casually to the rear of the room. "Sergeant," I whispered to the marine noncom, "will you go up the street and have a glass of wine with me?"

His face not far from the color of his uniform because of the heat and his addiction to tippling, he looked around the room. Then, evidently convinced that there was no need to worry in a garrison town and that we would be back before the judges finished with Captain Black, he nodded. Telling the marines to watch Black, he walked up the street with me.

"Good of you, sir," he said.

"Not at all," I said. "It's warm and it appears that we'll be in the courtroom quite some time."

"That it does, sir."

Soon we entered a wine shop on a corner with a door opening on each street. At once I ordered a glass of rum for each of us from a sad-eyed Spaniard. To my surprise the sergeant emptied his in a gulp.

Smacking his lips, he said, "Now, sir, you take your time, but if you don't mind, I'll stand in this door and keep watch for officers. Then we must get back to the courtroom."

When I had been kidnapped aboard the *Ginny*, not only had the letter from Crawford been taken but my money also. Black, however, had come aboard the *Beagle* with his pockets full, and before we left for the hearing, I had borrowed a few gold pieces from him, giving him a note promising to repay sometime in the future. I now placed a Spanish dollar on the counter, and as the Spaniard started to make change, I shook my head and put my finger to my lips. Praying he would remain silent, I slipped out of the room by the opposite door, crossed a little square in front, and turned the first corner.

I had now really committed myself and knew I had to hurry. Grateful that I had been in Gibraltar once before with Uncle Tom and remembered something of the street pattern, I headed, not toward the Peninsula, but down toward the Land Port Gate at the northwestern end of the town. I knew my first test would come when I approached the sentry. If I couldn't get by him, my chances for escape would be slim, for the hue and cry would soon be after me. Quickly I straightened up and now walked with something like military precision, hoping that my clothes would enable me to pass for a British naval officer.

Then came the sharp challenge. I gave the sentry a stern look and told him to let me pass. He drew back respectfully and saluted me, I returned his salute, and in a moment I was outside the defenses of Gibraltar.

Hardly daring to breathe, I walked rapidly down to the mole, where I ran the gauntlet of boatmen begging me to let them take me to my ship. I pointed to one, who led me to his boat and seated me in the stern.

"Captain, where is your ship?" he asked when we were clear of the mole and out in the bay.

I gazed at the fleet of merchantmen crowding the anchorage. They flew the flags of many European nations, but I could settle on none until I spied a galliot flying the Norwegian flag. I knew that as a people Norwegians were great sailors and traders with a reputation for honesty and trustworthiness. After only a moment's hesitation, therefore, I pointed to the galliot. "There's my ship," I said; and was soon rowed alongside.

Once aboard, I asked three crewmen who were mending sail where I might find the captain. As one of them started to answer in broken English, the captain himself appeared. An elderly, broad-shouldered man of about my height, he introduced himself in excellent but accented English as Olaf Torgenson and asked what I wanted.

"Sir," I answered most respectfully, "I should like to speak with you in private, if you will be so kind."

After a long appraisal of me, he nodded. "Come to my cabin."

When he bade me be seated in a large, comfortable chair, I leaned forward. "Captain, I am in trouble," I said, "and I shall be deeply grateful if you will help me."

"Are you a criminal?" he asked.

"No, sir."

"Then tell me your story, and I will let you know if I can assist you."

This seemed fair enough, so without mentioning my connection with the *Argus*, I identified myself by name as an American who had been in Paris on business and was kidnapped at Bordeaux. The story from that point on was as I had given it to Captain Sage. Naturally I also told him of my escape from the Admiralty Court.

When I had finished, the old man was silent for a moment. Presently he said, "I think the court would indeed want to ask why you were kidnapped — I would myself, if I were a member, for there is an incompleteness about your story that makes me suspect you are not all you pretend to be, though you look honest enough." Then he smiled and reached for my hand. "But I am only a merchant sea captain of Norway and I will help you. You see, I was once a prisoner in Dartmoor myself, and I would not like to see you go there. Now the first thing to do is to pay off your boatman."

As I drew out a gold piece, he held up his hand. "You are too generous to him. I will pay him what he deserves."

"But I insist —"

"Mr. Dearborn, for the moment you are my guest and under my protection. If that man receives a dollar, he will talk about it along the mole, and when the British start asking the watermen questions, as they will, they will have no difficulty locating your waterman and then my ship. No, no, I will pay what is best for all of us. Then there will be no comment."

Soon he returned, and humming some song which sounded off key, he went to his trunk and drew out a pea jacket and a large fur cap. "Put these on," he laughed. "Ah, now you are a Norwegian. No, not quite!"

From his table he selected one of a half-dozen pipes. This one was stubby with a large bowl and felt heavy in my mouth.

"You smoke, don't you?" he asked anxiously.

"Yes," I said, "but not around home. My father is a minister, and neither he nor my mother approves of smoking."

"A minister's son," he grunted, and handed me his pouch. "Well, fill up with tobacco and let us go on deck."

Once outside I was certain the crew would stare at me and talk. Instead, they gave me hardly a look.

"They won't betray me?" I asked Captain Torgenson.

He chuckled throatily and shook his head. "They're good seamen and loyal to me. You can trust them to keep their mouths shut."

After we dined in his cabin, he said, "I will now go ashore, Mr. Dearborn. I have ship business to attend to, but I will learn all I can about your escape and what the British are doing."

Early in the evening he returned, looking pleased and amused, and over a glass of wine he told me that Gibraltar was swarming with search parties. "I think the whole garrison is looking for you," he laughed. "At least all the military and civil police are hunting in every corner for an escaped American. They say no one has escaped before, though I do not believe it. That other man with you has been put in prison, and the marine sergeant and the naval lieutenant have been arrested."

"I am sorry for that," I said. And I was. Black would have been sent to Dartmoor anyway, but I hoped my escape hadn't hurried his departure. I was also sorry for the sergeant, and even for the arrogant Eustis.

"Come, come, young man," said the old captain impatiently. "You must not feel bad. Your country is at war with England, and you were entitled to try to escape. It was the duty of the lieutenant and the sergeant to guard you, and they did not do so properly. I do not think they will suffer too severe a punishment because, if you will forgive me, you were not that important a prisoner. Besides, Mr. Dearborn, you are not out of danger. Your escaping is proof that you must be more than an American businessman in France, and by tomorrow, perhaps even tonight, the guard boats will be out to search the merchant ships in the harbor."

"Captain," I said, "I do not want you to get into any trouble on account of me."

"I do not intend to," he said gruffly. "No, no," he added, sensing my uneasiness, "I will not give you up to the English. I have been thinking of another way out for you. I would take you in my *Helga,* but I cannot leave port for several days."

"Captain Torgenson, you have been so fair and aboveboard with me I will tell you what I really am and then you will see why I must get away from here if possible." I then disclosed to him that I was the second officer aboard the American privateer *Argus,* was landed in France to report to our minister in Paris the evidence of one of my countrymen's treachery, and had returned to Bordeaux with a formal report for our government from Mr. Crawford. I told him about Bierce's following the stagecoach, the Judge's desire to return on the *Argus,* and India's anger that I should suspect Bierce of malign designs and disloyalty. Likewise I mentioned the relationships of Rudd and Bierce and Rudd and Black, both of which had led to my being where I now was.

When I finished, he drank the last of his wine, and his little eyes twinkled as he said, "Mr. Dearborn, you are scarcely a much-wanted spy, but you must indeed get out of here. I would not have it on my conscience to see British marines board my little ship and take you back to Gibraltar."

"Thank you," I said, and waited as he lighted his pipe.

"The best thing I can do for you," he said between enormous puffs, "is to get you over to Algeciras. Then, if I were you, I would go over the mountains to Cadiz and find myself a passage on some ship bound for America."

"But how do I get to Cadiz?"

He grinned. "Don't worry about Cadiz. First you must get to

Algeciras across the bay. Have you ever seen a Spanish smuggler, Mr. Dearborn? No? Well, in twenty minutes you will see one. He will look just as dreadful as you would imagine him, and there is no doubt he is a dangerous man. But he will take you across the bay — for a price. I would prefer to wait until tomorrow night so that I could enjoy your company further, but for the sake of all of us, especially your own, I must send you on your way tonight. You see, since I often put in at Gibraltar, I have become pretty well acquainted with this man, who is the leader of a gang of smugglers working out of Algerciras. I often sell him gin, tobacco, and other articles. He stops at my ship about ten o'clock and leaves for Algeciras about midnight when he has completed his trading with the ships in the Bay."

"I am not sure I can meet his price," I said.

"Don't worry about that," he said. "A few dollars will be sufficient, and if you do not have enough, I will lend you what is necessary."

He waved aside my thanks and said, "After all, you are going with him as a paying passenger with business in Algeciras. He need not know you are an escaped prisoner. Indeed he had better not know — I would not trust him that far."

He had hardly finished talking when there came a knock on the door, and one of his crew stuck his head inside and said something to him in Norwegian.

"They are about here," Captain Torgenson said, jumping up. "Come, let us go on deck."

We arrived in time to see a long, low boat, its oars dipping smoothly, glide under our lee. Four men climbed aboard, and I never looked at such walking arsenals of swords, dirks, and pistols. The leader, a big, swarthy man in a black hat and black clothes, and wearing a bright red waistcoat, spoke English with fluency. This surprised me until I realized that since their livelihood must depend on trading with ships at Gibraltar, they would have to know at least some English.

After the four had bought a number of articles and had had a glass of gin, Captain Torgenson asked the leader, "Captain Perez, what time do you intend to go back tonight?"

As Perez's eyes flashed suspiciously, Torgenson said, "This is my nephew John — Juan in your language — and he wishes to go to Algeciras for a few days on business. Could he return with you and stay the night at your house? I told him he would be safe with you."

Perez's eyes flicked me up and down. Then his lips drew back in a quick smile like a donkey showing its teeth, and he put out his hand. "I will be honored to have the señor go with me and stay in my home. He may stay as long as he likes."

"Thank you, Captain," I said, and gently withdrew what was left of my hand. He had a grip like a blacksmith's.

"I will be back at midnight," he said to Torgenson.

When the smugglers had gone, Captain Torgenson put his arm around my shoulders and led me back to his cabin. "Now, Mr. Dearborn, you will need another shirt and an extra pair of stockings."

When I insisted I could not trespass further on his kindness, he hushed me, and, folding a shirt and stockings into a tiny, compact bundle, he instructed me to put it inside my hat. I promised to send back both hat and pea jacket through the American consul in Algeciras.

"One more thing," he said, looking at me sternly for the first time. "These are desperate men you are going with. There are those who fear them, especially their own government. Spanish brigands can be savage, as the government and the French found out so recently. But they can also be kind. Take nothing that is theirs unless they press it on you; then it would be an insult to them not to accept it. Above all, Mr. Dearborn, leave their women alone. Diego Perez has a wife, Joanna, a strange woman. I know of two men who liked her too well. Each died by a knife thrust: one by her hand, the other by Diego's."

"Thank you, Captain," I said. I hope I sounded properly impressed. Actually I thought the kind, old man underestimated me and overestimated the hazards.

But at midnight, when I boarded the smuggler boat filled with silent men armed to the teeth who looked surly and grim, I began to wonder if I hadn't acted a little too superior in the face of Captain Torgenson's well-meant advice. Perez motioned me to a seat in front of him in the stern; he was handling the tiller himself. Unsmiling, he put his finger to his lips enjoining silence and then tapped a knife in his belt.

The two gestures were too explicit not to be understood. I could imagine myself laughing at them under other circumstances, but not now. I watched with a flicker of apprehension as we drew away from the friendly galliot and swiftly threaded a course through the anchored ships. Not a man spoke, not an oar splashed water. We heard the cries of the watch aboard a frigate near us, and somehow the sound of an English voice seemed infinitely friendly when I thought of my present company. Then we dropped the frigate astern and sliced through the dark waters toward Algeciras.

# XII

WHEN we approached Algeciras, the smuggler showed a lantern twice, covering it each time with a jacket. Not until an answering two flashes came from the waterfront did he bring his heavily laden boat to shore.

It was about three o'clock when we finally entered the small, low house belonging to El Capitan Perez and situated on an embankment above the water. The house contained but one room partitioned by latticed shades hanging from the ceiling. Perez kept his voice down as he explained that he had to leave to dispose of his merchandise and would not be back until noon. His wife and two children would look after me. Then, taking the stub of candle, he brushed one of the shades aside and told me to stay there and he would be back in a moment with something for me to sleep on. He was gone, almost soundlessly, before I could thank him. Evidently he went to his wife for I heard a furious whispering, which soon ceased, and he came back with straw and blanket and bade me sleep well. Uneasy in the strange house, I took off only my jacket and shoes and lay down. After listening to the breathing and stirrings just beyond the latticed shades, I eventually fell asleep myself.

I awoke to the smell of coffee and to the light of the sun, already high. Quickly I dressed and went to the kitchen. A blackened coffee pot rested in hot ashes in the fireplace, but no one was present in this neat, little house. Someone, however, had drawn up the latticed shades to the ceiling rafters. Going to the open door, I looked up and down the dirty street with its litter of refuse, chickens, and pigs. Then a voice behind me said, "Señor, if you will have breakfast, I can serve it to you."

Startled, I turned around and saw a little, blue-clad girl with snapping, black eyes holding a very small boy by the hand. Both were barefoot. "You speak English!" I said in surprise.

"Of course," she said, studying me with disconcerting care. "Many Englishmen come here, and it is good for business in Algeciras that people speak English."

"I am Jonathan Dearborn," I said. "What is your name?"

"I am Elena, and this is my brother Francisco. Our mother is at the market, and she will be angry if I do not give you coffee and a roll for your breakfast."

Such a breakfast, though hardly substantial for a New Englander, was a pleasure chiefly because of Elena, who talked like a little adult but with a directness and frankness that no adult would have thought of using at a first meeting. The boy, meanwhile, stared at me with black eyes as still and solemn as his sister's were animated and gay.

We were still talking when the little girl fell silent and both she and her brother stared over my shoulder. I glanced around and instantly rose to my feet. Behind me, having come in from the rear door, stood a woman in black. She was dark-haired like India but with black eyes, a deeply tanned skin, and an impression about her at once sad and powerfully vital.

"Señor?" The voice was deeper than India's and harsh where India's was mellow. The eyes, huge and inquiring, looked intently at me. "I am Joanna Perez," she said.

"And I am Jonathan Dearborn," I said. "Did Señor Perez speak to you about me?"

She nodded. "I am sorry I was not here to give you breakfast, but I was at market. Bah! a dreadful year for vegetables — too dry."

"Señora," I said, "I insist on paying for everything you spend on me."

[ 117 ]

She brushed my remark aside with a gesture. "We will talk about that later."

"But I —"

"You insist, Señor?" She placed the vegetables on the scrubbed wooden table. "If you insist on paying, why did you not go to an inn?"

I felt my face grow hot. "I did not know there was an inn in town. Perhaps I should indeed go there."

She shrugged. "If that is your pleasure, then do so — but not now. My husband will not like to find you gone so soon, I will not like it, and I can see that Elena and Francisco will not like it. Besides, my husband says you do not speak English like your uncle, Captain Torgenson, and I can tell that you do not speak it like an Englishman. We think you are an American, Señor, and if you are seen and the English at Gibraltar want to pay enough for you, there are men here in Algeciras who will take you to them."

"Señora, you have convinced me," I said, smiling. "I will stay, but I am sorry to inconvenience you."

"You are welcome here, Señor."

The words were kind, but the voice was so cold I felt repelled. It was a relief to turn to the children. Even this pleasure was soon cut short by the mother's calling Elena to come and help prepare dinner. That left me only Francisco, who, now that his sister was gone, became so shy it was impossible to carry on a conversation.

"Did you sleep well, Señor?"

I spun around to see Diego Perez just behind me. The man had a silent way of walking like a cat.

At my start Perez laughed. "What is the matter, Señor? There is nothing to be afraid of."

"I'm not afraid," I countered, more sharply than I meant. "It's just that you surprised me."

"A thousand pardons, Señor."

He was in a great, good humor throughout the meal, which consisted of coarse brown bread, goat cheese, black olives, a salad drenched in oil, and quantities of a pale, sour-sweet wine. When we were finished, he said, "You must not go out of the house for two days more."

[ 118 ]

"That is what I told Señor Dearborn," his wife said, looking intently at her husband. "As an American he would be in danger."

Perez nodded vigorously. "Sí. There are spies everywhere in Algeciras. We are but eight miles from Gibraltar. In two days, maybe three, people will forget about the American prisoner who escaped from Gibraltar."

"Then you knew from the start?"

He grinned. "I knew when I returned to El Capitan Torgenson at midnight, not when I said I would bring you here. I thought you at first truly a man of business."

"We should have told you then what I was," I said.

"Then I might not have taken you with me, and you would have been brought back to Gibraltar. I am glad I did not know — I have been a prisoner of the English and of our own government, and I am sorry for prisoners. That is one reason I do not take any."

I nearly choked on the bread. "You mean you kill them?"

"Those I do not ransom. Why should they live, Señor? They cannot be set free to tell what they have learned, and they are unhappy unless they are free. So —" He left the sentence unfinished but drew his hand across his throat.

"I wouldn't want to be a prisoner of yours," I said.

He laughed as though I had cracked the funniest of jokes. Then his face sobered. "I like you, Señor Dearborn. You will want to see the American consul, I know, but not for two days. You see, I do not want all Algeciras to know I brought you."

"But your men know. Surely one of them might tell."

"My men will say nothing," he cut me off. "You are my guest for two days more. I will not be here, but my Joanna and my Elena will look after you. On the third day from now, you may go to your consul, Señor Horatio Sprague."

Just before he left, the good humor in his face vanished as if one had suddenly blown out a candle. "Señor," he said, and his voice was deep in his throat and harshly rattling, "remember what I said and do not leave the house."

Then he was gone and I was left confused. This was no request, no admonition even, but an order. For a while it didn't weigh heavily on me, though I didn't like it. I reasoned that he had in mind my safety and naturally his own, and what he demanded was, after all, simply a wise precaution. It was only when I noticed a lean, youngish man in dirty white shirt and pants sitting in a chair with his back against the wall of a house diagonally opposite from Perez's that I began to wonder. The male population on this street, at least what I could see from the window, seemed wholly unconcerned about supporting their families, but even most of them would occasionally stroll along the street and talk with their neighbors. Not this man. His eyes rarely left the house of Perez, and when he wasn't smoking a long, thin cigar, the ash of which he flicked away with a deliberate gesture, his hands caressed the butts of two pistols thrust into his belt. Sometime in the course of the afternoon I began to feel that my role in the Perez house was something other than that of a guest and that I had merely changed prisons.

After supper that evening, for want of anything else to do, I began to tell the children about the early days in Maine when the forest came up to the backdoor, when moose and bears were commonly seen along the coast, and when the Indians lurked in the meadow grass and among the trees to kill or capture the settlers. I mentioned the tunnel from house to shore that my great-great-grandfather, Nathan Dearborn, had built as a place of refuge or an escape route should the Indians attack.

The children sat motionless, their eyes wide and staring. When I finished, they asked me many questions, especially Elena, such as what a moose looked like, if I had ever seen an Indian myself, how bear meat tasted, whether the flowers in Maine were like those in Spain. The questioning might have gone on indefinitely if Señora Perez had not sent the children to bed, though not after first bidding them thank me for my stories.

Later she said, "You were kind to the children, Señor."

"I like children, Señora, and yours are lovely."

"Do you have any of your own?"

"No." Then I added, "I am not married."

She smiled, and momentarily the deep lines of her face vanished. "Do you not like the women in your America?"

"I like one woman very much," I said, and felt the conversation suddenly so awkward I wanted to end it.

"She does not like you?"

"I don't know."

She said nothing but went to the open door and looked out. When I came near her to get a breath of air, she turned to me and said, "Señor, it is best that you stay back in the house so that no one will see you."

"Señora Perez, you are making me feel more and more like a prisoner," I said, half amused and half irritated.

"Why do you say that?" she asked. "Just because it is not safe for you or us that someone sees you?"

I nodded toward the man leaning against the house, only this time it was another, his relief. "Between you and that guard how could I help but think I'm a prisoner? And I suppose there's another guard somewhere near watching the backdoor."

"Then if the Señor is not stupid, he will not try to escape," she said.

"So I am a prisoner! Why? So that Perez can collect a ransom on me from the British?"

She said nothing but tossed her head and motioned me away from the door.

It became clear, as I lay down on my pallet that night, that I must somehow reach the American consulate, wherever that might be. I figured that Perez would probably not appear until the next night or the day following so that I still had time to plan. Perhaps, with daylight, something would occur to me, but at the moment brilliant ideas avoided me, and I fell into an uneasy sleep.

I couldn't have slept more than a couple of hours when the heat and the mosquitoes awoke me. It was stifling in the house and silent except for the breathing of Señora Perez and the children and the whine of the insects. Had I been a dog, I'd have panted from the heat. Determined to get some air, I tiptoed to the door. As I reached it and started to lift the bar, something hard prodded me in the back.

"Señor, leave the door alone and go back to your bed!" Señora Perez said in a fierce whisper.

"I'm not trying to escape," I said as calmly as I could.

"Raise your hands, I tell you. Now go back to bed."

Remembering what Torgenson had said about her willingness to use a knife, and troubled by the hysteria in her voice, I raised my hands and, in response to a sharp prod from what was obviously a pistol, turned slowly toward my "room" behind the latticed curtain.

But at this point I had had enough of the situation. I suddenly whirled, stepping aside as I did so, and grabbed her pistol wrist. Though she tried to bring the pistol up, I knocked it from her hand. For a few moments she struggled furiously, and she possessed a strength that surprised me. I had never manhandled a woman before, at least not in quite this way, and I took no satisfaction in pinning her arms behind her. After holding her there briefly, I let her go.

For a few moments we stood staring watchfully at each other and breathing heavily. Then I suppose I did a foolish thing. I picked the pistol off the floor and held it out to her.

"Bah!" she said in disgust, and threw it aside.

Then, with a movement almost pantherish, she slid into my arms and, taking my face in both her hands, kissed me hard on the lips.

That I was surprised is putting it mildly. Within seconds, however, as she leaned against me, warm and womanly, I swung from aversion to attraction. Yet even as my arms tightened about her, she suddenly beat on my chest with her fists and stepped back.

"Señor, you must go!" she whispered hoarsely.

I suppose my mouth just about dropped open at that point.

"Perez will be back before daybreak, and you will have no chance after that," she said.

"But I don't understand," I said. "Don't you want the ransom money?"

"I? Perez share anything with me? My children and I mean nothing to him. Money — that is what he loves, and sometime he will die of it. Some prisoner he has betrayed will kill him. No American — you are our first — but some Spanish smuggler he has betrayed to the government. And if no one else will kill him, then — come, Señor," she said urgently, "you must go."

I was about to ask how she expected me to get out of the house undetected by the guards watching it when she lighted a lantern and, carefully hooding it with a shawl, bade me open a trap door. She then led me down a short but steep ladder to the cellar. It was a dank and musty place, smelling of the empty wine casks that filled much of the space. Going to the wall on the side nearest the embankment she handed the lantern to me and bent down and ran her hands over the stones nearest the earthen floor.

"Here," she whispered, "here they are."

As I crouched, she said, "Remove these stones."

Carefully I removed several large, thin stones standing on edge and saw behind them a small wooden door. Grasping the ring, I pulled it open and was startled at how silently it swung back on its hinge; someone kept that hinge well oiled. A draft of cool air at once came through the space.

"Now listen, Señor Dearborn," she said, placing her hand on my shoulder. "This is a tunnel — a short one — that leads down the embankment. No one knows of it except Perez and myself. We built it together. You will have to roll a few stones away to get out, but they are not large. Be sure to replace them."

As I started to thank her, she put her hand over my mouth and told me how I could reach the American consulate. "If you see any civilian, act like a man with too much wine in him. If a soldier or a policeman stops you, ask outright for directions to the consulate. But try not to be seen by anyone. Stay close to the houses — not in the middle of the street." Then she kissed me again, and said, "Don't try to understand why I do all this for you. Just be as kind to your own children — and may God grant you will have some — as you were to mine tonight."

"But you," I said. "What will happen to you now?"

Her whispered laugh was both angry and amused, if that is possible. "Señor, in ten minutes I will start to scream and shout, and when the guards come, I will convince them that you escaped through the front door, and I will accuse the guard across the street of sleeping. And he may in fact be sleeping, but we can't take a chance on that. Now, go, go quickly."

The tunnel was indeed short, but it seemed endless. My shoulders and hips kept bumping protruding rocks and I scraped my knees. When I came to the mouth, it was partially blocked by stones, as she had said. But after glancing down the beach and seeing no one, and hearing only the lapping of wavelets, I pushed the stones aside.

[ 123 ]

My first few moments as I turned into the street I felt as if eyes were staring at me from every house. If a cat had crossed in front of me, I'd have probably thought it a soldier. To my unbounded relief I encountered no one and was already approaching the house where the American consul lived when an uproar broke out from down where I had come: shrieks and shouts; even a few shots were fired.

A young American about my age and physique answered my urgent knocking. He had obviously drawn his trousers up over his nightshirt and his "Yes, who are you?" revealed the annoyance of a man awakened from his sleep.

Quickly I told him who I was and that I was in danger. I mentioned my escape but said nothing about how I had accomplished it.

"Come inside, man, come in," he said, and barred the door behind him. "I'm William Leach, and my uncle, Horatio Sprague, is consul. I'll find a place for you to sleep, and you can tell him all about yourself in the morning."

After breakfast I did indeed tell Mr. Sprague about my experiences. He was a kind-hearted man who would have helped me anyway, but the fact that he had formerly been consul at Gibraltar, that his nephew knew and liked my cousin Paul in Boston, and that Sprague himself was from Massachusetts and acquainted with many people in Maine, combined to make him especially interested in my "case."

"You must lie low until we can get you out of Algeciras, my boy," he said in his easy, pleasant way. "The town is filled with smugglers and their friends."

"Uncle Horry, he'll have to go to Cadiz," Leach said.

"Of course. That's the nearest place where he'll be likely to find a ship for America. We'll have to find an honest guide today, Bill."

"That won't be so easy," his nephew sighed.

"You see," Mr. Sprague said to me, "the mountain roads are infested with robbers, and the robbers work hand-in-glove with the guides of unwary travelers. These robbers won't hesitate to kill if necessary."

Fortunately by noon Sprague and Leach had found a guide who had previously escorted Sprague himself over the mountains. His name was Manuel Esposito, and he was a ragged, wiry Spaniard with sad, black eyes and a leathery skin as filled with wrinkles as a ploughed field with furrows. Manuel appeared after siesta, so I was at once keen for starting off. Sprague, however, convinced me I should wait until morning since there were supplies to buy, a mule to hire, and the matter of safety to observe.

Early the next morning, therefore, after giving the consul Captain Torgenson's clothes to return, we set out for Cadiz, forty miles distant. For protection I was dressed as a peasant here in Andalusia, but I hoped I'd never be called on to exchange more than a few words in Spanish. Sometimes I rode the mule; at others, I walked with Manuel; and occasionally I permitted him to ride. At this last, his sad eyes would invariably crinkle in a smile that convinced me he was more melancholy in appearance than in actuality.

The road from Algeciras to Cadiz was often no more than a winding path among high rugged mountains. For a while we had a glorious view of the Straits and the Atlantic, but more often we could see only peaks and rocks and trees. We wound through wooded ravines, one so heavily overgrown that we scarcely saw the sun for half an hour. In fact, our progress was so slow that by early afternoon we were only ten miles from Algeciras and as many more from Medina, our objective for the first day. Because of our fatigue and the heat we stopped at a little *posada* to rest ourselves and the mule. It was a wretched, fly-ridden inn, but we bought glasses of thin, sour wine to wash down the bread and cheese we carried with us. Then, after an hour, we set out for Medina again.

As we approached this city built on a high hill, we could see its walks, churches, and houses — all plastered a dazzling white — from a great distance. The surrounding country was pleasant with olive trees, orange groves, and meadows. Cattle grazing in the meadows lent a pastoral aspect to the scene that contrasted sharply with the savage countryside we had passed through.

As we plodded up the high hill to Medina, I looked forward to a big meal and a soft bed at a hotel. Instead, Manuel turned in at a *posada* almost as miserable as the one we had stopped at for our noon meal. When he saw how disappointed I was, he shrugged his thin shoulders. "Cadiz is still far away, and, señor, if you will pardon me, you are not dressed like a gentleman."

[ 125 ]

I therefore dined off two hard-boiled eggs and more sour wine and slept on a straw pallet on the stone floor of a little box of a room with only my cloak for a covering.

Next morning we were up early and made our way more quickly over the better roads and less mountainous country to Cadiz, twenty-two miles away. After spending the night at one of the numerous comfortable hotels, I settled accounts with Manuel and then sought out the United States consul, Joseph E. Bloomfield.

The day I called at the consul's office, a tall, slender man was present whom Bloomfield introduced as Richard W. Meade of Philadelphia, a merchant then residing in Cadiz. During the week I was in the port city, these gentlemen showed me a number of civilities. Among them was a ticket to a bullfight, by courtesy of the consul, while Mr. Meade gave me a ticket to his box in the theater.

It was to Mr. Bloomfield, however, that I pointed out the urgency of my finding passage to America.

He picked a piece of lint off his coat cuff while I looked at him, sitting at a little mahogany desk with claw legs. His face was drawn and sallow from overwork or illness. "Mr. Dearborn," he finally said, "has it occurred to you that Captain Vail or the first privateer captain to whom Mr. Crawford gave the letter is already close to our home shores? After all, it's been several weeks since you were kidnapped."

Had it ever occurred to me! It certainly had, and it wouldn't have troubled me if I could have been sure that Brad had escaped Bierce and been safe and sound when "Little Ben" and the *Argus* called at Bordeaux. Brad would have told Vail what he knew and Vail would have headed for America at once. I realized, of course, that the other privateer might have slipped through the British blockade off our coast, but I had no such faith in her as in the *Argus* under Vail.

In all honesty, however, though I said nothing of this to Mr. Bloomfield, what bothered me most of all was the thought of what might have happened to India. I had no doubt that she was alive, though I wasn't so sure about the Judge. But for India to be forced to submit to a man like Bierce, to have to lie in his arms, made me writhe. Yet I felt certain that if India was in Bierce's arms, it was as his wife — Bierce with his desire to possess India and his passion for the appearance of respectability would have insisted on this.

"Yes, I suppose the government will learn about Bierce and a possible British invasion long before I could get home," I said. "But," I added, "I still want to reach Maine as soon as possible."

"Of course you do," Mr. Bloomfield said in a manner which was intended to soothe but which irritated me. "Now there's a brig bound for Boston on the first tide tomorrow. You can go on her, I'm sure, if you have passage money."

"I can give the captain a draft on the Brun Frères of Bordeaux," I said. "Captain Vail set up accounts there for all his officers."

He looked at me for a moment, then smiled. "Very well, Mr. Dearborn, if Captain Johnson — Elmer Johnson — won't accept the draft, I'll go surety for you."

"Thank you, sir," I said in great relief. "I'm very grateful."

"You may not be grateful for long, Mr. Dearborn," he said briskly. "Captain Johnson will have to run the blockade, you know, and British cruisers will be thick off our coasts now that Napoleon is at Elba."

I then asked about a rumor Mr. Meade had mentioned, namely, that a British expeditionary force destined for the Chesapeake was gathering in Bordeaux. A man who spoke with great deliberation, Bloomfield nodded. "It's more than a rumor. I'm afraid we are in for some difficult times at home. The British have been ravaging the Chesapeake for a long time, and now it looks as if they may drive on Washington and Baltimore. They're also building a fleet and assembling an army on Lake Champlain."

"And they may be planning to invade Maine," I said.

"That is possible," he said. "And this brings up the point I want to discuss with you. A good deal of information reached me yesterday from France concerning the Chesapeake expedition. I'm sure our people in France have tried to send to Washington what they know, but whether this information will get through is problematical. So since it's the duty of consuls everywhere to keep their governments informed, I'd like you to carry a letter for me. As soon as you land, please give it to the nearest United States government official for forwarding to Washington."

"I'll be happy to oblige," I said.

And so I was, but as I stood on the afterdeck of Captain Johnson's

*Nancy* as the brig slipped out of Cadiz under cover of darkness, I couldn't help but feel apprehensive about the future of our republic. Unless we settled our differences, we might easily lose the independence we had won thirty years before; redcoats would soon be swarming all over our country.

The only aspect that lifted my mood briefly was that I was at sea and on my way home, where I might see India Mitchell again.

But the thought that she might not be India Mitchell any longer threw me back into the depths. Even the heeling of the brig, as the rising breeze began to fill our sails and send us rushing westward, failed to cheer me. I was a poor companion to Captain Johnson at breakfast that morning.

# TWO

## The British Seizure
### of
## Castine and the Penobscot Country

[August and September, 1814]

# XIII

THE voyage across the Atlantic was fast and uneventful, and despite the blockade we slipped safely into Boston harbor one chilly August evening after being sighted by a British frigate, too late for her to cause us anything but mild apprehension.

I spent the night at the home of my cousin, Paul Dearborn, in Louisburg Square. Older than I was by several years, he had graduated from Harvard and soon entered the mercantile firm of Bacon, Lovett, and Hall. He married Cynthia Lovett, a girl as blond, cool, and remote as himself. They were still childless after six years of marriage, a condition that troubled the families on both sides and was just about the only scratch on my cousin's smooth confidence. Tall and slim, with Aunt Betsy's elegance of manner, he had an ingratiating tongue that rarely underestimated his own abilities, which were considerable, I must admit. He was an outspoken Federalist, but this did not prevent him from heading a syndicate that sent out two privateers with the hope of making a handsome bit of change from the war. One of the privateers had been fairly successful.

Though I hadn't seen Paul and Cynthia since before the war, they welcomed me with about as much warmth as they were capable of, dined me royally on roast beef — a blessed relief after the salt pork of the *Nancy's* table, and listened with flattering interest to my tale of Captain Vail's voyage, though I said nothing of Bierce, Rudd, or the *Ghost*. They then launched into a denunciation of the war and the Madison administration.

"I assure you, Jonathan, our country is lost unless we make peace at once," Paul said as we sat in their stately living room with its Hepplewhite furniture, its paintings by Gainsborough, Richard Wilson, and our own Copley, and its white marble fireplace with pleasantly glowing logs. "Our shipping is ruined, and I'll show you evidence of that tomorrow morning. In fact, there's a big meeting at Faneuil Hall about the war, so why don't you plan to come to it with me? There will be a lot said about the threat of invasion."

"Where?" I asked.

"Possibly right here in Boston. You know, of course, that the British are already in Maine."

"What? Where?" I sat up straighter than a deacon in church.

"They took Moose Island in Passamaquoddy Bay and Eastport in July. Didn't you know that?"

"How could Jonathan have known that, Paul?" Cynthia asked. "He was at sea then. Isn't that so, Jonathan?"

"Yes, I was at sea, Cynthia." I stared at the fire as a log suddenly crumbled into bright fragments, my mind a tumult.

"The British have actually annexed Moose Island," Paul said. "They say it's rightfully theirs since it is within their boundary line set by the treaty of 1783. The next thing they'll probably do is to start moving along the coast and annex all of Maine."

"Come, come!" Cynthia said. "How could they presume to do that?"

"Oh, they could, and they would, too, my dear! Who is to stop them, pray tell me? We have neither the ships nor the men to prevent them from landing at any point they choose."

"That's probably true," I said, "but if we can raise enough troops, we can make it hard for them to hold on to any place for any real length of time."

"Only if the federal government lets Governor Strong keep control over our own militia instead of turning it over to the Washington generals. Madison would dearly like to send the militia off to Canada under regular army leadership. Why, we've no real quarrel with Canada, or with Britain herself, for that matter!"

"Has Strong called out many of the militia?" I tried to keep the anger out of my voice.

"Just a few units as yet," he said; and I thought he looked a little embarrassed.

"With invasion so imminent?"

"But there is no need for an invasion," Cynthia said in a kind of cold fury. "There would be no necessity for calling up even a few militia if only Madison would make peace! Then we could all go back to normal living. Oh, that stupid Madison, I could shoot him — and that silly, showy wife of his, too!"

I looked at Cynthia, her handsome face distorted by a snarl, and was relieved that she was Paul's wife, not mine. I wondered what it was that made so many women I knew lose all sense of perspective when they engaged in a political discussion; they seemed to commit themselves so fiercely they invariably became intemperate and personal. Fortunately I remembered in time that I was a guest in my cousin's house and a self-invited one at that, so I checked the retort that was on my lips. Instead, I inquired about Cynthia's parents; and presently Paul suggested that all of us go to bed.

The next morning Cynthia told me that Paul was not feeling well, so I took my leave of them with thanks for their hospitality and said I was going to try to find passage to Maine.

The first thing I did, however, was to visit Captain William Bainbridge, commandant of the Navy Yard, as the leading federal officer in the vicinity in order to report the activities, known and suspected, of Warren Bierce. It was my misfortune that Bainbridge, who had commanded the *Constitution* in its great victory over the frigate *Java*, had not yet returned from an inspection tour on Cape Cod, so I sat down in the Yard office, wrote out the report for him, and marked it "Urgent." I also left him the letter from Consul Bloomfield for forwarding to Washington.

After that, I walked along the waterfront, vainly trying to find passage to Portland. To be sure, the wharves were filled with ships, barques, brigs, schooners and sloops; in fact, I counted more than two hundred craft of all kinds tied up or moored in the harbor. But almost all of them had their topmasts housed, while empty tar barrels or canvas bags protected their mastheads from rot. I had seen enough of these barrels before in Portland — "Madison's nightcaps" was the longshore name for them — but never so many as in Boston. These silent ships and the crowds of idle seamen hanging around the corners or fishing from the wharves were melancholy reminders of the effectiveness of British sea power. Some of the seamen even talked

[ 133 ]

excitedly of a possible invasion by the British, but no one seemed to know if Governor Strong intended to make more than a show of resistance. It was evident from what I heard that they blamed the government in Washington for their plight even more than they criticized the British.

Reminded, by what I overheard, of the town meeting late that forenoon at Faneuil Hall to discuss a possible invasion, I decided to attend. A market on the first floor, the Hall has been one of the great seminaries of our liberty here in New England ever since Peter Faneuil constructed it back in 1742. It was almost filled when I arrived, a quarter of an hour before the meeting was scheduled to start. Most of those present were men of some substance, to judge from the quality of their clothes, but it was reassuring to see at least a few sailors with tarred pigtails present; if the war was to be discussed, it was only fitting that the people most severely affected by it should be represented.

Yet the gathering was a strange one. I heard more than one well-dressed gentleman say that Boston should not resist if the British should land in force since Englishmen always respected private property. Although this was hardly the story coming out of the South with the British marauding in the Chesapeake area, and although it certainly did not square with accounts of what had happened along the Maine coast during the Revolution, I doubted that anyone could have convinced these men they might be mistaken. I felt better at overhearing tags and ends of conversation from a group of younger men who were talking over in one of the corners.

"We ought to start building forts at once," one of them was practically shouting. "I may be a Federalist, but I'm no British lover, and I think Governor Strong's too trusting."

"Strong is usually all right," another said, "but now he's doing Boston harm. I'm with Dexter — we should get ready to fight."

As if in response to the fierce roar of approval, two men strode in and took their places on the platform. One was the lively Samuel Dexter, once a fiery Federalist who had had a distinguished career as Congressman and Senator, Secretary of War and later of the Treasury under John Adams, and as a lawyer pleading cases before the Supreme Court. Though still nominally a Federalist, he supported the war policy of the Madison administration, and for this defection, his name was anathema to all steadfast Federalists. While I could not find him at all sympathetic with his long horse-face, elongated nose, and sad eyes, I admired his courage.

The other speaker was Harrison Gray Otis. I looked carefully at Otis; he was, after all, the high priest of Federalism even if not one of the most extreme members of the party like Timothy Pickering of Salem and his cronies who comprised the Essex Junto. Otis was tall and broad, and his clothes were simple but elegant. Abundant hair slightly receding revealed a high forehead. His eyes were bright, almost dancing in fact, and his mouth was wide and mobile above a firm chin. I distinctly received the impression of a man of strength but one whose affability, to judge from his pleasant expression, would prevent him from exciting fear or awe or even, perhaps, the most profound respect. He was here today, according to opinion in Faneuil, to protest the supine attitude of Governor Strong. To this extent he was therefore presumed in agreement with Dexter.

But, to the surprise of many, instead of condemning Strong, he set forth a series of resolutions in support of Strong's refusal to let the national government maintain the militia for fear the Secretary of War would order it to be sent to Canada or, at the least, out of the state. At the same time he turned on Dexter and searingly criticized him for being a turncoat.

This was too much for Dexter, who jumped to his feet, scored Otis's lack of patriotism, and exclaimed, "By heaven, I'd like to pull your nose!"

Otis started toward him at these words, and only the intervention of mutual friends prevented the two politicians from having a Donnybrook then and there. In the end the meeting supported Otis's resolutions, one of which provided that Bostonians would assist the defense of their city with their money and their hands if that defense was devised by proper authority. A number of people were as indignant as Dexter at the outcome, but their anger could not prevail.

As for myself, I was deeply relieved to put Boston behind me as I set out for home that afternoon. Since I could find no passage by sea, and my available cash was so low I could not afford to hire a horse, I started on foot, begging rides on farmers' carts and gnawing away at some bread and cheese I bought at a market.

It took me the better part of three days to reach Portland, and I was footsore and caked with dust when I turned in at our gate after dark. I'd have been even grimier if I hadn't bathed my face and hands near Stroudwater before climbing Bramhall's Hill. I thought at first of walking right in as I would normally have done; then, realizing my parents might be startled enough as it was, I let the knocker fall.

Presently I heard my father's footsteps and the idea of being home again after nearly a year's absence almost overcame me. And when he opened the door, holding a candle high and peering at me over his spectacles, I could only stare and struggle with my feelings.

He seemed to be similarly afflicted for a moment. Then he thrust out his hand. "Jonathan," he exclaimed, "Jonathan, my boy!"

I clasped his hand, hugged him, and could only say, "Yes, Father, it's me," and feel completely inadequate.

"Jonathan — oh, Jonathan!"

I spun around at the sound of my mother's voice and took her in my arms.

But being my mother after all, she soon broke away and brushed the dust from her dress. "What a sight you are, Jonathan! You must bathe at once. Then you shall have something to eat and we shall talk."

After a mountain of creamy, scrambled eggs and a number of thick strips of bacon, with bread and grape conserve and several cups of hot tea, I felt more like sleeping than talking. But talk I did, on and on, and they listened practically without comment as I gave a reasonably full account of what had happened since I had left Portland the previous fall.

When I finished, my father's face lighted up with a mischievous smile. "Jonathan, you may not know it, but we've heard a good deal about what happened to you up to the time you were kidnapped."

"You mean Brad Pettigrew is back?"

"Sit down, Jonathan," my mother said with a note of asperity in her voice. "Yes, Brad is back but probably not for long. The *Argus* is refitting to go out again."

"Then I must see Brad tomorrow. And Captain Vail, is he all right?"

My father laughed. "Just ask your mother!"

As I looked at her, she sniffed. "That man!"

"It's like this, Jonathan," my father said, chuckling. "Vail and Brad came to see us as soon as they arrived, a fortnight or so ago. In fact, Brad has come over several times. But on that first visit we were shocked, naturally, to hear that you had disappeared, and your mother gave Captain Vail a piece of her mind for letting you out of his sight. Well, you should have heard Vail scold us for not realizing you were a man with a man's duties and responsibilities."

"You'd have thought we were wrongdoers instead of bereaved parents!" my mother said.

"Now, now, it wasn't as bad as that," my father said. "But he told us you were a man he relied on and that was why he put you and Brad Pettigrew ashore on the French coast. He said you believed in the war and that we should be proud of you. Now isn't that right, Alice?"

My mother shrugged. "I suppose so. Yes, Jonathan, in all fairness he said some highly complimentary things about you."

"Of course this was hard to believe," my father said.

Mother stared at him. "Hard to believe?" Then she smiled. "Well, perhaps. But neither of us gave up hope, Jonathan. You were always resourceful, and Captain Vail assured us you still are. I must say, too, your Uncle Tom has been a tower of strength to us. Evidently he knows you better in some ways than we do."

"Tom is very fond of you, Jonathan," my father said. He paused: "And so is your Aunt Betsy."

A glance at my mother's face when Aunt Betsy's name was mentioned was warning enough. "Is Captain Vail in port now?" I asked.

"He told us yesterday that he hoped to leave before the weekend for a brief visit to his family in Castine," my father said. "He may take Brad with him."

"Brad is very restless," my mother explained. "He cannot reconcile himself to settling down to the law again the more the war goes against us. Some of his friends are being quite critical of him about this, for here in Portland, as you might guess, the sentiment is still strong against the war."

"But there are some like yourself, Jonathan," my father said, "who favor giving full support to the administration and they're really angry with Governor Strong for doing nothing to help. In fact, there are people who regard his attitude as treasonable."

Briefly I told them how Paul and Cynthia felt and what I had heard at the town meeting in Boston; then, trying to be as casual as possible, I asked what I had wanted to ask at the very first but dared not to, namely whether India Mitchell had returned to Portland.

I noticed them glance at each other, and at once I felt myself grow tense.

"Jonathan, weren't you a little sweet on India?" my mother asked, such sympathy in her voice that now I really knew something was wrong.

"Well — yes, I was," I admitted.

"Then I hope you have long since got over it. She returned to Portland as Warren Bierce's wife."

There are times, as everyone knows, when a person feels a sense of unreality, that in one corner of his mind he is certain what is happening is not so and in another corner he knows it to be true. This was one of those times, and momentarily I could not speak. Though I had suspected this very thing might happen, it hurt deeply. At the same time I was determined not to let my mother see how I felt. "I thought highly of India Mitchell," I said, and let it go at that. "When did the *Ghost* return?" I asked.

"About a month ago," my father said, glancing at me, not at all deceived, I suppose, but accepting my silent plea that we say no more about India. "The *Argus* arrived a fortnight afterward. There's been no love lost between the two crews. In fact, rumors have been flying around that the *Ghost* was seen coming out of a British port and that Warren Bierce was actually in London."

"Has Bierce said anything?"

"He has issued a scornful denial and said he would gladly meet his calumniators individually on the field of honor."

I smiled at the old-fashioned language. While I had little doubt that Bierce had said something like that, it was hardly in those words. What was interesting was that members of the *Argus*'s crew must have done some tall talking in town, perhaps even some of the *Ghost*'s crew as well.

My mother, however, was not to be so easily put off. "Jonathan, I always felt a little sorry for India Mitchell. Living with the Judge couldn't have been easy. Do you suppose her marrying Warren Bierce was a way of escaping her uncle?"

"My dear, how can Jonathan do anything more than speculate, just like the rest of us?" my father asked, as if to spare me.

"All I can really be sure of," I said, "is that, despite their differences, she was fond of the Judge."

I didn't want to talk any more about her, and I think my mother at last realized it. Though she had always admired India for her independence, she had often predicted that sometime India would land in trouble as a result of it. I was in no mood to listen to an "I told you so" discourse tonight.

We talked on and on, mostly about the war, until the clock in the hall struck midnight. Yet it was long before I could sleep. India married to Warren Bierce! I was prey to anguish, anger, and remorse, and broke into such a sweat that I felt as if I were in another bath and an uncomfortably warm one, at that. But I decided to remove India's white scarf from my sea chest that Vail had returned and send it back to her.

Nor could I keep my mind off the war, and wondered if anything was being done about another British invasion of our Maine coast. From what I had picked up in Boston, it was clear the government in Washington was helpless. In fact, Washington itself was likely to be attacked at any time. Massachusetts, it was also evident, would do nothing: if Maine was threatened, the District must stand on its own. Yet it was almost as opposed to the war as Massachusetts. There still were a number of Captain Vails around, though not enough, I feared.

The next morning, after carefully wrapping the silk scarf and sending it to India by Jackie Fisher, the boy across the street, I went down to the waterfront and had no difficulty finding the *Argus*. Among the lines of moored ships with their topmasts down and their masts hooded with the "Madison nightcaps," the spars of the *Argus* soared cleanly.

Her decks were cluttered as I had seen them when I first met Captain Vail, but it was an orderly disorder as men worked with block and tackle, easing the bulky supplies down through the hatchways, while other men moved from wharf to deck and below with the slabs of meat and sacks of flour. The *Argus* was readying for sea, and quickly, too.

As I began to skirt their activity and watched for a chance to board the brig, an unforgettable voice roared out my last name. Before I could even turn around, a powerful hand caught my arm and spun me about. "Jonathan Dearborn, so help me!" And I winced in "Little Ben's" crushing grip.

When I replied that I was certainly glad to see him again, he said I was supposed to be at the bottom of the sea or lolling around in a British prison. "At least those were the rumors," he added. "Go aboard, Jonathan. I'll join you as soon as I've finished with our ship chandler here, Mr. Wilson."

As he wheeled abruptly toward the big, worried-looking man beside him, I leaped aboard the *Argus*, and was surrounded at once by old shipmates — Lester Jordan, Oliver Jones, and Philip Adair. All shook my hand warmly, while Jones slapped me on the back, and shouted, "Damn all work, this is worth havin' a drink for!"

"Not till we're finished," Lester Jordan said, thinly. "We're squeezed for time, Jonathan," he explained. "The Captain wants us out tonight, if possible. You'll excuse us, won't you?"

As I assured them I'd never forgive them, they grinned and left, but not before Philip shook my hand again and said, "We know all about what Bierce and Rudd tried to do to you and Mr. Pettigrew, seh. I for one will not forget."

I thanked him and watched the big Negro catwalk his way through the clutter. Sometime he would settle many old scores with Rudd, and that would be a contest worth seeing.

"Well, Jonathan, shall we talk?"

Vail's question came like a gun blast, and I jumped. "Yes, sir," I said.

Over our rum in his cabin I told him what had happened to me, though I was considerably briefer than with my parents.

He nodded from time to time, and when I finished, said, "I made the Garonne before that storm broke. Afterward, I heard from Petti-grew what had happened. You see, Brad escaped into the hotel from Rudd's bully boys, and by asking questions along the river he learned about a carriage going to this ship *Ginny* and a man being brought aboard. It may have been dark, but some of those Frenchies never go to sleep, it seems, and a little extra wine and a gold piece will do wonders getting them to talk."

"Was the *Ghost* in port when you arrived?"

He shook his head. "Rudd must have cleared Cordouan Light just a few hours before I sighted it coming into port. As soon as I had watered and provisioned in Bordeaux, and waited for the wind to let us put to sea, I took the *Argus* out again. I can tell you it was a tricky business hunting for you off the French and Spanish coasts just when there were British troops and a big convoy assembling at Bordeaux right after we got out, all bound for the Chesapeake according to a couple of prizes we picked up. Course we didn't linger long after giving up looking for the *Ginny* because of the letter Mr. Crawford wanted me to deliver."

"But I lost the letter — I mean it was stolen."

"That's what we assumed must have happened, and though I real-ized that without the letter whatever Pettigrew or I might have to say about Bierce wouldn't swing much weight in Washington or even here, I felt it necessary to get home as fast as I could and make a report."

"What about that privateer, the *Good Hope*, that carried the duplicate copy?" I asked, a little hurt, I must admit, that Vail hadn't continued searching a while longer.

"She was captured trying to get out of La Rochelle," he said. "It wasn't an easy decision, Jonathan, to leave off looking for you. But I knew you are a pretty resourceful young man and I didn't give up hope that you would work your way out of whatever mess you were in. Well, when we reached Portland, I went up at once to see Cap-tain Bainbridge at the Navy Yard in Boston. Luckily, unlike the day you visited him, he was in his office."

"I suppose he turned thumbs down on any action."

"He said there were no grounds for any legal action against Bierce, since we just didn't have the evidence to make a case. As for the expedition, he granted the possibility of a major stroke here in Maine, but he thought an attack on Baltimore or Washington was probable after the shambles the British were already making of the Chesapeake area."

"But I've just heard a lot of speculation about an invasion being made near Boston."

"I doubt there'll be one there," Vail said, draining his glass of rum. "Boston is too large a population area. A landing somewhere on our coast is more likely."

"I understand you're putting to sea at once," I said, changing the subject.

He looked at me. "Tonight. But I've no place for you, Jonathan. I'm sorry, but I've moved Oliver Jones into your place and taken on Jed Green from over in Pooduck in Jones's berth."

"Any chance of signing on before the mast?"

"Not on your life!" Vail said. "It would be bad for discipline to have a man who has been second officer serve as a common seaman."

From my point of view I thought it might be good for discipline, but I didn't press the point.

"Look here, Jonathan," Vail said in a kindly manner, "you've just come home after months away, so why don't you see more of your family and friends for a while. Mind you, I'd like to have you, but I had to sign on a crew, and I've done so, sooner than I thought possible. This town is getting angry at Governor Strong for doing nothing and at the British for snapping up anything that shows up outside our harbors, even fishing smacks. Looks to me as though some of the people in Maine have about reached the point of doing something to help themselves. If Strong and Otis and that crowd in Boston don't watch out, people down here will end up being in favor of the war."

"Unless we're British subjects by that time," I said. "Look here, Captain, is Brad Pettigrew going with you again?"

Vail glanced down at his hands, and I could have sworn he looked uncomfortable. "Yes, he's going as a gentleman volunteer."

[ 142 ]

"I don't understand."

"Brad was through with the sea when we got back. Two days ago, when he insisted the way you're doing now, I didn't have a place for him either. But I finally gave in and signed him on as a gentleman volunteer. He gets his food free, but no pay and no prize money." He warded me off with his hand as I rose to my feet. "But that don't apply to you, Jonathan. You've just got home, and your parents will be sick if you leave so soon."

"Then if you won't accept me, Captain," I said bitterly, "there's just one thing left to me and that's to challenge Warren Bierce."

"You'd lose, Jonathan. He's a dead shot."

Both Vail and I turned toward the door at the sound of Brad Pettigrew's voice. The next moment Brad and I were grasping each other's hands.

"Pettigrew, what do you mean by entering my cabin without knocking?" Captain Vail's voice was more than half serious; he was a real stickler for formality at times.

"I beg your pardon," Brad said. "I fully intended to, but as I was about to do so, I couldn't help hearing what was being said and didn't want to interrupt you."

"Well you certainly did. If you were still a marine, I'd skin you for this. Since you're a gentleman volunteer, I'll let it go by this time. But another breach of privilege, young man, and you'll not see the Penobscot with me."

"Is that where we're going?" I asked.

"I didn't say I'd take you, Dearborn. But in answer to your question, yes, I'm going to look into the Penobscot before we swing toward Bermuda. As a matter of fact, I've contracted to deliver some powder and shot to Lieutenant Andrew Lewis, the commandant of Fort Madison at Castine, though I've not announced that to the crew as yet and won't until we're clear of Portland harbor. I'll thank you both to keep your mouths shut."

"Then you'll take me?" I pressed him.

He shrugged his shoulder. "Oh, all right, Dearborn. I'll accept you on the same terms as Pettigrew. But I'll never dare face your mother again."

"Better that you face Mrs. Dearborn again some time, sir," said

Brad, "than have Jonathan try anything rash with Bierce." Then looking at me, he said, "I hate to say this, Jonathan, but I think we're going to have to leave that man alone. We really can't prove anything against him. It's his word against ours, and he carries too much weight in this town."

"I'll never leave him alone," I said. "For the present, yes, but eventually there's got to be a reckoning with him."

And thinking of his insults to my father, the marriage that he'd evidently forced on India, his would-be murder of me, and what I felt certain was his treason to this country, I could not have been more serious. Sooner or later Bierce would overreach himself. Possibly, in view of his pride and love of public esteem, to topple him from the pedestal he had created would be more effective than to see him shot or hanged. But then would India start to pity him as a broken man and in her pity find a love for him?

The thought was so disturbing I hastily scrawled my signature on the muster roll Captain Vail spread out on his table and left with Brad to break the news of my imminent departure to my parents.

# XIV

THE run down the coast was as uneventful as my parents' response to my announcement was calm. I think they had expected I would go with Captain Vail. My mother sighed when I told her, while my father shook his head resignedly. I was so keyed up to defend myself that I actually felt let down by their lack of opposition. As for the *Argus's* departure, we left at night, passing the dark mass of the *Ghost* moored in the harbor, and gained the open sea with ease.

But Vail took no risks. Once we picked up the southwest breeze, he took us downeast on a course near enough to shore to run in among the numerous islands and fingers of land if opposed by a superior force, yet far enough to seaward to run for open water if we should encounter a marauding man-of-war close in. Actually we saw no sail that day, and, the favoring breeze continuing, we presently sighted Vinalhaven and Isle au Haut. Then we swung into lower

Penobscot Bay and swept past Owl's Head and the heavily wooded Havens. Ahead on the western mainland towered the great, rolling hills of Camden, blue in the distance and lovely to behold in the afternoon light. Presently we left them behind and moved up the eastward passage between Long Island and Cape Rosier on the mainland, finally dropping anchor off Castine as candles and lanterns were being lighted in the white houses of that lovely, little peninsular town with its water battery, Fort Madison.

"I'm going ashore to report to the commandant," Captain Vail said to Brad and me as he waited for his boat to be lowered. "Tomorrow, if you'd like, I'll show you my home town."

His behavior was quite unlike what it had been when we were formally members of his crew. In our current status as gentlemen volunteers he treated us more like companions, though neither of us was ever in doubt of his own position as captain. The master of a ship is a veritable god in the authority he exercises. We eagerly accepted his invitation and watched as the boat took him ashore.

"Why didn't the *Argus* go in there herself?" Brad asked. "It would have saved those men a row."

I pointed to Fort Madison. "Those guns are trained on us right now until Lieutenant Lewis is satisfied with our identification. Sure, we're flying the flag, but still we might be British! If we had tried to go inside, we'd soon have had a shot off our bows."

Captain Vail returned late in the evening and, the next morning, took the *Argus* to the wharf below the Joseph Perkins house. Two wagons and a light carriage were waiting when our hawsers were looped around the bollards. With guards posted to keep the onlookers who gathered from getting close or smoking, the crew brought up the powder kegs and the shot and gingerly loaded them into the two wagons, which were bedded with hay. As the drivers cracked their reins over the horses' backs, a detail of soldiers from the fort fell in around the wagons, two marching ahead to clear anyone off the road. Vail now nodded to Brad and me to accompany him, and climbed into the carriage, which was driven by a droopy-shouldered, long-faced man badly needing a shave whom "Little Ben" introduced to us as Eph Curtis. Eph grunted his acknowledgment and slapped his horse's rump with the reins.

[ 145 ]

As we followed the creaking wagons, the Captain showed us places made famous by the siege back in '79. He pointed up the hill to the crumbling ramparts of Fort George built by the British, and seaward to the site of the half-moon battery that the Americans had stormed and held briefly one dark night.

"It was there, Jonathan, that your Uncle Tom was captured after he and Enoch Grant held off the British long enough to allow our people to get away. He was imprisoned in Fort George and escaped into the town. Later he swam out to our fleet." Vail pointed to the fleet anchorage between the northern tip of Long Island and the peninsula.

"Aunt Betsy hid him, didn't she?"

Vail grinned. "Yes, she hid both Tom and Enoch, and Tom once told me it was then he realized that he didn't want to live if he couldn't have her for a wife, even if she was a Tory."

"That doesn't sound like my sober uncle," I said with a laugh. "No one in these modern days would ever act like that."

"Oh, never!" Brad said — but so dryly that I glanced at him, then at Vail who leaned back in his seat and began to study some curious cloud formations.

At once I felt myself growing warm — depend on me to say something silly! — but as I groped for a fitting reply, "Little Ben" leaned forward. "You can see Fort Madison now."

Down on the point a large earthwork rose, its semicircular walls facing down the bay.

"Doesn't look very strong," Brad said.

"Well," Captain Vail said, "Lewis has four twenty-four-pounders and a couple of fieldpieces. That's strong enough to stop anything under a frigate. He's got about forty regulars in his command."

"Forty soldiers, even regulars, couldn't hold off a landing force," I said.

Vail shrugged. "No, but if they were supported by the local militia, they might put up a fight long enough to rouse the countryside."

"As a former militiaman," Brad said, "I should hate to see the militia have to fight against British regulars."

"What about Concord and Lexington, and what about Bunker Hill?" I asked.

"Those were fought under special conditions — all favorable to the militia. In the first two places there was cover from woods and stonewalls, and the British were strung out on a single road miles from home. At Bunker Hill our men were protected by entrenchments, and Howe took the regulars straight up in front of them, shoulder to shoulder. We couldn't miss. But here —" Brad shook his head. "I'm afraid militia wouldn't be much use to Lieutenant Lewis, and forty U.S. regulars won't be able to prevent the redcoats from landing if they should come here."

"Thank you, General," I said.

But though I laughed, the prospect wasn't cheering, and, once inside the small fort, I didn't feel any better. Lieutenant Lewis was crisp and efficient, and, once the powder and shot were delivered and signed for, he offered us all a glass of rum. If it was army issue, it was poor stuff, but what it lacked in smoothness, it made up in strength. Maybe if they were given a tot before they had to fight, the artillery-men would stand longer at their guns. Actually, the soldiers themselves looked competent enough. It was the fort itself that troubled Vail, Brad, and me — its smallness and the few guns, as well as its position: a landing force on the western side of the peninsula could nip it off with ease.

Later Eph Curtis drove back into the village. At Captain Vail's suggestion we stopped to glance up at the house where my Aunt Betsy had lived during the Revolution and where she had hidden Uncle Tom and Enoch Grant. It was in other hands now, her father having sold it after my aunt's marriage and moved to London, where he died in 1801, soon after Benedict Arnold was buried in St. Mary's Church in Battersea. We drove by the green, and later passed the Mark Hatch barn, which had been used as a hospital by the British, at the edge of the town.

Finally Eph whoa-ed the brown mare to a stop in front of a little one-and-a-half-storey, clapboarded house, with a large central chimney.

"This is where my mother lives," Vail said, getting out of the carriage. "Come on inside."

"I'll wait here, Ben," Eph Curtis said, pulling his hat forward and his shoulders slumping as if he were already asleep.

[ 147 ]

"Hadn't we better wait here, too, at least for a minute or so?" I asked. Captain Vail had rarely mentioned his family, but I remember Uncle Tom's having said that he lost his wife and two children, as well as half the crew of the schooner he then commanded, of yellow fever when that disease hit Philadelphia in the 1790's.

"Suit yourself," he said gruffly, and walked around to the back door.

"Does Captain Vail's mother live here by herself?" Brad asked Eph.

"Looks after her sister Lou," Eph muttered. "Lou got hit by the branch of an apple tree fallin' back in '98, an' there wasn't much old Doc Mann could do for her, 'cept stop the bleedin'. She thinks we're at war with France an' John Adams's President. Wish he was, instead of Jimmy Madison."

"I take it you're against this war with England," Brad said.

Eph spat. "I ain't got nothin' against England. But, then, I got a little farm nearby, so I don't have no cause to get upset about ships bein' stopped and sailors pressed."

"Do many people here in Castine feel the way you do?"

"Lot of 'em. We even got up some resolutions agin the war not long ago. Oh, there's them that wants to fight, an' Ben Vail's one of 'em. Look here, Mister, what you asking me all these questions for?"

"Frankly, I was just curious — that's all," Brad said pleasantly.

"Huh!" And Eph made it clear by his manner that he didn't want to be asked anything more.

"Look," he said, "if you fellers are aimin' to meet Ben's mother, you'd better get to it. Ben wants to be back to his ship soon, I'm tellin' you."

We took the hint and hurried around to the rear door just as Captain Vail opened it to bellow at us. Quickly he herded us into the kitchen with its Franklin stove, yellow curtains, and thin, little mistress with snapping blue eyes who stood up and welcomed us in a booming voice almost as loud as her son's.

"Glad to meet any friend of Ben, and this is my sister Lou Peters," she said, putting her arm around the even smaller figure in the chair beside her who was wrapped in a shawl on this warm August day and stared at us with dull, unblinking eyes.

[ 148 ]

"Who are they, Sadie?" Lou asked; she sounded frightened.

"They're friends of Ben, Lou, so don't you worry," Mrs. Vail said.

"They don't scare me, Sadie, honest they don't. But here's something else 'at does."

"What is it, Lou?"

Lou Peters looked at us with those filmed-over eyes, now at Brad, now at me, and then at Captain Vail. "Ben," she asked, "don't you hear it, honest now, don't you?"

"Hear what, Lou?" Captain Vail growled amiably.

"It's guns!" she whispered.

The hair seemed to stand up on the back of my neck, and all of us fell silent, listening intently.

Yet all I could hear was the subdued crack of an ember inside the stove, and a catbird mocking back in the woods.

"It's the French," Lou said. "You can't trust those frog eaters. They'll be in here murderin' us if someone don't warn us in time."

"I don't think we'll have to worry about the French, Lou — not in this war," Vail said; and the relief in his voice was plain. If there had been any guns, they would have been British and the *Argus* would have been trapped inside Penobscot Bay.

"Mother, we're leaving now," Vail said. "We've work to do."

"I understand, Ben," his mother said. "Now you look after these young men." Turning to us, she said, "Ben told me about both of you. I hadn't heard of your people before, Mr. Pettigrew, but I do know Mr. Dearborn's Uncle Tom. In fact, everyone here in Castine knows about Tom Dearborn and Betsy Morris, Tory Sam's daughter. I hope you're a credit to him, young man."

Sudden embarrassment tied my tongue, and Vail came to my rescue. "There's worse than Jonathan," he said with a grin. "Now let's go."

On our way back, we swung by the Customs House overlooking the harbor. "Little Ben" jumped out ahead of us and talked with the stocky, gray-haired man who was about to board a sloop that had just arrived.

"That's Josiah Hooke," Eph said. "He ain't doin' so well these days."

"What do you mean?" I asked.

"Hooke's the Collector — been so for years. He used to be busy — lots of ships put in here. But this summer —" Eph paused and shook his head.

"Too much blockade?" Brad asked.

Eph nodded. "It ain't often a ship gets through."

Soon Captain Vail called to us and hurried us aboard the *Argus*. Once on his own deck, his bellowing orders practically tripped over one another. The effect was like an electric jolt from a Leyden jar. Men literally jumped into action, and I was downright uncomfortable watching Oliver Jones perform the duties that had been my responsibility on the *Argus*'s European cruise. In my envy I turned away and looked down the Bay.

Instantly the sweat broke out on me yet felt cold down my back: standing up the Bay was a small frigate or a heavy corvette. If she was British, we were trapped. If she was American, why in God's name did her master take a chance on letting her be blockaded in here by British cruisers known to be just off the coast? Glancing at Captain Vail, I soon saw that not only he but every man on deck was staring down the Bay. Then Vail turned and said something to Lester Jordan, the *Argus*'s first officer. Instantly the deck broke into a whirl of rushing men as we cleared for action. Afterward, silence settled over the brig as we backed our topsails and waited until we were more certain of who the stranger was and what he proposed to do.

"Beg pardon, seh, I know that ship."

It was Philip Adair standing respectfully in front of Captain Vail. Vail lowered his glass. "Well, who is she?" he snapped.

"That's the *John Adams*, seh, I have seen her several times before."

"The *Adams!*"

"Yes, seh, a heavy corvette of twenty-eight guns."

"I know, I know," Vail said. "But the last I heard, the British had her locked up in the Chesapeake."

Fortunately Philip didn't make the obvious remark that she must have escaped from the blockading squadron.

"Notice anything odd about the way she rides, Mr. Jordan?" Vail asked.

Jordan took the glass Vail handed him, then, after a glance, returned it. "She's low in the water."

Until Lester mentioned it, I hadn't thought much about it. But he was right. If she had been a merchantman, no one would have remarked about her appearance, but for a man-of-war she was dangerously low and making almost no headway.

Presently Captain Vail boomed out another order, and the *Argus* went spinning toward the *Adams*.

As we approached, her low set was startling. It was also puzzling because there was no visible evidence of damage suffered in action.

Our run toward the corvette had evidently roused her officers' suspicions, for a puff of white smoke suddenly blossomed as one of her bow guns bade us keep our distance.

"What ship is that?" came the brusque hail from her quarterdeck.

Scorning a speaking trumpet such as the *Adams*'s officer had used, Vail bellowed, "Privateer *Argus* out of Portland, Vail commanding."

Back came confirmation of Adair's identification. It was the *Adams* under Captain Charles Morris. She had struck on a reef off the Isle au Haut during a heavy fog and was barely afloat. Moreover, she had put into Camden and sent ashore more than fifty prisoners and over a score of her crew who had come down with scurvy. She was now on her way up to Hampden for repairs. But to Vail's question if the *Adams* needed any assistance, back came a proud denial, with thanks.

Then Vail asked, "Have you heard of a British expedition bound for the Penobscot from Nova Scotia?"

"Yes," the *Adams* roared back. "That's why we're going as far up as Hampden. It will be here in a few days. There's a sloop-of-war off Isle au Haut right now. We chased her but lost her in the fog — she's the *Rifleman*. Keep us informed if you can."

Vail thanked the *Adams*, and after an exchange of good wishes, we headed seaward, hugging the western shore past Owl's Head and Thomaston, and threading our way in almost motionless air that slowed our progress to a crawl through the islands off Spruce Head.

It was only after we were clear of the Bay and darkness was falling that Vail summoned the crew aft. The air was still, and the brig rolled heavily with a squeaking and creaking of her blocks and yards.

With an order from Vail for no lights to be shown and no talking to be done on deck except what was necessary for the operation of the ship we were a hushed crowd as "Little Ben" stood before us. Though he was barely more than a short blur in the gathering darkness from where I stood, there was no mistaking that powerful voice, mute it though he tried.

Quickly he told us that even before we met the *Adams*, he had learned from the captain of the sloop arriving in Castine that morning that the British were preparing to seize the Penobscot and annex all the area east of the river. They had all heard what the *Adams* had told them, too, so there wasn't much doubt of the expedition. The only unanswered questions were when the British would arrive and how large a force they were bringing.

The crew had been silent throughout save when Vail mentioned the desire of the British to annex eastern Maine. Then there were some growls of anger which were quickly muffled as Vail continued.

"Now men," he said, "I intend to find out whether that expedition has sailed. We'll drop down the coast until we can be sure where the British are. When we locate 'em, we'll hot-foot it back to the Penobscot. Oh, I won't take the *Argus* into the Bay if I can help it," he added. "That would be asking for trouble. But I'll get word somehow to the river towns so that they can at least call out their militia and warn Captain Morris of the *John Adams*."

It was not long after the crew was dismissed that I learned how he intended to warn the Penobscot people. Brad and I were about ready to turn in when a seaman knocked on the door to our cubbyhole and told us that Captain Vail wished to see us. Hurriedly we dressed again and went to his cabin. He was writing when we knocked. Hardly glancing up at us, he waved us to chairs and continued to write. The two smoking candles, cradled in glasses for safety's sake, emitted an odor that was almost sickening in that stuffy, little cabin. I'm afraid that, stimulated by the heat and the stench, my stomach became uncomfortably aware of the tilting deck as the brig rocked in the swells. Presently, to my relief, Vail sanded the paper, pushed it aside, and looked at us.

"Can't guess what I've been doing, can you?" he challenged us.

"No, sir," we answered together.

"I've just written a report to be given to Lieutenant Lewis or Captain Morris or some person in authority in the Penobscot area."

"May I ask what kind of report, sir?" Brad asked.

"Not at all, Mr. Pettigrew, not at all. It's a report on the British expedition. All I'll need to do to it is to fill in a few details when I find the British fleet, sign it, and sent it off. Simple, just that simple."

"And who is to take your report to this person in authority?" I asked, but really could guess the answer.

He turned on me with a short, quick smile. "Mr. Dearborn, as a gentleman volunteer, you can be dispensed with. So can you, Mr. Pettigrew. So can I for that matter, but not right now; indispensability has a time limit. Jonathan, I want you and Brad to stand by to take the longboat into Penobscot Bay under sail. You'll deliver my report to Lewis, and if you are unable to reach him, see that it gets to someone in authority."

"But the British aren't likely to let us slip into the Bay," I protested. "Some cutter or schooner of theirs will gobble us up in no time."

"I'll try to have a start on the British," Vail said, "and will draw their attention away from you. They're not likely to go after a longboat when they can chase a privateer just out of range of their guns."

"You'd better not take any rash chances," I warned him. "The British won't have forgotten your last cruise in their home waters. They'd like to get their hands on you."

"I suppose they would," he acknowledged cheerfully, "but they'll need more than luck to catch me. Now are you willing to do this?"

When I said that of course I was, and Brad had agreed, too, Vail slapped the table. "Good! We'll get the boat ready right after daylight."

"Should we wait that long?" I asked.

"I'm sure it's all right. I figure we have at least another day or two. I may be a little long on the time but not by much. Are you clear on what you're to do?"

"Yes, sir."

His smile and jauntiness faded. "I needn't tell you it could be of the highest importance for you to get into the Bay in time. We can't afford to lose the *John Adams*, and if the militia will give their regulars a taste of Bunker Hill, they may not linger long in the Bay."

But remembering what Brad had said about militia and the sad tale of militia performance so far in this war, I felt by no means encouraged, particularly if the British should come into the Bay in force.

---

# XV

"Psst!"

I stiffened at the sound and turned quickly toward Oliver Jones.

The sky was intensely dark, the stars but dimly visible through a slight overcast. The breeze was so light we barely had steerageway, which is not the most comfortable of situations when one knows an enemy is somewhere just beyond eyesight. I had slept very uneasily and at two o'clock I had gone on deck. Almost as soon as I appeared the watch officer summoned me.

"D'you see anything?" he muttered.

I peered into the darkness and was about to say there was nothing to be seen when a light flared in the sky, then seemed to fall.

"There it is again!" Jones said. "I thought it was a shooting star at first — it's the month for them — then I wasn't so sure. It could have been a rocket."

That was my opinion, too, and we watched intently. After a few moments, a light again flared, blue and white.

"It *is* a rocket!" we said together; and hardly were the words out before a hail came from the masthead confirming us.

What troubled us was that the rocket soared from a point extremely near us and was followed almost at once by another from a different direction.

"We must be right in the middle of the British fleet!" Oliver said.

"I'll go wake Captain Vail," I said.

But even as I turned away, Vail appeared as if produced by a genie.

Orders crackled in whispers as the crew, many of them barely awake, swarmed aloft. Slowly, so slowly that it seemed forever, we came about and inched back along the course we had come.

Dawn still comes early in late August, and the lightening eastern sky revealed a great cluster of sails to the eastward. There were about twenty vessels of various kinds, three of them huge ships-of-the-line. Others included frigates, sloops-of-war, a schooner and a brig, and a number of transports. What soon became of immediate concern to us, however, were a frigate and a sloop which broke off from the fleet and headed toward us. Both were fast, especially the frigate, but, in this quiet air, neither gained appreciably on us for a time. Then, in the fickleness of air currents, they picked up a breeze and began to overhaul us.

For a few minutes it appeared that the *Argus* had but a short time left to fly our flag. Dartmoor or at least some huge stockade in bleak Nova Scotia stared us in the face, and I don't mind admitting that I was both angry and appalled at the prospect. To be captured almost within sight of the Maine coast after nipping in and out of harbors along the south shore of England!

Then the breeze died altogether, and the mingled relief and apprehension on all faces was a painful thing to see. Instantly Captain Vail ordered both the longboat and the dinghy into the water to tow us. The mast which had been stepped in the longboat was unstepped, and the crew put their backs into the rowing.

We were scarcely a minute too soon for the British had their boats in the water, too. At first they towed both ships; then the frigate sent most of its boats to aid those of the sloop-of-war. The smaller ship was thus to be our enemy and was to engage us until the frigate arrived on the scene.

After our boat crews were relieved at the end of the first half hour, Captain Vail beckoned to me. "You and Pettigrew will have to wait for a while before I send you up the river."

His voice was as harsh as his face at the moment, but his eyes twinkled.

"We may be lucky even to start," I said.

"Oh, you'll start, but not much ahead of them."

Brad squinted back at our pursuers, then shrugged his shoulders.

"No need to ask, Pettigrew," said Vail, and this time there was no twinkle. "We'll need a breeze for part of the time. If we don't get it, we'll be in trouble; they've more pulling power than we have. I want you young man to take your turn at the oars with the rest, but I also want you to be ready to take the longboat into the river when I give the word."

"Aye, aye, sir," I said.

But as I sifted the meaning of what he had said, the prospect was at least dubious. Our taking the longboat would occur if we succeeded in breaking free of the enemy, which looked improbable at the moment, or if the enemy closed with the *Argus* and the chance of the *Argus's* escaping was hopeless, which appeared likely since the sloop-of-war was steadily gaining on us. A longboat under sail would need a long lead indeed not to be overtaken.

I doubt that anyone aboard the *Argus* will ever forget that day. Everyone who could be spared tugged at the oars until his back ached and his palms grew sore. Even callouses proved no lasting protection. Brad's hands and my own were badly blistered, with the skin shredding as the blisters broke. Worse than the pain, however, was the anger, the frustration and the sense of despair as the sloop, now identifiable as the *Niobe*, eighteen guns, hung like a bulldog off our quarter and steadily drew nearer, with the frigate *Hero*, thirty-eight guns, not far astern.

"God damn Vail for comin' so close to them Limeys!" one lanky privateersman shouted in the longboat. And at the angry chorus of agreement, Oliver Jones raked them fore and aft with a withering roar that questioned every man's ancestry on his mother's side and loosed fire and brimstone on the crew's lack of courage with all the eloquence of an Old Testament prophet.

"Now, row, you bastards!" Oliver shouted, his chins aquiver with outrage. "If you want to rot in Dartmoor, just jump overboard — if you dare — the British will pick you up, maybe. But, by Jesus, as long as you stay in this boat, you'll row till you've nothin' but bones left!"

Good old Oliver! He'd said what had to be said, and the boatcrew responded. At the same time I could appreciate how the protesters had felt. Everyone was worn and depressed. Furthermore, by deliberately trying to find the British, in order to warn the mainland. Vail was using the *Argus* for a man-of-war's function, rather than a privateer's; and patriotic as these men were, they knew full well there was no reward in such duty and, obviously, too much hazard for a man's peace of mind.

Shortly after noon, a small cloud of smoke billowed from the *Niobe*, followed quickly by another as she tried the range with her bow guns. Fortunately for us she was still too far away, and, after ten minutes or so, she ceased firing. On our afterdeck, we had a six-pounder which Vail ordered moved into position as a stern chaser. Philip Adair was about to try a ranging shot when the *Niobe* fell silent. Vail then told Adair to ignore the *Niobe* herself if she opened fire again and try to sink the boats.

By midafternoon, with clouds beginning to overrun the sky, a light wind blew up from the south, and by tacking to take full advantage of it, we began to move swiftly through the water. The last shift of men from the boats we picked up practically collapsed on deck; sailorlike, however, no man was too weary to drink the ration of rum Captain Vail issued.

Though for a time we held our own under sail and close-hauled upon the wind, we could not shake our pursuers. In fact, the *Niobe*, a very swift sloop-of-war, began to close on our larboard quarter and at seven o'clock fired a broadside. As fountains of water rose barely a hundred yards from us, Vail called me over. By now, with Isle au Haut off our starboard bow, we were near enough to Penobscot Bay for Vail suddenly to tell me to stand by to take the longboat in while he made for the open sea.

Then, unaccountably, the wind died away to mere catspaws and finally to nothing. Almost at once the strong current began to sweep us ashore, and Isle au Haut with its high sides and great ledges and soaring surf is a nasty place to be in trouble. What to do? The question, I'm sure, was in every man's mind.

"Do we get the boats out again?" Brad asked.

"If we do," I said, "they'll have to fight the current, which will slow us down, and they'll also be exposed to the *Niobe*'s fire."

"But if they don't tow us, we'll go ashore!" And Brad didn't succeed in keeping the alarm out of his voice.

[ 157 ]

"There is another course Vail can follow," I said, "but it's a dangerous one."

Brad shrugged. "It looks to me as if anything he does will be dangerous."

"You're right, and this is especially dangerous. He can anchor."

"Anchor! Why the British would stand off and blow us to pieces."

For a moment I stared with him at the approaching *Niobe*, then said, "But Vail's got to anchor, Brad, or be swept ashore. The trick will be for us to drift as close as possible before letting go our anchor."

"I still don't see how that will prevent the British from chopping us up."

"They won't be able to get that close or they may be swept ashore themselves."

"But what if a storm blows up? It sure as hell feels like we're in for some dirty weather."

"Then they'll want sea room, and we'll have to try to claw our way out of here, too. It won't be easy."

"Jonathan," and for the moment the joy of arguing displaced the apprehension in his voice, "let's grant that Vail anchors. You'll concede that this prevents us from getting word to Castine."

"Yes, that's so," I admitted. "We can only hope that some fisherman will have seen the fleet and made for port."

"And, Jonathan, you must also admit that there's nothing to prevent the British from blockading us indefinitely — unless, of course, the weather intervenes."

"It's possible they may not think us important enough to occupy a frigate and a sloop-of-war," I said.

"I don't see why not. They've got enough other warships with their fleet, and the United States government certainly hasn't anything in these waters to frighten them with."

"It hasn't an active ship-of-the-line in the entire navy, and they've got three right with this squadron," I said bitterly.

"Then a storm looks like our only hope, and it may mean a grave for us somewhere there," he said, pointing shoreward, where yeasty waters were breaking over a line of black, jagged-edged ledges, formidable and cruel in the fading light.

I nodded, and had no heart for continuing so morbid an argument.

My speculation on what Captain Vail would do was borne out when, with men in the leads sounding, he took the *Argus* close in and anchored. What I hadn't anticipated was that he would go so near one long, menacing ledge. This seemed as risky to me as his having ventured so close to the British fleet. Yet even as he had had a motive in the latter, for all that the vagaries of the weather had frustrated his purpose, so now he undoubtedly had a reason for choosing the spot where he moored the *Argus*. And he was too good a seaman not to know that if a storm should chase the British ships from their stations, it could also smash us to bits against the rocks.

Just before darkness set in, both the *Niobe* and the *Hero* stood offshore and blasted us with broadsides that illumined the sky with great reddish-orange flashes of light and reverberated with a shattering thunder against the high side of the island. Occasionally a ball flew close enough to raise a fountain of water that splashed our decks, but practically all that deadly hail fell short of us. I think part of the reason was not only that the British feared to venture nearer shore but also that in the gathering darkness the *Argus* was not clearly visible; the brig tended to blend into the blackness of the island.

When the British finally ceased fire, Captain Vail had the crew mustered. "Men," he said, his voice lowered but still carrying powerfully across the deck, "there's a blow of some sort coming up. Before it breaks, the British will be gone, and we'll work our way out of here."

"If we live," someone said.

"But I want you men to understand," Vail went on, ignoring the angry voice, "that the British aren't through with us. In my opinion they'll be in here in boats within an hour to try to cut us out. Between those two bulldogs out there they can easily send a hundred and fifty men, maybe two hundred, against us. We've only fifty-five men, but, by all that's holy, they'll soon know they're in for a fight."

With that he dismissed the crew, and the brig's deck swirled with activity. The gun room was stripped of weapons — swords, cutlasses, boarding pikes, pistols and muskets. The pistols and muskets were loaded, and buckets of the former were placed near the bulwarks so that no time would be lost reloading during the action. Heavy cannon balls were stacked in the shot lockers with a view to hurling them from the deck through the fragile bottoms of the attacking boats. The two swivels on the after railings were crammed with musket balls and slugs. Then after a cold ration of biscuits and rum the crew lay down at their posts and waited. The *Argus*, not a light showing, was as well prepared as she could be against the expected attack.

It was about ten o'clock when Philip Adair, looking seaward with Brad and me, whispered, "They're coming!"

Instantly Captain Vail was beside him. "Good man, Adair!" he muttered. "I can't see a thing out there, but I'll take your word for it."

The word flew along the main deck of the brig, and I saw dark forms rise and peer over the bulwarks. These men moved to the guns on the larboard broadside and waited. Adair's pet, the Long Tom, could not be sufficiently depressed for this work, so he was moved to the stern chaser.

We could now hear the thump of many oars in their locks, and presently boats seemed to leap at us from the darkness. At once battle lanterns were lighted all over the brig; if anyone lived to board us, we wanted to see where they were. Now we were ready.

"Fire!" Vail shouted.

The *Argus*, rolling in the swell, was jarred sideways and perilously close to the reef by the force of the broadside. For a moment the blinding flashes from the guns and the acrid clouds of smoke hid the boats from our view. Then we heard the cries of wounded men.

Vail now ordered us to fire at will, and for two or three minutes our guns slammed in a continuous roar. Not that we could see anything because of the smoke. But whatever boat came through that curtain of fire was going to lose men.

Then from our bow came a wild shout, and British seamen poured onto our forecastle. But just as Jed Green, the stocky, quiet third officer, charged into them with a half-dozen men armed with pikes, a grim, cursing mass of boarders also swarmed over our stern, firing their pistols.

As coolly as if standing behind the great bulwarks of a ship-of-the-line instead of on the bullet-swept deck of a small brig, Philip Adair fired the stern chaser, then joined Brad, myself, and two other men in a wild rush to clear the stern. I fired my pistol point-blank at a big seaman, but it misfired. As I slashed at him with my cutlass, he struck my weapon so powerful a blow that it was torn from my hand. It was his last act. Big Philip skewered him with a boarding pike and thrust him overboard. Meanwhile Vail himself mustered a half-dozen more seamen and aided us in clearing the stern of the enemy.

For a moment we had a respite on our part of the *Argus*, and could see the plan of the enemy's attack. The British had attacked with a boat at the bow, one at the stern and five on the side. Actually two had slid around to the lee side but, after nearly capsizing between the *Argus* and the reef, came back to our weather side. We could now clearly see why Vail had chosen such a hazardous place to anchor. On our bow the British had likewise been driven overboard, but they had concentrated so heavily amidships that they had hacked a way through our boarding nettings and made a lodgement on our deck where Lester Jordan and most of our men were trying to contain them.

At once Vail, leaving Brad and two seamen to guard the afterdeck, led the rest of us except Philip in a smashing charge against the flank of the boarders. It was fire the pistols, then throw them at the enemies' faces, and follow up with the thrust of pike and the cut and slash of cutlass. It was hot, deadly work, but slowly we pressed them back until we had tumbled the last one overboard. Meanwhile Philip hurled heavy cannon balls down into one boat, which broke apart and sank.

But just as we thought we had beaten them off for good, two more boats arrived. This time the British seemed less eager. Not that one could blame them. We threw down cannon balls at them, blasted them with a shower of musket and pistol balls, while Philip, manning a swivel gun, smashed one boat so dreadfully it drifted away with apparently no man aboard able to hold an oar. Two boats had been sunk. As the surviving barges drew off and were joined by one additional boat, we manned our broadside guns again and hammered them until one more boat broke up and sank under a direct hit.

"That's enough — that'll hold 'em!" Vail roared.

We held our fire as the remaining craft picked up the survivors struggling in the water. Then as the boats drew off toward the men-of-war beyond, we broke into wild cheering. Afterward we heard yells of defiance. The British were game, there was no doubt of that. To cover the boats' retreat, the frigate and the sloop-of-war now opened a heavy fire on us. We jeered as the balls fell short with great splashes.

Suddenly, there was a tremendous crack overhead as one ball hit a spar, a lucky hit indeed for the British and an unlucky one for us. For as the spar tumbled to the deck, it sideswiped Captain Vail. He fell without a sound.

For a moment there was absolute silence broken only by the whirring sound of the rising wind in our rigging and the crash of the surf. We stared at our little Captain as if transfixed. Then Lester Jordan stepped forward.

"Adair, take the Captain to his cabin," he said. "Jonathan, you go, too. I'll be down as soon as I can. Mr. Green, douse those lanterns and get the boats ready to tow us clear of this reef. Mr. Jones, shake out the topsails and let's up anchor and get out of here!"

He was right, of course: the ship came first, even before the fallen Captain.

A nasty bit of irony, I thought, as I followed the giant Negro, who cradled the unconscious Vail in his arms like a child. The captain's plan was working: we had made a successful defense, the British — judging by their lights — were heading for the open sea with the storm now coming on swiftly, and Lester Jordan, a skillful sailor in his own right, would take us out of these dangerous waters. But at the very moment of triumph, when the enemy must have lost in dead and wounded and drowned nearly half his attacking force, "Little Ben" had fallen, and by a freak kind of mishap.

# XVI

WE had scarcely picked up our boats when the storm hit us. Fortunately, though mixed with gusts of wind and torrential showers of rain, it did not last long. But the sea, whipped into a frenzied froth, ran too high to permit Lester Jordan to turn Brad and me loose in the longboat. Before dawn, however, he let us go, with strict instructions not to let anything prevent us from warning Lieutenant Lewis at Castine as soon as we could, not even our sympathy for our passenger. For in the bottom of the boat, secured in a kind of cradle made of strips of canvas, lay Captain Vail.

The hours that followed were hours I shouldn't want to repeat. The sea was subsiding, but the waves ran so high for the longboat that we constantly shipped water. Small as our sail was, and closely reefed, we whipped along at high speed, yet pitched and tossed at times so badly that I pitied the injured man. I prayed he would not recover consciousness until we had brought him out of these lively waters into the shelter of the Bay; otherwise he would be in utter pain and misery. Yet I knew that for him to be unconscious all this time was a bad sign. It was this concern rather than fear of the British that made both Brad and me so apprehensive.

The sun was high up when we ran into the Bay and headed for Castine. Although I knew it most unlikely, I half expected to see the British fleet in the Bay. Actually, with the *Argus* having left the fleet far to larboard in her flight from the *Niobe* and the *Hero*, and with the brief summer's storm having blown up, I realized, when I mastered my alarm, that the fleet must have moved farther to the westward of Isle au Haut, possibly in shelter off Matinicus Island. It was therefore unlikely that the British would be in the Bay before nightfall or sunrise tomorrow. Of course, they might not be heading for the Bay at all but for Portland. Still, I felt sure their old stronghold at Castine, which they had held in the Revolution, was their objective. Besides, knowing the damaged *John Adams* was in the Bay, they couldn't help but wish to capture or destroy her. With possibly twenty-four hours of grace the militia companies could be mustered in the Penobscot towns and the *Adams* readied for defense.

"I still don't think the militia can save Castine," Brad said when I told him what I hoped. "The town is on a peninsula, after all, and, with their fleet, the British can surround it on three sides and, by landing troops, cut it off at the neck."

"I realize that," I said. "But the militia could certainly rally on the west side of the river to save the *Adams* at Hampden."

Brad, who was finishing his work with the bailing scoop, squinted toward the western shore sheltering such large towns as Camden and Belfast and numerous smaller towns all the way to Bangor. "There are enough militia over there to make it tough for the British if they'll only stand together and fight, but you can never count on them."

When we drew up off Fort Madison and shouted to Lieutenant Andrew Lewis who we were, I found myself regretting deeply that more regulars were not available than his capable artillerymen, who gently lifted Captain Vail ashore and bore him inside the redoubt.

When I told Lieutenant Lewis about the nearness of the British, his lips tightened. "My little fort was never meant to hold off a fleet of such strength, but we'll do what we can. Now can you get over to Belfast and take the word to the river towns?"

Although what he said was more an order than a question, I was stubborn. "First, I want to get Captain Vail to his mother's home and find a doctor for him."

"I'll take care of that," Lewis said. "My men will carry him home on a stretcher, and I'll get Dr. Oliver Mann to attend him. Meanwhile, it's essential that the west shore be warned and your boat is here and ready to go."

Reluctant as I was to leave Captain Vail in strange hands, I felt that since there was nothing more that we could do for him at the moment, Brad and I should be on our way. Besides, we knew that was what Vail would have wanted us to do.

So, a few minutes later, after a rasher of bacon, freshly baked bread from the garrison's cook-oven and a cup of steaming coffee, we started across the Bay to Belfast. Once there, finding no militia around, we went straight to the town clerk's office and asked that warning be passed down to Camden and an express rider sent upriver to warn the people, especially those at Hampden where the *Adams* was being repaired.

"You're just sayin' the same thing this note from Lieutenant Lewis says," the town clerk replied, looking up at us from over his glasses and remaining seated at his desk. "Can't see gettin' so excited about British ships outside the Bay. There's been Britishers there before."

"I doubt there's been a fleet of this size out there before," I said, trying to hold my temper in check.

"Maybe," and the clerk shrugged his shoulders. "Well, I'll get word to Cap'n Morris up at Hampden, an' if I can find someone else, I'll let the folks down in Camden know."

"Thank you," I said, though I felt small gratitude.

"Drat this war!" the man grumbled. "We didn't ask for it. It was those Madison fellers down in Washington."

We left him, still muttering, and returned to Fort Madison, where we reported our mission completed, then hurried for the home of Captain Vail's mother.

When we arrived, she answered our knock. Her face was gray, but her eyes were snapping with indignation. "If I could only get my hands on those Britishers!" she said. She told us the Captain was still unconscious, then led us into the kitchen and insisted on our drinking a glass of cool lemonade. Afterward she asked to know what had happened. Between Brad and me, we pieced together an account of events since our leaving her home. Yet even as she nodded at what we were saying, she looked every so often toward the downstairs bedroom, and the youthfulness in her face vanished, leaving it heavy with deep-set wrinkles and slack flesh.

"Mrs. Vail," I said, "if the British enter the Bay, Castine is bound to fall, and when it does, they will probably take a census of the inhabitants. Known enemies of the Crown will be locked up. We'd hate to see that happen to Captain Vail, so if it's possible, Brad and I would like to take him away. We should probably have landed him at Camden, but we were following our orders to waste no time in getting word of the British arrival to the fort at Castine."

"It would be better, Mrs. Vail," Brad added, "if we could move Captain Vail now that he is unconscious and would feel no pain."

"He would be safe if we took him up to Bangor," I said.

"Not that Godforsaken place!" she exclaimed. "It's the noisiest, dirtiest, busiest little town in these parts, and too important for the British to ignore. For that matter, no town in this whole Bay area is safe. No, my son stays with me. Doc Mann told me to keep him quiet, and I intend to."

"But if the British come, what will you do?" I asked.

Her jaw tightened. "If I have to, I'll hide him. But the British are a civilized people after all; they won't bother us — a helpless old woman like myself, my poor daft sister, and a son who can't talk at all! No, sir! I'll just get Lou to tell them about the spooks she sees, and they'll think we're all crazy and leave us alone."

"Let's hope so," Brad said.

She insisted that we stay the night but we declined and told her that if she changed her mind, she could send for us at Fort Madison.

"It's nice of you boys, but it ain't likely," she said. "Just you watch out for yourselves now, an' don't go gettin' too close to those red-coats."

We promised her we'd be careful and soon left for the redoubt, where we found the soldiers going through a gun drill.

"Lewis won't be able to stop a British fleet with only four guns, even if they are twenty-four-pounders," Brad said, after the sentry let us through.

I had too oppressive a sense of disaster to make any comment.

Lieutenant Lewis made us welcome, and issued us each a blanket for the night, which, though fair, would probably be damp, he said. He also issued us rations. In fact, he was such a thoroughly decent person and so competent an officer that I began to feel sorry for him. He must have realized that his position was hopeless if the fleet should move against him. Yet to evacuate the fort now would have been regarded as sheer cowardice. I thought that he might have wanted to talk that evening — I should have, in his place — but he kept his own counsel. He didn't even appear to be worried, or so I thought until I heard him up making the rounds several times in the night and talking with the sentries.

Once I dimly heard a conversation that went on for some time before I awoke to see Lieutenant Lewis and Brad standing on the parapet and staring down the Bay. While I was shaking my head free of cobwebs, Brad suddenly appeared.

"Jonathan," he whispered, "wake up! The lieutenant wants you."

Quickly I pulled on my shoes and jacket and followed him to the parapet.

"Dearborn" — Lewis was all soldier as he snapped out my name, though keeping his voice down — "Pettigrew and I think we see ships moving in the lower Bay. Do you see anything?"

My eyesight was pretty good, but though a faint light suffused the east, it was still too dark to see any great distance. Yet as I peered intently, I began to discern the movement of distinct and separate masses of darkness.

"They're ships for sure," I agreed.

"British?"

I shrugged. "We'll soon be able to tell. It's getting light fast now."

A few minutes more, and we were no longer in doubt. Ploughing up the east side of Long Island came a long line of men-of-war and transports. We couldn't see the end of the line, but there were enough ships to convince us this was no mere foray; it was a major invasion. There must have been several thousand troops aboard. Nor were the British taking any chances; in addition to frigates, sloops-of-war, and at least one schooner that presently came into view, there were at least three huge ships-of-the-line, 74-gun ships. Lewis could not possibly make any kind of effective resistance against such a force. But if resistance was futile, one would never have guessed it from Lieutenant Lewis's manner. The men were quickly awakened and served breakfast at the guns. Two soldiers, however, he sent scurrying townward for boats to evacuate the troops and the two fieldpieces. When three boats, manned by fishermen, presently nosed around to the battery, he said to us, "We could retreat by land if we have to, but that would mean losing the fieldpieces."

Back of us we could see scores of Castine citizens gathering to watch the great show of British power. A cloud of dust rising to the north was evidence that a number of residents were fleeing with their wagons, probably piled high with whatever they could pack aboard them.

Finally, shortly after sunrise, the entire fleet lay before us, and from their midst a little schooner darted toward the redoubt. Conversation in the battery now died swiftly. If the schooner was to test the fort, she stood no chance and must have known it, for she suddenly hove to and a tall, scarlet-clad figure stood up with a speaking trumpet in his hand. A moment later, a powerful English voice blasted shoreward, "Ahoy, the fort! This is Lieutenant Colonel Nichols of the Royal Engineers, and I speak for Sir John Sherbrooke, Governor of Nova Scotia. In the name of His Majesty, King George the Third, I command you to lay down your arms and surrender the fort directly."

We looked at Lieutenant Lewis standing on one of the guns. Cupping his hands about his mouth he shouted, "There will be no surrender!"

"Damn you, you haven't a chance!"

"I will give you two minutes to start back to your fleet or I will fire! Number One gun!"

The schooner made no movement, the officer continuing to watch us.

"Fire!"

The twenty-four-pounder bellowed, and though the ball missed, it struck the water just abaft the schooner's stern and doused the officer's handsome uniform.

As if by magic the schooner flung herself about and headed back for the fleet. Our guns now fired as fast as they could, but except for a couple of rents in her sails she was untouched.

Then as the men-of-war began to move toward us, and a few heavy shots whistled over us, our guns stopped firing. Quickly Lewis ordered the twenty-four-pounders spiked and the two fieldpieces with shot and ammunition placed in the boats. He personally supervised the laying of a fuse to the powder magazine. Then ordering all his men into the boats and directing the boats themselves to head up the Bagaduce River, he lighted the fuse and dashed to the *Argus's* longboat, which Brad and I and ten of his artillerymen sent flying along the shoreline.

Suddenly Lewis shouted, "Everyone down!"

We ducked to gunwale level as the magazine exploded with a crash that rang for minutes longer in my ears. Timbers, bricks, and sods fanned upward and out in a burst of white smoke that soon turned a dirty gray-black color. Butt ends of shoring supports burned furiously.

In the silence that followed, a silence so intense one could almost hear it, I stole a glance at Lewis's face; it appeared graven of stone, the very essence of calmness, but the eyes looked anguished. I could well imagine what the captain of a man-of-war feels like when he loses his ship.

Once at the Perkins wharf, we got the fieldpieces out of the boats with block and tackle, and placed them and their carriages on a big dray that Lewis commandeered over the protests of its owner. Then all of us took the road up the peninsula to Buckstown. Even as we were leaving Castine we saw the British fleet coming to an anchorage just north of the peninsula, the smaller men-of-war standing in close to the shore to cover the landing of the troops who were walking down the gangways of the transports into the waiting boats and barges in an endless scarlet stream. It was now about eight o'clock on the otherwise glorious morning of September 1.

By hard marching we reached Buckstown in the early afternoon, and pushed on until we reached a point opposite Hampden where we ferried across the river. Just up the river we could see the *Adams* lying at the end of Crosby's Wharf, her masts towering above the nearby storehouse. Her bluejackets had already removed her guns and partially dismantled her, preparatory to careening her and repairing her hull. Now they were swarming about her guns on the wharf and pushing and dragging a number of them toward the shore. It was obvious from the speed with which the work was moving that Captain Morris must already have been informed of the capture of Castine. Our arrival caused many of the *Adams*'s crew to pause in their work, but only momentarily. The harsh orders of the petty officers soon had the men at their tasks again.

Lewis shook hands with Morris, who was on the wharf supervising operations, and after quickly apprising him of the Castine seizure, introduced Brad and me.

"Glad to have you with us, gentlemen," Morris said.

His voice was deep and nasal, and as amiable as his manner. Yet I caught a hint of resources of energy in the rapid pace of speech and the abrupt way in which he shook hands and then turned to speak to his broad-shouldered executive officer, Lieutenant Wadsworth, who was in charge of placing a battery of nine eighteen-pounders on the high ground back of Crosby's Wharf. Morris's long nose twitched almost like a rabbit's as he talked. A native of Woodstock, Connecticut, this thirty-year-old captain had had an honorable career. He had been with Stephen Decatur when that great fighter took the little *Intrepid* into Tripoli harbor and, under the enemy's very guns, destroyed our frigate *Philadelphia* which the Barbary pirates had captured when it ran on a reef; Morris was the first man to land on the captured frigate's deck. When the *Constitution* under Isaac Hull fled from a British squadron at the outset of war in 1812, Morris was her executive officer. Later he played a gallant role in her great victory over the *Guerrière* and suffered a painful body wound in the struggle. Posted to the *Adams*, he had run the British blockade off the Chesapeake in January, captured several ships, and now was faced with the possible loss of his own ship in the Penobscot.

"Lieutenant," he said to Lewis, "an express rider reached me at noon with the news about Castine. I'm not one to pass judgment on your conduct, but I'd say you did the only wise thing in retreating."

"Thank you, sir," Lewis said.

"As soon as I could, I hurried off a courier to General Blake at Brewer. I have asked him to call out the militia and to come here as soon as possible."

"Then he ought to be here by tomorrow morning," Lewis said.

"Sooner I hope."

Lewis shook his head. "Militiamen aren't regulars, sir."

"But they're fighting for their homes, man!" Morris said. "Surely they'll turn out quickly — lots of 'em."

"Yes, sir."

But Lewis's mere acknowledgment was eloquent with doubt. Morris gave him a sharp look, then told him that he and his men could draw rations from the *Adams*. Though Morris did not include Brad and me, Lewis told us afterward that he would be glad to include us if we wished to make ourselves useful during the crisis. Naturally we agreed.

That evening everyone worked furiously setting up three batteries. One was a battery of nine eighteen-pounders on the high right bank of the Soadabscook back of the wharf. Another, containing most of the other cannon, was on the wharf itself commanding the Penobscot below where the Soadabscook enters it. The third consisted of one gun covering the communication between the hill and wharf batteries. The effort in manhandling these massive guns and their carriages into position was exhausting. Horses, requisitioned locally, helped greatly in dragging the guns up to the high ground lashed to stoneboats, but the work was still largely a kind that called for man muscle, human sweat, and some rather picturesque profanity! Torches and battle lanterns furnished a dim illumination for the work, which Morris interrupted near midnight in order to give us a chance to rest for a few hours.

In the course of the evening, General John Blake arrived with a small staff. "My troops are on the way," he announced to Captain Morris.

"Good, very good, sir," Morris said, and the two officers went off on a survey of the hill battery.

"Is he a fighter?" I asked Brad, as our gun crew paused to catch their breaths.

"I don't know," Brad replied. "He's a popular man up in these parts, but that doesn't mean he'll fight. I've seen him in Portland at a meeting of militia officers and liked him. Matter of fact, he's hard not to like. I only hope the militia will turn out for him."

But by noon the next day fewer than four hundred militia had arrived from Blake's brigade of the 10th Massachusetts Division. When Morris and Blake returned from a reconnaissance of the terrain and the battery sites, where a number of civilians from the area were now helping the bluejackets get the guns mounted, they looked down at the mouth. Not only were the militia surprisingly few, but at least a third of them were without arms, and most of those with arms — old fowling pieces, muskets, an occasional rifle — were short of ammunition. Morris therefore ordered muskets and powder and ball distributed among the militia from the *Adams's* stores.

"General Blake," I heard him say in hardly suppressed anger, "what is the matter with the militia? Has no inspection been held recently?"

"Our muster days are few during the year, Captain Morris."

"But, good God, General, haven't they had any training recently? After all, the British started grabbing parts of Maine in the east back in July!"

"Moose Island in Passamaquoddy Bay is a long way from Bangor, sir."

"Not when you have command of the sea, General, and the British certainly have that."

[ 171 ]

"You do not need to remind me, Captain. But I think you exaggerate the weakness of our militia. They will fight."

"Let's hope so," Morris said angrily. "They're up against British regulars who have been fighting the French for years."

"I have a lot of confidence in my men, Captain."

"I wish I shared your optimism, General. I'm afraid that unless they stand fast, I'll lose my ship and my guns."

He turned to his hard-faced executive officer. "Lieutenant Wadsworth, see that our twenty invalids are taken over Soadabscook Creek at once. If the militia don't hold, we'll have to leave in a hurry. With the two hundred of our crew remaining, we can manage a retreat if it comes to that. Lieutenant Lewis!"

Lewis, whose few troops had been assisting the *Adams*'s crew with the guns, reported at once.

"Lieutenant," Morris's voice was sharp, "the general has asked for you and your men to aid him. I'll give you an eighteen-pounder to stiffen the militia defense. I needn't point out that the safety of the *Adams* may depend on your efforts."

"We will do our duty," Lewis said, with just a suggestion of resentment that Morris might think he wouldn't.

Morris's voice lost its edge. "You may have to do more than your duty, Lewis. These militia are the greenest-looking crowd of would-be soldiers I've ever seen — brave enough, maybe, but bravery is no substitute for skill and experience. You're likely to find yourself the real core of resistance. But, Lieutenant, if you have to cut and run, just give me warning in time to spike my guns and save my men. The bridge across the creek will be nearer the enemy than us and the creek is fordable only at low tide. So give us time."

"Yes, sir," and with a salute, Lewis marched his little company of regulars out to join Blake's militia.

Brad and I followed since we had originally attached ourselves to the troops. Looking back at the batteries, I felt sure Morris could check the British if they came by the river. I'd hate to be in the landing boats facing such a fire as they would receive. But what commanding officer in his right mind would attempt such a thing when he could land troops below us, fan them out, and throw them against our flank and rear? Much as Morris would have preferred an

[ 172 ]

assault by water, he evidently suspected it might come by land. So did the nervous, confident-talking Blake. So did we.

And as Lewis's regulars took their place with Blake's militia, the prospect didn't look promising. Our position, to be sure, had much to recommend it. It was well-chosen high land in front of Hampden. Our left was flanked by the high hill where Morris had mounted his battery to command both the road and the river. Our right was likewise on high ground. In the center where, despite a dip in the land, a projection thrust toward the possible enemy approach, Blake had placed Lewis with his iron eighteen-pounder, supported by two brass three-pounders under a Captain Hammond of the General's own brigade. All these guns were in advance of our troop center and could rake the road and a narrow bridge at the foot of the hill which the British would have to cross in order to charge the hill. With United States regulars instead of militia in the line, I don't think I'd have feared the result. But with green, ill-trained militia in small numbers spread over too much territory, how could we possibly do more than fire a shot or two and run? If only the militia would stand and fight!

It by no means steadied us, after having for supper a partially spoiled strip of bacon no thicker than a wood shaving plus a couple of sea biscuits from the *Adams*, to hear that the British were rapidly closing in on us. The British Major General Gosselin had landed at Belfast with more than six hundred men and secured the town without any real resistance. This force was obviously to protect from the south and, if necessary, support an expedition of seven hundred redcoats coming up the river under Lieutenant Colonel Henry John and Captain Robert Barrie of the 74-gun ship-of-the-line *Dragon*. A harsh, outspoken man, Barrie had gained a reputation for ruthlessness in the Chesapeake. Barrie's own forces consisted of the sloops-of-war *Peruvian*, 22, and *Sylph*, 18, and the *Dragon*'s marines and a large body of sailors. His own men and John's filled the *Dragon*'s tender, a transport brig, and nine launches. Scared-looking boys dashed into our lines giving us reports before they were directed to General Blake. According to the reports, Barrie had earlier landed a detachment of troops at Frankfort on the headwaters of Marsh Bay, and this detachment moved along the river road without resistance to meet Barrie's squadron, which put in at Bald Hill Cove about five o'clock.

The enemy now was close to us, not more than two to three miles distant. To make matters even less pleasing, the weather turned very dark and rainy, with a tendency to fog. This was ideal weather for a skilled enemy to spring a surprise. I felt sorry for our militia sentries that night. Not only were they soaked to the skin, they probably saw a redcoat behind every bush. Actually, I don't think many of us slept. Three more companies of militia reported before daybreak, raising our forces to six hundred, but as they slipped and slithered through the lines to take position on our right, they looked as innocent of training as the rawest civilian. As in the first contingent, many arrived weaponless.

"Damn them!" I heard Lewis say as he watched them after making his rounds.

"Morris is probably God damning them and Blake, too," Brad whispered, pulling the blanket Lewis had issued him over his head.

It was indeed a miserable night with our fires sputtering out in the rain, and a dangerous day ahead. Yet toward morning, as the men settled down and snores rose gratingly among the sleeping troops, I, too, dozed off. Dimly I heard the call of some night bird, then dropped into a deep slumber.

# XVII

A RATTLE of accoutrements and a muffled sound of tramping somewhere off in the heavy fog brought our troops to life about five o'clock. Quickly we formed a thin line of battle about the eighteen-pounder and General Blake sent out two companies to reconnoiter and report the enemy's movements. As no attack came, our men rested in ranks and gnawed on whatever was left of last night's supper, which in my case was a sea biscuit so hard I had to hammer it to pieces on a stone with the butt end of my knife before I could even attempt to eat it. Brad shared half another with me, and we both washed down this sumptuous breakfast with the lukewarm, brackish-tasting water in our canteens. Some of the regulars had done themselves proud raiding the militia's kits and were toasting thick slices of bacon over little fires and stuffing their mouths with apple pie. We could smell coffee boiling in the militia lines to our left, and I heard one knot of regulars planning a raid on that coffee if the British didn't spoil the fun.

It was an eerie feeling waiting on that dark morning for something to happen, we knew not what. General Blake came up and spoke in a low, urgent voice to Lewis. A moment later, Lewis called to Brad and me. When we reported, he introduced us to Blake, then said, "I want you men to get back to Captain Morris and inform him that our scouts report the enemy within five hundred yards of our position and about to attack."

"Yes, sir," we said.

But as we started, he checked us. "For God's sake, don't run! If the militia see you running, they'll panic. Walk!"

Actually our troops were spread so thinly we saw only a few stray militiamen back of the main line of resistance.

Among the sailors there was almost a complete absence of sound, which surprised me since sailors are generally a garrulous lot. As we approached Morris on the wharf, our footsteps made hollow echoes on the planking, and we were fiercely hushed by a little midshipman who demanded our business. When I told him we bore a message from General Blake, he waved us on.

Morris received us with an air of impatience until I mentioned that we were from General Blake. He and two of his officers were staring off into the fog and appeared to be listening intently.

"Tell General Blake his militia must stand firm," Morris said. "It they don't, I shall have to burn the *Adams* and retreat."

"Burn the *Adams!*" The words fairly leaped from Brad's mouth.

"I shall have no other choice," Morris explained. "The militia are supposed to be protecting my rear, and I can't spare a man to help them. Now I want you men to go back to General Blake and tell him I'm expecting an attack from the river at almost any moment. D'you hear anything new?" he asked an officer.

"They're getting nearer," the officer said.

For a moment everyone listened. Despite the muffling effect of the fog, there was no mistaking the thump of many oars in locks some-where on the river.

"Tell General Blake they're moving toward my position in boats and barges," Morris said. "I've placed Lieutenant Wadsworth in charge of the hill battery with Lieutenant Madison and Mr. Rogers, my purser, to aid him. The wharf battery here is under Lieutenant Parker, Lieutenant Beatty, and Sailing-Master M'Culloh. Lieutenant Watson has his marine detachment and will watch the main body of the enemy and cover my flank and my retreat in case that is neces-sary. I can't spare a man to help General Blake, but the safety of the *Adams* depends on his militia. They must stand firm, they *must!* Clear?"

"Yes, sir," we said.

"I'm going to make a final inspection of the hill battery. If the British make a simultaneous attack by land and water, as I suspect they will, I'll take up my station on this wharf. Any communication from General Blake will reach me here."

We left barely ahead of him as he strode up toward Wadsworth's battery.

"Blake hasn't even issued orders to throw up a redoubt anywhere," Brad said as we hurried to find the general. "The only one we have is what the regulars have built to cover their gun crew."

After we delivered Morris's report to General Blake, who asked us to remain close to Lieutenant Lewis, we rejoined the regulars. There was a good deal of horseplay going on among the militia we passed. Evidently the fact that any minute now a battle would begin that might demand every bit of energy they possessed did not disturb them. But, of course, why should it? They had never been in a battle before. Nor, for that matter, had their officers, but surely these last should have possessed a sufficient sense of responsibility to keep their men in line rather than let them stray on account of their tomfoolery. A sudden attack out of the fog could be catastrophic.

When we recounted to Lewis what we had observed among Cap-tain Morris's men and Morris's apprehensions, Lewis nodded. "I know how he feels about the prospect of destroying the *Adams*."

Remembering his own act in blowing up Fort Madison rather than surrender, I could appreciate the remark.

I was just on the point of strolling over to look at the gun crew when a sharp rattle of musketry broke out. This continued for several minutes, and to judge by the intensity of the exchanges, our skirmishers were warmly engaging the British advance. Then men from the two reconnaissance companies burst out of the fog and raced towards us. "They're comin'!" one of the officers shouted. "They're right behind us."

The skylarking of the militia, which had largely subsided when the skirmishing occurred, ceased altogether: the regulars even stopped their grumbling. The entire line, thinly and unevenly spaced, and half obscured by the fog, seemed suddenly to freeze. For a moment we heard only scattered shots. Then unmistakably moving toward us from the fog came the heavy tread of many boots, and we heard a few British voices sharp and high-pitched in a tone of command. It was now between seven and eight o'clock. They must be about to cross the stream between Hampden and Hampden Corners, and no one had given orders to blow up the bridge.

"Lieutenant Lewis, give them a few shots!"

All of us turned around and looked up at Blake on his horse. Some half-forgotten picture of a Roman emperor seen in a book in my father's library long ago came to my mind.

"Yes, sir!"

Lewis's crisp acknowledgment broke the spell, and the crash of the eighteen-pounder swung all of us to the front. Two or three of the militia's small fieldpieces joined in at once. Soon the rank, acrid smoke hanging low over the field in the heavy air caught at our throats and started a wave of coughing. Lewis's eighteen-pounder, loaded now with grapeshot, raked the bridge, but the density of the fog prevented the gunners from aiming well. Then we saw them moving up the hill towards us, a heavy scarlet column, with a strong skirmish line ahead.

Even as we watched them and waited for an order to fire, Wadsworth's guns on the hill opened up with a roar that hurt my ear drums. Turning around, I saw bright streaks of reddish-white light ripping through the fog, and realized the enemy was using rockets from ships somewhere out in the river.

Finally, without waiting for the British to come close enough for muskets to be effective, the militia fired. Lewis held those regulars not at the eighteen-pounder tightly in hand. The enemy was still too distant for us to see "the whites of their eyes," as Israel Putnam had said at Bunker Hill, but they were within musket range when Lewis ordered us to fire. Quickly we reloaded while the cannon crashed again. This time, however, the barrel could not be sufficiently depressed and the charge went over the heads of the advancing redcoats. Our second musket volley did far more damage, halting the charge just below the gunners. In fact a counterattack with the bayonet cleared the area around the cannon.

I have often thought we could have held the British at Hampden if the militia had had even a small amount of discipline and training, or if, at the least, they had thrown up entrenchments. For a moment, the British were slowed, thanks almost entirely to Lewis and his few regulars. But only for a moment. To the left and right of us the militia began to flee, at first by twos and threes, then by larger groups. Many threw away their muskets and ran in stark terror. Only General Blake, a few officers with him, Lieutenant Lewis and the regulars stood fast.

"Dearborn! Pettigrew!" Lewis shouted. "Get back to Morris and tell him the whole line is collapsing."

We took off at once. Passing General Blake, we stopped. Evidently, however, he had seen Lewis speak to us, for he waved us on, pointing with his sword to Morris's position.

When we arrived at the wharf, the place was a bedlam. Men were swarming over the *Adams*'s decks and black smoke was already pouring up from her. From everywhere came the sharp, ringing sound of iron upon iron as sailors hammered spikes into the touchholes of the guns. The wharf was a miniature tumbling sea of blue, while from everywhere came shouts and orders. Discovering Morris as he paused for breath after a burst of orders, we gave him the bad news.

"I know, I know!" he snapped. "Lieutenant Wadsworth up on the hill saw the militia run — God damn them! Now you'd better get out of here yourselves while you can."

There was nothing for us but to retreat, and I can't say Brad and I were slow in reaching the bridge over the Soadabscook. Once across we formed a line with some of the bluejackets and prepared to cover the retreat of the rest of the *Adams*'s crew.

That retreat was something to watch; and if the militia had shown but a portion of the discipline of the *Adams*'s men, we could have made it rough for the British. Most of the men on the wharf were soon across the bridge. Lieutenant Wadsworth's men from the hill battery had to leave off spiking their guns to save themselves. As they rushed toward the bridge, the little unit of twenty marines under Lieutenant Watson covered their retreat with superb courage and skill. Unfortunately, Captain Morris and a knot of men still remained on the wharf, having seen that all the guns there were spiked and that the enemy could not possibly extinguish the fires on the doomed corvette. Suddenly a file of scarlet appeared on the hill across the wharf; it looked impossible for Morris to escape.

But Morris evidently saw the enemy even before we did, for he was already hurrying the men along. As the bluejackets rushed toward the bridge, however, the enemy opened fire and started down the hill.

"They're cut off — they'll never make it!" Brad shouted.

Sailors and marines from the *Adams* who were around us stormed down the bank and opened fire on the British skirmishers. Unfortunately a musket ball hasn't much accuracy at more than a hundred yards, and the redcoats ignored us. The commander of the *Adams* would make a rare prize for them.

But the British — and we — reckoned without Captain Morris. Instead of attempting to reach the bridge, the group now dashed down to the creek itself.

"The tide's rising," a man called out. "They'll have to swim."

"Most sailors don't swim," I said to Brad; and sounded, I'm sure, like a doom-ridden prophet.

Then with a series of great splashes the men hit the water. At first two or three tried to swim and made such little progress we thought they would drown.

"Stand up and wade across!" Morris yelled to them.

The surprise on their faces was easily discernible when they found they could walk, even if they sometimes sank to their chins. Strong hands pulled them to shore and up the bank. Then only Captain Morris was left on the opposite shore. Disdaining to look around, he ploughed across the creek, sometimes swimming, more often wading with the water up to his armpits. Although a number of us blazed away at the redcoats and kept most from venturing close to him, a few came near enough to make his fording the creek a very risky affair. Innumerable little fountains splashed about him as musket balls hit the water. But soon, his hand too was grasped by a big bosun who half dragged him up the bank. A great cheer went up from all of us to see him unharmed.

What to do now must have been on many people's minds as we raced along the road to Bangor. The militia had completely scattered, leaving their dead and wounded to be taken care of by the British and the people living in Hampden. General Blake and a few officers alone remained of the hundreds of civilian soldiers who had assembled for the invasion. Blake's face had the look of a man who had been struck by his dearest friend; he simply couldn't believe that his beloved militia had deserted him, and he was deeply hurt. Was there now any hope of saving Bangor with Lieutenant Colonel John's troops pursuing us by land and Captain Barrie's flotilla heading up-river? I saw Blake and Morris talking with great earnestness, and heard them call Lieutenant Lewis into their conversation.

Twice, while they were talking, I looked back. The fog was now dissipating rapidly, and the dense, black smoke from the burning *Adams* towered high, then flattened out over an enormous area. In the distance we could see a thin skirmish line of redcoats moving toward us. As men looked back over their shoulders and saw those scarlet figures, invariably they quickened their steps.

"What are you and I going to do?" Brad asked.

"Wish I knew," I said. "I guess it depends on whether Blake and Morris think there's any point in trying to defend Bangor."

"Maybe we'll find out about that right away," and Brad pointed up the road to a party of a half-dozen civilians, two mounted and the rest on foot, coming toward us, with one man carrying a furled flag of truce. "Looks like the city fathers are trying to persuade the General not to sacrifice the town by further fighting."

"He hasn't anyone left to fight with," I said. "Morris's and Lewis's men aren't enough."

"Oh, I realize that. I was just thinking that we Maine people aren't covering ourselves with much glory today."

Of course he was right, at least for the most part. The few militia who had turned out had been eager enough, God knows, but, unable to face volley firing or the bayonet, they had cut and run. Nor were other militia gathering on the flanks of Colonel John's force and making life uncomfortable for his troops as colonial muskets had harried the redcoats from Concord back to Boston. People simply didn't believe in this war even when their homes were threatened, or maybe they didn't believe the British were a menace to themselves or their homes. This would have been my Aunt Betsy's feeling, but, of course, she had come naturally by her friendly sentiment for the British.

Loud talking by the Bangor magistrates and General Blake ended with the civilians waiting under a flag of truce for the British to come up, while our straggling column hurried on toward the town. From what I could see of their faces, Blake looked even more stricken and Morris angrier. Then, as we moved past a scattered row of houses into the town, we came to a road winding up over the hills to the west. Morris shook hands with Blake, and motioned the sailors with him to the left.

"Well, this is it," Brad said. "Do you want to stay with Blake and watch the British occupy Bangor or go with Morris?"

As he saw me hesitate, he added, "If you're thinking you should stay on account of Vail, you're crazy. There's not a damned thing either of us can do for him now. He's hurt and he may be a prisoner, and Castine is swarming with redcoats. We'll be lucky if we're not captured ourselves here in Bangor."

Brad was right, of course, though I hated to admit it. If Vail hadn't been injured, it might be possible in the confusion at Castine to smuggle him out. But, then again, if he hadn't been injured, he'd be at sea somewhere with the *Argus*. We had done everything expected of us. It looked as if this whole area was to come under British control, and I had no desire to remain.

"Let's ask Captain Morris where he's going," I said, and ran up to the officer as he stood with Lieutenant Wadsworth while his column wheeled to the left.

"We're going to Portland, and you may come along with us if you want to," Morris said. "We'll head west to the Kennebec and then south. God knows how we'll eat, the farms are so few, but we'll

[ 181 ]

manage somehow. We'll have to break up into small groups, though."

As we fell in line, I saw men, women, and children in front of their doorways watching us. They stood, woodenlike and silent, evidently dreading the worst. General Blake had sent officers riding along the street telling them the British were on the way and they should evacuate the town. No one made a move to comply.

At the top of the hill our column paused for breath and looked back. Smoke was rising from the wharves down in Hampden, and the British flotilla was clearly visible closing in on Bangor, while a long scarlet column pushed along the road we had left. I could imagine what would happen to the numerous ships on the stocks — the torch or capture. But I wondered more about the people themselves and prayed the British officers could keep their men in hand and not let them loose upon the town. It gave one a strange feeling to see one's country occupied — and under such humiliating circumstances. Between anger and impotence, I felt half sick.

"God damn those bastards!" a sailor ahead said.

"But there ain't nothin' we can do," another near him said. "They got too many ships an' too many men."

"I don't mean the British," the first one retorted. "Damn them anyway. I mean the milishy. If they'd stood, we could have saved the *Adams*."

Maybe yes, maybe no. I suppose that unless more of the countryside had risen to help us, we could not have saved the *Adams* indefinitely. And the countryside had simply sat back on its haunches and let the British take over. Something was really wrong when men refused to rally in defense of their homeland. Neither the British nor their sympathizers like Warren Bierce could have hoped for a more satisfactory ending to the invasion.

Feeling both weary and sad, Brad and I presently fell in with the column and marched westward into the wilderness land between the Penobscot and the Kennebec.

# XVIII

THE trip to the Kennebec was a hungry experience but not to be compared with that my Uncle Tom went through following the loss of the American fleet in the Penobscot in '79. Now, at least, there were several rough roads through the forests, and, here and there, one came upon clearings and a handful of houses. The few people we encountered were reasonably generous with their food, but obviously had to take into account the long winter ahead and could not spare us much. When we reached Augusta, supplies became more plentiful.

While at Augusta, Brad and I looked over the crumbling ruins of Fort Western. It took no great feat of the imagination to see again the hundreds of soldiers of Benedict Arnold's expedition climbing aboard their bateaux and canoes and paddling up the Kennebec on that heroic but ill-fated drive to Quebec thirty-nine years before. If ever New England needed something of their spirit and of the indomitable courage of their then-loyal and scrappy, little leader, it was now. But nowhere in the whole country did it seem possible to find such leadership in the field unless it was from that fiery soldier from Tennessee, General Jackson. As for our Congress, there was no one to compare with the Adamses — Sam and John, with wise, old Ben Franklin, with Richard Henry Lee or Patrick Henry. What, in God's name, had happened to us?

From Augusta, the group of sailors we were with slipped through Hallowell and Gardiner, then, while other groups trudged to Portland by way of Brunswick, we cut across country through Lewiston, over the Androscoggin, and headed for New Gloucester. This lively, little farming town with its spacious farms and well-kept houses received us as if we brought good news instead of bad. We were invited to homes for dinner, and when our lieutenant in charge insisted we must press on, the good people pressed freshly baked bread, corn, and early apples into our hands. These provisions we finished while resting at the summit of the high hill overlooking the town. There are more spectacular views in southern Maine but few in my knowledge that give one a better vista of rolling meadows and woodland linking up with distant hills. Had this been Europe, a great castle would have stood on this hill, guardian in the days of old to the nobility within and to the serfs who worked the rich meadows below. Instead, on this hill now there were only pastures, a few scraggly trees surmounting a pile of rocks, and a narrow, coarse-graveled road. It was better so; we were a free people, and allegedly equal.

After twenty miles or so from New Gloucester through the cross-roads town of Gray and over a narrow, winding, deeply rutted road we reached Portland in the late afternoon of September 7. It was hard to believe that the attack on Castine had occurred only on the first, so much had happened in the meantime. Our group was the last to report, and Brad and I lingered just long enough to thank Captain Morris for his kindness. He brushed aside our thanks, expressed his appreciation for our service, and told us how proud he was of the conduct of his own men on the march from Bangor, especially the fact that there was not a single case of desertion.

"The navy may not talk much about patriotism, gentlemen," he said, "but it expresses it through the loyalty and good conduct and courage of its personnel."

We were hardly a gathering of citizens in a public hall that he should address us so grandly, but what he said was so true that we could only agree.

After arranging to go out to my Uncle Tom Dearborn's the next day, Brad and I went to our homes. I knew Brad was eager to see my cousin Eliza, while I simply had to get some advice from Uncle Tom that I knew my own parents, however well intentioned, had not the background for giving.

That evening I recounted to them what had happened since the *Argus* had left Portland. News of the British capture of Castine had reached Portland several days ago, my father told me. There was still great alarm that Portland itself might be next on the British invasion schedule. Militia units were being called out in all the coast towns, and units in the interior towns were alerted. Fort Preble over in Pooduck was being reinforced, as was Fort Allen on Munjoy Hill. It was rumored that the banks were even considering burying their specie or transporting it into the interior or to Boston for safekeeping.

"Boston!" my mother scoffed. "What's to prevent the British from capturing that, too? But it might be a good thing," she added, "if the Federalists there saw their beloved British seizing Federalist ships and camping on the Common!"

"Now, Alice, don't be bitter!" Father said with a smile. "Anyone would think you approved of this war."

"Hardly! But sometimes these Federalists make me sick. They've regarded the administration as our enemies and the British as our real friends. Well, the British have shown just how friendly they are by seizing our territory and destroying lives and property. Look at their burning of Washington two weeks ago, and now their depredations in Maine! Now those precious Federalists are all so alarmed they're getting ready to fight!"

"It's a little late," I said. "If they were going to fight, they should have done so before. But at least if enough of them rally to the Republicans, we can prevent the British from seizing any more of our land."

"You're assuming too much, my boy," my father said. "If the British stay the other side of the Penobscot, this furor will die down quickly, and the Federalists will be stronger than ever for making peace."

"Your father and I also want peace, Jonathan," my mother said, "but we don't want the price to be the disintegration of our nation. What you said you heard and saw in Boston has alarmed us. I'm afraid of Mr. Otis's influence."

My father nodded. "So am I, and I am praying that he will be able to control the Federalist hotheads who may wish to take New England out of the Union."

"If he doesn't take the lead in doing that very thing himself!" my mother said.

I looked at my parents in astonishment. Knowing how pacifically minded they were, I had thought they would want peace at any price whether that price was British occupation or secession. Did this now mean that they approved of fighting as an alternative to either?

They shook their heads at the same time like marionettes on a string. "Jonathan," my father said with a gentle smile, "you know we don't approve of war under any circumstances. It is man's greatest folly."

"His worst sin, you mean," my mother put in vehemently.

"Well, it leads from his worst sin," my father allowed. "Pride. I think any solution to our present situation is preferable to war. But that does not prevent me from deploring the British invasion of our country or condemning the Federalist wild talk of New England's going its own way."

"I admire both of you for your position," I said; I had not expected such candor or understanding. "It is not my position, as you know. But, though I support the war, I am beginning to think it is lost unless more people rally to the cause. And the irony is that the people around here won't do that unless the British move west from the Penobscot and seize more of our territory."

"Are you hoping they do?" my mother's voice was brusque.

I shook my head. "How could I wish our people more misfortune just so that the war would continue and help unite the factions?"

The next day when I had intended to go to my Uncle Tom, I succumbed to a weakness that may be the death of me one day. I came down with a heavy, late-summer cold that suddenly turned into pneumonia. For a week I was pretty ill, and for one night and most of a day evidently there was some reason to worry. I think the turning point came when I awoke to see a blue-clay vase filled with late-blooming roses standing on the sickroom table. My mother was nodding in her chair when I awoke, but with the sixth sense that nursing seems to give, she was alert at once.

After she audibly thanked God that I was conscious again, she said in a matter-of-fact tone, "You had a visitor this afternoon, Mrs. Warren Bierce."

I still had difficulty thinking of India Mitchell as Bierce's wife, and for a moment — perhaps because of my weakness — I floundered trying to make the identification.

My mother broke the awkward silence by adding, "She's as lovely as ever, in fact, more so now than before, I think. But she has suffered, too. I can tell it by her eyes."

"It's no wonder, being married to Bierce," I muttered, and was appalled when I heard how thin my voice was.

My mother got me a glass of cold spring water, then picked up her crochet work. "India seemed genuinely concerned about you."

"That's nice," I said.

She gave me a sharp look over her glasses, then resumed her crocheting. "The Judge has been a broken man since his return from France. I used to think he wanted India to marry Mr. Bierce, but I hear that he rarely enters their house now. Doesn't that seem strange?"

"Yes, I suppose it does, Mother," I said, and I felt as weary as I must have sounded. If there was anyone I didn't want to think of at the moment, it was Judge Kent, or Warren Bierce, or, for that matter, India herself. I was still too angry and too bitter over what had happened. Sometime, when I found a way, I'd have it out with Bierce. If only I could prove a connection between him and the British invasion of Castine, I'd see him hang. How my mother would be shocked if she knew my unchristian thoughts! As for India — but I couldn't think of India sharing that man's life in all its intimacies.

"Jonathan, are you all right?"

I looked up to see my mother leaning over me.

"I've called to you twice, but you've been muttering and look flushed. I wonder if your fever is back again."

She put her hand on my forehead and sighed. "Frankly I don't know whether you're feverish or not, but you'd better sleep. I shouldn't have talked with you."

I was relieved she let it go at that. For the moment I felt too disgustingly weak to plan anything so formidable as the downfall of Warren Bierce. As for winning India Mitchell Bierce, the roses on my night table somehow gave me a flicker of hope despite their obviously being simply a gesture of sympathy.

Three weeks later I felt as well as ever, and, with Brad, went out to see my Uncle Tom and Aunt Betsy. Brad had resumed his law practice, though in a half-hearted sort of way. He needed no encouragement to accompany me to the Cape Elizabeth Dearborns. As a matter of fact, he had been out several times courting Eliza since we had returned. The way my mother told him to look after me, anyone would have thought I was still an invalid. But Brad gravely assured her he would be a regular physician to me. My mother, whose sense of humor was not her forte, thanked him as gravely, and meant every word of it.

As we turned off Fore Street and down the wharf to catch the ferry for Pooduck, we nearly collided with Warren Bierce and Jake Rudd.

"Christ, look where you're goin'!" Rudd said. Then, seeing who we were, his eyes narrowed, and his face set in heavy, ugly lines.

It was Bierce who broke the silence as all of us stared at one another. "I hear you have been ill, Dearborn," he said pleasantly. "Glad to see you're up and about."

"That's kind of you, but it's no thanks to either of you that I'm even here."

"Or me, for that matter," Brad said.

"What the hell do you mean?" Rudd demanded.

"I don't think there's any need to explain," Brad said.

"I don't know what you are talking about," Bierce said.

"One of these days perhaps you will remember. Perhaps, indeed, you will have no choice but to remember."

"Are you threatening me?" And Bierce smiled with an arrogant confidence that graveled me.

"My friend isn't threatening either of you," I said. "He's merely making a statement of fact that I'll support."

Bierce shrugged. "You're welcome to do what you can. Just remember that slander and libel can be expensive."

"I shall be very careful," Brad promised him.

"Good. I hope Dearborn will be, too. Rashness can cost a man much, perhaps more than his reputation. Come on, Jake."

He bowed, took the glowering Rudd by the arm, and stepped around us, leaving us feeling a little silly and deeply angry. The honors were all his. Even Brad could not contest his command of the situation, while I, of course, was simply too heavy-handed and too personally involved to come anywhere near matching him. He had met our threat — for that is really what it was — with counterthreats; and both Brad and I knew all too well he would not hesitate to carry through with them. The only consolation was that if we could substantiate some of our suspicions, that evidence, supported by the information we already possessed, could damn Bierce even in this Federalist community. But to substantiate them would be a task probably beyond our resources. This, too, we realized sadly. In fact, we arrived at my Uncle Tom's a thoroughly subdued pair.

When we told him of the encounter, his head thrust forward, a mannerism that usually indicated he was disturbed. "Now you two watch your step. I know from Ben Vail that both Bierce and Rudd are dangerous men. And there's no doubt that Bierce is a power in Portland."

"He's a Federalist I am not especially proud of," my Aunt Betsy said in an icy tone.

Eliza got up and poked the fire alive. My cousin might not be the prettiest girl in the world, but she was still what we call "good looking" in Maine. She was mischievous, and she was vital. She had hardly got the tongs around one chunk of wood before Brad jumped to his feet and took them from her. Instantly she relinquished the tongs as if they were far too heavy for her and collapsed on the floor as though in utter weakness. One of these days there'd be a marriage, and I saw Aunt Betsy eyeing the two of them.

The early fall chill in the air outside made that large front room seem especially snug with only the fragrant apple-wood fire for light and the shadows dim but huge. We were staying the night, and after a dinner of roast pork with lots of crackling, a plum duff to finish it off, and the pleasant taste of Madeira on our tongues, the war seemed far away. But it wasn't, and we couldn't forget it.

"Is Castine still a lovely village?" Aunt Betsy asked.

"Yes," I said, "probably even more so since you last saw it, though what will happen to it now is anyone's guess."

"I'm sure the British will treat it well," my uncle said, looking uneasily at his wife, "especially if they intend to stay there for a while. What concerns me is Ben Vail's health. I only hope his mother will be sensible enough to get medical assistance for him even if she has to go to the British for it."

"Wouldn't they put him in prison?" Eliza asked.

"A sick man?" Aunt Betsy asked. "What do you think the British are, barbarians?"

"Of course not, Mother!" Eliza said. "But look at how they looted

Hampden and burned ships there and at Bangor. They ruined the meetinghouse at Hampden and smashed the pulpit and all the pews. They even made poor General Blake come into Bangor and surrender and give his parole. Now I don't call all those carryings-on nice behavior."

"Part of it was perfectly within their rights as belligerents, Liza," Brad said gently. "Not the looting and the wanton destruction of the meetinghouse, but the ships were fair prey."

"And so was General Blake," I said. "I never saw anyone more stubborn —"

"Stupid, if you ask me," Brad cut in.

"But didn't he stand and fight?" Eliza asked. "If you ask me, I'd say he was a patriot."

"Oh, he meant well," Brad conceded, "but that wasn't enough. He wouldn't attack the British just when they landed, which is what Captain Morris wanted him to do, and he forgot or refused to have the militia dig in and throw up breastworks."

"And, worst of all," I added, "he brought those militia into battle without training and many of them with no muskets — some of those boys didn't even know how to shoot. No wonder they're hanging and burning him in effigy."

"But you can't say he wasn't brave!" Eliza insisted; and by the tremor in her voice I judged her close to tears. She always had a soft heart for the underdog.

"No, Liza," I said, "General Blake isn't a coward, and he isn't a traitor — that's so much reckless, unfair talk. No doubt, too, he is a well-meaning Christian gentleman and a success in civilian life. But at Hampden he was an inefficient, ignorant officer who did his country and the District of Maine a great deal of harm."

"I think you're blaming our people more than the British," Liza said. "After all, it was the British who started that fight. They invaded Maine."

Brad, after a nod of permission from Aunt Betsy, lighted one of his pale, tan cigars with his ignition box. As always, he turned the glowing end of the cigar around to see that it was evenly lighted. We watched him in silence as he blew a streamer of fragrant tobacco smoke toward the ceiling. The little ceremony over, he turned to

Eliza. "The point is, Liza, the British are making war against us and we are so divided we're not offering any resistance worth the name. We're practically inviting the British to come in because of our own impotence."

"Oh, come now!" Uncle Tom's voice had such a harsh edge to it everyone jumped. "Don't make us out worse than we are. As soon as they heard the British were in the Bay, all the Penobscot and Kennebec towns mustered their militia, even as we did here in Cape Elizabeth. General King of Bath ordered his troops to assemble at Wiscasset, and so did General Sewall of Augusta. I realize the banks at Bath and Wiscasset sent their specie inland and the Portland banks buried theirs and many families fled from the coast, but all that was to be expected. The fact is, we were ready to fight the British. We might have been beaten, but we weren't so spineless that we'd let an enemy take over our homes without a fight. And that goes for us Federalists as well as for you Republicans."

The smile on his face as he finished took the sting from his remarks, and Eliza's applauding from the floor and crying, "Hear, hear!" relieved the situation.

Brad grinned, too, but he couldn't resist saying, "And yet, sir, as a militia officer myself, I can't help but be shocked that out of a possible twelve thousand fighting men in the counties bordering the Penobscot just a few hundred turned out for the battle at Hampden."

"I'm not defending the poor show we made in numbers or the fight itself, but you must realize that British command of the sea permits them to land a force of redcoats that will be stronger at a given point than anything we can muster against them. After all, our men can't fly from town to town. They're earthbound, and the roads are in sad shape."

"What troubles me now," I said, "is where all this is going to end. They captured Machias and now Sir John Sherbrooke has declared all Maine east of the Penobscot annexed to Canada. What's to prevent him from taking the rest of Maine?"

"It's more thickly settled down this way," Brad said. "The British would have plenty of trouble."

[ 191 ]

"But if there are many who feel as Warren Bierce does, the British might not have as much trouble as we'd like to think."

"I think the solution is fairly obvious, whether you young gentlemen like it or not," Aunt Betsy said.

No one in the family could forget that she had been a Tory and was now a Federalist sympathizer. But unlike many in Maine who had become almost rabid in their support of one party or the other, Aunt Betsy was a fair-minded woman.

"There is only one course, as I see it, that both parties should now work for. That is peace."

"Peace!" I said.

"Yes, peace. The Federalists want peace because the war has never made sense to them. The Republicans should now want peace because the country threatens to fall apart. And if peace doesn't come soon, all of us in Maine may find ourselves British subjects again. Oh, I know our ships have won sea battles and victories on the lakes," she added, as I started to protest, "but what does it all mean? An American merchant ship can hardly move out of port before it is captured. Our frigates are blockaded in our port towns. The British practically own Chesapeake Bay, even if they were repulsed at Baltimore. And now they actually do own eastern Maine by right of conquest. I tell you, distasteful as it may seem to you young men, you should now work for peace."

No one spoke after she finished. Eliza, Brad, and I stared at her. Then Uncle Tom coughed over his pipe, or was it to cover up the chuckle that now began to shake him?

"Betsy," he said, fighting down his laughter, "you've saved me having to give the same little speech and not half as well. These young folks scare me sometimes, they know so much. But there are times when they need to hear a sober truth or two from an older person; after all, no one generation knows everything. Congratulations, my dear."

My dignified aunt inclined her head in acknowledgment, but I could almost have sworn I saw her also wink, ever so slightly, at her husband — or was it my imagination?

# THREE

## *The Conspiracy to Liberate Captain Vail*

[November, 1814]

# XIX

THAT fall of 1814 was a desperate time not only in Maine but along
the entire Atlantic seaboard, as news despatches revealed. With the
full power of England's navy, backed by Wellington's veterans, now
available, towns everywhere took alarm. Citizens of Philadelphia
and New York formed militia companies and rushed to finish the
extensive lines of fortifications they had begun in the summer when
news of the depredations of Admiral Cochrane and especially Admiral Cockburn in the Chesapeake reached them. Though the stout
defense of Baltimore was encouraging, the earlier rout of our troops
at Bladensburg and the burning of Washington in late August lingered painfully in people's minds. General Jackson was reported to
have stormed Pensacola down on the Gulf Coast, but rumors of a
huge British squadron waiting in the West Indies with thousands of
redcoats fresh from victorious fields in Spain and France were terrify-
ing. Now the British were said to be headed for New Orleans, and
now for New York — the former especially after Commodore Macdonough beat the British on Lake Champlain in a terrific battle on
September 11 and the British army then withdrew from its siege of
Plattsburg. Off Cape Cod, however, British frigates still hovered like
hawks, swooping on any sail they sighted, plundering property ashore,
and forcing towns like Wellfleet, Brewster, and Eastham to pay large
contributions to save some of their public works from destruction.
Except for the activities of our privateers, there was little evidence of
our ability to convince the British they were in a war at all. Instead,
the initiative was theirs and they weren't hesitant to seize and re-
tain it.

The actions of the British, particularly in seizing private property, disillusioned many of our New England Federalists. In fact the British annexation of Castine and eastern Maine gradually tended to rally people, whatever their politics, to the cause of defense. In Boston, hundreds of citizens, including many of the most prominent Federalist leaders, worked on the town's fortifications. We saw similar enthusiasm in the rush to join the existing militia companies in Portland and to create new ones. My Uncle Tom had been right on this count: Federalists would turn out as quickly as any Republican if the country were invaded. Besides, down here in Maine there had been so much resentment at Governor Strong for not supporting us with troops after the Castine affair that in many places Republican strength had actually grown greater than that of the Federalists owing to so many desertions from the Federalist Party.

At the same time the demand to end the war rose with every week. We knew Mr. Adams and his colleagues were conferring in Ghent with their British counterparts, but these negotiations were endless, and people were growing angry at the delay. Meanwhile another development occurred which indicated that the Federalists were going to take an important step with regard to the war. It was in early October and I was in the Marston Tavern after court had closed for the day when Brad walked in and laid a copy of the *Weekly Messenger* in front of me. This was a Boston Federalist paper but more popular in Portland than the *Yankee*, a Republican sheet in Boston.

"They've done it," he said, calling for a glass of ale. "They've voted for a convention — the General Court has, I mean."

"Now take it slowly," I said. "You know I've been so busy studying property law again with Mr. Longfellow that I can hardly keep up with our political happenings." For the time being Mr. Longfellow was in Boston with the General Court and I had scarcely seen him since I started reading with him again. But he had laid out a mass of reading for me and I was back with Sir Edward Coke in the seventeenth century. I knew that the governor's speech on the war situation, when the legislature opened on October 5, was turned over to a joint committee for study. Harrison Gray Otis was chairman. But, beyond that, I knew little that had occurred.

"It's all in here if you want to read it," Brad said, tapping the paper, "but here's a summary. The committee reported in three days — that must have required some doing, believe me. I'm sure

Otis must have written the report; he's the only leader of the Federalist pack who has enough energy for two men, with some left over. Besides, it sounds like him."

"What do you mean?"

"Listen to this." He picked up the paper. "One of the principal points of the report was the necessity of uniting to repel any invasion. But another point was the urgency — listen to this now — 'to hold up to view, on all occasions, the destructive policy by which a state of unparalleled national felicity has been converted into one of humiliation, of danger, and distress.' "

"But that's what the Federalists have been doing all along. There's nothing new there."

"Patience, my friend, just be patient. Listen again: the committee recommended that 'a conference should be invited between those states, the affinity of whose interest is closest.' "

"The idea of a conference isn't new."

"No, but this is an official recommendation. Of all the resolutions they suggested the fifth is the crucial one. They want twelve men to be appointed from Massachusetts to confer with other delegates from the New England states about the best means of defense and — here you are — 'to take measures, if they shall think proper, for procuring a convention of Delegates from all the United States, in order to revise the Constitution thereof, and more effectually to secure the support and attachment of all the people, by placing all upon the basis of fair representation.' "

This was a surprise! "So they really do want to change the Constitution — it's not been all talk."

"It has never been just all talk. The town resolutions all over New England this year have insisted that New England needs special consideration through amendments in order to guarantee her security. No, it's not been all talk, and it certainly isn't now. The General Court accepted that fifth resolution. The Senate voted twenty-two to twelve on October 12, and the House of Representatives voted two hundred and sixty to ninety on October 16."

"How did the Maine District vote in the House?"

"There were thirty-four yeas and twenty-three nays, which was fairly close."

"Any more of these harbingers of good will for the Union?"

"Yes. On the seventeenth, Governor Strong was authorized to send the committee report and the resolutions to the New England governors, as well as an invitation to attend a convention. Then, the very next day, the General Court hammered the nail in."

"What do you mean?"

"Federalists from both the Senate and the House met and elected the twelve delegates to represent Massachusetts at a convention at Hartford on December 15."

"They really mean business, don't they?"

"They certainly do. And, Jonathan, I've more news for you." He studied me carefully over his own glass of ale. "Mr. Longfellow and Sam Wilde of Hallowell, who used to be on the Governor's Council, were among the twelve elected."

"Mr. Longfellow! I've always known he was a strong Federalist but not that strong."

"Well, you know now. And, if you should ask me, I'd say your legal studies are going to get short shrift until after that Hartford Convention."

I thought so, too, but that didn't disturb me so much as the talk from some Republican quarters that to hold the Convention was an act of treason. In fact, a number of Federalists, including my Uncle Tom, disapproved of it, particularly with the country going through such troubled times. Uncle Tom insisted that, whatever Otis might say about contriving the best means to protect New England from invasion by the British, and from the military and taxing policies of the national government, people would believe the Convention a seditious gathering interested in abetting the secession of New England from the Union.

"It would take New England a long time to live down that reputation, whether it was deserved or not," he said. "And it's likely to ruin the careers of many of the men who attend it as delegates."

While support for the Convention was strong in most Federalist quarters, local Republicans were loud in their denunciation of it. Our two Republican papers in Portland friendly to the administration, Francis Douglass's *Eastern Argus* and Jedediah Daniels's *Eastern Courier*, regarded the Convention as treasonable; Daniels was particularly critical.

[ 198 ]

My own parents disliked the summoning of the Convention, but my mother felt that someone should speak out against the proposed militia law of the Secretary of War, Mr. Monroe, which had been amended by a bill introduced by Senator Giles of Virginia. This was a very complicated and controversial piece of legislation bitterly resented by the states for numerous reasons but by my mother for the specific reason that men from eighteen to fifty could be subject to a draft and taken into the regular army.

"This is a dreadful measure!" she said at breakfast one morning. "If the Convention is to do anything worthwhile, it might protest this proposal."

"I know you as a peace lover would object to it as a war measure," I said, "but otherwise, why get so excited? Shouldn't all of us be liable to serve our country in an emergency?"

"Not at the youthful age of eighteen!" And my mother might have been spitting fire.

"But eighteen is a responsible age."

"Perhaps, but still young. Parents have a responsibility for the care and control of their children until they are twenty-one. To give the government power to draft boys of eighteen would break up the family and endanger the moral character and welfare of the boys themselves. Just think, they would be exposed to the contaminating influence of the regular army!"

Actually I knew little about our regular army. I had seen troops at the local forts before the war, of course, and, more recently, the regulars under Lieutenant Lewis. No one who wanted to amount to anything went into the army in peacetime. On the other hand, with a war on, so many thousands would be brought into service, and had been already, that I couldn't see that the new army as contemplated would be very different from the kind of society we had at any time. But to argue with my mother where she could identify herself with a moral issue was a futile undertaking. I told her I didn't think the situation was as serious as she thought, but I agreed with her that the Convention could do worse than to consider Mr. Monroe's proposals.

I didn't tell her that I thought one of the strongest objections to the bill was that a number of the states felt the government in Washington was undercutting their own rights. According to the laws of these states, parents were entitled to the obedience and services of their children until they were twenty-one and the children to the support and protection of their parents. The family was endangered, to be sure, but for many families there would probably be less concern about jeopardy to the moral character of boys than of the families themselves being deprived of the boys' services for three more years and employers finding that apprentice contracts were broken.

Something else happened that fall that angered many of us in western Maine, though it was also clear that others were not disturbed at all. I learned of it in a somewhat peculiar way. I had returned some law books to Mr. Longfellow's home after supper one evening, and Zilpah, his wife — always pleasant but always ailing, or so it seemed — let me take several more. We talked briefly about her husband's activity in the General Court, then hearing her children squalling, I thanked her and left.

The streets were very dark, the only light being from the lamps and candles in the houses. The air was crisp, the scattering of dead leaves — long fallen — crisp and crackling under foot, and the wood smoke from the numerous fireplaces wonderfully fragrant. I strode along feeling better than at any time since I had returned from the Penobscot.

I don't know just when or how I sensed that I was being followed. It wasn't a pleasant feeling, and I thought at once of when Brad and I were returning to our hotel in Bordeaux. Could this be Bierce again? I stopped under a tree. Though its leaves were gone, its trunk was large, and I stepped close to it. I peered around me but saw nothing. I heard nothing, either, except some leaves being blown along the street by the night wind.

Then came footsteps, crunching along the graveled walk, steps measured and slow, yet not stealthy. So with a backward glance and still seeing nothing, I started again for home. Nothing happened. But I had hardly deposited the books in my bedroom and joined my parents in the study when the door knocker tapped.

For a moment when I opened the door, I could see nothing except the outline of a huge man. Then as I peered at him, I realized he was not a white man.

"Philip Adair!" I said. "Come in, come in!" I shook his hand and led him, protesting, into the study.

My parents were graciousness itself, though my mother's eyes widened. I truly believe she had never had a colored person inside her house before. She looked even more startled when he began to speak, while my father's eyes lighted up. Even I had forgotten Philip's almost flawless English delivered in a deep but soft voice. His manner was, as usual, courteous but not deferential, dignified but not stiff.

"Philip," I said, "you must have been the person I heard behind me when I was on my way home from Mr. Longfellow's."

"That may be, Mr. Dearborn. I did see someone ahead of me but too far distant to distinguish his features. Then he seemed to disappear in the darkness."

"That must have been when I turned into our gate," I said. "Well, you gave me a start, I can tell you. For a few moments I wondered if you were Warren Bierce or Jake Rudd, though I couldn't see any reason for their trying again what they did in Bordeaux."

"I do not wish to alarm you, but, if I were you and Mr. Pettigrew, I should always keep a wary eye on both those men."

"Philip has good reason for distrusting Rudd," I explained to my parents, and let it go at that. This was no time to tell them of Philip's life. "Now what can I do for you, Philip?" I asked.

"I am greatly worried about Captain Vail," he said. "As you may know, the *Argus* has been off on a cruise ever since you and Mr. Pettigrew took Captain Vail to Castine. We returned at once to Portland and Lester Jordan received a certificate as master from the syndicate owning the *Argus*. After we replenished our ammunition and made our repairs, we put to sea without any delay. If the next British move was to take Portland, we wanted to be well at sea. We left the day before you returned and came in only a few hours ago."

"But if you have just come into port, how did you know when I returned?"

He smiled. "I had supper with Mr. Pettigrew, and he directed me here."

"Mr. Adair," my father said, "if there is something you would like to talk with my son about in private —"

Philip, for the first time, seemed to fumble for words. Then, as he was obviously puzzled as to what to say, my mother stood up.

"Mr. Adair, my husband is right. I think we should leave you and Jonathan alone. Come, Gerald."

But Adair was also on his feet in a swift, catlike movement, which left me no option but to stand up, too.

"Please, I beg of you, sit down and listen." Philip raised his hands almost entreatingly. "It is important."

"But I don't understand, Mr. Adair," my mother said sitting down. "We thought that you would prefer to be alone with Jonathan."

"Madame, what I have to say may save your son an explanation that will be difficult for him to make, if I have judged him correctly and his fondness for both you and your husband."

"Well, in that case, pray proceed, Mr. Adair."

"Philip," I said, with, I fear, a trace of annoyance at all the mystery, "you certainly have me puzzled, and I frankly don't know if you are doing me a favor or not."

"Seh, let me explain."

He folded his hands in his lap and leaned forward in his chair.

Looking at me, he said, "Captain Vail may be in great danger at Castine, seh."

"You mean he's dying?"

The words were wrenched out of me in a kind of gasp. I hadn't realized how truly fond I had become of "Little Ben."

"Why, Jonathan," my mother said, "you didn't tell us Captain Vail's injury was that serious!"

"Please!"

Philip's hands again came up, but his voice was so sharp we stared at him.

"Captain Vail is still not a well man, but that is not all the trouble. He has been thrown into prison at Fort George."

"What!"

"He has been declared a dangerous enemy and may soon be sent to Dartmoor."

"Then someone betrayed him!" I said.

"Of course. But it wasn't anyone at Castine."

"But it would have to be!"

[ 202 ]

Philip shook his head. "Mr. Dearborn, every since you and Mr. Pettigrew took Captain Vail home I have been concerned about him. He was good to me at a time in my life when I needed help, and I have never forgotten his kindness. Yesterday on our way here we stopped a fisherman off Thomaston for news. He was from Camden himself, but he had heard about Captain Vail's imprisonment from men who traded with the British at Castine. They said the word was passed to the British by someone down this way. A committee of the townspeople went to General Gosselin, the British commander, to try to get Captain Vail released because of his condition, but the General refused."

"But what a dreadful thing to do — to betray him!" my mother exclaimed.

"Do you mean to imply it was a fellow American who gave him away?" my father asked.

"I only know what we were told," Philip said. "At the same time I am prepared to believe it, and it wouldn't surprise me if Mr. Jonathan here doesn't know as well as I do the man who was responsible."

"You mean Bierce?"

But as Philip nodded and said, "Bierce or Rudd," I said, "We're only guessing, of course, Philip. We really don't know."

"That is true, but Castine has become a busy center for trade, and the British have reopened the customs house there."

"This I had heard," I said, "and Bierce and Rudd may be trading there, but that doesn't prove they betrayed Captain Vail."

"Oh, Jonathan, don't go 'legal' on us!" my mother exclaimed. "What is important is that Captain Vail is ill and may die if he is sent to England."

"Yes, that's a ghastly prospect," my father said, "but I don't know what can be done about it. I admired Captain Vail's honesty and forthrightness and compassion when he called on us after he returned from Europe without you, Jonathan."

"Gerald," my mother said brightly, "I have an idea. Why don't you go to that British general and ask him to release Captain Vail in your custody?"

"Why, my dear, I think you may have something there. Mr.

[ 203 ]

Adair," — my father sat upright in his chair, his eyes glowing — "why don't I go to Castine at once?"

"Seh, that is very kind of you — and of Mrs. Dearborn," Philip said. "But there was a minister on that committee, so I heard, who asked the same thing, and the General still refused."

"Are you sure?"

"No, seh, I am not sure. But if it was someone from Portland who betrayed Captain Vail, he would certainly not want General Gosselin to release him. In short, he must be afraid that Captain Vail knows something about him that he doesn't want revealed."

"So do I, for that matter," I said.

"But nothing you can prove, so I understand, seh. Captain Vail must have made an official report of the *Ghost*'s presence in England. No doubt the despatches taken from you in Bordeaux revealed this. Oh, there is reason enough for Rudd — and Bierce, of course — to want Captain Vail out of the country. But one doesn't have to contrive reasons, seh, so far as either is concerned. Hatred and fear and spite are enough."

"I gather you have some plan to rescue Captain Vail, Philip, and it must involve me since you're trying to save me having to explain all this to my parents."

I said this as calmly as I could for the sake of my parents who had now become very quiet, but inwardly I was all excitement.

"Yes, seh. I suggest that you and Mr. Pettigrew and I go to the Penobscot and find some way to get Captain Vail out of Castine."

It didn't surprise me. He had talked with Brad at supper, he had said earlier, and now he had talked with me. But to pluck Vail out of a British military prison would be no picnic. It would probably take some money, too, and some of the prize money due me had not come through. What I had I would surely be happy to use, and Brad and perhaps even the officers on the *Argus* would be ready with funds. More than money, however, would be required. It would take skill and nerve and perhaps, at some point, force. And we would have to act quickly.

"I would go by myself," Philip said, "but a black man on his own couldn't do very much. He would have to be someone's servant."

"I still think I should go to Castine," my father said, glancing at my mother whose face, as well as his own, was white and anxious. "Whatever plan you three men contrive will be dangerous for all of you, as well as for Captain Vail."

"Thank you," Philip said gently, "but, if you will pardon me, seh, I think your going would be useless and would only waste time. Captain Vail may be sent to England any day now."

I rose to my feet. "Philip, I will go."

He bowed his head. "Thank you, seh, thank you."

"What did my friend Pettigrew say?"

"He will go, too. He suggested we meet at his house tomorrow morning at eight o'clock to make our plans. He thinks we might be on our way by noon."

"So soon?" my mother gasped.

"My dear," said my father, "if a man's life is at stake, no time is too soon to try to save him." Then, walking to Philip, he put out his hand. "I think you are a good man, Mr. Adair. I still prefer my plan, but Mrs. Dearborn and I will pray for the success of yours."

---

# XX

IT was the third day of our ride to Camden. My Uncle Tom Dearborn had once said that if there was one animal in the world he hated, it was a horse. I don't feel that strongly, but as one who hasn't done much riding, I didn't find horseback the most comfortable method of transportation, and said so.

"If you're going to be a lawyer, you'd better get used to riding a horse," Brad laughed. "The strain of preparing a brief for a distant court isn't always on one's brains. Besides, it will be years before we have decent turnpikes."

"The only thing that keeps me going now is to watch Philip. He looks as if he feels the way I do."

Philip grinned, a rare gesture for him. "To think that some people ride for pure enjoyment!"

"Well, we're close to Camden now, so cheer up," and Brad couldn't resist cantering away from us just to show off. Then, seeing farther around the curve in the narrow, rutted road than we could, he rode swiftly back to us.

"I don't know what it's all about," he said, "but there are wagons coming down this road and coming fast, with outriders, too."

Instinctively we drew together and loaded our pistols. One never knows what to expect along these lonely Maine trails that pass for roads.

Then the wagons creaked and groaned into sight, the horses straining hard to the cracking of bull whips and some of the most fervent cursing I'd heard since leaving the *Argus*.

Seeing us, one of the guards rode up to us and told us we'd better get off to the side or we'd be run over. "Got to get these wagons a long way from Camden by nightfall," he explained.

Then he was gone, and a whole convoy of wagons of assorted sizes and shapes passed us. Two men riding as a rearguard waved in a friendly manner, so we rode up to them and I asked them what it was all about.

"This is the British *Mary*'s cargo," a black-bearded man said. "Noah Miller of Belfast boarded the *Mary* coming into Castine this morning. He didn't have no authority, so it was piracy. When he brought the *Mary* into Camden, old Hook, the Collector, declared the cargo U.S. property and shipped it out of Camden as fast as he could. It's all dry goods and all in these wagons an' worth forty thousand dollars, they say. We're bonded to deliver it in Portland."

"But why the hurry?"

He grinned, his black beard making his lips very red indeed. "Well, friend, the *Mary* happened to be part of a British convoy, so it's likely them warships over in Castine are goin' to pay Camden a visit. Town's so scared some of the people are gettin' out. If you're goin' there, mister, you'd better think twice. Me, I'm glad I'm headin' away from the old Penobscot."

We watched them out of sight and then rode on, more slowly now. With all this happening we might be running into developments that would complicate our task.

Before long we passed refugees, both individuals and families. Many looked terrified, and few wanted to talk. I thought this evidence of panic surprising, but when I recalled what some of our

[ 206 ]

towns in Maine like Hampden, Bangor, Frankfort, and Buckstown had experienced and those on Chesapeake Bay as well, especially Havre de Grace, where the enemy, out of control, looted and burned and raped and killed, I didn't blame these people. I could only hope that the militia might turn out more quickly and in greater numbers than at Hampden, and might fight harder, if it came to that.

When we entered Camden, darkness had fallen, militiamen were swarming through the streets, and their officers were drinking freely in the taproom of John Eager's inn where we put up for the night. We had already adopted the roles we intended to play at Castine: I, William Adams, a Portland merchant; Brad, Sylvester Eustis, my lawyer; and Philip, Ben Jones, my servant. Mrs. Eager, a sharp-featured little woman with a voice like a bluejay, was nothing if not competent.

She said, "I've three rooms left. I'd take the corner room with two windows if I was you. It costs more, but it's sunnier. Your servant can sleep in the attic with the help."

"I'm surprised, Madam," Brad said in his ingratiating way, "that an inn as clean and obviously well run as yours has three rooms to rent with all these militia officers around."

"Oh, them!" she sniffed. "They'll go home to sleep, most of 'em anyway. And some of my lodgers have skedaddled out of town, scared to death of what the British may do about Noah Miller's piracy. If my John wasn't up to Bangor, he'd have said 'Good riddance to bad rubbish!' Now, you gentlemen ready to sign?"

I had hoped to talk with John Eager about our plan. Like his wife he enjoyed a reputation for being a strong patriot. As an innkeeper he would have known someone who could have helped us with arrangements we had to make. So, with Eager away, I turned to Josiah Hook, the United States Collector of the Penobscot District. He had fled Castine with the customs house records when the British arrived, and at the moment he was the object of both praise and criticism for having confiscated the sloop *Mary*'s cargo. He had also issued a revenue commission to Noah Miller, predating it fifteen days. But no one seemed to think this act would deceive or dissuade the British from action. I called at his house the next morning, but several prominent Camden citizens were already there, and by the sound of their voices, they were in angry argument. Brad and I therefore decided to walk around the town.

It was clear that Camden was highly apprehensive over the possible British reaction. Groups of citizens stood around talking, though the air was quite sharp. Frequently we saw people glance up at Mount Battie, towering over the town. On the summit of the high, rounded hill was a flagstaff and a small battery manned by militia. No flag was flying at the moment, but if the watchers on Battie detected any movement of ships from Castine toward Camden, they were to hoist the national ensign. Meanwhile carts and carriages loaded with people and household goods were steadily moving inland.

Unsuccessful in a second attempt to see Hook, we watched the militia drill, then drifted back to the inn. Mrs. Eager was supervising the table settings, while from the kitchen came some wonderful aromas, especially that of bread baking. When I turned from warming my hands at the fireplace, complimented her on the quality of the breakfast we had had, and remarked that I was looking forward to dinner, she thanked me and said she enjoyed cooking for men; they were more appreciative than women and didn't "pick" at their food.

"But shouldn't you be leaving Camden along with the others?" Brad asked.

She looked at us, hands on her hips. "If you mean, am I afraid of the British? the answer is no. If they come here, I'll feed 'em, of course, and then maybe they'll leave this house alone — maybe. But you learn to take nothing for granted running an inn."

"I suppose you people have half expected the British here ever since they took Castine," I said.

"Yes, we have. And we might still have escaped if Major Miller hadn't turned pirate."

"I still don't see how he managed to cut that sloop out of the convoy."

"It was simple, Mr. Adams. There was a fog, and instead of following the convoy east of Long Island, the *Mary* went up the west side. Miller caught her off Turtle Head on the north end of the island."

"Did he bring her here directly?"

"No, he went to Northport where he put the supercargo and a

[ 208 ]

King's agent ashore — the supercargo had offered to ransom the sloop, but Miller wouldn't agree. The supercargo and the agent were supposed to rejoin Miller at Lincolnville, but it seems they hired someone to get 'em over to Castine. That's how the British know what happened."

"Then Miller came here?"

"No, he went to Duck Trap and talked with Major Ulmer, a deputy inspector for the customs there. Ulmer claimed the *Mary* for the U.S. government, and he was the one who then brought her into Camden."

"What about Miller?"

"Miller came walking into Camden. Strikes me funny, somehow," and she laughed, a shrill, high laugh.

"Then Mr. Hook went to work."

"Yes, an' Mr. Hook didn't waste no time. They got the *Mary*'s cargo loaded onto wagons an' off to Portland in four hours; then Hook sent men to hide the sloop somewhere up the St. Georges River. I don't hold with the British but if you ask me, the whole thing smells."

"You wouldn't be willing to surrender the *Mary* and her cargo to the British, would you?" I asked.

"Now? Why, it would be impossible. The cargo is miles away by this time, and likely not all of it will be sold in Portland. No, I'd stand up to the British just as our militia here in Camden intend to, but I could think of better causes to suffer for. Now if you gentlemen will excuse me, I've got to get dinner on the table."

While she went about her chores, Brad and I walked down in back to see if we could find Philip. A stableboy told us he had gone to the waterfront, so we went back to join the men, most of them militia officers, already gathering in Mrs. Eager's front room. When Mrs. Eager called us to a dinner of pea soup, baked ham and cabbage, I found myself sitting next to a tanned, vigorous militia colonel.

"My name's Foote, Erastus Foote," he said in a voice that revealed a training and modulation not acquired solely by barking orders at militia units.

When I introduced myself and Brad as from Portland, he shook his head and laughed. "If you're interested in trading, you should have stayed in Portland until the *Mary*'s cargo arrived. The women of Portland will have the best chance in years at laces, silks, shawls, and the good Lord knows what!"

"But isn't there already a considerable trade between Castine and the Kennebec towns?" Brad asked.

"Yes," he said with a grimace. "There's a lively trade between Castine and the Kennebec towns and a stage runs every day between Hallowell on the Kennebec and Castine. But there's even more between Castine and our own Penobscot towns."

"Isn't a lot of it smuggling?" I asked.

He shrugged. "Some of it is, of course, but it doesn't need to be, at least not until the river freezes. You see, Washington has ruled that neutral vessels and cargoes may come from any of the British dominions to any port of the United States. That's why Josiah Hook is opening up another customs house at Hampden and Peleg Tolman of Bath is accredited as Swedish consul. There are several Swedish ships right now at Castine. But when the freeze takes over and vessels can't move, then just you watch the smuggling across the ice at night!"

"Patriotism doesn't seem to stand in the way of business," Brad said.

Foote looked at him for a moment, then said, "Trading may be one way to convince the British there is no need to annex the territory on this side of the Penobscot, Mr. Eustis. Mind you, I don't hold with enriching the British customs, but neither do I wish to see this bank of the river become British."

"Isn't it possible Major Miller's action will encourage the British to annex it?" Brad asked.

"Unfortunately, yes. But the British won't have as easy a time here as they did upriver in September, no, sir! Our militia have been training!"

After having observed how the militia had broken at Hampden, I wondered how much longer the militia here, notwithstanding their training, would stand against an attack by Wellington's veterans. But I had no time to say anything, if indeed I would have done so, before shouts broke out in the street and a militia sergeant burst into the inn, throwing the door back with a crash that shook the house.

"Colonel Foote, they've raised a signal flag on Mount Battie!"

To a man we jumped to our feet. With a quick bow to us, Foote left, the others trooping at his heels.

Mrs. Eager had flown into the dining room at the shout and watched her guests running down the graveled walk. "Well, I never!" she exclaimed, and shaking her head, she and the waitress started to clear off the table.

Brad and I eased ourselves out as soon as we could without seeming to be in a hurry. We actually felt guilty at leaving the dinner only half eaten.

Once outside and down the street, we had to keep close to the houses as wagons thundered by, horses looking wild-eyed as their drivers whipped and swore at them.

"Is this how Camden meets the British?" Brad asked.

"The test will come when they land, if they do. Let's go down and find out what's happening."

At the waterfront a large group of people were clustered about Colonel Foote, Selectman Robert Chase, and the biggest businessman in town, Benjamin Cushing, a shipbuilder. Everyone seemed to be waiting.

"What's the latest?" I asked a militia officer.

"Frigate headed this way from Castine." He spat. "Damn Noah Miller!"

Between the creaking, rushing wagons along the main street and the excited chatter of the crowd on the wharf, the Camden waterfront was a noisy place. But as the last of the wagons disappeared in a cloud of dust people began to lower their voices. Finally, as the powerful frigate hove in sight and anchored off the ledges beyond the harbor entrance, the talk died like the flame on a torch thrown into the water. As she lowered a barge, which approached the entrance under a white flag, the selectman, Robert Chase, turned to Colonel Foote.

"Well, Colonel," he said, his voice quiet but carrying clearly, "let's you and I go out to meet them."

"I suppose we'd better," Foote grunted. "Look here, Jess," he said to a fisherman near him, "you'll take us out in your boat, won't you?"

"Guess it won't kill me — I hope," the man replied, and went down to the slip where his boat was tied up.

"That's Jess Moore," the militia officer beside me said. "Jess ain't afraid of anyone."

But Moore soon had more passengers than he'd agreed to, including the customs collector at Waldoboro, Joseph Farley, and a Lieutenant Russ of the militia. We watched in silence as the big fisherman rowed down toward the barge where Chase and Foote parleyed with a Lieutenant Sandon from the frigate *Furieuse*. Soon the boat came back up the harbor and the barge returned to the man-of-war.

"What's the word?" someone sang out as Moore brought his boat alongside the slip and held it steady while his passengers stepped ashore.

But Chase said nothing until he joined the crowd. He and Foote looked so serious I thought surely that Camden's hour had come.

"Gentlemen, we've got to have a town meeting right away," Chase said.

"Let's have it right here," the officer beside me shouted.

Chase shook his head. "We'll do this proper. We'll go to the meetinghouse, and I want that bell rung so everyone'll know we're holding a meeting."

Although there was some grumbling, the crowd followed Chase and Foote up the hill. Soon the clanging of the bell brought more people — actually the sound was more like tolling, and it was in something of that mournful, apprehensive mood that people crowded into the seats while Chase mounted to the pulpit.

It was an angry meeting. When Chase announced that the British demanded the *Mary* or eighty thousand dollars and would destroy Camden and Lincolnville unless the citizens of Camden complied, the meeting broke into an uproar in which shouts of "Damn Miller!" almost equaled in intensity those of "Damn the British!" In fact, a ship captain named John Pendleton favored paying the sum, but at once he was challenged by one Oakes Perry who said that all the houses the British might destroy weren't worth eighty thousand! The session now broke into such a fury of conflicting opinions that only after furious gaveling was Chase able to bring the meeting to order.

Yet when he asked if they wanted to give in to the British demand, the "No!" from the floor was like a cannon blast that must almost have been heard aboard the enemy frigate. Chase and Foote were then elected by the citizens to explain to the frigate's captain why the town could not surrender the *Mary* and her cargo.

But the master of the 38-gun *Furieuse* lived up to his ship's name. His terms still held. He would allow the town three days, however, to decide how it could meet his demands provided two prominent citizens came aboard the frigate as soon as possible and remained there during the grace period.

Back went the town into meeting and reluctantly agreed to designate as hostages Selectman Chase and businessman Benjamin Cushing. Jess Moore rowed them out that evening at nine o'clock, and as he cast off and headed toward the frigate's lights, an audible sigh went up from the crowd huddled on the dark pier.

"We'll never be able to raise eighty thousand dollars," a man groaned.

"And we won't try," Colonel Erastus Foote rasped. "Chase and Cushing know that, too."

"But what can you do, sir?" Brad asked.

"What can we do? I'll tell you what we can and will do. We'll fill this town with militia, and then let the British try to land! If they stand offshore and shell this town, we'll drop round shot on their decks from the battery on Mount Battie."

"Are you sure the boys up on Battie can really shoot their guns?" some skeptic asked.

Foote turned toward him. "Sure? Of course, I'm sure! Now all you people go home. We're going to come out of this situation all right, just you wait and see."

"I think he really believes it," Brad said to me as we walked up to Eager's inn.

"Well, who can tell yet?" I said. "Maybe he'll convince the British as well as our people here. But what troubles me is how we can slip over to Castine with that frigate lying offshore and watching the river bank for miles. It looks to me as though we'd better go up toward Belfast and try our luck there."

"You may be right," Brad said, "but it's too late tonight to do anything more than sleep on it. Wonder where Philip's been all day."

"Well, you can bet he hasn't been just letting the time go by."

I felt guilty — at our neglecting Philip and especially at not having made arrangements to get to Castine. That frigate had certainly messed up our plans, and I began to share the sentiments of those citizens of Camden who had shouted in town meeting, "Damn Noah Miller!"

---

# XXI

"Beg pardon, could I speak with you and Mr. Pettigrew?"

We had just stepped outside the inn after breakfast when Philip joined us.

"Well, Philip," and Brad smiled, "how do you like Camden? Didn't I see a colored girl in Mrs. Eager's kitchen?"

But Philip didn't return the smile. "Yes, sir, and she is still a nice girl," he said firmly. "May we walk down to the waterfront? There are others down there so it won't seem strange if we go there, too. Then we can talk."

Brad cocked an eyebrow at me, and I nodded. "Of course, Philip," I said.

When we arrived at the pier, Philip said that our problem was solved, though we'd have to wait for two more days, in fact until the *Furieuse* was gone.

His assurance annoyed me, as occasionally it had before. "Please explain, Philip," I said, rather curtly, I fear, and regretted it at once.

"Last night," he said, looking at me with a kind of hound-dog sadness, "I visited Jess Moore after he returned from rowing Mr. Chase and Mr. Cushing to the *Furieuse*."

"You're way ahead of us, Philip," Brad said. "That was what I was going to propose we do this morning."

"I didn't feel that my concern for Captain Vail would let me wait any longer."

The sadness in his eyes was reproachful, and half in annoyance I gazed at the frigate. She looked solid and competent, altogether too powerful for this little town, however spirited it was.

"What did you find out?" I asked.

"Moore will take us to Castine."

"When?"

"As soon as the *Furieuse* departs."

"Damn it, that may be forever"; and now I stared in anger at the bulldog out beyond the bar.

"Moore thinks she will leave on Saturday or Sunday. He says the town won't give the British a penny and if the militia keep coming in, Captain Mouncey of the *Furieuse* won't dare risk his marines and seamen ashore. He may set the town on fire with hotshot, but he will not land. After that, he will take Chase and Cushing back to Castine as a pledge of Camden's good behavior."

"Your man Moore is quite a prophet," Brad laughed.

"My man Moore, as you say, Mr. Pettigrew, is also a smuggler by night, and he will take us to Castine the night after the *Furieuse* leaves."

"I hope you didn't tell Moore anything more than you had to," I said.

Philip dug his hands into the pockets of his greatcoat and hunched against the wind. "I found Moore's house yesterday afternoon. As soon as I heard him agree to take Mr. Chase and Colonel Foote to confer with the British and saw the shrewd but daring kind of man he is, I thought sure we could do business with him. At once I inquired where he lived. It's barely more than a fishing shanty. His wife is dead, his son is grown up, and he lives there alone. An independent, difficult man. He hates the British, but he's greedy — I suppose that's why he smuggles. I've heard two or three say he has money to burn, though you would never know it from where he lives. I told him you were businessmen interested in buying European cloth, and he will see you Saturday night — day after tomorrow."

It was a long speech for Philip, but just another indication of how much he thought of Captain Vail. He was indeed, as Brad had said, way ahead of both of us.

Meanwhile the town continued to fill up with militia from the surrounding communities. Colonel Foote ordered up all companies of his 5th Regiment, belonging to the 2nd Brigade of the 11th Division. He also sent for assistance to Colonel Samuel Thatcher of Warren, who ordered a battalion to Camden under Major Isaac Reed of Waldoboro. Reed's command embraced companies from Warren, Union, Waldoboro, and Friendship. Troops from Belfast likewise arrived but not under their commander, Major Noah Miller. The major wouldn't have been popular in Camden at this time; besides, the British had offered a reward for his capture, and evidently there were enough men in the vicinity who could have used the money and who hated him badly enough for Miller to decide he'd best make himself scarce.

Except for a few militia officers Brad and I were the only guests remaining with the Eagers. When I mentioned at noontime that we were going downtown to watch Colonel Foote's regiment parade, Mrs. Eager laughed and said, "If you see the Warren company coming in, look sharp for Sam Thatcher."

"How will we know who he is?" I asked.

"You can't miss him. He'll be the only colonel besides Erastus Foote. But all you really have to do is to look for a man who sits and walks so straight he seems to be leaning backward."

"A good soldier?" Brad asked.

She shrugged. "I couldn't rightly tell. But he's a good lawyer — everyone will tell you that, includin' Sam himself. There's no love lost between him and Rastus Foote."

"Rival lawyers?" Brad asked, his eyes twinkling.

"Yes, an' they're both politicians, too. Foote's even a senator in the legislature. But it was over some court case they got to quarrelin', an' then they started after each other with their canes."

"Who won?" Brad asked.

She threw up her hands. "Wa'n't much to choose. Maybe Foote. He seemed to hit a little harder. Now wouldn't you think that two grown men, educated at that, would act better'n a couple of wild boys?"

"Mrs. Eager," said Brad, looking gravely at the bright-eyed little woman, "never expect anything but the worst from lawyers. They are as vain as soldiers, as greedy as merchants, as full of talk as actors, and as suspicious — and rightfully so — as innkeepers!"

[ 216 ]

"Oh, Mr. Eustis!" she exclaimed. "Lawyers can't be that bad!"
Then she clapped her hands to her mouth. "Dear, dear, how tactless
I am, you bein' a lawyer, too!"

"That is why I spoke as I did," he said, and laughed heartily.

What people remained in the town — and Camden was nearly
evacuated by this time — gathered to watch Major Reed's battalion
march in. In courtesy, and I suspect to impress the British with the
sound of his massed drums, Colonel Foote paraded his regiment to
receive the newcomers. Had there been any regulars present, they
would probably have scoffed at the variety of militia uniforms, from
handsome white pants and befrogged blue jackets to a simple scarlet
feather stuck in a cap. Hundreds of militiamen streamed by, but by
the pounding of their drums Captain Mouncey of the *Furieuse* must
have thought there were thousands present.

As the Warren company approached, a tall, haughty-looking man
on a handsome white stallion rode in front. Though the animal was
skittish, the officer kept him firmly in hand. No one could doubt the
officer's identity after Mrs. Eager's description. This was the proud
Colonel Thatcher.

When he drew near the spot where Colonel Foote held position
with his mounted staff, Foote turned to his officers and, in a sarcastic
voice that carried over the drums, said, "Now, prepare for the worst,
for here comes Death riding upon his pale horse!"

I couldn't be sure that Thatcher heard him, but his white horse
must have. At any rate, as Thatcher passed Foote, the animal became
noisily flatulent and couldn't stop his volleying.

Foote's face seemed to freeze in shock, while Thatcher's grew pink
with embarrassment.

Then it happened: the militia — both officers and men — and the
few civilian spectators burst into a roar of laughter. I'll never forget
that scene: the flatulent horse, the indignant and mortified colonels,
and the guffawing militia. If the captain of the *Furieuse* heard that
laughter as well as the drums, he must surely have wondered what
kind of enemy awaited him if he tried to put his marines and bluejackets ashore.

Fear that he might really be considering a landing swept the town
the next day and the troops were kept under arms and ready. In case

the British should try to land, Captain Calvin Curtis went up to the battery on Mount Battie to check on the guard there and the guns. To the alarm and anger of the troops in the town when they found out, he discovered all the artillerymen gone off to a husking bee except the corporal and he was asleep!

The fear of a landing was very strong on Saturday, and was increased by the visit of Squire Dorithy of Sedgewick to Camden. He came in his capacity as a justice of the peace, and the *Furieuse's* barge stopped his little boat and brought him before Captain Mouncey. The Englishman agreed to let him enter the harbor provided that he would report the condition of the town and the number of troops assembled there. Dorithy attended to his legal business, then called on the military leaders before returning.

"We gave him a good story to tell Mouncey," Colonel Foote laughed that dinner time. "And it wasn't a lie, either. Told him to tell the British the roads were filled with troops, the meetinghouse was overflowing, men were already pouring in from the back country and others were assembling in the inland towns to march whenever the guns up on Battie were fired to warn them the British were coming."

"Where's the lie, Colonel?" Mrs. Eager asked. "Ain't all that true?"

"Well," and the Colonel grinned, "we've got troops at a number of points, but we haven't as many on hand as we'd like the British to think. Anyway, we instructed Dorithy to make the story impressive and he will, I'm sure — in fact, he helped concoct it."

That afternoon, with the grace period expiring, rumors swept the town persistently that the British were going to land. Colonel Foote was constantly in the saddle checking on the defenses at Eaton's Point, Jacob's Point, and other areas. Before long, however, the belief became more prevalent that the British would bombard the town rather than attempt a launching, so many of the militia were organized into fire brigades. When darkness came on, and the *Furieuse* remained at her mooring, the tension subsided a little, but only a little. People realized that the next day, the Sabbath, must surely bring the crisis.

But for Brad, Philip and myself that Saturday night became even more exciting and important because of our appointment at Jess

Moore's house. Hardly larger than a corn crib, it was so close to the riverbank it practically overhung the water. Near it fish nets were drying over wooden racks. A light shone dimly through a curtained window. After I knocked at the door, Moore opened it, holding a perforated lantern high to see who we were.

"Mr. Moore," I said, "I'm William Adams from Portland, and this is Sylvester Eustis. Ben Jones here spoke with you a few days ago about our going over to Castine."

"Come in," he growled.

From what I had been able to see of it, I judged Moore's house to be a weatherbeaten, little structure and was certain it must be as shaggy and dirty inside as its owner looked. Instead, it was as trim and neat as any ship's cabin and cleaner than most. Though the room was small, it had a varnished pine interior which gave off interesting bronze lights from the fire on the hearth. Pans, well blackened but clean, hung in a row on the wall. A brass ship's lantern swung from the ceiling, while between a closet and a window a hammock was slung. Not one but three muskets with glistening barrels and locks hung over the fireplace, while a Pennsylvania rifle standing in the corner seemed almost to reach to the low-beamed ceiling. The room contained four straight-backed chairs, a large "easy" chair near the stone fireplace and a small table, scrubbed white and smooth, by the window. I didn't see a book in the room, but there were several newspapers folded into an old butter firkin by the "easy" chair. Pervading the room was a not unpleasant blend of fish and tobacco.

Moore motioned us to draw up our chairs toward the fireplace while he stood to one side, an elbow resting on the mantel, smoking strong tobacco from a broken stub of a pipe.

"Suppose you tell me what you want me to do — I've kind of forgot what your nigger here said."

Philip, a free Negro, was hardly my "nigger" but since he was filling the role of my servant, I let the comment pass.

"We're interested in buying European textiles in Castine," I said. "Venetian and Valencienne laces, French silks, English cottons and woolens, and the like."

"Couldn't you order them by mail? Some Swede would deliver your order to this side of the river or even bring it to Portland."

"I want to make a selection personally."

"Do you know anyone over in Castine who can vouch for you? The British are letting lots of merchants in, but they're also checkin' them pretty carefully."

"No, I know no one there in authority who could vouch for me. But that doesn't worry me — I'll take my chances."

"Mighty sure of yourself, ain't you?"

Bridling my temper, I shrugged. "I've a job to do."

"You know that's tradin' with the enemy, of course!"

"That seems to be a fairly general custom around here," Brad said suavely. "But I can see you're the kind of patriot who won't have anything to do with the British even if it means money in your pocket. Maybe we'd better go now, William."

"Now, you look here," Moore started, knocking the ash from his pipe, "I ain't said I don't want to make money. The catch is, I don't want trouble with the British, an' I don't want trouble here, so anyone I take over to Castine gets some questions flung at 'em. An' I'll tell you this, Mister Man," glowering at Brad, "I'll take most anyone over, if he's got the price, an' I don't care if he's a merchant, a trader, or what-have-you, so you mayn't call me much of a patriot, an' maybe you're right. But I'll have you understand I don't take anyone over who don't smell right, an' mister, I don't like your smell! Or yours, either!" he growled at me.

"I don't understand," I said.

"So you don't understand!" he sneered. "Well, I'll tell you what I mean. You been here about four days now. You ain't talked much about your business, but that's all right — no one tradin' with the British does. But both you men been askin' a lot of questions 'bout our milishy, our officers, where we've got our cannon, an' things like that. I ain't ever heard a trader ask such questions. 'Course you say this man here" — pointing at Brad — "is a lawyer, an' I'll believe it. Lawyers have a nasty, high-talkin' way about 'em, even Rastus Foote, an' he's the only lawyer I like. But you" — now staring at me — "you ain't no trader — you don't look seedy enough — an' you ain't no merchant."

"How do you know I'm not?"

He wagged his head like a shaggy dog but his deep-set eyes never left me. "You ain't got the down-to-earth manner. Maybe you've got the money, an' you've got a kind of air of power. I don't know what you are, mister, but you ain't no merchant, an' this nigger here ain't just no ordinary nigger. He don't speak like one, an' he don't act like one. I don't think you aim to go to Castine on plain business. If you're figurin' on doin' harm to this country, I ain't havin' anything to do with you. I tell you, I don't like the smell of you, so you can be on your way for all I care."

As he strode toward the door to show us out — and quickly, too, as if we really did offend his nostrils, I decided to be reckless. For all his greed, Jess Moore was in the last analysis a kind of patriot. Besides, it was just possible we might need someone's help in getting Captain Vail over to this side of the bay.

"Just a moment," I said as Moore reached the door, "would it make any difference to you if we were trying to carry out something that was both patriotic and merciful?"

He stared at us. "I'd have to hear what it's all about before I could answer."

"Let's go," Brad said, grasping my arm. "We're not dependent just on this man to get us to Castine."

"But I'd like him to be the one," I said, never taking my eyes off Moore. Difficult as Moore was proving, there was an impression of trustworthiness about him that appealed to me. Besides, he had been the one Foote had relied on to take him and the Camden hostages to the *Furieuse*.

"Don't take any chances," Brad begged.

"I think Mr. Jonathan knows what he's doing," Philip said softly. His assurance — and I hoped he was right — gave me confidence, so I plunged.

"Mr. Moore, have you ever heard of Captain Benjamin Vail who lives in Castine and masters the privateer *Argus* out of Portland?"

For a long moment, Moore measured me with those deep-set eyes, then released the door handle. "I knew you wasn't a merchant," he muttered. "Now, maybe we'd all better sit down an' you tell me what's on your mind."

"But do you know Captain Vail?" I persisted.

"Yes, I know Ben Vail. Who around here don't? Only right now Vail ain't at sea — he's in a British prison at Castine."

"Right," I said. "Now let's sit down, as you suggest, and we'll talk this out."

Though Brad's face only gradually lost its disapproving look, I explained to Moore our real names, our relationship to Vail and our hopes for releasing him.

He made no comment for a time when I finished. Then he repacked his pipe and lighted it with a spill of bark from the fireplace. Anxiously I peered through the swirling smoke coils, but for a few moments I could barely distinguish his face. Then at last he began to speak.

"Until I heard more about you through John Eager's wife — she and her husband are good friends of mine — I agreed to take all of you over. Ain't that so?" he asked Philip.

"Yes, seh," Philip said.

"Then I got suspicious you wasn't what you said you was, an' I guess I was right, wasn't I? But I didn't guess you had something like this in mind. If I had, I wouldn't have said what I said the way I said it. But, honest, Mr. Dearborn, if you're goin' as a merchant, you got to act more knowin', somehow. Some smart Britisher over in Castine's goin' to suspect you ain't what you're aimin' to be."

He was not only forthright, but was becoming garrulous as well.

"An' this nigger here — what's your name, Adair? — well, Adair, you got to remember you ain't an equal, even if you really are. Right now, you're a servant. Man, your attitude's too upright. You got to learn to crawl a little when you speak. Fact is, you speak too good, an' like a Britisher at that! Now, ain't that a hell of a way for a black man to talk?"

"As for you" — turning to Brad — "well, I guess you're actin' like a lawyer all right, kind of nosey and suspicious an' nastylike."

"Will you take us to Castine?" I asked him.

He spat into the fire. "If that bulldog out there leaves Camden alone an' goes back to Castine tomorrow, we'll leave this house after dark — you send your nigger here to me after supper, an' I'll let him know when for sure. I don't like to have people see me leave Camden in the daytime. But what I want to know is how you plan to get Vail out of Castine even if you spring him out of prison, which I doubt you can."

"Our idea," I said, "was to hire horses and wagons to truck the goods we'd buy out of Castine or hire someone in Castine to bring them over by sloop under a Swedish flag — we're not trying to evade the United States revenue service."

"That means you'll have to let someone in Castine know about your plan."

"That's possible, and we don't know anyone there yet."

"And what happens if your plan falls through and you have to leave Castine in a hurry?"

"If that happens, we'll have to go up the east bank of the Penobscot. I'd like to hide a canoe or a rowboat somewhere along the bank so that, if things didn't work according to plan, we could get back over to this side of the river."

"How and when do you expect to get a boat over there to hide?"

"Could we do it tomorrow night?"

He looked at me as if I were mad. "You mean you want to hide that boat, then slip back down the river and come into Castine innocentlike in the morning, as if from Camden?"

"Yes, Mr. Moore, that's what I'm proposing."

"It's risky," he muttered. "It's damn risky. An' it'll mean a hard row if we don't get a breeze, an' we'll have to get back down river before it's light. I don't know. I'll have to buy a boat, of course."

I drew a small sack of currency from my pocket, which he accepted with no show of reluctance. "You don't want a canoe, even if that would be faster," he said. "With a man aboard who may be sick, a rowboat will be better."

"I can't tell you how much we appreciate —" but he cut me off before I'd scarcely begun.

"Don't thank me!" he growled. "If you're a religious man, you'd better start prayin'. If you ain't, then hope for luck, lots of it. We may need it tomorrow night, an' you'll sure need it afterward."

"But we do appreciate your willingness to take us, Mr. Moore. And I know Captain Vail will be grateful, too."

"I don't know Ben Vail well," Moore said, and his voice was gruff, "but he's been doin' what a lot of us would have liked to do if we'd believed in this damned war. Least I can do now is to help you to help him. But, mister, you're headin' full sail into trouble, take it from me!"

# XXII

ALTHOUGH the next day was the Sabbath, divine service was lightly attended; people seemed mainly concerned about whether or not the *Furieuse* would attack. All the militia companies were alerted for trouble. I really think there were enough cool heads and good shots among the militia to discourage a landing party. But why the frigate didn't stand off and shell the town the way the British had destroyed Portland during the Revolution I doubt if any of us Americans will ever know. At any rate, about noon, to the astonishment of everyone, the *Furieuse* suddenly set sail for Castine, and as she headed back across the bay, cheers spread from company to company. One of the militia officers, a Major Wilson, capered along the shore on his horse, daring the British to take a shot at him. Sight of him must have been too much for the *Furieuse* to tolerate, for a puff of smoke suddenly burst from her side and a cannon ball landed within a few feet of the foolhardy officer, scaring both him and the horse. The *Furieuse*, though leaving the town alone, carried away Camden's two hostages to Castine.

After Foote dismissed his troops and they marched home to their various towns, the Camden company alone remaining on guard, I told him who we really were and what our mission was.

"Now, look here," he said, taking us both by an arm and walking us up toward the Eager Inn, "there's not much that I can do right here to help you in Castine. Officially I know nothing about your enterprise. Unofficially I'll do what I can for you, but I'll deny all connection with you — that's a lawyer's privilege, you know. As much as all of us around here admire Ben Vail, we don't want to run the risk of another visit by the *Furieuse* — this time we were lucky. Clear?"

"Yes, sir. I realize the British hold two hostages for Camden's good behavior."

"Exactly. On the other hand, if you should be chased within range of our batteries on Battie or along the shore, not even the British could reasonably expect me not to give you what assistance I can. But that's about the limit of what I can do for you."

"Fair enough," I said.

And so it was, but I couldn't help thinking he was being overly cautious. If we had to slip out of Castine quickly, we might need assistance from the west shore of the bay long before we reached the shelter of Foote's guns. It was clearer than ever that we should have to depend almost entirely on ourselves. It was also evident that, in an emergency, to try to work our way back here to Camden would be folly. First, we should get across the river and then worry about getting back to Camden. We could hire some farmer's wagon to bring Captain Vail along the river road.

Just before supper Philip returned from Jess Moore with word that we should be at his house at seven o'clock.

I don't know what Moore had told Mrs. Eager, but evidently enough to allay any suspicions. In fact, when I mentioned our horses, she assured us they would be well taken care of and for us not to worry. She bade us bood-bye with more than the innkeeper's professional cordiality, though the warmth was in her manner rather than in what she said. I was convinced now that she knew what we were about to do, and I made a mental note to caution Moore against revealing our mission to anybody else.

Moore's sloop was a small but sturdy craft, no different basically for many of its type to be found in our coastal waters. He had it rigged with sweeps, however, and as I noticed how slowly we slipped through the water, with the boat we intended to hide trailing from the stern, I suspected that all of us would be getting our share of rowing exercise before dawn.

It was a strange sort of night, the temperature rather sharp but not unseasonable. For miles we clung close to the shore. All along we could see lights in scattered houses and in villages, and the peaceful prospect added to my feeling of unreality. It was hard to believe that a state of war existed between the two sides of the Bay, and that we were bound on a desperate errand into territory annexed by the British. I simply couldn't get used to the idea of any part of Maine being enemy country. Yet if we had any doubts, we had only to recall, the *Furieuse*'s departure not many hours ago with the two Camden hostages. Nor was it possible to forget, despite the tranquillity of the evening, the very reason for our being out on the dark river.

Suddenly a hand grasped my shoulder. "Time for the sweeps. Wind's died," Moore grunted.

Brad and I bent our backs over those hellish sweeps until my muscles burned with pain. Then when it seemed that that damned big oar had become my master, Moore and Philip took over from us.

"Feel the way I do?" groaned Brad.

"I'm beginning to wonder whether I'll make it," I said. "I must be pretty soft."

"Shh!" Moore hissed.

Brad and I glanced up at him, then around us but saw nothing.

"What's troubling him?" Brad grumbled.

"Sound — I should have thought of it," I said. "You'd be surprised how far a man's voice travels over water."

"Um." But afterward, when he spoke, Brad muttered or whispered.

The night seemed endless. Every now and then a breeze would spring up and we'd gratefully sit back and rest. Unfortunately it couldn't be relied on, which meant we were soon back to the sweeps. Until we were above the northern tip of Long Island, using the sweeps, apart from the tiring effort, was not a serious matter; but when we began to swing eastward in the wide part of the upper bay between Belfast and Castine, we had to be doubly cautious about making any noise. The locks were muffled with canvas, but we could not prevent a faint thumping as we rowed. In another way, however, the easterly crossing was a little easier because we started to feel the river current, which was why in moving us down the Bay, Jess Moore took us considerably north of the point where he intended to hide our boat.

Now indeed we kept a keen eye for any guard boat that might be patroling above the peninsula on which Castine was located. We saw nothing, however, as we crept shoreward.

Moore soon quietly lowered his mainsail and poled the sloop so close to the bank he was able to tie up to a big pine tree.

"Remember this tree," he whispered. "You'd better haul the boat partly up the bank and cover it with leaves and brush so it won't be seen from the river. No one could find it from the landside unless he came right over here."

Taking off our shoes and stockings, and rolling up our pant legs, Brad, Philip, and I plunged into the water and drew the boat up the bank. Once Brad swore softly as he stubbed his toe, while I couldn't hold back a grunt as I stepped on something sharp. Still we hid the boat as best we could and at Moore's "Psst!" we hastily crawled back aboard his sloop.

"It's goin' to get light soon," he growled, "an' we've got to back out into the river, drop down a piece an' come over properlike from the west. They get suspicious mighty easy."

Up climbed the sail and out went those accursed sweeps, and as we headed back toward the western shore, I found myself wishing with all my heart that we had Captain Vail aboard now. The whole idea of smuggling him out of Castine began to seem ridiculous to me. We'd have to leave so much to chance that it wasn't possible to do more than plan in the most tentative sort of way. Some people seem to like to expose themselves to danger, and I confess it's given me a lift from time to time to do so. But I've rarely had less of a plan to cope with the danger than on that November morning. I struggled to control a sudden shivering, and it wasn't entirely caused by the bitter river dampness.

Before long we were far enough to the south for Jess Moore to swing eastward again, clearing Long Island as if we had come directly up from Camden.

"We'll go in with daylight," Moore said. "They don't like anyone brought in when it's dark."

Presently we could make out the outlines of Fort George, which the British had rebuilt on the ruins of their old Revolutionary War fort. I could see, too, the crumbled mound that had been Fort Madison housing Lieutenant Lewis's guns. Round the rocky, shelving shore we swung and headed up the Majabagaduce River toward the harbor. Past the *Furieuse* we slipped; already her crew were at work cleaning ship. Inside the harbor were two man-of-war brigs and, unloading or waiting for wharf space, a half-dozen merchant craft: three large sloops, two brigs, and a ship. Three additional sloops flying the Swedish ensign rode high out of the water, obviously waiting to tranship cargoes, once they had cleared through the Castine customs house, to the western, or American shore.

"Here they come," Moore said.

Moving swiftly toward us came a six-oared barge, all varnish and brasswork, with an officer in blue and a civilian seated in the stern.

"No guard boat?" Brad asked.

"Customs, and a Lieutenant Jenson who's the harbor master," Moore said. "Guard boats patrol only at night."

Quickly Moore lowered the mainsail, then both he and Philip checked our progress with the sweeps.

"So it's you again, Moore," the Lieutenant said as he boarded us, followed by the civilian. "Thought I recognized your sloop."

"Yes, sir."

"And who are your passengers?"

After Moore introduced us, the officer said, "I must see your papers, gentlemen."

We produced the papers we had had hastily drawn up the morning we left Portland.

Lieutenant Gordon squinted hard at each of us both before and after he looked at our papers. "Everything seems in order," he said, returning them to us after opening a black writing case he had brought aboard and noting our names in a registry book. "What's your purpose in Castine?"

I told him of my intention to buy European, especially English, textiles.

"Couldn't you wait until one of these Swedes in the harbor brought them over to Belfast or Camden?"

I shook my head. "I wanted to make the selection here in order to be sure I procured the right material."

As the officer glanced at the customs agent, the latter nodded. "It makes sense," he said. "My name's Gulvin, Edward Gulvin. I'm an inspector assisting our Collector here, Mr. William Newton. We've all kinds of material I think you might want to look at. Are you returning with Moore?"

"No, sir, they're not," Moore said. "I'm supposed to be over at Belfast around noontime to load with some Swedish goods for Camden, so I'll be getting out of here right away."

"Then how do you propose to get your purchases out of Castine, Mr. Adams," Lieutenant Gordon asked.

"That depends on how much I buy," I said, with a breezy show of confidence I was far from feeling. "I'd like to hire one of those Swedish sloops over there to take my material all the way to Portland, but if that's out of the question, I'll have to depend on Captain Moore here, or someone like him, to carry me down to Camden or Rockland, and then hire wagons for Portland. If that's not possible, I'll try to get wagons here and go upriver and cross on the ferry."

"I'll be surprised if there are any wagons left in Camden," the officer sneered. "Our intelligence here was that they had all been employed to rush the sloop *Mary*'s cargo out of town."

"Yes," I said, "I understand a number of my fellow Americans became so infatuated with pursuing this unfortunate war that they assisted in the removal of her cargo, but I think there are a few wagons left."

"Where do you intend to stay while you're here, Mr. Adams? You must realize that our officers are quartered in the inns and many of the private houses."

"Then, sir, may I ask where merchants like myself stay who come here?"

"They usually don't remain overnight. Or, if they do, they stay at the houses of friends. But there is one place, the Wells Inn, where you might inquire. Report to the provost's office when you land. He'll be able to help you if anyone can."

After the officials left us, Jess Moore took us inside the harbor and dropped us at the slip below the Perkins Wharf.

"Now, look," he said as we picked our way through the shipping, "if the provost can't find any place for you to stay, I'll give you a few names. Cap'n Joseph Perkins is one — he's one of the great men of this town. Bill Abbott's another."

"I know of him — he's a lawyer, and a good one," Brad said.

"Yep, an' then there's Cap'n Elisha Dyer, Job Nelson, an' Mark Shaw. They've been members of the Committee of Public Safety. Course they ain't active now with the British here, but if you need help for Ben Vail, try any one of 'em. Don't know what they could do, but they'll do what they can — least, that's my bet. Now, good luck to you."

We shook hands with him, stepped onto the slip and watched him edge out into the harbor with, for me, a kind of sinking, lost feeling. We were on our own for sure and with the enemy all about us.

After asking the petty officer in charge of the slip to direct us to the provost marshal, we headed at once for his office. The provost, a big, overpadded major named Burke, asked us much the same kind of questions as had the harbor master and customs inspector, though he bore down harder on our attitude toward the war, which we stoutly insisted was anti-administration and pro-peace. After a fierce stare, he told us that, as for putting up for the night, we'd have to go to the Wells Inn.

"Mrs. Wells is a sour Yankee bitch," he barked, "but she'll find room for other Yankees like yourself, even if she has to lay you four abreast across a bed!" He laughed explosively as if he'd just realized what he'd said. "She'll charge you plenty, too," he added.

Mrs. Wells's inn was on the south side of Main Street. It was a plain, square house, the white paint scaling from its clapboards, which looked as if its days of splendor had definitely been in the past. Mrs. Wells looked a little like that herself. A big-boned woman with a long, leatherized horse face and eyes of a pale, washed-out blue, she had an energetic manner and a voice like an auctioneer's.

"I've got one room," she roared, "but your servant'll have to sleep in the attic. How long you stayin'? British won't let you be here more'n three nights without a special permit, anyway."

"I hope we can finish our business in three days, madam," I said.

"Don't 'madam' me, young man. That's what the Britishers say, damn them. I'm the Widow Wells — 'Mrs.' to you people."

"Yes, ma'am — I mean, Mrs. Wells."

"That's better. Well, the room's at the head of the stairs — you can go look at it yourself. But you'd better take it. There ain't another in town."

She entered our names in her register. "Lawyer, you say?" she glanced up at Brad. "Gather you people don't like this war."

"Does anyone?" Brad countered.

[ 230 ]

"Hell, no. But ain't that like a lawyer to answer a question by askin' another? Suppose you're a British lover, too?"

"One doesn't have to be that to dislike the war," Brad said.

"Well, it's a blessin' to hear you say that. My husband, Cap'n Wells, had no love for the British. I don't trust 'em, but I can't say I hate 'em — some of 'em have been fair with me an' let me run my inn even when I made it plain that I didn't regard 'em exactly as my best friends."

"The provost seemed to have positive opinions about you," Brad said.

"Him!" she exploded. "That tub of spoiled lard! Well, I never!"

Quickly she closed the book and stood back to let several of her guests out of the dining room. "Dinner's at noon sharp in case you've forgotten," she said briskly. "See that you're on time! Now," — turning to us — "have you gentlemen had breakfast? There ain't much left, but I can scare up a little coffee, an egg, maybe, an' bread, of course. Your servant can eat in the kitchen."

In the end, after we deposited our baggage in the room and washed up, we had coffee and bread — and one egg between the two of us, which Brad won on a toss of a penny.

"The garrison takes most of the eggs, an' everything else, too," Mrs. Wells moaned. "The farmers and fishermen around here are makin' more money than they ever did in their lives. You can bet they're not unhappy with the British here. But most of us would like to see the redcoats go, even if they've given us good treatment. General Gosselin's a gentleman."

"I thought so," Brad said. "And I'll bet everyone gets a fair trial if he's charged with an offense."

She looked at us as she poured us a second cup of coffee. "Whatever gave you that idea, mister?"

"English common law is the noblest system of justice in the world, and under it we still believe that a man is presumed innocent until he's proven guilty."

"Well, that may be so, but I ain't never been guilty of anything yet — leastwise I ain't been caught at anything," and the Widow Wells neighed like a horse in such an excuse for a laugh that I couldn't help smiling. Then noisily sucking in a mouthful of coffee, she asked in a deep voice, "And what happens, mister, when a real patriot gets put in prison by the enemy?"

I knew Brad resisted glancing at me. "Was he guilty of an offense against the enemy?" Brad asked.

"Well, I — I suppose he was, sometime before."

"He will still have to answer for whatever offense he committed," Brad said. "The law demands accountability whether it's common law or martial law."

"But damn it!" she exploded, then dropped her voice to a whisper, and asked, "What if he was betrayed by one of his own countrymen?"

"That would be unfortunate, but it would not affect the course of the law in his case."

She finished her coffee in a gulp, and stood up.

We rose too, thanking her for breakfast.

"Don't thank me," she interrupted. "I charge plenty, especially to Americans who trade with the enemy!"

She stared hard at us, then, picking up the coffee pot, she strode into the kitchen.

We escaped outdoors as quickly as we could, and I wiped the sweat from my forehead and palms. "Didn't the provost call her a bitch?" I asked.

"Yes, but a Yankee bitch," Brad muttered, "and that makes a lot of difference. We know at least one person here in Castine who's sympathetic with Vail. She'll know of others, too, and we'll probably need her help and theirs as well in springing the Captain out of prison. Count it a good beginning, Jonathan, a good beginning."

---

# XXIII

Accompanied by Philip, who followed us at a respectful distance, we spent a large part of the morning inspecting the most impressive array of woolens, cottons, and silks that I had ever seen, not to mention house accessories, chinaware, brassware, iron pots and pans, leather goods from shoes to saddles. Much of the material, to be sure, was what a workingman would wear, strong, coarse osnaburg cloth cheap in price. But there was also much that would appeal to a man or woman of fashion. As I selected a number of bolts of cloth, I thought that the time might not be far off when Americans would compete with England in the world markets for goods of these kinds since much of our maritime capital, thanks to the blockade, was being diverted to the construction of mills and factories like those in England itself.

Bidding the factor at the warehouse put aside what I had selected as an initial purchase, I nodded to Brad and Philip and walked outdoors. "Hear anything?" I asked as we strolled up the street.

Brad had been with me only part of the time; the rest of the time he had observed other individual purchases or listened to the prices of spoiled goods being auctioned off. He had also talked with American traders from Bangor, Belfast, Augusta, Hallowell, and Gardiner, and with occasional British officers who stopped in to watch the trading.

He shook his head at my question. "Not really, though one man from Hallowell told me there's a good deal of feeling over in the Kennebec towns at Vail's imprisonment. Seems our captain has become something of a Maine hero."

"There are some things we've definitely got to find out, Brad: where Vail is kept and what civilians around here, if any, have access to the fort."

"We can try one or all of those names Jess Moore gave us, to start with."

"We might better start with the Widow Wells," I said. "I'll bet she knows more of what goes on here than any of the men Moore mentioned."

We were now passing the main gate of the fort. With apparent casualness we observed the sentries at the gate and along the ramparts. There was such a coming and going of officers, work details, and units that had been exercising on the firing range that I grew fascinated with the possibilities of entering without detection provided I could procure a British uniform, or, better yet, if I could take the place of some civilian — a sutler, vendor, deliveryman or what-have-you whose business took him inside the fort.

[ 233 ]

"Best not to look too long, seh," came the whisper from Philip behind us.

Unhurriedly I looked away. Then when we turned down the hill, I asked, "Do you trust the Widow Wells?"

"Jonathan," Brad said, "she seems loyal, but I wouldn't put it past the British to have paid her to report anything or anyone that seems suspicious. It so happens I think she's reliable, but that's only a guess."

I nodded but said nothing. As members of the local committee of public safety, the men Moore had suggested we contact were probably kept under surveillance, and a report of visitors would undoubtedly be made to the provost. With an early curfew in effect a night visit might be really hazardous. While I wanted to confer with Captain Vail's mother, I had even less doubt that a watch was kept on her house. However I went over the problem in my mind, I came back to the Widow Wells.

After dinner that noon, our fatigue from being up the night before caught up with us, but although I was sure that he wanted to nap, and that he disapproved of my action, Brad remained with me when I asked Mrs. Wells if there was some place where we could talk with her in private.

She gave me a quick, calculating look, then said, "Guess there is, but you'll have to wait until my hired girl an' I get these dishes finished. You go on up to your room now, an' I'll let you know when I'm ready."

"You're taking a big chance — I hope you realize it," Brad said when we took off our shoes and stretched out on the bed.

"We're taking a big chance just being here," I said.

"Well, it'll be interesting to watch you go to work on the lioness," and he began to smile.

I can't say I didn't feel nervous and somewhat apprehensive as we waited. The idea that I might be endangering Brad and Philip was not an easy one to live with. Fortunately Mrs. Wells must have been as aggressive with the dishes as she was in manner, for while I stood by the window watching the redcoats and civilians in the street, the door opened and our landlady stepped inside with no knock or invitation. Without a word she nodded to us, and we followed her a few doors down the hall to an upstairs sitting room.

The room was as plain and unadorned as Mrs. Wells herself, a faded brown wallpaper with white woodwork. There were only two points of color. One was a rose shawl or scarf which Mrs. Wells was knitting and which was thrown in careless folds over her sewing basket. The other was a vivid canary whose cage rested on a marble-top table. It ceased trilling the moment we entered and seemed to watch us before it began to try a few notes again.

"Surprised an old woman like me has a canary instead of a parrot, ain't you?" And Mrs. Wells sniffed as she waved us to sit down; I found my chair as straight-backed and uncomfortable as a church pew.

"Yes, I'm a little surprised," I admitted.

"Well, so are other people. They think a parrot goes along with a widow or an old maid. I tell 'em I don't want competition. I don't need a parrot to talk to or to talk to me. Besides, a parrot ain't always safe to have around. I don't know what you want to speak with me about, gentlemen, but a parrot might take a fancy to the sound of something you say and start blabbin' it. This could be embarrassin'." Then she looked searchingly at each of us and folded her arms. "I think you'd better say what's on your mind." Her voice, though deep and rough, was almost a whisper and her eyes were hard.

I came straight to the point. "Mrs. Wells, from what you said this morning, I concluded that you are sympathetic with Captain Vail."

"You didn't hear me mention his name, young man," she said. "Look here, what's it to you how I feel about Ben Vail?"

"What if I told you I was a friend of Captain Vail? Would you believe me?"

She looked at me steadily without saying a word.

"Just to make it more difficult for you, Mrs. Wells," Brad said, and his tone was as flinty as hers had been, "would you believe me if I said that I, too, am a friend of the Captain?"

She looked at him as she had looked at me, and for a long moment their eyes locked in combat.

At last she said, "I can't see what difference it would make if I said

I believed you. It certainly wouldn't help Ben Vail up there in Fort George. Or would it?"

"It might," I replied. "Regardless of what you think of us, we're interested in seeing Vail freed."

"They won't keep him here long enough — they're supposed to be taking him to Halifax in a week or so," she said.

"Then we must get to work at once. We'll have to gain access to the fort, and since Vail is allowed no visitors and we're not in British uniforms, we'll have to find someone in the village who can enter without suspicion and take his place. Or hers, for that matter," I added, "if the British are employing any cleaning women."

Mrs. Wells's laugh was harsh. "Who'll be the woman, you? Or you, Mr. Eustis? No, I think that's out. There are women admitted to the fort but not for that purpose."

"What men are admitted, Mrs. Wells?"

Again she studied us, but less hostilely this time. "Oh, there are farmers who bring in cattle and grain and vegetables, and eggs and butter, of course."

"Do you know of any townsfolk who work in the fort?" I asked.

She rose and walked to the window, staring outdoors while I listened to that damned canary twittering and chirping and fluttering about his cage as if he were anything but content in it — which was probably my imagination at work, since that bird probably wouldn't have been able to survive a condition of freedom.

After what seemed an eternity Mrs. Wells walked back and sat down. "Do you realize that everyone who puts up at my house is watched and none more carefully than myself? You can't talk with a soul in Castine without the provost knowing about it."

"Will he know about this little chat, Mrs. Wells?" Brad asked. "You told us this morning you make no bones to the British about wanting the Americans to win this war? Is this fine display of sentiment simply a trap for unwary patriots? You must be well paid, Mrs. Wells!"

I stared at him. I began to realize that, in time, he might become a formidable figure at the bar or in politics, if that was what he wanted. Right at the moment, though, I thought him rude to a woman whose help we needed.

To my surprise, she didn't tell us to take our baggage and leave, as I fully expected her to do when her face grew red with anger and she stood up, hands on her hips, and looked down on Brad as if she would like to hit him. Instead, she said, "If I were a man, I'd throw you out of my house, Mr. Eustis. I'm as loyal an American as you are — and you, too, Mr. Adams, if you gentlemen are as loyal as you say! But I'll give you a chance to prove how loyal you are: I'll put you in touch with one of the turnkey's helpers at the fort. Then you can work out your plans with him for freeing Ben Vail."

"Who is this man?" Brad asked, his voice still hard.

"His name's Bertie Lord, and he lives down along the waterfront. He's at the fort days and occasionally at night. You'd better talk with him this evening and say his aunt sent you."

With that she gave us directions and added, her eyes cold and steady, "Now, by the livin' God, don't either of you dare say again I'm not loyal! Besides, you can talk big about loyalty — you're just here for a few days, if you're lucky — but remember I live here."

When we went up to our room, I asked Brad what he meant by being so rough on her.

"Didn't it work?" he countered.

"But she would have talked eventually."

"Maybe. She's a scared woman, Jonathan, for all her manner. We haven't time to spare, so I had to bring matters to a head."

"But to accuse her of disloyalty!"

"Jonathan, I don't think she really believed us until I got rough with her. Now, tonight, we'll see what this Bertie Lord has to tell us."

Finding Bertie was easy. A scrawny man of middle height with pale blue eyes like his aunt's but which, unlike hers, never looked at one quite long enough, he evaded giving direct answers and fell back on monosyllables when he spoke. He was both blunt and uneasy when we introduced ourselves.

"Ain't ever heard of you," he said.

Through the rays of his lantern we could see his wife behind him, as scrawny as he and the image of worry and fretfulness.

"We'd like to talk with you about some matters of common interest," I said.

"Why?"

"If you'd be so kind to invite us inside, sir, we'll be happy to explain," said Brad, and he was at his gracious best.

"Bertie," his wife said, "I don't like their looks. You'd better send them away."

"Your aunt, Mrs. Wells, sent us," I said to Bertie.

"Vera?"

"Bertie, you send them away!"

He turned on her. "Hush your mouth, Daisy. Come in," he said to us and, barring the door, admitted us to the kitchen and told us to sit down at the table. "Well?" he demanded, and he and his wife sat down, too.

Briefly, and revealing as little as possible, I told him we were in Castine to buy goods but that we were also interested in Ben Vail.

"Why?"

"He's a good man, he's hurt, and he was betrayed," I said.

"Maybe. I wouldn't know."

"But he is hurt, isn't he?"

"Not so bad, not any more."

"Does he walk?"

"Yep."

"We've heard he may be moved to a man-of-war and taken to Halifax. Is that so?"

"Wouldn't rightly know."

"Well, that would be a shame, and if he's hurt, it might kill him."

"Doubt it."

"Why?"

"I dunno. Just doubt it, mister."

"Mr. Lord, I think you and Mrs. Lord are very intelligent people," Brad cut in smoothly and with such sincerity I wondered how I could have been so mistaken; personally, I thought them frightened to the point of stupidity.

"Uh. That so?" Bertie said.

"Exactly. Here we came in on you after dark, and you didn't know us at all. Mrs. Lord" — he bowed to her — "wanted you to send us on our way. She showed good sense. After all, this is an occupied town, there are mixed sentiments here, and one never knows how one's neighbors really feel, isn't that so?"

Brad barely paused for breath, only long enough, in fact, for Bertie to get out a single "Uh" before he plunged on. "Castine is a fine place to live, I'm sure. At the moment the British hold it, but, mark my words, it's going to be American again. No American peace negotiators will consent to any part of Maine becoming permanently British. Isn't that so, Mr. Adams?"

"Absolutely," I said.

"Now, Mr. Lord, I'm convinced that though you are presently working for the British, your heart is with the American cause. Like your aunt, I know you are praying — and you, too, Mrs. Lord — for a peace that is honorable to America."

I wondered if Brad wasn't overdoing it. Looking at those two shifty sets of eyes flicking back and forth between Brad and myself but mostly looking at Brad as if he'd cast a spell, I doubted that the Lords were praying people at all. I doubted that their hearts were anywhere except in the pitiful money Lord himself was making as a kind of minor jailer for the British.

"Mr. Lord," Brad went on, his manner and voice becoming gentle, "it is true that you and Mrs. Lord hope to remain in Castine, isn't it?"

This time it was Mrs. Lord who said, "Uh," and added "Huh," as if they were unrelated words, while her husband nodded.

"Now, Mr. Lord, you are employed by the British, and it stands to reason that when the British pull out of this town, anyone who has helped the British won't be very popular here, isn't that so?"

As the man's face grew sullen, Brad snapped, "You wouldn't want to be tarred and feathered and run out of town on a rail or have your fine house here confiscated and you and Mrs. Lord left hungry and homeless, would you, Mr. Lord?"

As his wife gasped, Brad smiled grimly at her. "Of course not, Mrs. Lord. Now, as all of us know, there is a brave American imprisoned up in Fort George. He was betrayed to the British by a fellow countryman, and we want to get him out of the fort before the British take him away. You know Ben Vail is a fine man. He's also a hero to a good many Americans. We want you, Bertie Lord, to help us free

[ 239 ]

him. If you do, we'll see that the Americans know about it when the United States recovers this town. Then you'll be a hero, too. Better still, you and Mrs. Lord will be able to stay in Castine."

I didn't know how the Lords felt for the moment, but I knew I was impressed. I stared at him as intently as the Lords.

"It ain't an easy job you're puttin' me up to," Lord croaked.

"Of course it's not easy," Brad said.

"An' I don't rightly know what you want me to do. That's a powerful strong fort."

Brad smiled. "Well, we're not asking you to storm it all by yourself. Who brings Captain Vail his food?"

"I do most of the time. Sometimes it's Matt Coombs, the turnkey."

"Good. Now we want you to get a note to Vail that he can trust you. He can, can't he?"

"I always liked Ben," Bertie said; then added, "but he'll have to get rid of that note."

"He can swallow it. I won't even mention your name. I'll just write one word, 'Courage!' "

"Uh. Is that all?"

"Not quite"; and dread quickly replaced relief on Bertie's face. "Do you have an assistant?"

"No."

"That's not so good. Now, let me see. Who cooks for the garrison, soldiers or civilians?"

"Both. I mean there are some men in the town who help out. There's quite a turnover, 'cause no one likes the work an' there's a mean sergeant in charge."

"Good. Now tomorrow I'm going to go up there and get hired as a cook's helper."

He looked at me, and for once I think I succeeded in looking as wooden-faced as I hoped. Brad a cook's helper! Of all the crazy ideas!

"Can you cook, Mr. Eustis?" Mrs. Lord asked.

"He don't have to," said Bertie. "He'll keep the fires goin' and lug in the meat and turn the spit and cut bread, an' things like that."

"Then I guess I can qualify," Brad said. "But, the next day, I'm

[ 240 ]

going to have to get hold of the keys to where Captain Vail is locked up. And, Mr. Lord," his voice becoming very gentle indeed, "I may have to knock you out or Matt Coombs, the turnkey."

Mrs. Lord gasped, and the silence grew long and heavy. Then Bertie mumbled, "It better be me. Then I won't have to answer all the questions they'll throw at me about what I was doin' while you was lettin' Ben out. Besides, I ain't so big as Matt. You can hit me after you bring me Ben's supper Wednesday."

Brad then pumped Bertie on the plan of the fort, the location of sentry posts, the names of some of the civilians who worked there, and a host of details. All this caused me to marvel. Obviously Brad had planned something like this beforehand — it showed too much forethought to have been contrived as we talked with the Lords.

After good nights to the Lords, and a sharp warning from Brad for them to say nothing, I turned to him.

"What a cook's helper you'll make!" I said. "And don't you remember that I was to be the one who was to get inside the fort?"

"Shh! Keep your voice down!" and he glanced around in the darkness. "The trouble with you, Jonathan," he muttered, "is that you're not guileful enough. This role calls for someone who's a bit devious, or who can pretend to be. You'd give yourself away the first time anyone asked you a leading question."

"Then what do you want me to do?"

"Get a team of horses and a wagon tomorrow and start loading it with what you've bought."

"But the British will wonder where you are."

"Let 'em wonder. They would miss you as the merchant more than me. Cover for me as best you can and get Mrs. Wells to do so, too. She'd better — she's in pretty deep now, and so's our friend Bertie. And keep Philip near you."

"Just one thing more," I whispered. "You're not going up to the fort as a cook's helper dressed like that, are you?"

I heard his soft chuckle. "I brought along some old clothes in a saddlebag, Jonathan."

While he went to the privy, I entered the house and started for the stairs. I barely had my hand on the railing when a voice rang out, "That's the man, Lieutenant!"

[ 241 ]

I spun around and looked into the amused and triumphant face of
Warren Bierce.

# XXIV

"I MIGHT have expected this of you, Bierce," I said, more startled for
the moment than angry. Then anger triumphed. I don't know
whether my face went red or white, but something in it must have
revealed how I felt, for the young officer stepped forward and asked
me if my name was Jonathan Dearborn. To deny it in Bierce's presence was folly, so when I acknowledged it, he said that I was under
arrest.

"On what charge?" I demanded.

"You will learn at the fort," he said.

"Do you have a warrant?" I asked. I realized it was a silly question,
but, standing by the staircase window, I played for time, hoping that
Brad would see me and not enter.

He smiled thinly. "A military necessity doesn't require a warrant,
Mr. Dearborn, at any rate not in occupied territory. Now you will
follow me, please."

It was an order, and I really had no choice but to obey, for a
sergeant and three enlisted men entered from the kitchen. At a nod
from the officer the sergeant quickly ran his hands over my clothing.

"No weapons, sir," he said to the lieutenant.

"Then take him to the fort. Mr. Bierce and I will be along
directly."

The sergeant knotted my hands behind me and marched the little
detail up the hill in cadence, with all the pride of a soldier who had
caught the greatest spy in the land.

Naturally I wondered on what charge they had arrested me, but
knowing Bierce, I feared the worst. My only consolation was that
evidently, for the moment at least, they had not discovered Brad.
Possibly Philip had also eluded them, though it was unlikely that a
black man could escape for long in a white community.

Presently we came up to the great earthern wall of the fort and
entered through the main gate. There were several structures inside,

masses of candle-illuminated blackness in the night, and into one of them the sergeant marched me.

The interior looked like a combination of inquisition chamber and gunroom, but the slits of windows and that curious smell composed of sweating humans, open latrines, and tobacco smoke left little doubt that this was the guardhouse.

"We'll wait 'ere," the sergeant growled. "Lieutenant Felton will be back soon from seein' the general. Now, wot you done, Yank?"

"Nothing, really," I said.

"So it's for nothin' ye're 'ere in the fort! Come off it!"

"No one has told me why I'm arrested."

"Well, it must be for somethin' important. When that merchant there — wot's 'is name, Bierce? — come in 'ere to see Major Burke an' the major sent Lieutenant Felton to get you, an' then the major hurried over to see the general, we 'ere say it must be important to get you. An' 'ere you are, Yank!"

Soon young Felton entered the guardroom. "Bring him over to the general's quarters, Sergeant."

Though General Gosselin sometimes stayed in the town, he was at the fort this night. As I was marched into his small combination living room and office, I was struck by the power of the man's sharp profile. He was not a young man, but the years sat easily upon him and his blue eyes were keen and his voice was crisp.

"What are the charges against this man, Lieutenant?" he asked, his eyes flicking from me to Felton to Bierce, then to the sergeant standing behind me. A Colonel Anstruthur and Major Burke sitting respectively at his right and left were the only officers with him.

"Trying to help Vail to escape, sir."

"Who preferred them?"

"Mr. Bierce, sir."

"Is that right, Mr. Bierce?"

"Yes, General." And Bierce explained that hearing in Portland that Brad, Philip and I had suddenly left town when word arrived of Vail's imprisonment, he put two and two together and decided the British should know about us since if anything should happen to Vail in an attempted escape, feelings between the British and the Americans would be exacerbated, a lamentable occurrence with peace coming on. After Bierce arrived at Widow Wells's inn this evening and looked at the register, he was certain we were present since one William Adams had listed a colored servant. He had therefore gone to the general himself who had authorized the provost marshal, Major Burke, to order Mr. Dearborn's arrest.

The General now turned to Major Burke and learned that he had sent Lieutenant Felton with a file of soldiers to verify the identity of the accused and apprehend them.

Felton responded at once, in answer to a question from the general, that he had carried out the order.

"Then you are indeed Jonathan Dearborn and not William Adams?" Gosselin asked me.

"Yes, sir."

"And you had associates? What were their names?"

"Sir, I would rather not answer those questions," I said, the palms of my hands starting to sweat.

"But I am ordering you to do so," he said.

"I must respectfully decline, sir."

The silence was formidable as he stared at me. Then Bierce broke it, reminding the General he had told him who we were when he had reported his suspicions earlier that evening.

"My memory is not so short as to forget this soon, Mr. Bierce," Gosselin said. "But I wanted the names from this man himself."

"I beg your pardon, sir," Bierce said, while I felt for the moment like cheering at the discomfiture obvious in his voice if not in his manner.

"Is Mr. Bierce right?"

I shrugged. What was the use of concealment now. "Yes, sir."

"You realize, Dearborn, you could be charged with espionage?"

"I suppose so, sir. But that was not our reason for being here. Even Bierce doesn't charge us with that."

"So I've noticed," and I thought the General's voice was somewhat dry. "But how did you propose to free Captain Vail?"

I looked at him. It was hard to lie to this man, and I didn't intend to more than I could help. After all, I didn't want to incriminate Brad or poor Bertie Lord. Furthermore, Brad's plan hadn't been mine; in fact, I had been relying on what we could make of the situation here in Castine first. When I told the general this, he shook his head.

"You mean you had no plan at all? Did you know nothing about the construction plan of the fort?"

"Not in detail, no sir."

"Did you hope to use any of the natives here?"

"We'd have probably tried," I told him.

"Would you have ventured to corrupt any of my soldiers?"

Though aware of the sudden rough edge to his voice, I could not give him a direct answer. So I said, "Well, sir, we didn't seriously consider it since there wouldn't have been time enough to develop that as a possibility."

I was also fully aware of the implication that if we had had more time, we wouldn't have hesitated to work on some redcoat, but I said nothing more.

"Where are your associates now, Dearborn?"

"I honestly don't know, sir."

Nor did I. And I must have sounded sincere, for he turned to his provost marshal with a lifted eyebrow.

"We have search parties out, sir," Major Burke said, "but we haven't found them yet." The fat hung in folds over his collar, and his face was almost as red as his uniform.

"Then keep searching until you do, Major. Now, Dearborn," and his voice became frankly curious, "why should you and your friends try to free Captain Vail? What is there about the imprisonment of a single privateersman that has you and evidently some other people of Maine so excited?"

I looked at him, looked at all three of those officers in scarlet sitting in that spartanlike room so far removed from the luxury of English country living that they were probably accustomed to, and also glanced sideways at Lieutenant Felton with that pink-and-white innocent face that so many young Englishmen have. I saw, too, the sardonic expression on Bierce's face, but I ignored it.

"General," I said, my voice so unsteady it nearly unnerved me, "Captain Vail is not a man of great importance, as the world reckons importance. He is not a statesman — he is not even a politician. He may not be, for that matter, as skillful a privateering captain as Boyle of the *Chasseur* or Dominique Diron, though he is very, very good, as Lloyd's of London could certainly testify, to their grief."

To my gratitude the tremor was leaving my voice, and though Burke looked angry and the colonel's aristocratic face was the picture of boredom, General Gosselin appeared interested, so I kept my eyes on him.

"What appeals to the people of Maine about Captain Vail, General, is the combination of ability and integrity of character and patriotism. He is not a great talker but a doer and a man who has kept the faith. As you know, he was wounded — hurt badly and at home when you people captured Castine. He is now your prisoner, and you have every right, I suppose, to treat him as a prisoner of war. But what has enraged people is that he was betrayed to you by an American, a greedy, selfish man without honor who will not hesitate to use you even as he has used his own countrymen to promote his own personal interests."

"There's no need to raise your voice, Dearborn," the General said quietly. "This is not one of your American townmeetings."

As I bowed in acknowledgment, Bierce stepped forward. "General Gosselin, I am sure you have long known how I, like so many New England people, have deplored this war between our two nations. I don't regard myself as less an American or a man of honor for trying everything I can do to prevent the effusion of blood. I do not question Mr. Dearborn's estimate of Captain Vail's character, but I would remind you that Vail by his privateering has helped prolong this war to the ultimate disadvantage of both our peoples and with the immediate disadvantage to the British people of loss of life and property."

"You do not have to explain your position here, Mr. Bierce," the General said. "You have indeed been a friend to us."

"And I hope you will continue to regard me as a friend, sir. I have exposed Dearborn as a man who, by trying to liberate Vail, would exacerbate the already bad feeling existing between Englishmen and Americans. I have said nothing until now that Dearborn is in an excellent position to testify to Captain Vail's so-called patriotism.

When the *Argus* made its cruise into European waters that was so disastrous for English shipping, Dearborn went as Vail's second officer. I'm sure he will be glad to tell you of his exploits."

The fat was really in the fire. The British now had more reason for putting me in prison along with Captain Vail than for my abortive attempt to help free Vail. I had certainly played into Bierce's hands, as well as those of the British.

"Well, Dearborn?"

I looked at Gosselin's cocked eyebrow. He seemed more curious than angry, and I wondered how much I should say. "Yes, sir," I admitted after a long pause, "I was Captain Vail's second officer."

"And your exploits that Mr. Bierce mentions?"

"Nothing unusual, sir. I simply did my duty — even if that meant reporting to the American minister in Paris evidence of Mr. Bierce's transactions with your government. Mr. Bierce followed the coach in which my friend and I were traveling to Bordeaux. There he had me set upon and kidnapped aboard a ship bound south down the African coast. I was lucky to have escaped alive."

Bierce laughed and said, "That's about as likely a story as I've heard in months! General, this man is a consummate liar."

"I don't know whether he is or not, Mr. Bierce," the General said. "But, after all, you are not on trial here. His Majesty's Government is grateful, I'm sure — I know I am — for every bit of assistance you have given us. This man" — indicating me — "and some other Americans may think differently, but that needn't concern us."

"No," I said, "it needn't concern you, and it needn't concern Mr. Bierce henceforth that some people regard him as a traitor: those who know most about his activities, Captain Vail and myself, particularly Captain Vail, are now your prisoners, sir."

"Indeed you are. Major," — turning to the provost marshal — "is the room in the officers' barracks where Captain Vail is confined the only room that's grated?"

When Burke acknowledged this was so, the General said, "Put Dearborn in with Vail."

"Sir," and Bierce bowed deferentially, "may I say something?"
"Well?"

[ 247 ]

"I think it unwise to put those two together. They just might escape."

Gosselin looked half amused. "You wouldn't like that, would you, Mr. Bierce? Well, sir, rest easy. I assure you they have not the slightest chance of escaping from my fort."

"But, sir," Bierce began, "you don't know how slippery these people can be."

"Perhaps not, but I have enough faith in British alertness not to be alarmed."

He leaned back in his chair and nodded to the provost. Instantly Major Burke ordered Lieutenant Felton to confine me with Captain Vail.

With Felton and the sergeant on either side of me and the sergeant's troop detail behind, I was marched to the officers' barrack close to the high west wall of the fort.

"In with Vail?" The burly turnkey, Matt Coombs, who had been sent for from the guardroom and who looked and smelled like a beer keg, hurried up with a key on a long chain. Opening the door of the officers' barrack, its numerous rooms aglow with candles, he led us down a corridor while a number of officers, in various stages of undress, watched us from their doors.

"What? Another beastly Yankee?" I heard one say.

The tone of disgust was what graveled me. In fairness to the British, I could not say that they had been other than correct in their treatment of me. But their contempt not only of me but of most Americans was infuriating. Had we been united as a people and opposed them manfully, they would have had more respect for us. People like Bierce did nothing to elevate us in British opinion despite the assistance they gave the Crown.

We stopped before a barred door in front of which stood a sentry. With Coombs holding his lantern high I could see through the bars a camp cot, a small bare table, and one chair. High in the wall and just under the boarded ceiling was a small window, also heavily barred.

"Vail!" the turnkey called out as he opened the heavy iron door. "You've got a visitor."

"Visitor!" Felton laughed. "He's going to be a full-time resident!"

Then someone got up off the bed and walked slowly toward us. I

[ 248 ]

stared at him, horrified by his gauntness and the pallor of his face, accentuated though it may have been in the lantern light.

As the sergeant pushed me inside, Vail held out both his hands. "Dearborn! Jonathan Dearborn!"

"Captain Vail!" I said, and gripped his hands. I was surprised how strong they were in spite of his condition.

"Jonathan, how in God's name did they get hold of you?"

"Look here," said Felton, sounding tired and bored, "I don't want to hear that story all over again. He'll have time enough to tell you that when we've gone, Vail. Sergeant!"

With heel clicks and a rattle of arms the detail left us.

"I'll have a cot in here in the mornin'," Coombs growled. "You c'n sleep on the floor tonight."

"Coombs, it's November and cold in here," Captain Vail protested. "Get him a cot and blanket now."

"Go to hell, Vail. If he's cold, let him sleep with you." And with a coarse laugh, Coombs clanged the door shut.

He walked off down the corridor, followed by the sentry.

"You've no guard for the night?" I whispered.

"Yes, I'm afraid I do. But when the guards were changed in the night, after I was put here, the officers protested, so they're now stationed outside the barrack. But forget about guards, Jonathan, tell me what's happened since I last saw you. I know you and young Pettigrew took me to my mother's house, and for that I'm grateful."

He cleared his throat, then carried the chair to his bed, repulsing my attempts to take it from him.

"Sorry there's not more light, but that lantern hanging outside the door will have to do. My supply of candles is getting low. Now sit down and start talking, but keep your voice down. And, if you don't mind, I'll lie down again."

He suddenly began to cough, a long series of short, hacking coughs that alarmed me.

"Captain Vail," I said in alarm, but he cut me off.

"Nothing, it's nothing. Just start talking."

So while he huddled under the blanket, I recounted all that had occurred. Twice I stopped, thinking he had fallen asleep, but he hoarsely said, "Go on!" And on I went. But, even as I spoke, I was a prey to anguish and compassion when I considered what Captain Vail was like now and then recalled the stalwart, dynamic little officer who had taken the *Argus* into desperate battle.

---

# XXV

THE next day Bertie Lord took over from Matt Coombs, but when I tried to talk with him, he refused to say a word. Only one thing came of my efforts. When he brought in my cot and chair and I asked him if the British had caught my friend and the colored man, he shook his head. Other than that, he was uncommunicative. I suppose, in his place, I'd have been, too; furthermore, the presence of the sentry was no encouragement to him to talk.

All that day I hoped with an aching fierceness that Brad and Philip could get off the peninsula. Captain Vail sought to encourage me in my hoping but I was frankly depressed. Vail's very sympathy hurt. Here we had tried to help him, and now he was having to help me.

It made me feel no kinder toward Bierce when Captain Vail explained how he had been imprisoned.

"I was pretty sick after you left me, then after lots of rest I began to feel better. People here in Castine knew I was at my mother's, but no one gave me away to the British, even the 'peace-at-any-price' folk. Then our friend Bierce appeared."

"In the *Ghost?*"

"No, that would be too much of a giveaway. He came up in that little sloop that he sails around Portland Harbor."

"Was Rudd with him?"

"I don't know. But somehow Bierce found out I was here. You know he's persuasive with his tongue, and maybe someone talked before he knew what he was saying. Anyway Bierce told the British who I was and Gosselin sent a guard to bring me in. I'll hand it to the general, though. He was fair and square. Said he was sorry for me but that he had no choice but to put me in jail."

"It's about what he said to me, too, though he omitted the regrets. After all, the circumstances were different. But I agree with you: he

[ 250 ]

seems a decent person even if he encourages a man like Bierce to be an informer."

"Bierce is more than an informer, my boy!"

"How right you are! Shall we continue with 'traitor'?"

"There are several other labels he deserves, you know."

"Yes, and if Captain Black of the *Ginny* were ever around to tell his story, I'd add 'would-be-murderer' to the list, though I suppose that applies more to Rudd than to Bierce."

"The principal instigator was probably Bierce," Vail said.

"Rudd's a bad man, but Bierce's a bad man with a brain."

He asked about Judge Kent but was tactful enough not to mention India, for which I was grateful. I couldn't think of her without feeling ill used and bitter and hurt, yet somewhat respectful and puzzled. To marry in order to save the Judge's life must have taken courage, though there was evidently much about Bierce that she found attractive. But to stay with him! Personally I've never been able to figure out why some women persist in remaining with the men they marry. They must have strong stomachs to put up with their husbands; or possibly an old Calvinist preacher, a friend of my father's, was right when he said that such women are either determined to reform their husbands or are drawn to the evil in them. Neither alternative seemed quite to fit India's case.

It didn't take long to become familiar with the routine of our prison. The frequent changing of the guard inside the corridor during the daytime helped break the monotony, though, in time, it became monotonous itself. Coombs was turnkey during the night, while Bertie Lord came on early enough to bring us breakfast and remained long enough to give us our supper. He did little lingering in the officers' barrack, nor, for that matter, did Coombs; their headquarters was the guardhouse, where evidently the regimental prisoners served their time. Once a day a British army surgeon checked over Captain Vail. He was a thin, sullen Scot so chary of words one would have thought they cost him money. When I mentioned the Captain's cough, he gave a high hoot. "Tis naething," he said. When I continued to voice my concern, he drew himself up and asked if I were questioning his professional knowledge and skill. As a matter of fact I was, but realizing that to admit it would not help Captain Vail, I explained that I was an old friend of the captain's and naturally concerned about him.

One morning while Lord was bringing in our breakfast, Vail and I were both startled to hear a bump overhead and the sounds of footsteps.

"For heaven's sake, what's that, Bertie?" Captain Vail asked.

And for the first time Bertie Lord opened up since I had arrived. "Two of the officers complained of a leak in their ceiling."

"So that's an attic up there?"

"Yep. Runs the length of the barrack."

"How do repairmen get up there?" I asked. "From the outside?"

"Naw. There's a middle passageway through the barrack to the west wall, an' they go up a trap door from the passageway."

Neither Vail nor I said anything more, but when Bertie had gone, I took a good, hard look at our boarded ceiling.

"I don't suppose you have a knife, Captain?"

He produced a small pearl-handled penknife and laughed helplessly. He was right, too: a man couldn't cut his way through that ceiling with anything so small and ineffectual.

"I've nothing myself," I said. "They took my clasp knife away from me. It's a wonder they didn't take my money."

"Oh, the British are honest, so far as that goes," Captain Vail said. "At least they play the game fairly as long as Gosselin is in command."

"Suppose we could bribe Bertie to get us an instrument we could use?"

"Depends on how frightened he is. I've known him a long time."

"What could we use up there?" And I nodded toward the ceiling.

He glanced at the sentry, who had stopped in front of the window in the corridor and was looking out onto the parade ground, which was beyond our line of vision. Then, walking over, Vail stared up with his hands in his rear pockets.

"I'd say a gimlet would help just above this barred window. We'd have to work at night and would have to depend on what light came through the glass. We wouldn't dare light a candle."

"One of us would always have to stand guard in case someone comes down the corridor."

"Right," and he squinted upward again. "We'd need a gimlet and a bigger knife than I have to finish the job."

"Shall we try to get them from Bertie?"

"Let's go for a gimlet first. And let me ask Bertie. If he won't do it for me, I doubt if he will for you. By the way," and he acted a little embarrassed, "are you ready to spend some of your money? Bertie won't do anything except for money. I'd pay him, but all I've got is small change."

"I'll take care of that," I said.

"You realize you'll have to do most of the work, son? I'm not tall enough, and, besides, I'll probably get to coughing so loud with the dust the night sentry'll come running in from outdoors thinking I'm about ready to slip my cable."

"Of course I'll do the work."

"Then we'll try old Bertie when he comes in tonight with our supper."

"Not this noon?"

"No, that'll give him too much time to think about it."

"What'll it cost, five dollars?"

"Hell, no, Jonathan! One dollar will be enough. If you give him more, he'll worry someone will find out. But a dollar won't scare him or make anyone else suspicious if it falls out of his pocket or something like that. Now you give me that dollar."

He burst into a fit of coughing that started both of us sweating — he with the effort and I with sympathy.

That evening, after Bertie had brought our food, I drifted between him and the door to shut off the sentry's view in case the redcoat became curious. Usually the sentries ignored us except when an officer passed. I had tried several times to engage them in conversation, but they had evidently had orders not to talk with us. Tonight, though, I tried harder than ever to get the sentry talking, in order to cover up the conversation between Captain Vail and Bertie Lord; it turned into a monologue; he ignored me completely. Still I kept up a stream of questions and comments until I saw Bertie get ready to leave.

Vail would say nothing, of course, until Bertie had left the building, Matt Coombs had made his inspection, and the new sentry had taken up his post outside the barrack. Then Vail cocked an eye toward me. "We'll get our gimlet."

"How did you persuade him?" I asked.

"I told him that if he wanted to live in Castine after the war, he'd better do something to square himself with his neighbors after working for the British during the war."

"That's what Brad told him."

"Well, it's a good approach. I feel certain he'll bring a gimlet to us."

And Bertie did, but in a manner that gave nothing away to anyone who might be watching. The very next morning, when he brought in our breakfast, a loaf of bread, as usual, flanked the ham on the plate. He said nothing, he didn't even look at us, and he left at once. But when Captain Vail served the food onto our two tin plates, there was the gimlet resting snugly between the bread and the ham. Quickly he slipped it inside his shirt, and I ate that breakfast with keener relish than any meal since leaving Camden.

But Vail would not let either of us eat the bread inside the crust. "We'll need the bread to plug the gimlet holes," he explained.

That night, following Coombs's inspection, I carried the table over to the spot where we decided to bore. Then, while Captain Vail kept one eye on the door and the other on how I was doing, I went to work with the gimlet. Our plan was that I should bore out a space large enough for a man to crawl through. Then when the boring was completed, I'd use a knife to cut through the parts that held the piece together. This would mean getting Bertie to bring us a knife. I soon discovered, too, that it would take many nights of work with the gimlet.

I worked for hours, until my hands were sore. Then we brushed the sawdust together. Since there was no place to hide it, I mixed it with the soft insides of our loaf of bread and sprinkled the mess with water from our jug. Afterward, rolling it between my thumb and forefinger into tiny balls of dough, I filled each of the gimlet holes. When I finally stretched out on my cot, I slept as if I were drunk, and indeed I was — with fatigue and hope.

But the work didn't go smoothly every night. There were nights when officers walked past our cell at such frequent intervals that we dared not move out of our cots. Several nights, hearing footsteps, we barely got the table back in place. Occasionally there was no time to fill the holes with dough, and we kept our fingers crossed that no one would spot the perforations in the ceiling.

Meanwhile Bertie Lord grew friendlier, though he continued more guarded with me than with Captain Vail. Nor did he object when Vail asked for a knife; Bertie left one beside the breakfast plate one morning. But the transaction was strictly between the Captain and Bertie, for I tried again to talk with the sentry when Vail made his request. It was a great relief when, to my repeated questions, he finally said the British had never caught up with Brad or Philip, and had given up the search. A fortnight had gone by when he supplied this bit of information, and I began at once to wonder if Brad himself had given up any idea of returning.

Matt Coombs gave me further cause to fret when one evening, just as we were about to start on our work, he lumbered over from the guardhouse.

"You men ain't got much time left here," he growled. "Maybe a week."

Coombs was an overstuffed giant whose belly hung over his waistband and whose face also sagged in heavy folds. If his brown eyes resembled a St. Bernard's at first sight, they had no kindness in them, and although his body was gross, it gave one the impression of power. I could understand why Bertie Lord was scared to death of him. According to Bertie, Coombs had come with the British, but his speech gave him away as being from New England or, more likely, from one of the Maritimes.

"And then where are we going, Coombs?" Captain Vail asked.

It was well he spoke, for I'm sure my face must have expressed dismay, which undoubtedly pleased Coombs. I thought I'd need at least a week to complete the boring and cutting.

"Well, it could be you're bound for Dartmoor, Vail, both you an' Dearborn. Point is you're gettin' the hell out of Castine, and soon."

"What are they sending us on, a merchantman or a privateer?" I asked.

"They ain't takin' any chances with you two. You're goin' on the sloop-of-war *Isis* as guests of honor — chained in the brig, Dearborn."

"We must be dangerous enemies," I said.

His laughter came in one sudden blast and then was over. "Oh, you're dangerous, all right! In a pig's ass!" he added in a growl. "I don't know why they think you're so important. If I had my way, I'd make an example of you — shoot you both. That'd put the fear of God an' the King into your stinkin' privateersmen. They'd leave British ships alone after that."

"I don't think you know American privateersmen very well, Coombs," I said.

"Haw! All you Yanks know is money. You ain't got guts enough to back your own government against us. Why? 'Cause it keeps you from makin' money. And it ain't enough that you don't help the rest of your dirty country, you come down here to Castine and trade with us. God damn customs house is makin' so much money they don't know what to do with it all!"

Both Captain Vail and I were silent: there was enough truth in what he said to sting. Then as he stood there, gloating and glowering, I said, "Look here, Coombs, does that man Bierce, Warren Bierce of Portland, come down to Castine often?"

"Him? Mr. Bierce? Well, now, wouldn't you like to know!"

"Frankly, I would," I said.

"Dearborn, you can God damn well keep on wantin' to know. All I'll tell you is this: you can bet he'll be down to see you safe aboard the *Isis*. Don't know what you did to him, but he sure don't seem to like you two."

"Will Rudd be with him?" Captain Vail asked.

"Who? Rudd? Jake Rudd! Well, now, I wouldn't wonder, wouldn't wonder at all. Them two is friends, good friends."

"That's certain," I said.

"That Rudd," Coombs said with admiration, "he's an ornery bastard. Glad I ain't his enemy. He got into a fight with an army cap'n here over cards an' beat him so bad the cap'n an' his friends have sworn to shoot him on sight. There was such a stink Bierce ain't allowed to let him ashore. But that don't mean he won't be along in that sloop of Bierce's to see you two taken aboard the *Isis*, no sir!"

With that he left, and Vail and I went furiously to work on the ceiling; at least I did, while the captain kept a sharper watch than ever.

On the third morning after Coombs's announcement, when Bertie brought in our breakfast, I was sure I detected a little white cylinder pass from him to the Captain, which Vail palmed quickly and then thrust into his coat pocket as he reached for his handkerchief and burst into a fit of coughing. When the spasm subsided, he could eat barely anything and soon went to his cot and lay down. I thought Bertie looked concerned, but he said nothing.

When Bertie had gone, I took my chair over and sat beside the captain. "Are you going to be all right, sir?" I asked. "Shall I send for that damn doctor?"

"I'll be all right," he said, but so feebly I grew alarmed.

Then to my surprise his eyelid closed in a slow wink and he reached in his pocket for his handkerchief and brought it out along with the cylinder. Glancing toward the door, I waited until the sentry walked past, then nodded.

The Captain quickly unrolled the slip of paper, read it, and thrust it into my hand.

Waiting again until the sentry had returned, looked into the cell, and moved up the corridor, I glanced at the paper. All that it contained was a cryptic symbol in ink:

$$\mathrm{B}\!\begin{smallmatrix}1\\5\end{smallmatrix}$$

Even as I stared at it, Vail took it from me, popped it into his mouth and, macerating it, swallowed it. Instantly I brought him a dipper of water which he gulped thirstily.

"Feel better?" I asked him as the sentry looked in on us.

"Yes, much better, thanks," he sighed.

When the sentry passed, the Captain whispered, "Did you understand the message?"

"It's Brad all right," I said, "and the only thing that makes sense to me about the one and the five is that it must mean the fifteenth day of the month."

The Captain grabbed my wrist so tightly I winced. "That's tomorrow, son, tomorrow! We must try to get out of here tomorrow night!"

Suddenly I realized how much an escape meant to him. But could he make it? What if he had a spasm of coughing when we were trying to slip out of the fort? And why and what had Brad planned that we must make our attempt on the fifteenth? How, in fact, did he know we were so near to being ready? Bertie Lord, to be sure. But we could expect no real help from Bertie; he was much too cautious.

I then glanced up at the ceiling, and any elation I felt vanished when I realized how much work remained to be done before tomorrow night.

---

# XXVI

THE day set for our escape attempt seemed endless. The night before I had used the gimlet for the last time; all that remained was to cut along the rectangle inscribed by the gimlet holes and remove the piece of the ceiling. If anyone looked carefully, of course, he could not help noticing the difference in color between the bread and sawdust filling we had used and the natural wood. But at a distance, with the bread having dried after we had chewed it, the difference was not so obvious. Bertie Lord never mentioned it, but both the captain and I were sure he had seen the rectangle; after all, he was not so stupid that he couldn't guess what we had wanted the gimlet and knife for. Furthermore, he must have told Brad how far along we were, else Brad would not have designated the date on which we should try to break out.

In the late afternoon, it began to rain. Occasionally we even heard sleet against the window near the ceiling. This might lull the British into relaxing their vigil — sentries would be less apt to think prisoners would try to escape on a night such as this promised to be — but when I thought of what might happen to Captain Vail as a result of being exposed to such weather, I began to wonder if we hadn't better call the whole thing off. I put it up to him frankly before darkness set in, but he shook his head.

"I'd rather chance one night of this than six months of confinement in Dartmoor," he said with a wry grin.

When Bertie Lord brought our supper, a greasy lamb stew, he hovered over us so much I grew nervous. "Well Bertie, is it still raining?" I asked.

"Can't you hear it? Listen!"

Captain Vail paused, spoon in midair. "I'd say it was bucketing right down. Awful night, Bertie, real bad."

"That ain't the only thing that's bad, Cap'n," and Bertie twitched his head around to see if the guard was near.

"What's the latest calamity?" Vail asked.

"Bierce an' Jake Rudd arrived an hour ago, an' the man-o'-war you two are goin' to England in is due in sometime tomorrow."

This was a shocker for sure. We looked at him, then at each other. But only for a moment. Dipping his spoon into the gray mess of stew, Captain Vail said, "Well, now, Bierce and Rudd in at the kill, wouldn't you guess that of them? Bertie, you stay away from them. They're bad news."

"Yes, sir," said Bertie. "Fact is, I may get outa here myself sometime, an' if I couldn't get out the regular way, I'd follow the river shore north'ard. I sure wouldn't let fellers like that catch me."

"I wouldn't if I were you, Bertie," said Vail. "Our luck, Jonathan, that we're prisoners of the British instead of Bierce and Rudd."

"Right," I said. But my mind was on Bertie's remark about following the shore northward. That just didn't slip out of him, I was certain. Was Brad going to meet us at some point beyond the fort or the peninsula? And his having indicated tonight as the night to escape must mean that he, too, had heard of the British warship's impending arrival.

After Bertie left with a good night that sounded suspiciously like good-bye, Captain Vail again went over with me, as he had many times before, the plan we'd follow: to the attic until we reached the middle entry, down a trap door to a ramp that moved up to the wall of the fort, along the wall to a spot midway between sentry boxes, then down the outside of the wall by means of blankets lashed to a picket post. It sounded so simple, so indeed like a routine exercise, that I could almost persuade myself there was nothing to worry

[ 259 ]

about — until I realized how quickly I was breathing and how sweaty my palms were.

Suddenly heavy footsteps sounded outside the cell door, a key grated in the lock, and Matt Coombs stepped inside. "You men ready to leave tomorrow?"

"We haven't much to get ready, Coombs," Vail said. "We'll be waiting for a look at our new home."

"Huh! You'll be wishin' you was back here tomorrow night. Look, I got a visitor for you. Know him?"

We glanced around, and there was Bierce standing outside the grated door.

Instantly I asked Coombs, "How did he get in? I thought only military personnel were allowed in this barrack."

"Just checking to see that you and Captain Vail are still safe here, Dearborn," Bierce said with a grin.

"Well, take a good look. I guess it'll be the last time you'll see us for quite a while."

"I'm weeping, Dearborn."

"This thought of not seeing you shatters me, too, Bierce. But you don't belong here now, I'm certain. I don't believe you have permission from anyone but Coombs, and you probably bribed him."

"What do you mean, bribed me?" Coombs's voice was ugly.

"I don't think General Gosselin would like to hear about it," I said.

"Dearborn," said Bierce, "did it ever occur to you that the general is a friend of mine?"

"The more fool he, then," I said.

"Coombs," Captain Vail's voice was calm but the tone was sharp, "what do you and Bierce want of us? If it's all the same to you, we'd like to sleep."

"Sleep! My God, Vail, you'll get enough sleep at Dartmoor! For that matter, just cough long enough an' you'll hawk up your lungs, an' then you'll sleep for a long time."

"Bastard!" I said.

"That's enough out of you!" Coombs shouted, and rounded on me.

But it was Bierce who poured oil on this particular piece of troubled water. "I think I've seen enough, Matt," he said. "Let's get out of here. They're secure until morning. Once they're in England they'll be secure until peace is signed."

"You can have us put away in Dartmoor," Captain Vail said, "but one of these months we'll be back."

Even as he spoke, he burst into a spasm of coughing. After it passed, Bierce's eyebrow arched. "Maybe," he said, "maybe. But, by then, it won't matter, will it? Who will listen to you? The war will be over, and no one will be interested in what happened during it. Every one will be wanting to forget these days and will only be interested in the new opportunities of peace."

"Peace will still be a while coming," I said.

"To be sure. But the commissioners are hard at work in Ghent, as you know, and even John Quincy Adams won't be able to prevent the British from annexing permanently all this part of Maine east of the Penobscot. As far as I'm concerned, the sooner we have peace, the sooner the markets of the world will open up for those who want to make money, and candidly I'm one of them. You two men are an obstacle to good relations between the British here in Castine and the rest of Maine. That's why I'll be relieved to see you aboard the *Isis* and bound for England."

"Well, Bierce," I said, "I think you're a traitor, a would-be murderer, and a mercenary devil if there ever was one. But at least, in your way, you're being honestly a scoundrel, which I suppose is something in your favor."

His face went liver-red, then white with rage, but he kept his voice under control when he said with heavy sarcasm, "Good of you to concede something to me, Dearborn. I'll try to think as kindly of you."

"You do that. Now why don't you and Coombs leave us alone and let us get our last good sleep ashore for a while?"

Once the door had closed on them, I looked inquiringly at Captain Vail and nodded toward the ceiling.

He shook his head. "Too early. We'd better blow out this candle and get ourselves some sleep."

"Sleep! How can you sleep when you know what lies ahead of us?"

"I don't know, not really. Do you? Maybe that's why I can sleep.

[ 261 ]

Now you'd best bed down, son. I'll have no trouble waking up in time."

But sleep was impossible. I went over all the steps we'd have to go through in order to get out of the fort and tried to anticipate what we'd do if we encountered obstacles we hadn't planned on. I wondered especially if Bierce himself were not taking measures on his own to prevent our escaping. I realized, too, that some people in Maine shared his views regarding the war and the peace. Had all the suffering and bloodshed and gallantry in this conflict been for nothing? Was there no one who could restore the reputation of our country for courage and honor? Could General Jackson down in the South do that if given a chance? But he had few troops and a reputation here in New England for having so violent a temper and such wild political views on the rights of the people that sober men of property like the Federalists had nothing good to say of him. Damn it, we New Englanders were always so sure we were right and the rest of the country wrong! Would we never learn to pull together?

Suddenly my shoulder was being shaken and I saw Captain Vail standing over me. "Let's go, Jonathan," he whispered.

I didn't know whether I had fallen asleep or not, but I had certainly not heard him get up. At any rate, I quickly stuffed my stockings into my shoes and placed one shoe into each of the side pockets of my jacket which I stripped off. Then after we carried the table over to the barred window, I leaped onto it and went to work with the knife, cutting through the line of perforations. It was a trying process, hard on my patience and my hands and wrists. It also made considerable noise. Occasionally I slackened the cutting, waiting for the bursts of sleet against the window to drown the sound of the knife; then I worked furiously. Once, at a warning "Psst!" from Captain Vail, I jumped off the table, the two of us quickly whipped it over to its place, then we fell onto our cots and lay motionless. A moment later, the officer of the day and the sentry looked in at us, the lantern the officer held high casting flickering beams over us. After what seemed an interminable time he left. Never before had a check been made on us so early in the night; this extra precaution on our last night made me even more uneasy than I had been before.

The redcoats gone, Captain Vail and I quickly rose, and I went to work again with the knife. At last the ceiling rectangle came free and I passed it down to Vail, who gently laid it on the floor. Then we caught up our coats, with our pocketed shoes and our single blanket apiece, and stood on the table. Carefully I poked our shoes, coats and blankets into the attic. Afterward I bent down and, taking Captain Vail onto my shoulders, I stood up while he scrambled through the aperture. Vail now tied the blankets together and, looping one around a beam, let the other down to me. Momentarily I swung like a pendulum until, climbing with a hand-over-hand motion, I grabbed the edges of the opening, thrust myself through, and lunged forward onto the floor. For a few seconds I lay there gasping. Then at a tap on the shoulder from Vail, I rose, and the two of us, bent double, groped our way toward the middle entry.

Thanks to the candle, hurriedly ignited with flint and steel, we had no difficulty locating the trap door which, after a good deal of frantic tugging, I succeeded in removing. Now putting on my coat and looping the blanket around my waist, I dropped easily into the passageway. For an instant the bitter cold bit through my feet almost as if it were a flame. Then Captain Vail was beside me and the two of us slipped up the passage, gently lifted the latch of the door toward the wall, and slid through.

Dark as it was out here, it was still lighter than in the passageway. For a moment, however, the mixture of sleet and rain prevented us from seeing more than a few feet in front of us. But there was no missing the wall looming ahead, a mass of dark earth and rocks covered white from the sleet.

Glancing around, we quickly moved forward in a crouch and picked our way up the wall. To move directly up was out of the question because of the steepness and the slipperiness, so we slanted toward the right, leaning in against the wall. It was rough on our feet, but we dared not put on our shoes because of the noise they might make. Twice Vail paused for breath, and once he slipped. With the greatest of efforts I reached up and steadied him.

We headed toward a point between sentry boxes on the wall. Reaching the top of the wall, we crept along, hugging the rampart as closely as we could. We knew it was about time for changing the sentries and, consequently, those on duty would soon be walking past and would be doubly alert. Up to now the storm had kept them in their boxes, so we moved as fast as we could before they should come outside onto the wall.

Midway between two boxes we stopped, and tying our blankets together, I knotted one end around a picket. Then, while I kept watch, Captain Vail lowered himself to the ground outside. A moment later I joined him, and we threaded our way through the jagged points of the *chevaux de frise* which the British had placed against the wall to slow up any storming party the Americans might throw against the fort.

We were clear of the fort but still deep in danger. It would only be minutes before our escape would be noticed either in our cell or along the top of the wall where, if the sentries missed our footprints in the snow, they couldn't miss the blanket on the picket. Yet, danger or no danger, we stopped to put our shoes on our freezing, bruised feet. Then with Captain Vail in the lead, since he knew the area, we rushed across an open field and into an old woodlot where we groped our way among the stumps, bushes, and rocks.

No sooner had we reached this place than a gun boomed and we heard the clatter of steel on steel as armed details rushed from the fort. Almost at once answering guns echoed hollowly from ships in the harbor. We knew that it wouldn't be long before boats from the men-of-war would be scouring the shore, and the possibility that we might be caught made me press Captain Vail so closely he waved me back.

"Save your strength," he whispered. "We've a long way to go."

Then we reached the cove where General Wadsworth had made his escape from the same fort back in 1780.

"Let's go!" Vail said, and plunged into the water.

Fortunately the tide was far from full so that we went in only up to our waists, but the water was so cold I nearly doubled up when it reached my genitals, and before we had gone a third of the half-mile distance to the opposite shore, my teeth were chattering. I could only guess how it must be affecting Captain Vail, for he ploughed on through the freezing water as if the temperature were that of August. It was only when we were about one hundred yards from shore that he began to falter. Instantly I was at his side. Though he shook me

[ 264 ]

off at first, he presently let me support him. Once we reached the beach, I half dragged him into the protection of a clump of alders, where we both fell to the ground and gulped in the cold, wet air. This set off a spasm of coughing which he tried to smother, and, in doing so, he sounded as if he were strangling.

When he began to cough, I stood up and looked around. Through the murk I could see the torches of search details, and occasionally heard a shout. Gradually the redcoats were bearing over toward where we were but following the curve of the land rather than cutting directly across through the water. We had a few minutes start on them, but only a few.

"Can you go on?" I asked.

He started to get up, and I helped him. "Go on? Hell, yes, we can't waste any more time."

Our idea now was to reach the Penobscot. The woods were thick and the brush was tangled, but somewhere up along the river bank was either Brad or a boat — of this I felt sure; and Brad would know I would remember where we had hidden the skiff originally intended for the escape.

But pushing through this mass of wilderness was rugged work. I don't know how Captain Vail kept moving, but from some source, some inner strength of spirit I suspect, he found the energy to stumble along. Once we heard shouts along the peninsula road to the east, and we knew that if the British threw a file of troops from the road directly to the shore and, like a line of beaters in a hunt in India, worked southward, they would be almost certain to catch us as we moved northward ahead of another body of pursuers. Something like panic began to grip us as we slipped and lurched along.

All at once I heard a subdued shout so near that we halted, breathing heavily. Again came the shout — it was my name being called — "Jonathan!"

"It's Brad Pettigrew!" I said, and, cupping my hands, shouted back.

In a few moments we saw him just below us in a boat. Quickly we scrambled down to the shore while he and another man we soon recognized as Philip Adair brought the boat in and helped us aboard.

"Are they close?" Brad asked as he and Philip bent to their oars.

"Very close, I think," I said. "They were hemming us in by land."

"What about boats?"

"The men-of-war know we've escaped, and Bierce and Rudd are up here in their sloop."

"Damn them. That means boats will be out and maybe Bierce will bring his sloop around, too, though he's probably manned a boat."

With that I wrapped a blanket from the boat around Captain Vail and handed him a bottle of whiskey Brad had brought along. I then reached for another bottle, and the whiskey, scorching my throat as I gulped it greedily, gradually warmed me to the point where I no longer shivered uncontrollably.

Suddenly Philip whispered, "Here they come!"

Peering through the rain and sleet, I could see two boats skirting the eastern shore. For a moment I believed we were undiscovered. Then farther down the river but also farther out, moving to cut us off, a dark mass was dimly visible. Suddenly orange flame blossomed from a small cannon aboard her, but we never even heard where the ball went. What troubled us was that the third boat's cannon shot had called the attention of the two inshore boats to us so that they now headed our way.

When General Wadsworth and Major Burton escaped in 1780, they crossed the Penobscot at a point higher up. Where we now were, the river was wider. The obvious course for us would seem to have been up the river, but that would have meant bucking the current as we aimed diagonally for the western shore. I doubted that we'd ever reach land before being overhauled by one of the heavily manned British boats.

"Brad," I asked, "have you alerted anyone on the western shore?"

"The Belfast people will have two boats out looking for us, and Jess Moore will be up from Camden in his sloop."

"Moore!"

"Yes, Moore. He figured this was the one scrap in the war he wanted a part in. Camden is plenty mad over the British keeping their hostages so long, and the whole western shore is sore about the British shipping Captain Vail off to England."

"Of course you didn't do a thing about spreading the story!"

Philip Adair laughed. "Mr. Pettigrew here is going to make a fine lawyer. How's Cap'n Vail now?"

At mention of his name Vail raised his hand. "I'm all right, Adair," he said in a surprisingly strong voice. "What's the situation, Jonathan?"

Quickly I told him. He thought for a moment, peered over the gunwale, then said, "It stands to reason we can't stay on this course much longer."

"Yes, sir," I said. "I'll relieve Brad in a moment and later he can spell Philip, but that won't help us much, not unless Jess Moore or those Belfast boats get here in time."

"Is Moore armed?" Vail asked Brad.

"He's got two three-pounders mounted."

"Popguns. How about men?"

"Nothing to worry about there. Half of Camden wanted to go. Wouldn't be surprised if Colonel Foote himself is aboard."

"How about the Belfast craft?"

"One sloop — I don't know how she's armed. The other's a whale-boat with a three-pounder and well manned."

"Good. But we'll play for Moore. He could probably hold his own against whoever's after us. Now, Jonathan, take Brad's place. Brad you come back here and be my eyes. We're going to cut down toward that third boat."

"That's pretty risky, Cap'n," I said.

"Of course it is, but it'll soon be more so if we stay as we are now. When that boat comes about to keep us from ducking between her and Castine, we'll come about in the opposite direction and head down toward the western passage."

"Then she'll come about, too."

"Of course — there's a numbskull in command if she doesn't! But when she does, we'll try something else. You bring any muskets for us, Brad?"

"Two muskets and two pistols."

"Good lad. We'll use 'em if for no other reason than to attract Moore's attention. I hope they fire that cannon again, too. That'll make even more sound and light."

I don't know whether I was more amazed or delighted. A few minutes ago Vail seemed like a broken man, wheezing, coughing, and shuddering with cold. Now he was like his old, vigorous self, though the fact that he remained huddled in his blanket in the bottom of the boat, raising his head only to peer through the snow, was evidence enough that he was ill. He leaned his head against Brad's knee, while Philip and I put our backs into the rowing.

"Take it easy, you two," Vail cautioned us. "We've still a long way to go. Save your strength for maneuvering."

The words were no more than out of his mouth when the cannon boomed again, and this time the shot went over our heads with a great "whoosh!"

Then Captain Vail gave his order, and we swung sharply downriver. As we did so, the snow swirled about us so densely we lost sight of our enemies. We must have disappeared from their view for the moment, too. But only for a moment.

"God damn it, there they are!" came a bellow.

All of us recognized the voice as Jake Rudd's.

"Give him a shot, Brad, if your priming's dry enough," Captain Vail said.

Brad fumbled with the musket for a long time but finally fired. Again he fired, and this time the cannon replied, but to no effect. At Brad's third shot, we heard a yelp of pain followed by a storm of cursing as oars clashed.

"Good man!" Vail said. "That'll keep us respectable. Now let's come about again, and you spell Adair this time, Brad."

It had been a daring maneuver, and it succeeded, but only for a brief time since Rudd was soon churning after us. Had it not been for the storm, he would soon have taken us. Luckily the snow prevented us from ever being a clear target for either his cannon or his muskets. Yet this maneuvering about and firing served only to bring the two British boats closer to us. Philip and Brad were now back rowing, and I was firing one musket as fast as I could load it, while Captain Vail, who had thrown off his blanket, was pot-shotting away with the other.

All this, of course, couldn't keep up for long. We'd soon be captured, if not killed, but the sheer relief of fighting back, even if there wasn't much chance of scoring a real hit in the storm and with the waves beginning to hurl us about, gave me a kind of fierce joy.

Then a bullet from Rudd's boat struck my musket just as I was bringing it down to aim. In a flash the weapon was torn out of my hands and flung into the water while I was thrown onto Captain Vail, my head striking the gunwale.

Blazing pinwheels whirled in my brain, but I straightened up, grabbed a pistol and fired at Rudd's boat. The shriek that followed gave me a vivid but brief satisfaction for I realized that in a moment Rudd and the British would be upon us. Frantically I reloaded the pistol, praying there might be time to get in one more shot. Then Captain Vail broke into a cheer in that monstrous voice of his, and as I turned to where he was pointing, I saw a sloop crowded with men, its sweeps driving it powerfully forward, crash into one of the British boats. That little area of the Bay then broke into a wild melee of shooting, shouting, and cursing.

Our pursuers turned at once on the sloop, and this was too much for Vail. "Let's get back there and help!" he shouted.

Quickly Philip and Brad brought us about, while I reloaded a second pistol. Then, shouting like madmen, we drove toward one of the barges. Both Vail with his musket and I with the two pistols fired at the same time. Which of us hit the British who fired at us I'll never know, but our attack must have seemed even more formidable than it was; and it was formidable enough as Philip Adair, using his oar like a great scythe, knocked over two British seamen. His efforts, however, nearly capsized us and sent him sprawling into the water.

But Philip was under us and in from the other side with a swiftness that was startling.

"Rudd! Rudd! Let's get after Rudd!" he yelled.

Having lost one oar, he now wrenched Brad's oars from him and started rowing us to the other side of the sloop.

Despite the fighting the three of us stared at him. He seemed demented.

Then from the west a cannon roared, and we heard the shouts of many men. "Belfast! Belfast!" came down the wind.

At this the British and Rudd gave up and fled, and, weeping with rage, Philip Adair pulled us alongside the sloop.

"That you, Ben Vail?" Jess Moore called out.

"I'm Vail," the Captain said.

The Camden men burst into cheers, and a dozen pairs of hands eagerly hauled us aboard.

A few moments later a huge whaleboat hove in sight.

"You got Vail?" a man in the bow asked.

"You bet I have, but you fellers came just in time," Moore said.

"Thank God, Vail's safe!" the Belfast leader said, and his crew also cheered.

"Look here," Moore said, "we better all get back home before something else happens. It's gettin' rough, too."

"Got any rum aboard, Moore?" someone on the Belfast boat asked.

"You come alongside an' I've got a whole keg for you," Moore said, and as the cheers and laughter died, he added, "compliments of Colonel Foote. Got some for ourselves, too."

The night had ended well: we'd made our escape, our rescuers had suffered only a few casualties and nothing very serious at that, and we'd given the Castine British a taste of defeat, small encounter though it was. For all this I was deeply grateful.

But my sympathy now lay with Philip Adair; he had wanted to deal with Jake Rudd in his own way as I wanted to deal with Warren Bierce in mine — and I wasn't sure that at the time the ways differed greatly. Both Rudd and Bierce, however, seemed to flourish despite us. On the other hand, the escape must itself be a blow to them, certainly to Bierce, if one could judge from his eagerness to see us off to England.

"Philip, let's get some rum," I said to the big Negro.

He shook his head, but when I returned with a pannikin of rum for him, he accepted it with a gracious acknowledgment and drained it in a single gulp. Then, sighing, he rose to his feet, swaying with the movement of the sloop.

"Mr. Dearborn," he said, his voice half resigned, but only half, "the Bible says that vengeance belongs to the Lord. I believe this, but I also believe He acts through men, and I surely want to be one of His instruments."

"If that's what you want to be, I hope you'll get the chance," I said; and went to the keg to refill his pannikin and mine.

My own role I could never envisage in such lofty and dreadful terms, but I surely shared his desire to bring a ruthless enemy to a reckoning.

[ 270 ]

# FOUR

## *The Hartford Convention*
## *and*
## *the Last Hours of the* Ghost

[December, 1814–February, 1815]

# XXVII

ONCE we had reached Camden, Colonel Foote took Captain Vail into his house, brought a doctor to care for him, and posted guards around the house. Only then, when we felt there was nothing further that we could do for "Little Ben," did we leave for Portland.

On the way home Brad told me what had happened after my arrest. At first he and Philip had fled to where we had concealed the skiff and thence to Camden until the search was halted. Then he slipped back to Castine, where the Widow Wells concealed him. While in Castine, he had kept in touch with Bertie Lord, whose courage he had constantly to bolster. When Bertie told him about our progress with the gimlet, Brad rowed across the Penobscot, informed Jess Moore and Colonel Foote, who quietly alerted patriotic elements in both Camden and Belfast. Later when he returned and learned through the Widow of the impending arrival of the man-of-war that was to take us to England, he sent us the hurry-up message through Bertie and went far up the Penobscot to signal by fire to Philip who had camped out on the opposite shore. Philip then sent messengers galloping to both Camden and Belfast, and rowed across the river to join Brad and wait all that next day for us. All three of us, however, knew that without the help of Moore and the others, our lot now would be miserable indeed.

We discovered, on arriving in Portland, that the excitement over the Vail case quickly subsided and that the talk was now all about the Hartford Convention, which was due to meet on December 15. Admire Mr. Longfellow though I did, and deeply respect him, too, I could not cheer his election to the Convention. In fact, I disapproved of the Convention as a divisive factor in the political life of the country and especially dangerous in view of the war.

All this welled up in me one evening in Marston's Tavern when Brad and I were nursing a glass of rum. Perhaps I had drunk too much already; at any rate I expressed my opinion of the Convention and New England's attitude toward the war in a voice that must have carried. Had I not enjoyed, together with Brad, a little local notoriety because of my role in the Vail incident, I think the murmurs and growls of disagreement that my opinions touched off might have turned into something more formidable. As it was, I heard numerous allusions to me as "the God-damned Republican!" "that Jeffersonian jackass!" and "a Madison fool!" Brad finally persuaded me to leave with him before anyone became violent.

At noon the next day, while we were at dinner, a little colored boy arrived with a note from Jedediah Daniels asking me if I could find it convenient to call on him that afternoon.

I handed the note to my parents and watched their faces as they read. My father looked surprised; my mother, alarmed. Though I had never met him, Jedediah Daniels had a reputation as a redoubtable follower of Jefferson and Madison. More to the point, perhaps, at least as far as my mother's expression was concerned, he was the present editor and publisher of the *Eastern Courier*, a weekly newspaper founded years before to support Jefferson and the cause of democracy. Like his fellow Portlander, the forthright Francis Douglass, and his *Eastern Argus*, founded even earlier, in 1803 to be exact, for the same purpose, Daniels and his paper had many enemies, but numerous supporters, too, especially among the poorer folk.

"Whatever does this mean, Jonathan?" my mother asked.

"Yes, Jonathan," my father said in his quiet way, "I know Jedediah Daniels fairly well. He is a good man, a brave man, too, but he's a bloodhound for news as you can tell from the story in his paper of Captain Vail's escape. Have you done anything else to prompt his interest?"

"Absolutely nothing," I said, "unless it was my foolishness last night, and I can't see how that would be news worth publishing."

My first impression of Jedediah Daniels was that there was little remarkable about him. He was a mild-mannered, loose-jointed man, whose brown coat was flecked with dust and bits of paper from the stacks of newspapers and foolscap on his desk. He glanced up over his spectacles as I opened the door of the printing house and the bell jangled my entrance.

"Glad you dropped in, Mr. Dearborn," he said in a voice almost as soft as Philip Adair's.

He got up, slid the bolt on a cage door to his office, and asked me to come inside. He must have noticed my surprise, for he said, "I had this cage installed around my office at the outbreak of the war for extra protection in case a mob didn't like what I printed. You may remember the Baltimore riots in 1812 when a mob stormed a printing press office and a jail, killing General Lingan and wounding 'Light Horse Harry' Lee so that he'll probably never recover. I don't want to take any unnecessary chances."

"What about your press? Is that protected, too?"

"Yes, Mr. Dearborn, that's protected the same way and my printer and his assistant are armed. So far we've had nothing but threats, and every newspaper gets those. Now, then, sit here," and he removed a pile of old newspapers from an extra chair in his office.

As I sat down, I could hear the voices of the two men back in his shop as they set type for the next issue; they were so loud I had to strain to hear what Mr. Daniels was saying. The air smelled of ink, damp paper, dust, and stale tobacco. It was also chilly in the room; the Franklin stove used to warm both the shop and the office was hardly sufficient. Altogether, this must be an uncomfortable place to work, and yet I had to admit to myself that there was a kind of pleasing excitement at being at the very center of where all that happened in Portland and Maine and the country — and the world, too, for that matter — was recorded and editorially appraised.

"Now, Mr. Dearborn," and Mr. Daniels gave me a long, searching look, while his nose twitched like a rabbit's, "I was at Marston's Tavern last night. You were very eloquent. *In vino veritas?*"

I shifted uncomfortably. "The rum may have made me what you call 'eloquent,' sir, but I've held those opinions for some time."

"If I remember correctly, you were firmly in favor of the war. Now I gather you are really opposed to it."

"At this stage, yes. Reluctantly."

"Why?"

"I think this war was a just one, but with the country now threatening to fall apart, from divisions of opinion and lack of a concerted will to fight and with the British winning just about everywhere, I feel the sooner we make peace, the better."

"Isn't that what the Federalists also believe?"

"I suppose it is — essentially. But it's in good part owing to their opposition to the war that the country is now in this situation, and the Hartford Convention will only make things worse."

"Do you think the Convention intends to propose the separation of New England from the Union, Mr. Dearborn?"

"I don't know, sir."

"A separatist movement would be an act of treason, would it not?"

"That is my opinion, sir."

"It is mine, too, Mr. Dearborn." He picked up a quill and spun it in his fingers. "Do you intend to accompany Mr. Longfellow to Hartford?"

"No, sir. He's been in Boston, and we haven't talked for weeks. Besides, if Mr. Longfellow takes anyone with him to assist him, it will more likely be a young Federalist than a Republican."

"Would you like to go to Hartford?"

"Well, I'd never thought of it, but, yes, I would, though I feel certain Mr. Longfellow will not ask me."

Though his longish face remained expressionless, the nose began to twitch again. "Mr. Dearborn, if my information about you is correct — and I have taken the trouble to procure more than you suspect, young man — you and Warren Bierce of this town are not exactly the best of friends. Do you know that one of the strongest supporters of the Convention is Bierce and that he is leaving for Hartford as a spectator to the sessions?"

If I knew Bierce, his would not be exactly a spectator role — he'd pressure every delegate he could get his hands on. "I'm not really surprised, Mr. Daniels," I said, "I've questioned his loyalty to this country a long time, but I still don't see what you're driving at."

Daniels sat back in his chair, folded his hands over his small paunch, and looked at me with those deceptively gentle eyes. "Mr. Dearborn," he said, "the Hartford Convention may be one of the most important events in the history of our young country or it may go down in history as New England's folly. Whichever it is, it will be news of consummate interest to our people in Maine, or should be. If you are not accompanying Stephen Longfellow to Hartford, I should like you to go as a special agent of mine. You can say, to those curious, that you are reporting the Convention's proceedings for this newspaper, and so you will be."

For a moment I could only look at him like a schoolroom dunce baffled by a long word he was asked to spell. Then, grateful yet suspicious, I said, "That's very good of you, sir, but . . ."

He raised his hand, if not his voice. "You have not been delinquent in this war, Mr. Dearborn, but this is a patriotic duty I am charging you with."

"But it would be like spying on Mr. Longfellow!" I protested.

"Nonsense! I want you to go to him and tell him exactly what I wish you to do. I'm sure he will not object."

"You see, Mr. Dearborn," he continued, "I have already taken the trouble to communicate with him, and he graciously said that he would be at least as open with you as with other reporters — and there will be a number in Hartford, I assure you. He also said he thought that your working for me would be a valuable experience for you."

Daniels's voice was as dry as a twig as he said this last; two men could scarcely be farther apart politically than he and Stephen Longfellow. "But, by all means," he went on, "see Mr. Longfellow and satisfy yourself."

"I will," I said.

"Should he, by any chance, have changed his mind since I spoke with him this morning —"

"You spoke with him this morning?" I interrupted. "Mr. Longfellow is back from Boston?"

"Arrived last night. But, as I started to say, should he have changed his mind, I hope you will give serious attention to another consideration. It concerns Warren Bierce. I am a member of the syndicate that owns the *Argus*, Mr. Dearborn. We are certain that Bierce is a traitor — not just a smuggler or an antiwar Federalist — and we are assembling evidence in this country and abroad. When we have enough, we will go to court. I understand that your experiences with him not only help confirm our suspicions but also expose him to other serious charges. Naturally we shall want a complete deposition from you and anyone else whose statements may help us."

But as I was about to burst into a flurry of questions, he again held up his hand. "Bierce is a highly regarded man in Portland for all the rumors about his connection with the Vail case, so we must be careful and thorough. In Hartford your duty will be to observe him and keep a record, however trivial it may appear at times. But do not quarrel with him, Mr. Dearborn, and do not give him the slightest suspicion that you are other than what you appear to be, a reporter for the *Eastern Courier*. Is all this clear?"

"Yes, sir."

"Good. I shall expect your answer at nine o'clock tomorrow morning."

Hartford is a gracious little river port of a little more than six thousand people, smaller and cleaner than Portland but lacking the hilltop view of our Casco Bay. As between the waterfronts of the two cities, that early winter of 1814, there wasn't much to choose — both were dead. Hartford's Main and State streets are wider than anything Portland has, and its shade trees challenge Portland's in number and height, though then, as at home, they were like gray skeletons. I don't think Portland need doff its hat to Hartford's private residences, but, of course, none among Portland's public buildings, nor any in Maine, for that matter, can compete with Connecticut's State House, designed by Charles Bulfinch of Boston and constructed for $52,480, which the state had a hard time raising; Connecticut's religious politicians even tried a public lottery which failed.

On another count, however, Connecticut could boast superiority not only over the District of Maine but also over any New England state or any state in the Union with the possible exception of Delaware: the prevalence and intensity of its Federalism. Coming down on the coach from Portland, and while stopping over in Boston for two days with my cousin, Paul Dearborn, at his Louisburg Square home, I heard little talked about but the Convention. Paul and Cynthia were Federalists to the core and quoted prominent Fed-

[ 278 ]

eralists like Timothy Pickering and John Lowell as feeling the Union was practically dissolved and being very glad of it, especially Pickering. There was widespread suspicion, however, that some of the Convention delegates who were leaders, like George Cabot and Harrison Gray Otis, were too moderate. In the November elections, people throughout New England had voted overwhelmingly for peace, and sent most Republican candidates down to defeat. They had also voted strongly for the Convention, which they hoped would alter the fundamental law with respect to the powers of the federal government and the states, giving the states far more authority. Among the Federalist objectives were the prevention of a national draft, a denial of power to the national government to take over the militia, and the use of federal taxes to support the militia. The Boston *Centinel* was virtually advocating disunion, while Republican papers like the *National Intelligencer* and the *Patriot* became increasingly pessimistic about the possibility of saving the Union unless peace was declared. But neither these papers nor our own *Eastern Courier* and *Eastern Argus*, nor, for that matter, most of the Maine Federalists, let alone Republicans in both Maine and Massachusetts, were willing to accept peace on the terms that Pickering and Lowell and Governor Strong found acceptable. These terms were the British terms, which included the Crown's annexation of eastern Maine. There were, therefore, differences of opinion in Massachusetts and Maine, both as between Federalists and Republicans and within the Federalist ranks themselves.

These differences were less noticeable in Connecticut. I arrived in Hartford three days before the Convention opened on December 15, found a boarding house not too unreasonable in its charges and not too far away from the State House, and at once discovered that, even more than in Boston, wherever I went the Convention dominated conversation, and there was much discussion of the intense Federalist sentiment that had led to its election. I knew, of course, there were many Republicans in Connecticut, but I met few. Federalists were everywhere in evidence and controlled the state. It was, in fact, largely a one-party state ruled by an aristocracy of property, particularly in the small towns and villages, and dominated by the Congregational Church. When, earlier in the year, the Madison administration passed the hated conscription law, the Connecticut Assembly declared it unconstitutional by a vote of 168 to 6. Connecticut Federalists were every bit as active as those to the north in condemning the war as a means of preserving the dynasty of Republican presidents from Virginia, of securing for the West the Indian lands and even Canada, and of aiding the South in its expansionist aspirations toward Florida and Mexico. The war was viewed as a conspiracy against New England, and support for the Convention was very strong in the Assembly, which had voted in favor of it, 153 to 36. To read such organs of Federalism as the *Connecticut Courant* and the *Connecticut Mirror*, though not the *American Mercury*, which was Republican, led one like myself to wonder if Americans could ever recover the unity they had once possessed.

Except for the extreme Federalism of some of their number, my father and I had enjoyed reading about the Hartford Wits and what they wrote, especially Joel Barlow's epic poem, *The Columbiad*, and John Trumbull's caricature of the Tories, *McFingal*. Before I left for the Convention, however, my father showed me a yellowed newspaper clipping of a poem a clergyman friend had sent him years ago from Philadelphia. It was by some unknown anti-Federalist who loathed the Wits and their politics and bore lines which I could not help remembering now when I heard so much of the Convention:

> *Hartford! curst corner of the spacious earth!*
> *Where each dire mischief ripens into birth. . . .*
> *Hartford, detested more by faction's race*
> *Than hardened sinner hates the call of grace.*

Yet fear and decry the Convention as I did, I could not deny the distinction and qualifications of many of its members. Of the twenty-six delegates, whose average age was fifty-two years, twenty-two were graduates of colleges and law schools and nine of the twenty-two were judges. Many of them had splendid records of public service in the army during the Revolution, in their state legislatures, and in Congress. To mention a few members from Massachusetts proper, there were George Cabot, white-haired and affable, one of the founders of the Federalist Party; Harrison Gray Otis, a lawyer not quite fifty whom I had heard speak in Boston and who had a notable record of service in Congress and his state legislature; Nathan Dane, who in the Continental Congress had proposed the Territorial Ordinance of 1787 with its antislavery provision; Timothy Bigelow, the one extreme Federalist present and a prominent lawyer, who had recently been elected for the sixth time Speaker of the Massachusetts House of Representatives. From our District of Maine came Samuel S. Wilde of Hallowell, a lawyer and a former member of the Governor's Council, and my own respected mentor, Stephen Longfellow, Jr., graduate of the Harvard class of '98, member of the legislature that had voted for the Convention, and a man who was generally considered as possessing the ablest legal mind in Portland. Connecticut sent, among its delegates, the distinguished Chauncey Goodrich, lawyer, former mayor of Hartford, former Congressman and U.S. Senator, and presently lieutenant governor of Connecticut; tall James Hillhouse, Revolutionary soldier, treasurer of Yale University, former member of Congress, serving in the House and then the Senate; John Treadwell, old and fat, but with a remarkable record as a veteran of the Revolution, member of the Continental Congress, judge of probate for twenty years, lieutenant governor for two, and a writer of theological works; Nathaniel Smith, brilliant and eloquent, former member of his state legislature and of Congress, and presently judge of the Supreme Court of Connecticut.

Among all the remaining delegates Colonel Samuel Ward of Rhode Island towered like a Maine pine. His grandfather had been a governor and his father had founded Brown University, which, of course, lent him some prestige. But in his own right Ward had marched with Arnold to Quebec and had been captured in the attack on the city. A lieutenant colonel when the war ended, he went into the East India trade and became a great merchant. He had also been a representative of his state in the famous Annapolis Convention of 1786 and was greatly esteemed and respected. Close behind him in the regard of his fellow Rhode Islanders was Daniel Lyman of Newport, likewise an officer in the Revolution, surveyor and inspector general of Newport for twelve years, chief justice of Rhode Island, and president of the Society of the Cincinnati.

Anyone who takes the trouble to consider these men will easily see that one would look far to find a group of greater distinction and respectability. Timothy Pickering and John Lowell might complain of the temperate views of the delegates even before the Convention started, but that such "Wise Men from the East," as Gouverneur Morris, a New York Federalist, alluded to them, should be here in Hartford at all was alarming to many of us Republicans.

At first I thought I'd have little opportunity to meet any of them, but at one of the small hotels where I was dining and feeling lonely and a little sorry for myself I saw Stephen Longfellow enter with three men. He waved to me, and after I had finished and was on my way out, he asked me to join them for coffee.

"This is a young man whom I have high hopes for some day as a lawyer," he said, and introduced me to George Cabot, Harrison Gray Otis, and Timothy Bigelow. "Unlike us," Longfellow said with a smile, "Jonathan believes in this war, or did until recently."

"Ah ha, a Republican!" Otis said, and the cordiality seemed to go out of his smile. "Do you think Jefferson and Madison are still in favor of the war, young man?"

"I don't know that Mr. Jefferson ever was, sir," I said. "As for Mr. Madison, I presume he wouldn't have peace commissioners at work in Ghent if he weren't anxious to bring the war to an end."

"Good point, good point!" chuckled Bigelow, a big, cherubic-faced man.

Mine had been a cheeky reply, but Otis, though a kind-hearted man, had a smoothness of manner that made me want to ruffle him. I was grateful, however, that Bigelow cut in when he did.

"Actually, gentlemen," Cabot said in beautifully articulated English, "Jefferson, so I understand, is as anxious for peace as we are. What man with an iota of common sense is not, even Madison?"

"But you told us, Longfellow," said Otis with a smile that made me wary at once, "that this young man believed in the war until recently. Whatever changed his mind?"

Longfellow glanced at me. I couldn't say that he winked, but then I couldn't say that he didn't. "Jonathan left studying with me to go off privateering. He was with Benjamin Vail in the *Argus*."

"Vail!" Bigelow exclaimed. "Now there's a name to reckon with. He's right up there with Boyle of the *Chasseur* and Samuel Reid of the *General Armstrong*. By Jove, what a fight Reid put up in the Azores when the British tried to board him with boats. Pity he had to scuttle his ship."

"We faced the same sort of action off the Isle au Haut," I said, "but Captain Vail beat off the British."

"Great odds, I know," Bigelow said. "Just the same kind of fight Benedict Arnold would have loved. My father didn't get along well with Arnold — he even voted against Arnold's proposal to storm Quebec — but I remember when he said Arnold always had courage to the point of rashness — no one can take that away from the traitor."

Bigelow was one of the fiercest Federalists in New England despite his being "good company" and enjoying the role. But at the moment he seemed to have annoyed Otis. "I'm still curious why you lost your appetite for the war, Mr. Dearborn," Otis said with a slight frown at Bigelow.

Mr. Longfellow's eyes were on his coffee cup, though I knew he was listening, and not idly, despite my having gone to him after my interview with Jedediah Daniels of the *Eastern Courier* and explained my position on the war and my interest in accepting both of Daniels's proposals: that I report the Convention for his paper and that I keep an eye on Warren Bierce. Longfellow had said it would be a good experience for me, though he doubted that I'd learn much about the Convention proceedings and he warned me to be extraordinarily careful about Bierce. While he knew everything I would now say to these gentlemen, I felt that he was appraising me carefully as he toyed with his coffee cup.

To the other three, therefore, I related the fall of Castine as I saw it, the futile battle at Hampden, and the smuggling that developed between the Americans and the British at Castine. Mindful that they were busy men, I kept my account brief, especially of Vail's imprisonment, my own incarceration, and our escape. I told them candidly how I felt: that, in view of our defeats almost everywhere, the lack of concerted resistance for which our own New England must bear a large share of responsibility, and the disintegrating force of a fierce sectionalism, the United States should agree to peace.

"But not peace at any price!" I added hotly.

"What do you balk at, Mr. Dearborn?" Otis asked.

"The cession of eastern Maine to the British, sir."

They were silent when I finished. Then Jove-like but mild, Mr. Cabot said, "At least, Mr. Dearborn, we are agreed that we must have peace, though we arrive at it by different roads."

"And you mustn't think us wholly devoted to the disintegration of the Union!" Otis said with a flash of humor that completely passed Cabot by.

"Heavens, no," Cabot said, shaking his head. "I won't deny there are Federalists to whom that might not be unwelcome. But as I said to a young friend who asked me what I intended to do in Hartford, 'We are going to keep you young hotheads from getting into mischief.' We are not mischief-makers ourselves despite what you and your party may think of us, Mr. Dearborn."

He spoke as if I were a wayward son, but his smile, when he finished, helped still my annoyance. I thanked them for their graciousness, but as I started to leave, Otis stopped me with an eloquent gesture of his hand.

"Mr. Dearborn, do give us the benefit of the doubt," he said with the polished accents of an orator so that I felt as if he were addressing rather than speaking to me. "The future of our country lies with patriotic young men like yourself. I would not have you think that, though we are older, we have aught but the welfare of our beloved land at heart."

"Right, you're so right," Bigelow growled. "We're not traitors, whatever else the damned Republican press may call us."

"Hear, hear!" said Mr. Longfellow, and the others joined him.

And with that I left, feeling honored, annoyed, embarrassed, and, above all, puzzled. These men were Americans and absolutely sincere, yet the very act of holding a convention, particularly at this time, showed a lack of confidence in both the administration and the Constitution that could be fatally divisive in its effects on the country at large. Were they too shortsighted, too parochially minded not to perceive this? God knows, there were enough Republicans who were pointing to the dangers!

One subject I had not mentioned in my account to the delegates was Warren Bierce. While I had difficulty not naming him, I remembered Mr. Longfellow's words of caution and said nothing about him. Bierce might be in Hartford to persuade these men, but if they were of such wisdom as the *Connecticut Courant* claimed, they could surely recognize the falseness in a man like Bierce. Bigelow might be taken in by the man, and possibly Otis, though I doubted it, but never George Cabot.

I had inquired among various reporters from the local papers if they knew of Bierce's being in Hartford. Though they were generally a congenial group despite their politics, they said they knew only that a number of prominent New Englanders who were not delegates had taken up lodgings in Hartford for the duration of the Convention. I was advised, however, to see Colonel Thomas S. Jesup, commandant of the military district of Connecticut and also commander of the 25th Infantry, who was in the city at the time. Jesup was a man in his late twenties whose bravery at the battle of Chippewa in early July had earned him a brevet as lieutenant colonel and whose conduct at the battle of Niagara later in the same month had won him a full colonelcy. At Niagara he had been severely wounded but was now about recovered. He was ostensibly present in Hartford, I was told, for recruiting duty but actually to watch the Convention. He had made it no secret, either, that, at the first indication of an insurrection, he had been authorized to call on New York for additional troops to suppress the revolt. "Jesup knows everything that goes on here," they said.

Jesup, when I was reluctantly admitted to his headquarters by an officious aide, after he had conferred with the Colonel himself, turned out to be an officer whose deep wrinkle between his eyebrows gave him the appearance of being perpetually annoyed. He spoke in bursts of words which tended to confirm the impression, and his accent was unmistakably from south of the Mason-Dixon Line.

"My aide tells me you're a reporter. That right?"

"Yes, sir," I said, "I'm from —"

"I've given instructions to turn all reporters away. I don't want to see them. Understand?"

"Yes, sir, but —"

"But you're from the *Eastern Courier*, and that's favorable to the administration, so you told my aide. Right?"

"Yes, sir."

"What's your problem?"

"Colonel Jesup, I've been told that you know everything that goes on in Hartford right now and every stranger that enters the city."

"Nonsense, sheer nonsense! Wish it were true."

"I'm looking for a man named Warren Bierce. He's a merchant from Portland, Maine, and he's supposed to be down here for the Convention."

"Delegate?"

"An observer, I'd say."

"If he's like some of these arrivals who are not delegates, he intends to do more than observe. He probably hopes to get them to vote some kind of treasonous action."

"That's quite likely," I said. "He's opposed the war from the start."

"The more fool he."

"I couldn't agree more." Jesup seemed interested. I'd like to have told him more about Bierce, but, again remembering Mr. Longfellow's advice, I was cautious.

"What do you want me to do about him?" Jesup asked. "I can't arrest those who simply oppose the war. It would be unconstitutional. Besides, if I did, I'd have most of Connecticut in jail."

I shook my head. "I came to you, Colonel, just to inquire if you knew where Bierce is to be found. I'm not asking you to take any action against him."

He stared at me so long from across his desk that I felt uncomfortable. "Then why do you want to know where he is, so you can do something to him?"

"Not here and now, sir. I want to watch him and listen to him — nothing more."

"You sound more like a policeman than a reporter." Then he shrugged. "If he's the kind of man you indicate, Dearborn, I'll want to keep an eye on him myself. It looks to me as if this Convention intends to plan sedition, and if that turns out to be true, I'll throw the delegates into jail and all the hangers-on, too, on suspicion. If your man's among 'em, he'll get his, believe me. If he isn't, he's either too shrewd or not guilty, or you're a liar, Dearborn."

[ 286 ]

"Yes, sir — but I'm not."

"That remains to be seen. Where are you staying?"

"The Trumbull House."

"Very well, Dearborn. If I find out where your man Bierce is lodging, I'll let you know. Now are you attending the opening of the Convention tomorrow?"

When I said that that was certainly my intention, he shook his head. "My advice to you, Dearborn, is stay away. There may be trouble in and around the State House. Governor Smith and the city fathers here in Hartford don't like me or my authority, but I represent the government of the United States, and I won't see that government betrayed without taking action."

"Yes, sir. But you are aware, of course, sir, that the states voted the Convention no real authority and told the delegates to recommend nothing 'repugnant' to the states' 'obligations as members of the Union.'"

"I'm aware of that without needing you to remind me. By God, you sound like a supporter of the Convention yourself!"

"I deplore the Convention, sir, and I'm afraid of it despite the fact that many of the most distinguished delegates are moderate Federalists."

"Well, I deplore it, too, Dearborn, and I'm not afraid of it, and, so help me, I don't care how distinguished those men are, if they recommend anything seditious or treasonous, I'll throw a cordon of troops around the State House and arrest the lot of 'em. Good day, sir."

As I later walked through the windswept streets of Hartford, I wondered what, in the long run, the country had most to fear: the mercenary aims of corrupt men like Bierce, the narrow provincialism of well-intentioned men like the Convention delegates, or the hasty resort to force by patriotic soldiers.

# XXVIII

THE crowd around the State House at the opening session of the Convention on the morning of December 15 was large and generally friendly. There were more cheers than jeers as the delegates arrived, most of them in small groups and afoot, others by carriage. I noticed uniforms here and there and received the distinct impression that their presence was not happenstance. Realizing, to some extent, how Colonel Jesup felt, I suspected he visualized his role as less one of protecting the Convention from the crowd than one of protecting the crowd from the Convention. But how a man can isolate ideas, keep people from being "infected" by them, has still to be discovered — and may no one ever find the formula! Far better to let people appraise and make their own decisions, and if one is reduced simply to praying they may not be mistaken, at least there is the consoling thought that the voice of the people, even if only of a portion of the people, is to be preferred to the dictate of a single ruler.

Nowhere in the crowd — and I made it my business to sift my way through it — did I see Warren Bierce. Though I made a note of this in the record I was keeping for Mr. Daniels, I said nothing about the curiosity I felt as to why Bierce was not here. It wasn't like him to miss something so important as the opening of the Convention.

But if I puzzled over Bierce's absence, I was even more puzzled and disturbed by a rumor spreading through Hartford during the late afternoon and evening of that first day of the Convention. It was reported that the Convention had voted to keep the meetings secret.

"That does it!" a reporter named Ed Dyson said when the announcement was made by our landlady as we were getting up from the dinner table that night.

Everyone around the table had just looked at one another when we heard the news. Nor did it seem unlikely; Mrs. Burton's son worked for the *Connecticut Courant*, which was certainly not unfriendly to the Federalists!

"Go for a walk?" Dyson asked.

We got our coats and hats and went out into the streets, which were cold and dark in the vicinity of the boarding house except for the flickering glimmer cast by candles and lamps in the houses we passed.

Dyson was a fiery Republican from Davenport in the southwestern part of Connecticut. He was reporting the Convention for the *Gazette* there. "These damn Federalists!" he said. "They're so sure of themselves they don't care what people think. You watch what happens because of this secrecy business."

"What do you mean?" I asked.

"I mean they've laid themselves wide open to suspicion of treason."

"I can't believe men of their quality are considering treason."

"I didn't say they are. But now it makes no difference — people will think they are, and that's what will count. Mark my words, Dearborn, the Hartford Convention will stink of treason from now on, and the country will accuse us New Englanders of wanting to break up the nation. When you think of Lexington and Concord and Bunker Hill —"

He left the sentence unfinished, but he strode on faster than ever, his coattails flapping in the wind, and I was hard-pressed to keep up with him. Then as I was trying to find words to express my own indignation and yet not agitate him further, he stopped and turned on me, thrusting a long, bony forefinger at my chest.

"If I thought that the hatred the rest of the country will feel toward us would change the situation here in Connecticut, I'd rest a little easier, but I can't. Dearborn, do you realize the Federalists completely control this state? Do you realize that a Methodist like myself couldn't hold office? A man has to be a Congregationalist to get anywhere. Oh, I know there are exceptions, but they're even worse than the rule. Take Roger Griswold, for instance. A lot of us who aren't Congregationalists supported him for governor because he wasn't a church member and we hoped he'd try to disestablish the Congregational Church. What happened? He got more conservative than almost anyone. When war broke out and Madison asked for troops to invade Canada, he wouldn't let any leave the state and called Madison's request unconstitutional. Then in 1813 the Federalists elected John Cotton Smith, an old Puritan bastard who's bucked the war even worse than Griswold. I think Republicans hate him worse than your people hate Caleb Strong."

"Now, hold on there!" I protested. "I don't think we need put our governors into an unpopularity contest, but I'll tell you that, in Maine, we Republicans, and a lot of Federalists, too, feel just as sore about Governor Strong. We think he's deserted us. In Maine he's being called the 'hero of Castine' and there's a petition running around that the people of Maine should present him with a sword — and I can quote, Dyson — 'as a mark of their estimation of his patriotic and gallant defense of Castine, and the prompt and efficient protection he afforded that District when invaded by the enemy!' That sword's to be of the best white pine, Dyson, and it may even be painted white just to make sure Caleb Strong notices the color."

"Oh, I grant you, Strong's been no help to you people in Maine, but at least you can vote to separate from Massachusetts after the war. Here in Connecticut, though, we're stuck with Smith and the Federalists, particularly the Federalists, for a long time to come unless we can get up enough sentiment to change the Constitution. And we might just be able to do that. Meanwhile, here we are with Smith."

"But at least Connecticut has produced some war heroes," I said. "Think of Captain Isaac Hull of the *Constitution* and Commodore Thomas Macdonough on Lake Champlain."

"Sure, sure," he said. "But they're individuals. I suppose the state has contributed two thousand men to the war, but as individuals who've enlisted. The militia have stayed at home — and a fat lot of good they've done. They didn't prevent the British from raiding Essex back in April and destroying a lot of property. Colonel Randall's militia may have prevented Sir Thomas Hardy from landing at Stonington in August — though that's doubtful if Hardy had sent enough of his marines and sailors ashore — but the state had no real defenses to keep him from pounding Stonington for three days. Oh, the town itself had three guns, and they did quite a bit of damage, but they were the town's, not the state's property."

"In Maine we heard that Hardy did almost no damage to Stonington."

"Not much, and he wounded only one man and a chicken — fancy that! Quite an achievement for an officer who was Nelson's flag captain at Trafalgar! But, there, maybe Hardy didn't try too hard. They say he isn't in favor of this war."

"I've heard many of the English aren't," I said.

"Maybe. But I'll bet that for every Englishman opposed to the war, there are five Americans. And I haven't heard of any Englishman who refused to serve his country, which is more than I can say for New Englanders. Jesus! What's that?"

There was a sound as of a pistol shot behind us and a clatter of hoofs and wheels. We leaped to the shelter of the trees lining the road and barely cleared the street before a coach with four horses thundered by, its driver cracking a long whip over the horses' heads. A dusting of snow on the ground rose like smoke as the coach flew by.

As the coach passed, we slipped back into the street and watched it draw up in front of a brightly lighted house, a block away.

"Let's go watch this," Dyson said.

We broke into a run, but kept close to the tree trunks so that we couldn't be observed. Then, nearing the house, we stepped again into the shelter of the trees.

Despite the darkness I recognized the tall, proud figure of India Mitchell Bierce as a servant rushed out of the house and handed her down from the coach. She walked with great deliberation to the house, seeming to ignore entirely the man behind her whom it required no skill to identify as Bierce. After the trunks and boxes were carried into the house by servants, the coach drove off.

"Well, now, who would that be?" Dyson asked as we walked by the house. "Can't be one of the delegates — they're all here. But he was sure in a hurry."

Briefly I told him who Bierce was, though I said nothing of India. "Why he's here I don't know," I added, "but I think he'd certainly like to see New England break away from the Union, and he'll probably try to talk to as many delegates as he can corner."

"There are plenty of others like him here," Dyson said in a bitter voice, "and I wish him as bad luck as the rest of them."

The next day Colonel Jesup sent a note to my boarding house by an enlisted man informing me in one sentence that Bierce had arrived in Hartford and where he was staying. It was interesting to

was keeping such a close surveillance of the little
was also a little reassuring when I thought of Bierce and a
little disturbing when I thought of the possible threat to our right as
Americans to assemble.

But if the Colonel had any curiosity as to what Bierce was up to, it
was surely no greater than mine as to why he had reached Hartford so
late. Colonel Jesup must have had his curiosity satisfied first because
Bierce presently began to give a series of quiet dinner parties to
delegates, important citizens of Hartford and the state, and editors
and publishers of Connecticut newspapers. People spoke not only of
Bierce's hospitality but also of the graciousness of his lovely wife.

"Your man Bierce is the next thing to a traitor," Jesup growled at
me after summoning me to his headquarters a few days after Bierce
and India had arrived.

"You're not telling me anything new," I said. "In fact, I'm convinced he is a traitor, but proving it isn't so easy and getting a
favorable verdict would be impossible here in New England. Besides,
what good would it do now?"

He stared at me. "Why do you ask that?" he demanded.

"Isn't the war about over?"

"There's no treaty of peace yet, at least none that we know of. The
British are down Louisiana-way, and, by God, Andy Jackson's getting
ready to fight 'em!"

"I wish I were with him," I said. I was swept away momentarily by
the idea of positive action in support of something I believed in
fervently instead of following a gray, middle-ground course of peace
sought without honor and simply to keep the country from falling
apart.

"I could wish the same for myself," Jesup said, "but my duty's here
in Hartford raising troops for the United States Army and keeping an
eye on the Convention."

"I don't think you're hearing much about treason there, sir."

"Mr. Dearborn, I'm hearing nothing. They're keeping their proceedings secret, as you know, and they're saying damned little out of
session. I don't *think* they're talking treason, but I don't *know*. What
I do know is that I'm making it as difficult for them as I can by

marching a recruiting detail back and forth near the State House, and that drummer has orders to make his drum heard in Hartford."

Jesup's recruiting detail wasn't earning the United States Army or the Madison administration many friends in Hartford, but when I told him so and inquired if his device wasn't a bit childish, his temper flared like a Roman candle.

"By God, Dearborn, nothing that makes treason difficult for the enemies of the government I serve is childish!"

"But you, yourself, said, Colonel, that you didn't think they were planning treason."

"I also said that I didn't know for sure, and I don't intend to give them the benefit of the doubt until I do know."

"There's talk that the city government may ban the detail."

"Let 'em try!"

"And" — quoting Dyson, who had a trained ear for the latest rumor — "I've heard the governor may even call out the Footguard."

To my surprise Jesup's fierce face relaxed in a grin, though there was nothing amusing about it. "That's the governor's privilege, Dearborn. But let me tell you, if he orders that crowd of Beau Brummels with their fancy uniforms against United States troops, even raw recruits like I have here, there'll be a scene on these streets that Hartford won't forget in a hurry. Besides, you can't tell me the people of Connecticut are ready and willing to take up arms against the United States government."

"I'm not trying to tell you that," I said. "In fact, I'm sure they're not, even as I doubt the Convention is planning treason."

"But we don't really know about the Convention, do we, Dearborn? I'll continue to make it difficult for them to conduct their business. Meanwhile, my eye is on Bierce, and, states' rights or no states' rights, I'll move in and arrest him on suspicion of treason if he gives me the slightest provocation. I'll do that, Dearborn, mind what I say, so help me God!"

I knew little about Colonel Jesup — he might be a blowhard for all I could tell — but at the moment he was a man who would have welcomed an opportunity to strike at someone. At the same time, I doubted that he could trap Warren Bierce into committing himself publicly to a treasonous opinion. Nor did I believe that the Connecticut authorities would permit their opposition to Jesup and his officers to reach the point where the fashionable Footguard would actually take up arms against elements of the 25th United States Infantry. A lot would depend, however, on whether or not Jesup moved against the Convention. For the time being, the very secrecy to which so many of us objected was, ironically, their protection.

On Friday, the twenty-third of December, at noon, I had occasion to mention this matter of secrecy to Mr. Longfellow. I would never have presumed to bring it up to him had he not sent for me to come to his lodgings.

"Jonathan," he said after we had exchanged pleasantries, "there are two items I wanted to speak with you about. One concerns your work for Jedediah Daniels of the *Eastern Courier*."

"Yes, sir?" I was suddenly on guard.

"I realize that the *Courier* is an opposition paper and that our secrecy at the Convention is a fine opportunity for such papers to speculate about a conspiracy."

"I have sent home no reports of that kind, sir," I said. "It's true that I have mentioned how a number of people, especially Republicans I have met down here, and some of the papers I've read feel about the Convention, but I've indulged in no speculation of my own."

"Why not?"

"I don't consider speculation part of the work I'm doing for Mr. Daniels — I leave that to him. Besides, I cannot believe that the Convention contemplates treason, certainly not you, sir."

"Thank you, Jonathan," and he smiled faintly.

"But I do believe the secrecy decision a great mistake, sir."

He looked at me steadily for a moment, then nodded. "You may be right, Jonathan, and Zilpah would agree with you, though her father sides with me."

He drew a letter from his wife out of a mass of papers on the table in his room. "Listen to this portion she wrote on the seventeenth. She says of General Wadsworth, 'He thinks it would be best to deliberate with closed doors, from prudential motives, and because a concourse would put a restraint on the freedom of debate, and the business would be done in half the time without spectators. You

[ 294 ]

might afterward make as full communication to the public as you thought proper.' "

"Peleg Wadsworth," Mr. Longfellow went on, "may be a believer in the Federalism you distrust, Jonathan, but he is a wise and patriotic man. I think he is absolutely correct, particularly when I think of how efficiently and harmoniously our sessions have been going at the Convention. And we shall undoubtedly make a statement at the conclusion of our session."

"Is all that reportable, sir?" I asked.

Though he looked startled for an instant, he nodded. "Yes, if you will kindly not mention any names, I think it would be a good idea to inform our people in Maine, especially those of your persuasion, that we Federalists are cooperating effectively for the welfare of New England and the country at large."

"But what of Mrs. Longfellow's opinion, sir?"

He glanced at the letter again. "She asks a question — and here there is nothing to be quoted."

"Of course not."

"She simply asks '. . . would not a secret consultation give more plausibility to the cry of treason that will be raised?' "

"She's right, Mr. Longfellow! If you will forgive me, I think she's wiser on that point than the delegates."

"Including myself?"

I flushed. "Yes, sir," I said, greatly daring.

The silence found both of us staring. Then he smiled. "Time will tell who is right, Jonathan — you and Zilpah or the general and myself. Now the second reason I asked to see you is to invite you to drive to Middletown tomorrow afternoon. Several of us are going, and while we intend to pay our respects to Judge Trumbull, who wrote McFingal, we're also visiting one of your heroes, Commodore Macdonough."

"Macdonough!"

"Yes, the 'hero of Champlain,' as everyone is calling him."

"And with reason, sir. It was a brilliant victory."

"It was indeed, and, Jonathan, I'll have you understand that even we Federalists rejoice in his victory as Americans, though we regret the war that brought it about."

[ 295 ]

"I think I understand, Mr. Longfellow," I said.

"I hope you do. Well, will you go?"

"I'd love to," I said, "and I'm grateful to you for thinking of me."

He waved aside my thanks, and I left, excited at the prospect, and relieved that our difference in views hadn't resulted in any hard feeling, though for a moment or two there had been tension between us.

When I returned to my boarding house, Ed Dyson strode into my room, waving an envelope. "I thought you and Mr. Warren Bierce were enemies," he said.

"We're hardly friends," I replied, watching the letter that he swung to and fro in front of him.

"Do you know the beauteous India, Mr. Man-from-Maine?"

When I nodded, his brows drew together. "Is she as Federalist as he is or Republican like us?"

"She's a Federalist. But why do you ask?"

He dropped the letter in front of me. Quickly I broke the wax seal and read an invitation in India's own handwriting to attend a party — "festive occasion," she called it — at the Bierce's temporary residence the night after Christmas.

As I looked up, something more than astonishment must have appeared in my face, for Dyson waved a finger at me. "Don't build too much on this, Dearborn. I got an invitation, too, and I'll bet men from other papers did as well. If you ask me, the Bierces have decided to cultivate us plain gentlemen of the press. Now ain't that a caution, as you Maine people say?"

"Dyson, he's up to something."

"A profound observation, my friend."

"I wonder if he knows I'm here in Hartford."

"He may not, but Madame certainly does. Think I'll go along just to watch Bierce's face when he sees you. Or maybe there'll be even better entertainment."

"What's that?" I stared at his eyes that looked so weary and cynical.

"Watching you and La Bierce."

For a moment a gust of anger swept me, and my face grew hot. As

I started to rise, he put a hand on my shoulder and gently pushed me back. "No offense, Dearborn, believe me, and I won't pry. But you'd better cover up your feelings about those people that evening, especially how you feel about Mrs. Bierce. Gentlemen of the press may not be so gentlemanly in writing up an incident involving, shall we say, misplaced affection."

"By God, you go too far, Dyson!" I half shouted and rose quickly.

He leaped for the door, then spun around. "My apologies, Dearborn. I really meant no offense. But I also meant what I said."

He was gone before I could say another word, and I was so furious I could have thrown anything at him, even the lamp. Had he given me wise counsel? Of this I had no doubt, but it graveled me that I should have been so obvious he would think it necessary to speak to me. In fact, my anger was really directed more at myself than at him, something I realized after I began to cool off. I could have declined the invitation, but I had no idea of doing so. My curiosity over that "festive occasion" was too keen. I wanted to observe Bierce in action again and look him in the eye and stare the bastard down. I also wanted to see India.

I took up her invitation again, so impersonally phrased. I sniffed it, hoping to identify some clinging bit of fragrance. But all I could smell was some damned stinking kind of lotion that Dyson used in his mop of hair.

---

# XXIX

SATURDAY afternoon was pleasant as we drove the fifteen miles down the river road to Middletown. There were five of us in the carriage besides the driver: Mr. Longfellow, Timothy Bigelow, Daniel Waldo, a wealthy hardware merchant of Worcester, Samuel Sumner Wilde, a lawyer of Hallowell in Maine, and myself. Waldo, in his early fifties, was a charitable, affable man and the only nonlawyer present except myself. Wilde could talk a blue streak but seemed often to defer to Mr. Longfellow, who, at thirty-nine, was the youngest present, again except for myself. In fact, Mr. Longfellow, in manner and presence, seemed as old as Waldo and considerably the elder of Bigelow, who was in his late forties.

I mention this matter of age and manner because I was unprepared for their lively enjoyment of the drive. I had thought that as delegates to one of the most significant assemblies of our time their conversation even in these relaxing minutes would be of the serious concerns they were considering in the State House. Indeed, I had hesitated briefly to accept Mr. Longfellow's invitation since I felt I should be an intruder. Happily for me, they greeted me warmly and scarcely mentioned politics or the Convention all the way to Middletown. They spoke instead of the river landscape (Wilde preferred the Kennebec country in Maine), the hills (which Bigelow compared unfavorably with those of Massachusetts), the warmth of the people (though Waldo assured us he had discovered little warmth in any Connecticutter with whom he had had any business transactions). From all I could infer, they liked Connecticut but thought that it was not even in the running with Massachusetts or the District of Maine and that Hartford and its environs could not begin to match in appearance or activity or future promise the particular towns where they lived. Yet the saving grace of such provincialism was that they recognized it as such and, while loving it, yet laughed at it, and at themselves for cherishing it.

Bigelow was the only one to remind me of my Republicanism when he said, with a sly glance at Mr. Longfellow, "I trust you have found out all that's going on in the State House, Dearborn. Your Republican friends in Maine will become even more suspicious if they don't soon know."

"I haven't been able to find out much, sir," I said.

"What! You mean Longfellow here hasn't been relaying to you all that we've done?"

I shook my head. "I wish he had, but you gentlemen are evidently taking seriously your oath of secrecy. Unless, sir," I added, "you would kindly oblige me with information now."

"I'd like to," he said, smiling, "but your Republican readers wouldn't understand what we've accomplished, and my Federalist friends wouldn't understand why I told you."

Waldo gently patted his shoulder. "I think you are being unjust, Tim."

"Unjust, maybe," he conceded, "but not unwise. 'Least said, soonest mended' is pretty good advice."

"But you don't often follow such advice," Waldo reminded him.

Bigelow laughed and nodded. "I think I'm a better teacher than a student: I never learned how to keep my mouth shut. As a matter of fact, I'm pretty proud of my discretion so far in the Convention, though Tim Pickering and John Lowell will probably think I've been too discreet when they examine the record of what's been accomplished."

At the sudden silence I felt rather than saw the eyes glance my way, but I prudently kept looking at the river as we drew into Middletown. If my ears, however, had been rabbit ears, they would have stood straight up. Was the Convention less radical than we suspected? Was Bigelow serious when he implied that its measures would be too mild for such extreme Federalists as Pickering and Lowell? As if sensing that I might have heard something I shouldn't, Mr. Longfellow quickly steered the conversation into questions about Middletown, which Waldo seemed to know most about.

The little city, spread along the side of low hills on the west bank for about a mile before the river narrows and bends to the southeast, was fully as large as Hartford, perhaps larger. The waterfront was quiet, a cluster of ships with hooded masts waiting for the British blockade in Long Island Sound to lift and the ice to break up. It was a melancholy sight. As we drove onto the main street intersected by streets moving from the river to the top of the hill at the west, we encountered many carriages and wagons as people went to and from their weekend marketing. I was surprised by the numerous trees preserved along the streets and the number of fine houses, especially on the west side of the main street. Past the Washington Hotel we drove where the greatest ball in Middletown's history had been given on the twenty-first in honor of Commodore Macdonough. Then to the home of Judge John Trumbull.

The Judge, a man in his middle sixties, was no ordinary person. At the age of two he could read and write and entered Yale College at thirteen, though he had passed the entrance examinations at the age of seven! While he had studied law in John Adams's office before the Revolution, he later chose his home in Connecticut, where he had served as state's attorney, as a member of the legislature and the highest courts of the state, and as treasurer of Yale.

But it was not primarily for his legal activities that he was so widely admired in New England; he was also a writer of popular poems and essays. His piece, *The Progress of Dullness*, written when he was only twenty-two, mercilessly criticized the educational system of that day especially for its toleration of idle sons of the wealthy and its neglect of talented girls. During the Revolution he wrote patriotic verse and essays, gaining wide fame with *McFingal* in 1782, a satire in which he held the Tories up to such delightful ridicule that he endeared himself to the whole country. Later he was one of the most active of the Hartford Wits and a friend of Joel Barlow, who died while accompanying Napoleon on the retreat from Moscow.

When a maid ushered us into the heavily draped living room, the Judge rose from his tall escritoire and made us welcome with a gracious manner one rarely sees today. Though his white hair and gaunt cheeks, accentuated by his high cheek bones, made him look older and more ill than he was, I have rarely seen such animation in anyone's face or eyes — the latter flashed with a lively intelligence.

"How nice of you gentlemen to take time from the Convention and call on me," he said in a rapid, almost musical voice, after Bigelow had introduced us and we had sat down, "though I can't believe you came to see me so much as Commodore Macdonough. Now, confess, aren't you going to see him, too?"

"Yes, Judge," said Waldo, smiling, "we decided that if we could pay our respects to both of you in one afternoon, we should consider ourselves doubly blessed."

"Handsomely said, sir," Trumbull acknowledged, bowing, "but Macdonough is the man you must see. How splendid his achievement on Lake Champlain! I considered myself honored to be invited to the ball for him on Wednesday last. He looked the very image of a hero — tall, broad — his uniform a tailor's masterpiece, his manner becomingly modest. Yes, yes, you must see him and not waste your time with me."

He waved aside our protests. "I know what it means, even at my age, to see a hero in the flesh and admire him. Why, young man," he said to me, "your face was all aglow when I spoke of Macdonough. You realize, of course, that Federalists like us shouldn't become excited over heroes of a war we deplore."

I felt myself flushing. "Well, sir," I said with a firmness I was far from feeling as I gazed into those twinkling eyes that missed nothing and, despite their liveliness, looked slightly cynical, "in the first place I greatly admire the Commodore. My fighting experience at sea has been limited to privateering, but even that helps me appreciate the extraordinary work he did on Lake Champlain."

"You, a Federalist, are also a privateersman?"

"Sir, I am not a Federalist. I am a Republican, but Mr. Longfellow, whom I'm studying law with, has been kind enough to overlook our political differences."

"That is indeed kindness," Trumbull said, and the twinkling eyes no longer twinkled for a moment. "May I congratulate you on your magnanimity, Mr. Longfellow, and you, Mr. Dearborn, on your good fortune. What do you think of our Federalist convention in Hartford, Mr. Dearborn?"

I hesitated, then said, "I like it less than I do its delegates, sir."

"Well said, young man. I suppose that, in your place, I'd feel the same. I remember when a number of us Federalists were rallying around President Washington and it seemed impossible that any patriotic American would not support us. In fact, I doubt if any president will even be so calumniated as was that great man. As I look back, I still deplore the calumny, but naturally I recognize the right to differ."

"And yet, Judge," Bigelow asked, leaning forward, "aren't there times when a government must take note of differences and do something about them?"

"You touch upon weighty matters, Mr. Bigelow. Now let me ask you, what happens when honest men disagree as a matter of conscience?"

"Mr. Jefferson, Mr. Madison, and the Republicans would say that the judgment of a majority of men must be accepted as finally right."

"But what do you say?"

"I say that the majority is more likely to be mistaken than an informed minority. People, sir, are often ignorant and **passionate** and should not be trusted with authority."

"You sound like Alexander Hamilton, Tim," Waldo said with a smile. "Remember his alluding to the people as a beast?"

"I agreed with many of Hamilton's ideas, and still do," Bigelow muttered.

"Yes, yes," Judge Trumbull said, pointing his finger at Bigelow, "but what of the dilemma of conscience, Mr. Bigelow? With a government such as ours today which accedes, at least in theory, to the majority, what is a member of the minority to do who loves his country as profoundly as any of the majority and yet feels the government is leading the country to destruction?"

"By God, sir, he gets like-minded people together to plan a campaign of action!"

"The Hartford Convention, for instance," Wilde interrupted.

"Exactly," said the Judge, as if he had uttered "quod erat demonstrandum" at the conclusion to a demonstration of a theorem in Euclid.

"Does that mean the minority is being treasonous?" he asked.

"No, sir!" Bigelow roared, and there was a growl of agreement from the others.

"What do you think, Mr. Dearborn?" and the Judge seemed to look clear through me.

"I think, sir," I said, "the question of treason depends on precisely what that minority proposes and how it plans to put those proposals into effect. If the proposals involve an outright separation from the Union, the use of arms, or even a refusal to obey laws enacted by Congress, the minority, as you know far better than I do, sir, is committing treason against the United States."

"Your protégé here isn't afraid to speak his mind, Longfellow," the Judge said, the twinkle back in his eye belying the frozen panels of his cheeks. "Does he come by this combative tendency naturally or is this the result of your instruction?"

"Jonathan comes of a line of fighters, Judge Trumbull," Mr. Longfellow said. "During the Revolution his Uncle Tom Dearborn fought at Valcour Island with Arnold and at Castine with my father-in-law, General Peleg Wadsworth. His father is a minister who is against war for any reason and holds his position against Federalist and Republican alike. Jonathan himself sailed with our Captain Vail as second officer on the privateer *Argus*, and he has just recently returned from the Penobscot where he helped Vail escape from a British prison in Castine. At the moment I'm afraid he's a battle-ground of conflicting desires. He sees the necessity for peace as we Federalists do, but he doesn't want it for our reasons or on British terms."

My face burned at becoming the subject of conversation, and I stared intently at the floor where a shaft of sunlight illuminated the veil of dust flecks that hung in the air.

"Mr. Dearborn," the Judge said in a kindly manner, "cling to your principles — never give them up for sake of expediency, but I beg you to consider that you may be mistaken. Gentlemen," he added, rising, "I honor you for what you are attempting to do in Hartford, though I admit to being as mystified about what is being decided as our young friend here probably is, even if I am not so apprehensive. Mr. Longfellow, see if you can make a convert of Mr. Dearborn; he would be a worthy addition to our cause. Thank you, one and all, for coming to visit me."

As we shook hands, he said to Mr. Longfellow, "See that Commodore Macdonough learns that Mr. Dearborn has seen action, too. I fear that most of us at the ball the other night were civilians or military men who had hardly smelled powder. The Commodore will be interested, too, that Valcour is in Dearborn's family background. After all, the Commodore's Champlain victory was not far from Arnold's battle."

We found that Macdonough, though gracious, and modest about his exploits, seemed more pleased to be with his family, particularly his slender wife, Lucy Ann Shaler, who hardly tried to conceal that she adored her husband, than to receive the congratulations of people who were strangers to him. Mr. Longfellow he had met while in command of a gunboat flotilla in Portland in 1812, but he had never seen the rest of us. When he discovered, however, that I had sailed with Ben Vail, he grew interested at once.

"Up there on the lake, Mr. Dearborn, we used to envy you privateersmen and the crews on our men-of-war that managed to get to sea," he said.

"Now they're envying you, sir," I said. "Your victory over the British fleet on September eleven was a remarkable demonstration of seamanship and courage."

"Well, Mr. Dearborn, as you know from your own experience, an officer can do only so much on his own. He needs brave, gritty men aloft and at the guns, and those men of mine would have done honor to Nelson or St. Vincent."

He patiently answered questions the delegates asked him, he acknowledged their congratulations with a modesty that in no way discounted the splendor of the victory, but he would not be trapped into giving political opinions. During tea, which his wife and her tall and dignified mother served, Bigelow tried to draw him out on his views of the Hartford Convention. Though Macdonough's face grew almost the color of his hair, his voice was even and calm when he said, "I'm sorry, Mr. Bigelow, but I must decline to answer your question. An officer in the regular navy, or regular army, for that matter, serves the government of his country to the best of his ability whatever party is in power. Now, sir," he said, turning to me, "it must have been a rare experience to have been with Vail on his great cruise."

"It was, sir," I said.

"How we wished we had been you people sweeping the coasts of England instead of being tied down on Lake Champlain building a fleet that we felt reasonably sure would never be used again if it was lucky enough to survive the battles."

"But what you did on Champlain, sir, was tremendous, just tremendous — defeating the British fleet by superb seamanship and fighting ability and thereby causing Sir George Prevost's army — Wellington's veterans, at that! — to withdraw to Canada. You saved the whole northeastern United States, sir!"

"Thank you. But I can't tell you how confining that lake seemed. A lake or a river is no place for a blue-water man."

"I'm sure Captain Morris of the *John Adams* felt the same way," I said.

"Poor Morris," he sighed. "It's rough to lose your ship."

It was then I remembered that he, too, knew what it was to lose a ship. For shortly after the *Philadelphia*, back in the war with Tripoli, had captured a ship and placed Midshipman Macdonough aboard with a prize crew, the big frigate had run on a reef and been captured by the enemy. Later Macdonough, like Morris, had been one of the heroic band that sailed with Stephen Decatur aboard the *Intrepid* into Tripoli Harbor and set the *Philadelphia* afire.

"Captain Morris lost the *Adams* — no doubt about it," I said, "but he and his men fought hard at Hampden to save her and the west bank of the Penobscot from capture. If the militia had stood fast, we might have driven the redcoats back into the river."

"You were at Hampden, Mr. Dearborn?" he asked with swift interest.

"Yes, sir, and the *Adams*'s men behaved well then and all the way back to Portland — not a single deserter."

"How did you happen to be at Hampden?"

Quickly I told him about Brad's and my bringing Captain Vail back to his mother at Castine and our flight from the town with Lieutenant Lewis's troopers.

"Good heavens, man, you certainly have been active. You didn't have anything to do with Vail's escape, did you? We heard that he'd got away."

"Jonathan and the lawyer friend of his, Bradford Pettigrew, were responsible for bringing Captain Vail out of Castine," Mr. Longfellow said.

"Man, this gets better all the time!" the Commodore exclaimed. "Tell us about that escape, won't you?"

The Commodore's wife looked mildly interested, but one glance at her mother's face discouraged me. "I'm afraid it would be pretty boring," I said.

"Nonsense! Tell it!"

This was like a command, sharp and authoritative, and the room was instantly hushed as I related as tersely as I could our escape from Castine. Despite the telling, the story itself must have carried through, for there was a sprinkling of applause when I finished and Macdonough reached for my hand and complimented me warmly. I felt honored, of course, but I am afraid there are times when I talk too much.

The conversation now turned to other subjects, and I could relax and try to be myself again. Holding the center of the stage twice this afternoon had just about unnerved me, good practice though it may have been for that elusive legal career.

As we were leaving, the Commodore detained both Mr. Longfellow and me a moment. "Mr. Dearborn," he said, "you said nothing in your account about why the British should have imprisoned Vail. How did they find out he was in Castine? Did some old enemy in the town give him away?"

"No native of Castine, sir," I said, "but an enemy without doubt."

"Do you know who it was?"

"Yes, sir."

"Are you going to do something about him?"

"I'm trying to, sir. In fact, a number of men are. But this enemy of his is rich, capable, and well regarded — and supports the Federalist Party, though he's only interested in his own welfare."

"Dearborn, you must keep after him. This is an issue that transcends party. Mr. Longfellow, I don't know much about politics in Maine, but please do see that our young friend here doesn't get discouraged in his suit."

All the way back to Hartford the men chatted about the vigor of Judge Trumbull's mind and the magnanimity and modesty of Commodore Macdonough. Mr. Longfellow was less a contributor to the conversation than the others, and I saw him glance occasionally at me. For my own part I was by turns exhilarated and depressed by Macdonough's urging me to continue to keep the Bierce case alive. I surely wanted to, but how ultimately to bring him to justice seemed as perplexing as ever. Though I had no hopes that the coming party at the Bierces' would be of any help, I now began to look forward to that with about as much curiosity and eagerness as I had anticipated in meeting Judge Trumbull and Commodore Macdonough.

The cap of enjoyment — and surprise — was placed on the day when the carriage stopped at my lodging house and Mr. Longfellow leaned out the carriage window and said, after I had bade all good night, "Jonathan, when this Convention is over and we are all back home again, you and I must have another long talk about Warren Bierce. Meanwhile, I entreat you, as I have done before, to be watchful in what you say and do."

"Yes, sir," I said, "and thank you. Good night, sir." And I walked up to my room, trying with the utmost difficulty to keep from letting out a war whoop and taking the stairs two at a time.

---

# XXX

THE reception at the Bierces' was scheduled at eight o'clock according to the invitation. I have what I am convinced is an odd belief, not widely shared, that the time to appear at a business or social appointment is the time specified. Apparently I am far off the mark, especially for a social engagement. So when I tried to hurry Ed Dyson along, he laughed at me, stropped his razor some more and attacked the rippled mound of shaving cream covering his left cheek.

"Don't hurry me, Dearborn. I make time a servant, not a master. Besides, if I were you, I wouldn't arrive at this affair too early."

"Why?"

"If Bierce doesn't know you're coming and decides to throw you out after he sees you, he's apt to think at least twice with a lot of people around, especially newspaper reporters who are hungry for news. And, believe me, Dearborn, a fight at the Bierce menage would be news. Coming right after the Lord's birthday, it would really make an impression."

The end result was that after we had bucked a blustery wind until we were thoroughly chilled despite our mufflers and greatcoats, we arrived at the Bierces' a full half hour late, which Dyson insisted was still too early.

I was looking forward, if warily, to the evening. It wasn't so much because of India, though the prospect of meeting her again excited me, as because of a growing feeling of confidence since Christmas Eve when we had returned from Middletown that sooner or later the net would close around Bierce. I confess that on Christmas Day, which, falling on the Sabbath, was treated like any other Sabbath here in Connecticut, I had had something of a letdown in spirits. Indeed I was divided in my feelings. On the one hand, I was a little suspicious of the invitation. It seemed almost like a trap, and I had had enough experience with Bierce not to be surprised at any duplicity — unless, of course, he knew nothing of the invitation. On the other hand, it seemed most unlikely that anything personally menacing would occur in such a gathering. Christmas Day ended, therefore, with an upturn in feeling; the fact that others in Maine were committed to the Bierce case and that Mr. Longfellow himself seemed at last interested made me hopeful that Bierce might get what he richly deserved.

As we entered the house, servants took our coats and hats, and one of them, his hair powder sprinkled like snow on the collar of his cherry coat, led us to where India and Bierce were standing in the drawing room. At least fifteen to twenty people were already present, and servants carrying trays of wine glasses were busy keeping the guests occupied. Everyone seemed to be talking at once, and voices went up in volume as the wines went down. Candles and a blazing fire in the fireplace with its pink marble mantel added cheer to the room.

Then the butler introduced us.

I have seen shock on many faces at various times and occasions, but the look of surprise and outrage on Bierce's face was something I'll never forget.

He had nothing against Dyson, but he barely touched Ed's outstretched hand as he glared at me. Then as I stepped into Ed's place, neither Bierce nor I made a move to shake hands. He bowed slightly and belatedly, as if suddenly recollecting that people would be watching, and I returned his bow with the same lack of enthusiasm. Neither of us said a word; it was a contest of eyes that was broken up only when Dyson moved on and India bade me good evening in her cool, throaty voice.

"How nice of you to come see us, Jonathan," she added. "You remember Jonathan Dearborn from Portland, don't you, Warren?"

Of course it was malice on her part, and driven home by a warm, innocent-appearing smile as she looked at her husband. The man was actually white with fury. Still, give the devil his due, as they say:

though violently angry, he kept his voice low and controlled as he said coldly, "You rarely give me a chance to forget him, India."

Then he turned to meet another latecomer.

"I'll see you in the course of the evening," India murmured as I bowed over her hand.

"What's it to be, pistols at twelve or six paces?" Dyson asked as we moved away from our hosts.

"Was it as bad as all that?"

"Friend, you're dead as far as he's concerned. Have you got anything on you that you can call a weapon?"

"Now? Of course not."

"I mean in your luggage."

"I've got a pistol, yes."

"Well, get used to wearing it. There's death in his eye, Jonathan."

"You're not serious."

"From what you've told me about Bierce and from what I just observed, I was never more serious. And his wife may not fare much better than you."

"Dyson, I don't understand. You've seen Bierce and his wife for maybe five minutes, and here you're predicting dire things for both India and me."

He drained one glass of wine and reached for another from the tray of a passing servant. "Wish Bierce would serve whiskey instead of wine," he muttered. "I'm a man of low tastes, Jonathan — I like whiskey. So do half the people here. But Bierce is trying to impress them with how respectable he is. Now you were asking me a question, friend Dearborn?"

"I just want to know the secret of your clairvoyant powers."

"Oh, those! Think nothing of them — I don't." And he raised his hand holding the glass so abruptly to acknowledge a friend's greeting that the wine slopped over. "Damn!" he exclaimed, and pushed the wineglass into my other hand while he reached for his handkerchief and dried his hand.

"Your friend Bierce is a dangerous man," he said with a glance at Bierce and India, who were now moving among the guests. "It's not just that I've got used over the years to appraising people, though that helps. What I've also done is to put what I observed in the context of what you've told me. It all adds up to danger."

"I think it has for some time," I said.

"Maybe. But, if you ask me, I'd say something new has been added. He hates his wife."

"What? I don't believe it. But even if he does, why should he be more of a danger to me now that he hates her than when he loved her? I should think it would be the reverse."

He shook his head. "Didn't you hear her? Didn't you hear and watch both of 'em? She deliberately tried to humiliate him, not that I blame her. He blazed back that she didn't give him a chance not to remember you. In short, she keeps throwing you up at him. He's a proud man, Jonathan, a dangerously proud man. He hates you probably for many reasons, and his wife now for attacking his pride and self-respect. And, friend, you're probably the principal weapon she uses against him. Why do you suppose she invited you here tonight? I'm convinced he'd love to see both of you dead."

I looked at him, tall, scrawny, his lean face flushed, and his hair awry. At the rate he was drinking, he'd soon be swaying, and I dreaded the prospect of somehow getting him home dead-drunk. But whatever he might be like then, the wine had seemed for the moment to give his mind a brilliant clarity. He had told me nothing about Bierce's attitude toward me that surprised me, and certainly nothing that intimidated me. But that Bierce should hate India had not occurred to me, and that he should wish her dead horrified me. Though Dyson had really sounded persuasive, I couldn't go quite so far as to believe this last, and I told him so.

He shrugged, and the lift of his shoulders made him look more than ever like a scarecrow. "I'll tell you this, my friend," he said, squinting at India in her white gown, "if that young woman didn't like you so much, Bierce would put up with both you and her much better."

"But she doesn't like me, at least not the way he thinks."

"How do you know?"

"We've had some pretty sharp disagreements just about every time we've seen each other."

Dyson laughed so loudly heads turned our way. "Nonsense, Dearborn! Haven't you heard that loving and quarreling are two sides of the same coin? But how do you feel about her? No, don't answer, I know already. Friend Dearborn, you be careful."

It was a strange conversation, and even stranger taking place where it did. I was relieved when a couple of Dyson's newspaper friends started talking with him and I was able to drift away. It's uncomfortable to be in the presence of a prophet, and I hate being advised, admonished, and lectured to all at once, even if my counsellor has the best of intentions. I therefore shrugged off much of what he had said, drank wine and munched cakes, and, while chatting now with this guest and now with that, kept glancing at the Bierces and calculating my chances of being able to see India alone.

At last she skillfully disengaged herself from a persistent guest, whose indulgence in the flowing bowl was even more impressive than Dyson's, and moved toward me, unhurried and casual.

"So you dared come after all," she said. Only her occasionally fanning herself with a highly figured Oriental fan revealed her nervousness; the room was hot, but hardly that hot.

"It wasn't a question of daring," I said, toasting her with my wineglass. "It was curiosity and —"

"Oh, just curiosity!"

"— and a desire to see you again."

"That's better, but it took second place to curiosity, didn't it?"

"Not really. But you must admit, India, that it's not the usual thing for a lady to invite me to her home for any social occasion when her husband and I are not friends."

"This 'lady' you speak of might want the two of you to become friends."

I looked hard at her for a moment. In the candlelight her eyes, usually gray-green, now accentuated by the fairness of her skin and the night-darkness of her hair, took on a deeper coloration. They appeared innocent, as did her face, as she spoke; too innocent.

"I think not," I said. "I doubt that the idea ever occurred to her. In fact, I wonder if even she and her husband are friendly at this point."

"Now you're being presumptuous!"

But the eyes did not hurl lightning at me as the India Mitchell of old might have done had she been serious. Instead, her features assumed a curiously guarded look and the eyes remained calm but no longer looked so innocent.

"Am I really presumptuous?" I challenged her. "This lady and her husband should be more careful in the way they speak and look at each other in public if they wish people to think them still devoted." At this she blushed faintly. "Is it so obvious?" she asked. And the way she spoke, the question seemed to be asked as much of herself as of me.

I said nothing. Actually, it hadn't been obvious to me, but a keen eye like Ed Dyson's had apparently detected everything.

"No matter," she said. "Perhaps the time for pretending has passed."

I was interested, of course, but also embarrassed, and so continued to say nothing.

"Tell me," she said, "is the Convention going to vote for separation?"

I felt relieved at once at the turn in the conversation, but considering why Bierce was in Hartford, I was also wary. "No, I don't think so. As far as I can see, the delegates have too high a regard for the Union to break it up."

"How can you be so sure, Jonathan? Aren't you judging solely by Mr. Longfellow?"

"No, I don't think so."

Nor, as I thought of the delegates I had met since coming to Hartford, did I think so. On the other hand, I wasn't sure, even if I sounded so, and some appearance of uncertainty must have become evident in my face, for she shook her head and said. "Oh, no, you don't think so! If you ask me, you're afraid to admit that you really do think so!"

"You're wrong, India," I said, and regretted being so blunt the moment the words were out of my mouth. It didn't help my conscience to see her eyes open wide in astonishment. "I mean," I added, "you're partly wrong. I'm afraid they might vote for separation, but I doubt if they do, though I'll grant you I was more fearful when I arrived than I am now."

"Has anything happened that accounts for the change in your opinion?"

"No, unless it's having met a few of the delegates and listened to them talk."

"Surely they'd say nothing to commit themselves in your presence."

"No, it's just little things here and there, plus a certain feeling I can't quite explain."

"Such a rational basis for an intellectual opinion — 'a certain feeling.'!"

I began to get warm. "Damn it, India, what do you want me to say — that I think it's possible they'll vote to separate but hope they won't? All right, I've said it. But I'll go further, too, and say I don't believe they'll commit treason by voting separation or anything like it. I don't *know*, of course, and I could be wrong, and I've no rational basis, if you wish, for thinking as I do. But that's how I feel. Now what the hell else do you want me to say?"

"Nothing," she said with a suddenly mischievous smile, "you've said quite enough. And, Jonathan, you weren't brought up to use such language in front of a lady!"

"But you —"

"Tsk, tsk! Don't say I'm not a lady, Jonathan!"

"I never intended to say anything of the kind!" I protested, the sweat breaking out on my forehead. Depend upon me to say something to offend her!

"Good! Just as long as I can be sure of that," she laughed. Then her face sobered. "I only hope that Mr. Longfellow and the other delegates won't let themselves be led to take extreme views or actions."

"India, I agree with you, but Stephen Longfellow, for one, is not a rash man, and he has a mind of his own, believe me! He certainly doesn't want to build up a store of trouble for this country."

"Trouble, Dearborn? Has my wife been giving you trouble?"

I froze at the sound of Bierce's voice, now self-possessed and amused; then I slowly turned toward him, my annoyance with India becoming cold anger at the arrogant, proprietary way in which he said, "my wife." "Hardly," I said in as calm a voice as I could muster.

"How remarkable! You looked as if you were up before the Spanish Inquisition."

"Looks can be deceiving, you know."

"So I've heard, but yours are eloquent, Dearborn. She was making you sweat, wasn't she? How could you be so rude to one of our guests, my dear?"

Though India kept her composure, her eyes flashed at the sarcastic tone. "Rude? Was I rude, Jonathan? If I was, please forgive me — at my husband's request."

"Your conversation must have been charming," Bierce said, looking first at her and then at me.

"It was interesting, if that's what you mean, Warren," India said.

"Only interesting? I thought you more of a gallant, Dearborn."

"If I told you we were talking about the Convention, would you believe it, Bierce?" My voice was harsh, and I felt such anger and contempt that I'm afraid the sound carried pretty far. I saw Ed Dyson break off his conversation and look my way.

"The Convention? Surely you and my wife could find other things to talk about than the Convention!"

Had they not been where so many could observe them, I think India would have slapped him then and there. As it was, her hand started to move, and Bierce caught it instantly and raised it to his lips. Though she winced at the pressure of his fingers, she inclined her head as if in appreciation of a gentlemanly gesture. The amenities were thus preserved and people could stop their excited whispering, but there was murder in the smiling look she gave Bierce.

"So you find the Convention an interesting topic of conversation, Dearborn," he said, placing his wife's hand on his arm and holding it there.

I felt so outraged, yet so helpless, at what had happened that I could only stare at him for a moment. "Very," I finally succeeded in saying, with a curtness that could not possibly convey the extent of my feeling.

"Then you may find what I am going to say now 'very' interesting, too, Dearborn. It's also about the Convention."

He held up his hand for silence. When he had the attention of his guests, he thanked them for coming and hoped they had enjoyed themselves. Then he said, "Mrs. Bierce and I — like so many of you — are merely transients in this lovely, little city, which we hope to visit again when times are less disturbing than they are now. We are all observing in the Convention a noble effort to win a freer hand for New England, to show the Madison administration that they cannot compel us to send our troops out of New England, that their conscription law is unconstitutional, that these states should have more control over the federal monies raised within them for the purpose of defense. As one of you in favor of what the Convention is deliberating, though not a newspaperman myself, I ask you to support the delegates even more firmly in their position than you already have done. We do not know just what is going on in the State House because they have kept so well their vow of secrecy. But if any of us detects the slightest degree of wavering on their part, let us rally to their side and assure them they have a duty to perform. If, however, they should press for a latitude of movement for New England greater and more significant than many, though not all, Federalists anticipate, let us not challenge their wisdom but stand ready to consider how to apply it and then act upon it."

He thanked them again for coming, hoped they would continue to enjoy themselves the rest of the evening, and wished them the best of the season.

As they responded with genuine enthusiasm, he gave me a mocking glance of triumph, and moved off with India on his arm.

"Ready to leave, friend Dearborn?"

Dyson's sardonic voice brought me out of my daze. "I may be nearly half-seas over," he said, "but you and I had better leave. You look as fussed as I feel. The fresh air will do us both good — for different reasons."

He spoke with only a slight blurring of the words, but his mouth worked as if every word were an effort to utter.

"Let's get our coats and hats," I said.

"Coats? Hats? Oh, yes! But let us first say good night to Beauty and the Beast!"

Both Bierce and India were correct but cool as we thanked them, and I left, astounded and saddened that evidently he had her thoroughly in hand.

Outside, Dyson and I took deep breaths of the winter air before either of us said a word.

"Dearborn, we've just left a house of desperation," he said in a pontifical manner, then slipped on a patch of ice and would have fallen had I not caught him by the arm.

"I don't understand," I said when I had righted him.

"Didn't expect you would," he giggled. "Where Bierce and his Beauty are concerned, you miss the obvious. Or did I say that before?"

"You did!"

"Then I've said it again for good measure. But, in addition, Bierce is scared the Convention's not coming through all the way, and he wants the newspapers to put pressure on it."

"By 'all the way' you must mean separation."

"What else?"

"There are only two kinds of people in New England who could wish for a separation: the extreme Federalists or traitors."

"Not sure you can separate the two, Dearborn, though I'll concede the extreme Feds the motivation of ideas and the sincerity of their motivation. That's not true of most traitors as such, Dearborn. Look here, do I sound like a schoolmaster? Well, I was one right after Yale."

"Where do you place Bierce?" I asked, and leaned toward him to catch his reply.

He was silent for a number of steps; then he said, "We just listened to a plan for separation and its approval. It was oblique, of course, but it was there."

"Are you saying Bierce is a traitor?"

"Dearborn, if I were a man of good sense and not half drunk, I'd refuse to answer your question. But I don't refuse. I'd say the man's a traitor on the basis of what I've heard, and there's no doubt at all if what you've told me about the past is true."

"It is!" I said.

"I wonder how much he's charged the British."

"How much?"

"His price, man! This is a nasty kind of traitor, Dearborn, a real materialist. The 'idea' traitor I can respect even if I hate him. But the

[ 316 ]

money traitor — Jesus, I despise him!" He spat in disgust. "Let's get the hell to our rooms, Jonathan, and have a drop of whiskey to cut the taste of that bastard's wine."

# XXXI

I DIDN'T know exactly what to expect after the evening at the Bierces. It seemed likely that with Bierce's little speech being noised about and losing nothing in the telling, Colonel Jesup might move to arrest him. On the other hand, there was so much sympathy in Hartford with the gist and the spirit of what Bierce had said that Jesup would probably have difficulty explaining his move and, in any trial, could not make a charge of treason stick. Moreover, Bierce's acquittal on any such charge here in Connecticut would not help his accusers if he were ever brought to trial in Maine. So I bided my time, hearing what I could about the Convention's activities and trying to keep track of what Bierce was doing and saying.

I had not seen Jesup for days, but a man couldn't be with any group for long before the officer's name came up. If ever anyone was unpopular, it was he, and I'm sure it bothered him little. The chief complaint was his recruiting detail with its drummer marching back and forth past the State House while the Convention was in session. Then one day the detail simply didn't appear. Though public pressure had been severe, Jesup wasn't the man to knuckle under it. The only explanation that made sense to me was that he had decided the Convention was no longer dangerous.

As far as I was concerned, there would still be danger until the Convention published its report, but I could find out almost nothing about what was happening. Perhaps Jesup had learned something unknown to the rest of us who were reporting for various newspapers. In fact a number of Connecticut papers had withdrawn their reporters. Fortunately for me, Ed Dyson remained in Hartford. He had gone home for Christmas and went back again for New Year's, but otherwise was in the capital most of the time. During Christmas I had not minded being away from home because of the Middletown visit the day before and my curiosity about the Bierce invitation the evening afterward. But New Year's Eve and Day found me at loose ends, and a little morose. Dyson apologized for not inviting me to his home in Davenport; said that the only place for me would have been on the floor, since he had six wild kids around and an invalid mother. He seemed a bit relieved himself when he reappeared in Hartford the day after New Year's, and immediately proceeded to restore his sanity, so he said, by breaking open a bottle of whiskey.

While he was struggling with the cork, our landlady called upstairs that the mail had arrived, including a letter for me. I leaped down the stairs so quickly that she looked hard at me and reminded me that stairs were to walk on, not run on. I bowed, took the letter from her with thanks, and sedately mounted to our room.

The letter was from Brad, who, after pleasantries, soon came to the point:

Have you seen India? Rumor here has it that she refused to go to Hartford until almost literally forced to do so. I presume Bierce used much the same tactic that he did in persuading her to marry him: some kind of threat to Judge Kent — a physical menace or an exposure of his reputation. It is probably the latter, but I wouldn't discount the former. The night before the Bierces left, Jake Rudd brought the *Ghost* into port. He and Bierce then brought the Judge over to Bierce's house, where Rudd has lived ever since. He is obviously a watchdog over the Judge. Mrs. Adams, who was the Judge's housekeeper, was denied entrance to Bierce's house on two occasions by Rudd. Yesterday Rudd let her in, and she found the Judge so ill Rudd permitted her to call Dr. Harding. Harding told her she'd better send for India, but when the doctor had left, Rudd told her not to dare get in touch with India. She then came to me since she knows we are friends and you are in Hartford. She begged me to ask you to tell India of the Judge's condition. Evidently he has had a seizure of the heart and is struggling with pneumonia. If it is possible for you to communicate the information to India, you should most certainly do so. Should you see Bierce, pray give him my worst, as usual.

"Trouble, Dearborn?"

I looked across at Dyson watching me with half-closed eyes as he nursed his glass of whiskey. "Trouble enough," I said, and handed him the letter.

"Two sweet characters there, Bierce and Rudd," he said after a quick reading and, passing the letter back, nearly finished his whiskey at a gulp.

I said nothing for the moment, then got up and took my coat off the hook.

"Off to notify La Bierce?" Dyson asked.

"Right," I said, shrugging into my coat, and strode to the door.

"Just a moment, friend Dearborn."

As I stopped and looked at him, he shook his head. "Thought better of you, Dearborn. D'you expect to be admitted to Bierce's house? If Bierce is at home, d'you expect he'll let you speak with his wife? If he's out, you sure don't think his butler will let you in, do you? And if you have any little notions about forcing an entry, let me tell you the accommodations at the jail here in Hartford aren't very pleasant."

"Damn it, you confuse me, Dyson," I said.

"Good. Now just you sit down at that little table over there and write a note to Madame Bierce — and don't forget she is Madame Bierce, so don't be personal."

"But if Bierce is keeping her under guard —"

"Probably surveillance, not guard," he said.

"Well, it amounts to the same thing. Anyway, he won't let her see the note."

"He won't see it if I deliver it personally."

"You, Dyson!"

"I'd like to write an article for the Davenport *Gazette* on the loveliest hostess here in Hartford during the Convention."

I stared at him; beside his approach my rash proposal looked callow and would surely have landed me in trouble. Then as he began to grin, I reached over and shook his hand.

"Mind you, nothing personal," he said as I threw my coat on the bed and sat down at the table.

But late that afternoon before supper when next I saw Dyson, he waved my excited questions aside. "Nothing to it and nothing really important to tell you. Bierce wasn't at home, but he had two flunkeys around who didn't want to let me in. Then India suddenly appeared and asked me to have tea. They couldn't get rough at that, but one of 'em hung around on the edges all the time we talked — and that wasn't long."

"You gave her the note?" I asked.

"Yes, but it wasn't easy. And if you think your name was mentioned even once, you're wide of the mark. We talked about the holiday season here in Hartford, so calm yourself, my friend."

I thanked him for what he had done but half regretted that I hadn't attempted to deliver the message myself for all the fact that I might have had to fight to keep myself from being literally thrown out of the house. In fact, I began to realize that the more unattainable India became the more I was inclined to make a fool of myself in her behalf. And I didn't regret that at all — only that she was unattainable. This, of course, didn't make me feel more kindly disposed to Bierce.

A few days later, Mr. Longfellow sent me a note asking me to stop by his lodgings after supper. We went up to his room where he had a small fire going. The main log was green and sputtered and sparked without giving out a great deal of heat. Mr. Longfellow blew out the candle, and we sat close to the fire for warmth, enjoying its flickering light and the shadow play on the ceiling and walls of the room.

"Jonathan," Mr. Longfellow said at last, "I asked you to come here for two reasons. I wanted to talk with you briefly about Warren Bierce and also give you a little information about the Convention."

He sat back in the wing-back chair and put the tips of his fingers together. I couldn't be sure whether he was looking at the fire or at me, but I suspected the latter and I wondered if I could ever behave with him as if he were not my teacher. I suspected that when I was years away from his tutelage I'd still look upon him in the light of our existing relationship, which was never on my part without a feeling of profound respect mixed with a certain apprehension. It was not simply that Mr. Longfellow possessed both erudition and a presence. It was also that I craved his respect of me so sorely I was afraid I might be weighed in the balances and found wanting, as the scripture says. Furthermore, there was no doubt that I was eternally trying to control an impulsiveness that prompted me to do and say things I'd later regret. I now sat up in my straight-backed chair, crossed my legs, and, folding my hands, hoped I revealed none of the excitement I felt at whatever he was about to say.

"Now, about Warren Bierce —"

"Yes, sir?" And, in spite of myself, I leaned forward.

"Mr. Bierce has not been exactly a model of wisdom since he arrived in Hartford. His little addresses to the two recent parties at his house were ill-advised and unfortunate."

"I heard the first one," I said.

"Yes, I realize you must have."

"I'm sure there were those who sympathized with what he said."

"Oh, I have no doubt. But, Jonathan, he was totally mistaken to think the delegates could be persuaded to take the extreme steps he recommends."

"You mean, sir, the Convention is not coming out for separation from the Union?"

"Of course not," and his annoyance was plain. "I told you sometime ago that the delegates were not traitors, whatever your party may think us. Nor are we timid, whatever opinion our fellow Federalists may have of our recommendations. We are Americans who are sincerely distressed by the policies of the Madison administration, especially its treatment of New England. We wish to set limits to the powers of the national government in favor of the states. After all, Jonathan, this Union is a compact of the states, which have a sovereignty of their own that should not be invaded by the national government. But here I am speaking to you about the Convention before taking up the case of Warren Bierce, so I suppose I should finish. We expect to wind up the Convention by the fifth and we are drawing up a general report for the *Courant* to publish on the following day. Actually the Convention will have only minor matters to deal with after today, for we completed our revisions on the report of the Otis Committee which was submitted to us on December 30."

"Could you tell me anything about the report itself, sir?"

He smiled. "Jonathan, we are bound to say nothing specific to anyone about the recommendations of the Convention until the report appears in the *Courant*. Much as I should like to see the Convention's work placed before the readers of your newspaper, I cannot make an exception, even of you."

"Of course not, sir."

"But if you wish to send off a despatch giving your paper the timetable of developments as I have given it to you, you may do so."

I thanked him. Actually I doubted whether it was worthwhile to spend the postage since the Convention was so near adjournment. Not that I balked at the postage, though Mr. Daniels had warned me to "practice economy," as he expressed it, while I was on this mission. Rather, a copy of the *Courant* on the sixth would be more warmly received in Portland. I intended, however, to include in my final report Mr. Longfellow's mention of the work of the Otis Committee and the Convention's revision.

"Now as to Bierce again," Mr. Longfellow said, "the more thought I give to his known and alleged conduct during this war, the more distressed I become at his association with our party. I realize I have urged you repeatedly to be cautious about what you have said of the man. I would do so again for, though you may be correct in your suspicions and in your actual charges, you could have great difficulty making them hold up in the courts and could lay yourself open to legal reprisal. At the same time, I am impressed with the possibility that he may be a dangerous man, and there's no doubt that he is a rash one, especially in view of his little speech at his last party."

I could have laughed long and bitterly. Stephen Longfellow's reluctance to see Bierce as other than a reckless, or possibly a dangerous man might be a credit to his caution, to an exaggerated sense of fairness, but hardly to his truly remarkable intelligence. At the same time, even such a concession was evidence of a certain amount of progress.

"I hope you will forgive me, sir, for being presumptuous," I said, "if I commend you on your good judgment."

He glanced at me, and the fingers began to tap together. "I realize you think I am tardy in reaching such a conclusion, Jonathan."

"Yes, sir, I do."

"But, of course, I haven't had exactly the association with him that you have."

"That's right, sir."

"Nor do I have a prejudice against him that may have its origin in personal as well as political considerations."

"You're quite right."

"So let us say that I may be moving toward your opinion but in my own way and at my own pace."

"Personally I feel grateful that you are beginning to see him as I think he really is, Mr. Longfellow."

"Whatever that may be, Jonathan, and I shall not necessarily assume the worst. The state does not hang men on suspicion."

"No, sir," I said, but knew, as well as he did, that history was filled with instances of hangings on suspicion. Being a man of ideals, however, Mr. Longfellow really meant that men shouldn't hang only on grounds of suspicion, and I doubted if he would ever reach the point of agreeing that there was enough evidence to indict Bierce for treason. I felt sure that the syndicate in Portland could not count on Mr. Longfellow to assist them. Yet that he had come so far as to make the remarks he had about Bierce was something.

All the next day and through the morning of the fifth, Ed Dyson and I waited and walked and talked and wondered. What would the Convention recommend? Stephen Longfellow could imply, when he did not actually say, that there would be nothing treasonous in the Report but what he as a delegate might think, nondelegates might differ with drastically. Both of us also speculated on whether India would be able to return to Maine. As of the evening of the fourth she hadn't, and I could just imagine some of the scenes at the Bierce residence. India was a high-spirited girl and, unless Bierce kept close watch, likely to take off for Maine herself.

The morning of the fifth, when word spread that the Convention was to assemble at nine o'clock and would soon adjourn *sine die*, Dyson and I hurried to the State House. As we walked along the streets, we passed occasional houses where flags were flying at half mast, a Republican expression of disapproval of the Convention. Several times during recent days Federalist gangs of men and boys had tried to raise these flags and near riots occurred before order was restored. Approaching the State House, we saw that a crowd was already gathering and was kept in check by details from the 25th Infantry. Along Main Street in front of the State House a fife and drum unit, consisting of a dozen elderly men dressed in the tattered remains of their Revolutionary War uniforms, played a funeral dirge while boos and cheers greeted them as they passed. In general, the crowd seemed good-humored, certainly far less apprehensive and belligerent than when the Convention had assembled before Christmas. People, I suppose, had become used to the Convention, even to its secrecy. Besides, rumors persisted that peace was not far off.

Suddenly, by one of those curious manifestations of mass response, the crowd became silent and heads turned toward the State House. The doors opened, and the delegates walked out as a group. As if reluctant to leave, perhaps even a little afraid of the crowd, at whom some of them looked over their shoulders, they stood chatting for a few minutes, then shook hands and finally broke up. There were a few cheers from the crowd and a good deal of hand-clapping but more demands for information than applause. To these questions most of the delegates I saw smiled, including Harrison Gray Otis, who also bowed courteously. A few delegates, however, frowned, while Timothy Bigelow shouted, "Read tomorrow's *Courant!*" He sounded angry, and he looked angry, but people cheered him regardless. Knowing him to have been one of the less temperate delegates, I began to feel easier. Evidently the results of the Convention hadn't been entirely to his liking.

The rest of that day wherever we went people speculated excitedly about the Convention. Still, no one knew for sure what it had decided; the delegates had kept their secret well. Dyson and I called at Mr. Longfellow's lodgings, but he was out.

That evening after supper Ed left the house, saying he might not be back until late. Meanwhile I walked past where the Bierces were staying. The curtains were drawn, and, feeling like a Peeping Tom, I walked briskly by the house. Once back in my lodgings I brought my account of events up to date for Mr. Daniels. I must have been completely absorbed in my writing, for I heard no footsteps on the stairs, only the violent opening of the door as Ed Dyson swayed inside waving a newspaper.

"Here 'tis, Jonathan, here 'tis, by God!"

I reached him just in time to keep him from falling and helped him to a chair.

"They crawled out!" he said. "They didn't dare!"

"You mean this isn't treason?" I asked, snatching the paper from him, a special issue of the *Courant* dated the next day. "How did you get hold of this?"

He grinned. "Pays to know some of the boys at the *Courant,* friend Jonathan. Where d'you suppose I've been this evening?"

"Well, where have you been?"

"Down helping get the *Courant* set up and printed. You might think, the *Courant* being a weekly, they'd be all set up and ready to print, but they didn't get the copy of the Report until late. Expect those boys'll work a good part of the night."

"Is it all here?"

"All there. Not much of it for three weeks' work."

Then as I hastily looked through the Report for its main points, Dyson shook his head. "No need to do that now, Dearborn. I can tell you what you'll want to know."

He then gave me a digest of that strange document which the delegates said they had drawn up to strengthen and, if possible, perpetuate the Union. They wanted to remove the grounds for jealousy, provide for a fair and equal representation, and set limits to powers which in their opinion had been misused. To accomplish all this, they proposed seven amendments to the Constitution. The first would apportion representatives for the United States Congress only on the basis of the free population, which seemed a good idea to me. In the second amendment no state was to be admitted without a favorable two-thirds majority of both houses of Congress. Thinking this over, I said that this would make it fairly easy to block the admission of any Western state.

Dyson nodded. "You bet it would! Here in Connecticut people are getting the 'Ohio fever' and after the war you watch 'em get the hell off these rocky hills and go where the land's open and lush. That's just what the Convention's afraid of: New England would be out-

[ 325 ]

voted by the West. Mind you, it was the West that pushed hard for this war, and the delegates didn't forget."

He then went on to the other amendments. By the third and fourth the Convention wanted to limit an embargo to sixty days and make it impossible to vote a nonintercourse act unless it received a two-thirds majority from the Senate and the House. I saw nothing startling in either of these; the Massachusetts legislature had actually voted for the first back in 1809.

On the fifth Dyson and I differed sharply. This one provided that there must be a two-thirds majority in both Senate and House for a declaration of war. He felt that if it took a two-thirds majority in the Senate to ratify a peace treaty, the same should be required for a declaration of war. In my judgment the amendment would rob the government of the power to act quickly, perhaps the power to act at all, if more than a simple majority were required.

"Hell," Dyson said, "the proposal still makes sense to me. Once we're at war I'm all for waging it with everything we've got, but I'd make it mighty difficult to get into war. There are too many glory boys in this country."

The sixth and seventh amendments were low blows. The Convention wanted to make it impossible for naturalized citizens to hold elective or appointive office in the national government, and proposed one term for the President, with no state to have two Presidents in succession. This last being clearly aimed at Virginia and the sequence of Jefferson and Madison, we damned the Convention for its narrow-mindedness.

"Does the Convention say anything else that's important?" I asked.

"Yes, one last point. The delegates insist that a state has the right to interpose its authority when the national government tries to create 'a military despotism' by acts such as taking over control of the militia or conscripting people. The sovereignty of a state and the liberties of its people must be protected."

"Of course, you know," I said, a little troubled, "that's what Jefferson and Madison said in 1798 in the Kentucky and Virginia Resolutions as a counter to John Adams and the Federalists' Alien and Sedition Acts."

"Sure, sure," Dyson said testily, "they've turned our own language against us, but, unlike them, we've been at war for over two years. It's a different situation in a different context. Then they were throwing men into jail for the slightest criticism of the government. I tell you, Dearborn, if the Madison government were as repressive as the Federalists, that bastard Bierce would have been in jail within hours of his appearance in Hartford. For all I know he may be there now."

"What! Has anything happened?"

"There was some talk down at the *Courant* office that Bierce had found out about the proceedings of the Convention and was so damned mad he was going around saying there weren't any real patriots left in New England — Federalist or Republican — outside of the Essex Junto."

"That sounds like him," I said.

"Well, that wasn't so bad. What seemed to get under people's skins was that he said the British were our best friends and we were all too blind to see it."

"Now that really sounds like him!"

"If the Great High Mogul here in Hartford — your friend Jesup — hears about him, he'll heave him into the local Newgate on a charge of treason — and maybe he wouldn't be far wrong, at that."

"Not far wrong!" I said. "He wouldn't be wrong at all. He'd just be late, that's all."

"Wonder if he's still in Hartford."

"He was still here in midevening. At least there was light behind drawn curtains."

"Were you keeping an eye on him or hoping to see La Bierce, Dearborn?"

I looked at the sly smile. "Maybe both, Dyson."

"Well, I've told you before — mixing romance with business has its perils, and not the least of these is loss of a man's peace of mind."

"Do you have peace of mind, Dyson?" I asked.

"Hell, no — never had, never expect to have it, and probably wouldn't know what to do with it if it came to me. But it's something I advise people to cultivate."

I laughed. "I'm afraid I'm like you, Dyson. Peace of mind is so remote it's practically irrelevant."

"Irrelevant — irrelevant." He seemed to be turning the word over and over again in his mind. Then he got up. "Dearborn, that's about what the Convention's Report here is — irrelevant, like the Convention itself."

# XXXII

A SHARP knocking on the door woke Dyson and me the next morning, and when I asked what the matter was, the landlady told me in by no means dulcet tones that a soldier had just brought a message summoning me to Colonel Jesup's headquarters at once.

It may have been because I liked neither being awakened nor going without my shave and breakfast that I accompanied the soldier to Jesup in a bad humor. When he tried to start up a conversation, I refused to be drawn in. I presume I was mainly annoyed because the military had summoned me, a civilian; I suppose that I was hardly different from my fellow New Englanders in my dislike and suspicion of military authority. At the same time, as we neared Jesup's headquarters, I couldn't deny an upsurge of curiosity as to the reason for the summons. This, however, Jesup soon satisfied.

"Dearborn, been keeping an eye on Bierce since he arrived, haven't you?"

"Yes, sir," I said. "I told you earlier I intended to watch him and listen."

"And so you have."

"Have you been watching me, too, Colonel?"

He smiled, a trifle bleakly I thought, and said, "You were too interested an observer to go unwatched yourself, Dearborn."

"You must have quite a dossier on me, Colonel, and my treasonable activities!"

He shrugged at my sarcasm. "Hardly. But I can't say the same of your friend Bierce. He got out of town just in time, Dearborn."

"Bierce is gone?"

"Left last night just before midnight. If he'd been around this morning, I just might have arrested him. At the least, I'd have had him in for a questioning he wouldn't have forgotten in a hurry."

"Then you, too, think he's a traitor, sir?" I asked eagerly.

"Of course he is. But a damned clever one. He's also more than just a traitor who goes over to the enemy — he actively works with the British."

"Can you prove it, sir? Have you got enough evidence?"

"What he said while here in Hartford was damning enough, though it couldn't stand up by itself in a court. But the people from whom he rented the house he used left him the entire domestic staff. After you first spoke to me, I managed to persuade two of them to work temporarily for the United States government. They report that while he was in Hartford, Bierce had two conversations with a British agent on successive evenings. I have their affidavits as of an hour ago. So if your people in Maine are building a case against him, Dearborn, what reports I have accumulated could add another block to the total evidence."

"Could I have copies, sir?"

"No, sir," he said, shaking his head. "But if I should receive a legal request, the army would likely be happy to comply. I thought you'd be glad to know that."

I thanked him and left, more disappointed than I knew I had a right to feel. Jesup, though officially and properly cautious, had been trying to be helpful, but I had the feeling that despite what evidence he had acquired, even the affidavits, Bierce was too smart for us, and too lucky as well, ever to be brought into court.

Meanwhile, with the Convention over and Bierce gone, I had no official reason for remaining in Hartford; in fact, I had a real duty to get to Maine as soon as possible to deliver my report to Mr. Daniels and give him the account of the Convention published in the *Courant*. I therefore reserved a seat on the stage going to Boston the next morning. It took two days to reach Boston, two more to find a place on the Portland stage, and another two to arrive in Portland, with a heavy snow cover from Portsmouth east. Though to have slipped down to Portland by schooner would have required barely more than overnight, the blockade was so tight only fishermen dared venture out and then not out of sight of land. I could have hired a relay of horses, but this arrangement would have been expensive and I couldn't see that the need for haste was that urgent.

On the route through the coastal towns between Portsmouth and Portland we passed a number of vehicles belonging to what we called in Maine the "Horse Marines." The blockade had forced a heavy use of road transport — great sledges drawn by oxen and loaded with merchandise, or fast horse-drawn sleighs. Jokingly our driver referred to the big fellows as schooners and the lighter sleighs as cutters. He said that a lot of this merchandise was contraband out of Castine and that customs officials in fast two-horse cutters often overhauled the slower craft and inspected their contents.

For a time I had thought I might overtake the Bierces, but the delay in Boston had made that impossible. Word of the closing of the Convention would therefore have reached Portland before me. This might have irked me more than it did if I hadn't realized I could still arrive in time to get the news into the next issue of the *Eastern Courier*, which was a weekly. Once arrived in Portland, I went immediately to my parents' home and then to the office of the newspaper. It was late afternoon and the city darkening, but I found Jedediah Daniels still in his cage of an office reading proof with the aid of a whale-oil lamp that had a wick so uneven the office was a haze of smoke.

"Ah, Jonathan Dearborn!" he said, looking over his Ben Franklin glasses at me and rising to open the cage door. "Now, young man, what have you to report?"

This, even before I had sat down or finished shaking his hand. I handed him my detailed journal and the "extra" of the *Courant*.

"I'll read your material this evening," he said, pushing it to one side. "Please tell me briefly about the Convention and then about Warren Bierce."

The soft, almost whispering voice was insistent, so I responded with a quick summary of the Convention and a more detailed account of Bierce.

"Bierce and his wife arrived in town last night," Daniels said when I finished, and I thought I could detect a note of reproof in his voice.

"That's the advantage of not having to depend on public transportation," I said. "I came back as quickly as I could, Mr. Daniels."

His nose twitched. "I am not criticizing you, Jonathan. I am merely pointing out that they arrived before you did. The only way you could have reached here sooner was by horse."

"That would have been more expensive to you, sir," I reminded him, my voice probably as resentful as I felt.

"So it would have been, yes, indeed," he said, his fingers drumming incessantly. "Have you submitted an account of your expenses with this material you've given me?"

"Yes, sir."

"Good. I will look them over tonight, too. Tomorrow we shall have a longer talk. Now, of course, you will want to see your friends and more of your parents. Pray give my kindest regards to Mr. and Mrs. Dearborn. I hope you appreciate them properly."

"I hope so, too, sir," I said, and rose to leave.

"Tomorrow morning at nine o'clock here, Mr. Dearborn. Pray be on time."

"Yes, sir."

When I described Daniels's reception, my father and mother exchanged one of those knowing looks that always seemed to exclude me and used to infuriate me when I was a boy. "Jonathan," my father said, his eyes twinkling, "Jedediah Daniels's whole life is his business."

"Getting his old newspaper out," my mother added, "is like converting the heathen. He has the zeal of a missionary."

My father nodded. "Exactly. To find out what is happening in the world and get a report of it into the *Eastern Courier* ahead of any other newspaper is a sacred mission for him, and he expects, I'm sure, that all those who work for him will be burning with the same fervor."

"But what did I do to offend him? I got here as soon as I could."

"The Bierces arrived before you did; that's all, son. It's winter and the roads can't be in the best condition, but you still made splendid time — Daniels realizes that. But the fact remains that Warren and India Bierce were here before you. You may not have loitered, but you were outsmarted: that is Daniels's feeling."

"And your being outsmarted means Jedediah Daniels and his precious newspaper were also outsmarted!" my mother said tartly. "I always did think him an unreasonable man where his work is concerned."

Brad agreed with my parents' view when he came over for dinner and later went up to my room for a talk. "I hadn't known Daniels at all well until I started to work with his syndicate. Since then I've had occasion to observe him fairly closely. He has to be at least two steps ahead of the other fellow in his planning — one step is not enough. And he will accept no excuses, no matter how valid. I suppose he's really something of a fanatic. I'm glad he's on our side. Oh, yes, and there's something else: he has developed a hatred of Warren Bierce that goes far beyond whatever feeling we have about the man."

"You mean that somehow he holds Bierce responsible for the *Argus* losing money?" I asked, and meant the sarcasm.

Brad blew out a long streamer of cigar smoke and laughed. "He watches his pennies all right, though he'll spend them, too — after all, didn't you go to Hartford for him? No, he honestly thinks Bierce has deceived everyone, including Daniels himself, and is a traitor who should be hanged publicly. Daniels is not a bloodthirsty man — vindictive, perhaps, but not bloodthirsty. His view of Bierce has become something like Philip Adair's view of Jake Rudd."

"I'm not sure I see exactly why."

"Oh, yes, you do," Brad said. "Philip holds Rudd responsible for his wife's death. Daniels was once a friend of Bierce, and so feels a sense of personal betrayal."

I didn't worry the point further. Instead, I asked about Captain Vail and learned that he was still very ill in Camden and continued to be heavily guarded. This news depressed me, and though I was weary, sleep was a long time coming that night. Before it overtook me, however, I had become so sympathetic with Jedediah Daniels's position that I was critical of myself for having let Bierce return to Portland before me.

The next morning I was present promptly for my appointment with Mr. Daniels. He looked drawn and tired as if he hadn't gone home, but his mood was markedly different.

"Dearborn, your report was interesting, very interesting," he said,

[ 332 ]

waving me to the chair by his desk and folding his hands over his little paunch.

I was to learn that if Jedediah Daniels liked something, he found it "interesting"; never did I hear him utter words of outright approval of anything. He was even chary of using handsome adjectives about people; he rarely went beyond "fine" in describing a person he liked. He actually seemed afraid of expressing approval. On the other hand, if he disliked anyone or anything, there were no limits that I could discern, except outright profanity or obscenity, to his vocabulary of derogation. I thanked him now for what he had said and remained silent as he idly patted my report and the copy of the *Courant* "extra." "Dearborn," he went on in his whispery voice, "I understand that you know Philip Adair."

When I said that I did, he pursed his lips. "Adair was here last evening. Your friend Pettigrew, who is working closely with our syndicate, introduced him to me a fortnight ago. I think he's a fine man, Dearborn."

"I think so, too," I said, and wondered why Philip had been there.

"He has given us a lot of information on Rudd as well as Bierce," Daniels said. "Rudd is an unhanged rascal, fully as traitorous in his way as Bierce but with less influence, and therefore less dangerous. I hope we can bring both to justice, but Bierce is the man who really must stand trial if only we can build a convincing case. Now this is an interesting report you submitted, Dearborn."

"Thank you, sir."

"But it's not complete," and my little bubble of elation collapsed as he spoke.

"You see, Dearborn," he went on, "Colonel Jesup's deposition with respect to Bierce's conduct in Hartford will be necessary. I wish he had given it to you, but I can understand his reluctance. I am therefore having the two lawyers of the syndicate, of whom your friend Pettigrew is one, draw up a request in behalf of the syndicate. And, Dearborn, I want you to go back to Hartford again with it, present it to Jesup, and bring back Jesup's deposition. I am sorry to send you on the road so soon again, but the mails are uncertain and speed is urgent."

I could have declined, of course; I had no desire to travel the wintry roads again. Besides, I had the feeling that something was going to break very soon in the Bierce camp, and I wanted to be around. At the same time I realized how important it was to secure Jesup's assistance, so I consented to go.

When she heard of my decision, my mother was all for going to Jedediah Daniels and giving him a piece of her mind. Fortunately my father was able to calm her, though even he thought Daniels might have sent someone else. Nor did he like it better that this time Daniels instructed me to hire horses down and back. This, however, was a relief to me.

The next morning, therefore, found me bound for Boston. Luckily the roads were hard-packed, better in fact than in summer, so I made excellent time with relays of horses. Colonel Jesup seemed surprised to see me so soon again and said that if I hadn't spoken to him about a report before I had left Hartford, he'd suspect me of simply using the syndicate's need of a deposition as an excuse to return to Hartford to court a girl. Fortunately he promised me the deposition, with copies of the affidavits from his two agents, within twenty-four hours; and I was presently on my way back to Maine with an alacrity that satisfied even my impatience.

If my return trip was less easy and swift because of the snow that fell on the three days it took me to reach Portland from Boston, ordinarily a two-day journey, I didn't feel cast down. I knew I was adding yet another brick to the case the syndicate was building against Warren Bierce.

What surprised me on my return was that Jedediah Daniels seemed less pleased than I thought he should be by the deposition. Very properly Colonel Jesup had not let me read it, but knowing what must have been written, I thought that surely much of what Jesup had said would have been damning. When I said so, Daniels shrugged.

"Yes, it's fine, and it will help, but it's only part of what we need. I want you and Pettigrew to make depositions of your own — complete, mind you. I'll give you three days here in Portland to rest and draft yours; and be sure to have it properly notarized by someone other than Pettigrew. Then I'm sending you on another journey."

By this time I had come to feel as if I had enlisted in the army or navy. Few commanding officers could have been more demanding of their men than Daniels. Yet I was so committed to the purpose that he and the syndicate had in mind that I did not think of objecting. I didn't even ask where he wanted me to go now. I merely said, "Yes, sir," and waited.

If he was surprised at my apparent lack of curiosity, he didn't show it. (Actually I was fairly aching for him to reveal what he had in mind.) Instead, he cleared his throat and said in his whispery way, "I'm sending you and Pettigrew to Camden to bring back Captain Vail's statement. While you were in Hartford for the Convention, I asked Colonel Foote to help the Captain prepare the statement. Vail is at Foote's house."

"Can't I go get the paper by myself, sir? Surely there's no need for Brad to break off from his work here."

But Daniels shook his head. "The roads are worse to the eastward than what you have just traveled, and it is so important for us to have Captain Vail's statement that I don't want to send only one man."

"I could take Philip Adair with me," I said.

"I have other uses for Adair, Dearborn."

So Brad and I went to Camden, and pleased indeed I was to have his company; being a courier can be a lonely business. We went armed with pistols, while I brought along a cutlass as well. Not that we expected any trouble. On the other hand, the mission was important and the coastal road often had lonely stretches. Besides, enemy territory lay just across the Penobscot and British raids down along the western side of the Bay were not unknown.

Fortunately we reached Camden without mishap and took a room at the Eager Inn. Mrs. Eager welcomed us warmly. Then her face sobered.

"Come to see Ben Vail, have you? Well, you'd better see him quick."

"He's that ill?" Brad asked.

"Mighty sick. Fact is, they say he's out of his head part of the time with fever. You better go up there right away."

It had taken us more than three days through the drifting snow to reach Camden, but, tired as we were, we went over to Colonel

Foote's house as soon as we had cared for our horses and washed up. Dinner could wait.

Colonel Foote himself met us and bade the sentry let us in. "Good, good, glad you've come!" he said, keeping his voice down. "Ben spoke of you just this morning, Dearborn."

"How is he, Colonel?" I asked. "Mrs. Eager sent us over just as soon as we arrived."

"He's sick all right, and the prospect doesn't look good at all. For a while, he seemed to get better and was up and around. Now he's in bed again all the time."

"Mrs. Eager said there were times when he wasn't rational."

"When the fever shoots up, he babbles away without making much sense."

"How is he now?"

"Not bad. Come in, he'll be delighted to see you."

Foote knocked at the door, and the nurse let us inside. "Don't excite him," she said, and looked so large and fierce it seemed as if she must have growled. Nor did she leave the room: instead she stood, back against the door, and folded her arms. I'm sure she handled Captain Vail as if he were a child.

Though we tiptoed toward the bed, he heard us and turned quickly.

"Jonathan!" he said, and held out his hand.

"Captain Vail!" I said, marveling at the power still in his voice and the strong handclasp.

"And you, too, Brad Pettigrew! Thought I'd never see either of you again."

He held out his other hand to Brad, and for a moment we stood on either side of the bed holding his hands. Then we gently dropped them.

"When are you going to be well enough to come home with us?" I asked. "My father and mother want you to spend some time with them, and my Uncle Tom has been claiming priority rights on the grounds that he knew you before they did."

The skin on Captain Vail's craggy face hung slackly, and his grin came through in an oddly distorted manner. "Tom wrote me," he said. "He thinks Cape Elizabeth is healthier than Camden."

"Healthier, my eye!" Colonel Foote laughed. "Think of all that fog down there! And when there's no fog, there's wind."

"I'm doing all right here," Captain Vail said.

"Of course you are, Ben."

But the Colonel's heartiness had a hollow ring in my ears, and the silent moment that followed was endless and anguished. Fortunately the nurse stepped forward and told us the Captain needed to rest.

"Rest!" Vail protested. "That's all I do, Minnie!"

"The doctor said you was to rest, an' I'm to see you follow his orders."

"You run a taut ship, Minnie Thompson."

"Then see that you obey." She pulled the comforter up over him with a rough gentleness and nodded us out. "Your friends will be back if you're good."

Colonel Foote led us into his living room and poured each of us a tot of rum.

"Is there any hope?" I asked, my voice so harsh it startled me.

Foote shrugged. "Who can tell? He's getting good care. Minnie Thompson's an old school friend of his. Her husband was lost at sea years ago, and she's been cook, midwife, nurse — whatever and whenever she's needed in this area. Now about Ben's statement. I have it in my desk, all signed. But of course I'll want to add my few words, too, for whatever I know about the situation. How long are you men planning to stay?"

Brad and I looked at each other. "I hate to say so, but I think we'd better get started tomorrow," I said; and Brad agreed.

"Very well," Foote said, "I'll have both statements ready for you in the morning. You're planning on seeing Ben before you leave?"

"Of course," I said.

"Good, good."

But in the morning Captain Vail was running a fever again. "He wouldn't know you if he saw you. You'd better leave him be," Minnie Thompson said. "I'll tell him you was here."

So we turned back toward Portland without again meeting the man who had come to mean so much to both of us. I was poor company on the way home. For that matter, so was Brad, despite his valiant attempt to cheer me up by reminding me that Captain Vail had eagerly insisted on carrying through the escape regardless of the stormy night or the enemy. Altogether, it was a sad and silent return.

# XXXIII

The day after I returned home I came down with a violent cold that turned into a light case of pleurisy. My winter travels had evidently caught up with me, though I was inclined to believe that the bitter and sorrowful mood which remained with me all the way from Camden to Portland had lowered my resistance to whatever causes colds. Even the relief at arriving home and the glass of steaming whiskey my father had insisted I drink — not entirely with my mother's approval — had not cheered me greatly. From the next day on for a week, I fought fever on and off, coughed, and held my back when I coughed because of the pain. It was my good fortune, however, to possess a strong constitution, despite my propensity for lung ailments, so I was presently on my feet again, though shakily so, and not until after the beginning of February.

While I was ill, Judge Kent died. Though I hadn't known him well, and didn't like him, what I had seen of him in Europe made me feel sorry for him. Yet I resented him, because, without him, India Mitchell, with her almost terrible sense of loyalty to him, would not have married Warren Bierce — of that I was convinced. What might happen now, with her uncle dead? Would she stay with Bierce, if she hated and feared him so, or would she leave him? If she remained with him, then that was that. But if she left him, there might be a chance for me, though a divorce was no easy achievement, nor pleasant enduring, given the spiteful tongues around. Moreover, if she could not secure a divorce, this would really make life difficult. Of course I could by no means be certain that India would listen to me, but this time I was not going to take any chances; I would be heard. At any rate, knowing India had been fond of the Judge after a fashion, I sent her a note of sympathy.

I also learned from Brad that since Judge Kent's death news had leaked out that the Judge had invested heavily in slaving, something we had long suspected. But he had also had a ship engaged in smuggling opium from India to China and occasionally had some brought into New York and Boston for secret buyers. Worst of all, in some ways, was the rumor that while on the Bench he had deliberately suppressed evidence that led to the hanging of a man who knew the Judge had protected a gang of wreckers; these men changed the light on a point on the Maine coast, which caused several ships to run ashore. If all this was true, it was easy to see how Bierce, who had a nose for such information, had such a hold on him. As long as he lived, the Judge treasured what was generally a respectable reputation, but now that he was dead and people knew about him, few had any good thing to say of him. Brad said some evidence had come to light that for many years the Judge had been secretly supporting the family of the wrecker he had hanged but that such "conscience" effort could scarcely counter the effect of the original revelation. Brad also believed that Bierce was responsible for the leakage of information about Judge Kent because of his anger at India, whom he kept virtually a prisoner in his house.

A few evenings after I sent my sympathy note, we were finishing supper when our door knocker thumped, an oddly uncertain thump followed by an unmistakably decisive thump. My parents and I glanced at each other. Then, as I started to push back my chair, my father rose.

"You remain where you are, Jonathan. I'll see who it is."

Before I could protest, he was out in the little hallway and opening the door.

"Jonathan Dearborn live here?" a harsh voice asked, or, rather, demanded.

"Yes, he does," my father said amiably, "and may I have your name, sir? I am Jonathan's father."

"My name's Black," the man said, "and your son owes me some money."

"Then come in, Mr. Black, and let us talk about it."

"I don't want to talk about it — I want to get paid."

"Well, you can't be paid out here in the dark, Mr. Black."

There was a stamping on the steps as the man shook the snow off his feet. Then my father entered with Captain Black of the schooner *Ginny*. Quietly my father introduced him to my mother, whose presence seemed to disconcert him. He turned his cap around in his hands as if it were a wheel, mumbled, "Your servant, ma'am," and then turned with relief to me.

"Dearborn, you look sick. What's the matter?"

"A cold and a touch of pleurisy, but I'm all right now, thanks. I understand you've come for your money."

"Yes, I have. Got it with you?"

"Not here, no. But I can give you a draft on my bank, and they'll pay you in the morning."

"Huh. Well, that's better'n not getting it at all."

"Look here," I said, "I thought you were in Dartmoor."

"Well, it's a long story," he said.

"Why don't you two men sit down?" my mother asked.

"I never thought," I said to him, "that I'd be entertaining in my own home the man that Jake Rudd and Warren Bierce hired to drop me overboard. Luckily for me you changed your mind."

Black's stubbly face grew red. "Maybe we ought not to talk about all this in front of your parents, Dearborn."

"Oh, don't mind us, Captain," my mother said gravely. "My husband is a minister of the gospel, and there aren't many human frailties that we aren't familiar with."

"Exactly," my father said, nodding. "The lure of money is an understandable weakness."

"Well, it wasn't just that, Reverend," Black said. "I like money, sure. An' I've done some mighty bad things to get it. But I don't make a practice of dumpin' people in the ocean for money, no, sir."

"But you were going to throw Jonathan overboard, weren't you?" my mother asked.

"No, ma'am, that wasn' in my calculations at all. I might have had other plans, but I didn't intend to kill him, no, ma'am!"

"Then why —"

"Ma'am, do you know Jake Rudd?"

"Other than meeting him once, Captain Black, I've been spared that indignity. But I realize he is a formidable creature."

"I learned a long time ago not to argue with Jake, but that don't mean I'll do just as he says if he ain't there to see that I do."

"And if he is there?" my mother pressed him.

Black half strangled on a cough. "Well, ma'am, he wasn't there, an' I'm glad, so let's let it go at that."

"How did you get out of Dartmoor, Captain?" I thought it high time to intervene.

"I never got *in* there. They put me on a hulk in the lower Thames, an' seven of us broke out one night. The mud flats was too much for four of 'em, but I made it. I ain't a young man, ma'am" — he looked at my mother — "but I'm strong, an' I don't lose my head. I caught a ride with a farmer goin' to market — course it took a little persuadin' for me to get his clothes."

"Killed him?" I asked, while my mother looked horrified, yet fascinated.

"No, but I bumped his head a bit so he didn' even know I was takin' his clothes off of him. I hid out in London for a while, then signed articles on a brig bound for Jamaica. She was taken by the *General Jackson*, privateer out of Boston. The *Jackson* was finishin' a long cruise so we ended up in Boston. Lots of Britishers off the harbor, but we made it through all right at night. Figured I'd come down here an' collect my money while it was still on my mind."

"Did you just get into Portland today, Captain Black?" my father asked.

"This afternoon."

"Do you have a place to spend the night?"

"Yes, Reverend, I do. I've a room down at the Anchor Hotel. Food's not bad, judgin' by supper."

The Anchor was a shabby seaman's inn down on Fore Street, but at least the fact that Black had already established himself there kept my father from inviting him to stay with us. I could see my mother was relieved, and I didn't blame her; Black was clearly no favorite with her. At the same time, had it been necessary, she would have seen her Christian duty and done it — grimly, to be sure.

Then, while my father explained to Black that since I was convalescing, he would go to the bank himself for me in the morning and obtain a draft, I had an idea. Since Black was a mercenary fellow, would he be willing to draw up a statement of Rudd's arrangement with him and have it sworn to and notarized? Of course he would have a price, but Mr. Daniels might be agreeable to his terms. It would be a case of fear versus greed, and there was no doubt that the idea of being on bad terms with Jake Rudd would terrify him. I might not be able to persuade him to make such a statement, but if Jedediah Daniels could convince him he had little to fear, and could also make the price appealing, Black might reach for a quill without great hesitation.

"Father, I'll be able to take Captain Black to the bank," I said.

At once my mother began to protest, but my father, after glancing at me, shook his head at her. "Come, come, Alice, Jonathan wants to go, so let's stop babying him. Just be careful, Jonathan. I'll have Jackie Fisher across the street bring a sleigh from the livery stable. Will ten o'clock be satisfactory, Captain Black? If so, Jonathan will call for you at the Anchor at that time."

When Black assented, my father at once stood up, thanked him for coming, and bade him good night.

Of course Black had hardly left the house before my mother turned on my father and scolded him up one side and down the other. He took it without a murmur; then said, when she paused for breath, "Alice, didn't you see that Jonathan had thought of something valuable for his case? He wanted to talk with Black without us around. Now, isn't that so, Jonathan?"

"Not quite, Father," I said. "I want Jedediah Daniels to talk with him and persuade him to make a statement about Rudd's employing him to do away with me."

"He'll never do that," my mother said. "That man Rudd frightens him."

"He'll do it if Daniels makes the price right," I said. "A man who will come from Boston to Portland in winter weather to collect fifty dollars will listen carefully before he turns down a chance to earn the same amount, or possibly twice as much, for subscribing to a few simple statements of fact."

"I think that might depend upon the fact and how quickly Captain Black could disappear from these parts," my father said. "You could never expect him to remain for the trial, if it comes to that, and a notarized statement wouldn't weigh as heavily with a jury as the man's appearing in person."

Of course my father was right, but I was still confident when, after picking up Black at the Anchor the next morning, I drove him first to the bank, then to the office of the *Eastern Courier*. I had written notes to both Daniels and Brad announcing my arrival with Captain Black. Though I explained nothing in either note, I knew that Brad would need no explanation, while he would acquaint Daniels beforehand with my relationship with Black if Daniels didn't already remember it from my detailed report.

When I arrived, one of Daniels's apprentices ran out and held the horses's head while we got down from the sleigh, then drove the sleigh in back.

"Ah, Dearborn, glad to see you're on your feet again," Daniels said, and after I had introduced Black to him and to Brad, he said, "Pettigrew, you can now bring on that hot rum."

"Hot rum in the morning! I'll be ruined for the rest of the day," I laughed.

"It'll save the day for me," Black grunted. "Soon's I leave here, I'm settin' a course for Boston. Now that I've got my money" — and he patted his inside coat pocket — "a little rum'll help me get ready."

"How are you getting to Boston, Captain Black?" Daniels asked. "There's no stage until tomorrow morning."

"Oh, I'll get a ride somehow," Black said.

"That may not be so easy, and this is no weather to be caught out in."

"I want to get to Boston," Black said. "I'd have caught a stage this mornin' if Dearborn here could have paid me last night."

"I'm sorry I wasn't able to," I said. "But there was no stage you could have taken today, either. In the winter, we're lucky if there's a connection between here and Boston once a week, and often there's no coach at all. It depends on the weather and the business. Once this war is over, we may have a regular service established."

"Once this war is over I want to get to sea again," Black growled.

"I think that time may be very close, Captain," Daniels said. "Meanwhile here in Portland there are powerful interests who wish

[ 343 ]

to bring two evil men to justice, Warren Bierce and his henchman, Jake Rudd."

He explained the situation in some detail and then pointed out how Black could serve the two causes of patriotism and justice by making a written statement of the murder arrangement as it had affected me.

To all this Black shook his head. "Mr. Daniels, I'd be makin' myself a party to the deed by writin' anything like that."

"But you were evidently moved by fear of Jake Rudd," Daniels said.

Personally I wasn't convinced it was solely fear that had motivated Black; there must also have been a tidy little sum of money involved. Bringing this up, however, would scarcely help now.

"I ain't no coward," Black said, "but, then, Rudd ain't just another man, an', if you'd ask me, I'd say you people ain't got him cornered yet, no, sir!"

"Do you sympathize with what we are trying to accomplish, Captain Black?"

"You mean, put Rudd an' this Bierce in jail, maybe hang 'em? I'm all for it. But I don't know you people, Daniels, an' I do know Rudd. You don't suppose he ain't on to what you're up to, do you?"

"I think both Rudd and Bierce probably are aware of our intentions," Daniels said. "After all, this is a small town, and people will talk, even when they're sworn to secrecy."

"Then you can bet they're not goin' to sit back an' let you invite 'em to go to jail. They'll have plans, too."

"What kind of plans?"

"Well," and Black scratched his ear, "they'll have plans to escape, if they feel you're closin' in on 'em. Now, wouldn' you?"

"I suppose I would."

"You bet you would, an' so would I. But they may have other plans, too, and that could mean strikin' back at you — an' hard, mister, hard!"

"That's always a possibility, of course."

Black was silent but glared contemptuously at all of us.

"Am I to infer," Daniels asked, "that you will not assist us, Captain Black?"

"I ain't goin' to do anything to get in Jake Rudd's way," he said stubbornly.

"There is nothing, not even a little financial recognition of what you did for Dearborn here — say five hundred dollars in hard money — that would alter your decision?"

Black licked his lips and stared at me. The offer was no small one in these times, and unusual as hard money, since banks were suspending specie payments all along the seaboard because of the way the war was going against us. Yet though I have to admit to being astonished that Daniels would propose such a large figure, I was a trifle piqued that I wasn't worth more.

Again Black shook his head, though by no means vigorously. "No, sir, I don't think so," he said; and the words seemed to be dragged out of him.

"I could see that you received this money without delay, sir," Daniels went on. "I'm sure it would help tide you over until peace comes."

"Oh, I could use it, all right. But it wouldn't help me much if I'm dead."

"You really are afraid of Jake Rudd, aren't you, Captain?"

Black flushed, but he nodded and said, "Rudd ain't a man who forgets, mister."

"Very well," and Daniels rose to his feet, as did all of us with much scraping of chairs. "You realize, Captain Black, that, whether you write it or not, you actually were a partner in the plot to murder Dearborn. This is not a light offense. Testimony from the British officers aboard the *Beagle*, which could be obtained in time, might be pretty damning about the likelihood that you were engaged in piracy, not privateering, at the time of your capture. The laws of the United States, Black, do not endorse piracy even in wartime. Now, my offer of five hundred dollars is hardly what you would receive from a successful piratical cruise, but it is substantial. A pity, Black, that it does not attract you. Good day, sir, and a safe trip to Boston."

Black thrust his hat on his head and walked to the door without a word or glance at any of us. Then as he reached the door, he asked hoarsely, "Did you say there's a stage for Boston tomorrow, Dearborn?"

"That's the only stage this week, Captain," Brad said pleasantly.

"Well, gimme a night to think this over," Black said, and plunged into the snow, his head bowed and his hands deep in his pockets.

Daniels, who rarely smiled, arched his eyebrows and looked so pleased, without actually smiling, that if he had been a cat, he would have purred.

When I soon left, too, Daniels patted my shoulder, a rare gesture for him, and said, "Get well, Jonathan. I can use you here with the paper."

I attributed such an expression of approval to his good feeling about Black, but, as for myself, I still had my doubts about the man; in fact I had heard little to cause me to question any longer my parents' assessment of Black's fear of Rudd. Mercenary he truly was, but his life was dearer to him than money. Yet there was something peculiar about his fear: Rudd seemed, to him, like a god, albeit an evil one, but a god nevertheless who was ever knowing and powerful beyond comparison. Compounding his fear was profound respect and admiration. With the proper gesture from Rudd, Black would make an obeisance.

Brad drove me home in my rig, then returned it to the livery stable. He was more optimistic than I was. "Black's a greedy fellow, don't forget that," he said. "I'll admit it looked hopeless at first, but I think Daniels handled him pretty effectively."

He paused to let some children sledding clear the street, then drove on. This confidence made my doubts seem so groundless I began to think I had been too suspicious of Black. When we drove up to my house, Brad bade me cheer up and said he would be over to visit in the evening. Aware that his practice was picking up rapidly now that he had settled again into the law, I told him not to make any promises in the event he had a sudden press of business.

"I'd like to see that 'sudden press,' Jonathan," he laughed. "Business is starting to come my way but hardly like that. I'll be over — there's something I'd like your advice on."

My advice! Usually I asked his. I wondered later if, in view of the half-deferential way in which he spoke, it had anything to do with my cousin Eliza. Was he about to ask Uncle Tom for Eliza's hand? Or had it come up to the point of marriage itself? In which case my mind balked at the very possibility that Brad, who was far more of a man of the world than I, should have any questions to ask of me, unless they had something to do with Eliza as a person or with her family. Actually I wished he and Eliza would marry. I was sure that both Uncle Tom and Aunt Betsy liked Brad and wouldn't disapprove, though I suspected that, in Uncle Tom's view, no man was good enough for his Liza.

Whatever his questions he never had a chance to ask them that day. We had an early supper, for my father had a meeting that evening with his deacons in his study. He had just risen from the table, leaving my mother and me sipping a second cup of strong tea, when Brad rushed in without knocking. Mother's face grew stony with reproof at such an unceremonious entrance, while my father's look of surprise was almost comical.

"I'm sorry to break in like this," he said, and his face was drawn and sad, "but word has just arrived that Captain Vail has died."

I stood up. "Dead! Captain Vail dead!"

"Jedediah Daniels received a message from Colonel Foote and notified me at once. The Captain died two days ago in his sleep."

My father bowed his head. "May God rest his soul."

"If only we hadn't tried to escape, he might still be alive," I said, trying to keep my voice steady. "It was the exposure that dreadful night that was responsible."

"We might have done better to have left him in prison," Brad said.

"Now, you young men stop talking like this," my father said, and his face was almost stern. "Don't you believe in your hearts that Captain Vail weighed the possibilities of being shot or drowned or recaptured or at least wounded in an attempted escape?"

"Yes, sir," I said.

"I'm sure he did, too," my father said. "It is tragic that what has happened, has happened. But I do not think you should reproach yourselves if a mistake was honestly made — he would be the last to want you to do that. And if it was the will of God, after all, it would be presumptuous of you to reproach yourselves. Again, let me insist that you stop this regretting. Better to let him serve as an inspiration to you and support what he believed in if that is what you also believe."

We were both silent when he finished but I noticed my mother nodding agreement.

This new sadness, however, made me even more determined as, I'm sure, it did Brad, to bring Bierce before the bar of justice before the war ended and our own countrymen forgot the perfidy of a man who had deceived and betrayed the republic and its defenders.

# XXXIV

Two days after the news of Captain Vail's death reached the city, the *Eastern Courier* in its very next issue carried an account of his life. I won't deny that I had a part in the writing of that article, which subsequently led Jedediah Daniels to urge me to consider becoming a newspaperman, a goal I found attractive despite my parents' disappointment that I did not prefer the practice of law. Daniels, however, went to work on my article, pruning, condensing, and reshaping my language in such a way that I hardly recognized what I had written. Likewise he added vivid details of our escape from Castine that I would have found embarrassing to develop since they emphasized, without mentioning names, to be sure, the part Brad and I had played and the rescue by forces from the western shore of the Penobscot. Still, I could see what Daniels was driving at, namely, to underscore the degrading role of Bierce and Rudd by depicting the hazards accepted by numerous Maine folk in rescuing a wounded hero.

Then Daniels went on to arraign Bierce and Rudd, particularly the former, before the bar of public opinion. It was one of the most scathing indictments I have ever encountered outside of a courtroom, and while our laws of libel are as yet very loose, the *Eastern Courier* was clearly vulnerable to a suit unless it could prove its allegations; this, of course, left unresolved the matter of intent. Furthermore, within the code of honor leading to the duel, which had no legal standing but which proud gentlemen still insisted on observing, it was not beyond possibility that Bierce would challenge Daniels. After all, it must have been disturbing to a man like Bierce, who was less imperturbable than he appeared, and who ardently pursued respectability, to read in the long indictment two paragraphs like the following:

Every age produces its traitors: Athens, in the time of its struggle with Sparta, had its Alcibiades; our country, during the Revolution, its Benedict Arnold. Now, in the present struggle, one of divided sympathies, it is not surprising if there are aiders and abettors of the enemy. What is surprising is the depth of perfidy to which certain men may stoop. Fortunately this category of miscreants is small, but it includes a merchant in this town, who, though making gestures of respectability and appearing to espouse the principles of Federalism, has in fact been a creature of the British, not out of a belief in the righteousness of their cause but in deference to his own desires for mercenary gain.

The charges are numerous. Throughout his connivings he has associated with himself a scoundrelly sea captain hardly less nefarious than the master he serves. With the aid of this wretch, our pseudo-respectable merchant did not hesitate to advise the enemy with respect to the seizure of Castine. He planned the murder (happily unsuccessful) of a patriot in France who had been on an official mission to report such treason to the American minister in Paris. He betrayed our heroic Captain Vail, lying wounded and ill at his mother's home, to the British in Castine. He assisted the British in their vain attempt to prevent the escape of Captain Vail. More recently he has been in Hartford during the Convention, endeavoring to separate New England from the Union in order to pander to his own acquisitive instincts. Now, in our hour of grief, let us not forget that more than any single individual, he remains responsible for the death of Captain Vail.

There was more of the above in detail, great detail. Though not a single name was mentioned other than Vail's, no one familiar with the Portland scene and with developments in Maine could have any doubt about the identity of Bierce or Rudd.

My father was disturbed at what he read. "Jedediah Daniels must feel a great lack of confidence to launch this open attack, and I'm not sure I approve of it," he said to Brad and me when Brad stopped by

[ 349 ]

at noon with copies of the newspaper and my mother promptly invited him for dinner.

"Aren't you in favor of bringing Bierce to justice, sir?" Brad asked.

My father put down his knife and fork, "Justice, yes. Vengeance, no. And this indictment has the odor of vengeance to it."

"I'm afraid I don't catch the distinction here, and I don't know why you say Mr. Daniels lacks confidence," Brad said politely.

"What I think Mr. Dearborn means," my mother said, "is that if Mr. Daniels had all the evidence necessary to convict Warren Bierce and perhaps that horrible creature Rudd in a courtroom, he wouldn't feel impelled to attack him as he has done in the press."

My father smiled and bowed to her. "You read me well, Alice. That's precisely what I meant. Now, Brad, be honest with us. As one of the lawyers for Daniels's syndicate, do you really believe you could win a case against Bierce and Rudd?"

Brad stared at him a moment, then shrugged. "A good deal would depend on the jury, sir."

"Of course, and let no one discount emotion as a basis of appeal. But what of the evidence itself, Brad? Is it sufficiently convincing? Could it stand by itself?"

"No evidence can stand by itself in a courtroom, sir," Brad said, and he looked a little uncomfortable. "It is what one does with the evidence. But I grant you this much: Bierce is not without friends and influence in this town, and Mr. Daniels wanted to get the essential facts of the case to the public before a defense counsel starts distorting them."

"But if we believe in our system of justice, Brad, a man must be tried in a courtroom before a duly accredited judge and jury, not in the marketplace."

"I understand that, sir," said Brad, flushing, "but the only counter to the possible exercise of influence is an informed public opinion."

My father smiled. "Evidently you do not have much faith in the integrity of a jury."

"Rather, sir," said Brad, "I have a well-developed — perhaps over-developed — respect for Warren Bierce's capacity for evil."

"That is a theological word, and —"

"But it is also a moral word, Gerald," my mother interrupted him. "Theology is your province, my dear, but morality is everyone's, and the time has come to bring Warren Bierce's career in crime to an end. I cannot agree with you that publicizing his offences is an act of vengeance. Of course, I understand your viewpoint," she added hastily.

"I'm glad to hear you say so," my father said. "I've been feeling a little lonely the last few moments."

"But, if I may say so, sir," Brad said, "you are among friends and relatives. That is more than poor Harrison Gray Otis can say."

At our puzzled looks Brad laughed heartily. "As you know, Governor Strong appointed a commission of Otis and two of his friends, Thomas Perkins and William Sullivan, to take the Convention report to Washington and arrange for Massachusetts to raise its own troops for its defense and support the effort by federal tax money collected within our borders. Well, it seems the commissioners were dogged by bad luck. They were held up one Sabbath in New Haven by the Blue Laws and lost another day because of ice in the Hudson. Then on their way into Philadelphia their coach was preceded into the city by three black crows."

"Good heavens, what an augury!" my father laughed.

"I wonder what happened in Baltimore," I said. "News of peace? That would make the Convention look futile and the commissioners ridiculous."

"It surely would," my father agreed. "I'm sorry for Otis. Though I question his judgment on many issues, I have no doubt of the good intentions governing his motives."

"Nor I," I said. "But he's a compromiser, and while I admit that we need these men of middle courses and that he and George Cabot kept the Convention from recommending anything so extreme as separation from the Union, I prefer a forthright man, even a radical conservative like Timothy Bigelow."

"That's probably because you're forthright yourself, or like to be, Jonathan," my mother said.

"And relatively uncomplicated, praise be," my father added.

[ 351 ]

"Well, let's not discuss me," I said, feeling uncomfortable at the turn in the conversation. "What I'd like to know is what happens now to Bierce and Rudd."

"Warrants will go out tomorrow, or the day following," Brad said, "and from then on you'll hear some opinions expressed in this town, believe me."

"If it's only opinions, we can all be grateful," my father said.

Brad had to leave at this point but promised to return after supper.

Meanwhile I went out walking that afternoon for the air and the exercise. It was a gray, lowering day with an occasional spit of snow and whitecaps running in the harbor. In the distance I could see the topsails of the British 38-gun frigate *Vulcan* that had been patroling off Cape Elizabeth in recent days, so that even our Portland fishermen dared not venture outside the harbor. A more pleasing sight was the people I met who graciously inquired after my health and mentioned their regret at Captain Vail's death. The matter of my health irked me, for I felt better than I evidently looked, but I appreciated their concern. As for the Captain's death, it still cut too keenly for me to want to talk about it; I was hard pressed not to tell them so.

I was feeling at my most depressed when I nearly bumped into a little boy who ran ahead of his mother and slid toward me on a strip of ice. I caught him as he tripped at the end of the strip and swung him high.

"Henry Longfellow, you're getting so big I hardly know you!" I said.

"Well, I know you," he said, "so you ought to know me."

"And me, too," his mother added.

Zilpah looked healthier than I had seen her in a long while, her eyes twinkling and her cheeks rosy with the cold. After we exchanged greetings, she said, "Those were splendid accounts you wrote of the Convention, Jonathan. Both Papa and Mr. Longfellow thought highly of them — despite their Republicanism," she said, shaking her finger at me mischievously.

That I was pleased goes without saying. "Papa" was General Peleg Wadsworth, that pleasant but formidable man of whom even Stephen Longfellow seemed to be a little in awe. He was even more of a Federalist than his son-in-law, and that both found my articles acceptable was indeed gratifying. I told Zilpah so, and also mentioned my appreciation of her husband's kindness in Hartford.

She thanked me and said, "But, Jonathan, Stephen fears you are lost to the law. He thinks you prefer a newspaper office to a courtroom. It isn't so, is it? Or is it?"

"I'm afraid it may be, Mrs. Longfellow. I like what I have seen of the work, and Mr. Daniels seems to think I have 'possibilities' — at least that's the word he uses, and you know he doesn't go overboard with praise."

"No," she laughed, "it's as if praise cost Jedediah Daniels money. But Stephen thought you would also do well at law."

"He is very generous. I'm grateful for all the attention he has given me, but I'm afraid I have wasted too much of his time."

"Stephen doesn't think so."

"Is he home now?" I asked.

"No, he is still in Boston. I don't see him often when the legisla ture is in session," she said sadly.

Nor did she. It was fortunate that her father was so accessible, else she might have been quite lonely. Still, I wondered if, occasionally, Stephen Longfellow didn't find the presence of his father-in-law a little unsettling. For all Longfellow's reputation as a brilliant lawyer and an upright and able politician, "Papa" Wadsworth was an elder statesman whose opinions, growing more pontifical as the General aged, elicited an enormous respect in Maine.

"With peace coming soon," I said to Zilpah, "you will have him home."

"If only this wretched war would end," she sighed.

"I don't think we'll have to wait much longer," I said.

But as we parted, I began to worry anew that peace would come before the trial of Bierce and Rudd would have progressed far enough for people still to be interested in seeing them secure the kind of treatment they deserved.

When I reached home, I was so thoroughly chilled my teeth were actually chattering. I hadn't realized it was so cold or that I had been out so long. Naturally my mother scolded me and roundly expressed her opinion of my common sense, or lack of it. More to the point, however, and despite my mother's headshakings, my father broke out a bottle of Jamaican rum and made me a hot toddy. In a wing chair with my feet propped up before a nicely drawing fire and a glass of steaming toddy in my hand, so hot that I had to set it on a stand after sipping, I soon felt the chills subside and a delightful drowsiness set in. I slept until suppertime.

We had just finished supper and were awaiting Brad when the windows suddenly rattled and a moment or two later there came the thud of a heavy gun.

"Gracious! What was that?" my mother asked, her face white.

"That's a cannon, Alice," my father said, and rose to look out a window, though there was nothing to be seen except the loom of houses across the street.

Another crash, and my mother leaped to her feet. "The *Vulcan* must be in the harbor!" she exclaimed.

But I was already at the front door and barely heard her. Outside I could see nothing, and the opening of other doors presently showed neighbors as curious and as apprehensive as we were.

Then came a third thud, as evenly spaced from the second as that had been from the first.

"Those are minute guns!" I called out to my parents.

"What does that mean?" my mother asked.

"That means something important has happened."

"Pray heaven it is peace," said mother.

My father nodded. "I'll add Amen to that, Alice."

After the next crash we heard a wild ringing of church bells, and this was too much for my father and me. Despite my mother's entreaties to me to stay home, we shouldered into our greatcoats and hurried toward the center of town. Even before we arrived, we could see a fiery reflection in the sky. Thinking it was the start of a conflagration, we started to run toward it. Finally we saw, not a building ablaze, but a huge bonfire and heard the cheers of an ever-growing body of people. Just before we reached the outskirts of the crowd a boy appeared with a drum almost as big as himself and beat a sharp rat-a-tat-tat that touched off in even louder wave of cheering. Then someone started to sing "Hail, Columbia!" and others joined in.

"What's it all about?" I asked an old sailor with a wooden leg.

"It's Andy Jackson!" he shouted. "Ain't you heard? He beat the British at New Orleans!"

There is something peculiar but amusing and, in a way, reassuring, about an opposition party in America. Federalists might deplore this war vehemently, but, come a victory, their patriotism overcame their sectionalism. I saw numerous people in the firelight whom I recognized as Federalists cheering and singing and praising to the black sky overhead a Republican general they hated. It was a little like the visit to Middletown of Mr. Longfellow and his fellow delegates to the Hartford Convention. Though they opposed the war, they regarded Commodore Macdonough as much their hero as that of the Republicans. Tonight Andrew Jackson, who said that, had he been Colonel Jesup in Hartford, he would have hanged all twenty-six members of the Convention, was acclaimed an Alexander the Great, and even greater than Alexander because he was an American! Soon kegs of rum were rolled up, and the boasts became so absurd my father shook his head as we turned to leave.

"If all these men had stood together earlier as they do now, Jonathan," he said with a wry laugh, "this war might not be the debacle it has now become."

"Yes, and Captain Vail might still be alive," I said with a bitterness I was unable to suppress.

"Possibly," he said, glancing covertly at me.

Then Brad, breathless with running, found us. "I've been to your home, sir," he explained to my father, "and Mrs. Dearborn said you and Jonathan had left to find out what all the excitement was about. Well, Jonathan," he said, turning to me, "it's glorious news, isn't it?"

I clasped his outstretched hand, my bitterness vanishing in the exultation he felt.

"Andy Jackson," he went on, "British mistakes including a frontal attack, and the good shooting eyes of American riflemen did it. Two thousand British casualties against almost literally a handful of Americans — think of it!"

"Dreadful!" my father exclaimed, and his voice was hoarse with pity. "Does the value of the individual human life mean nothing to you young men?"

[ 355 ]

What could one say? Of course he was right, and we certainly would have agreed in principle. But still I think we were justified in feeling as uplifted as we did. The moment was awkward, however, as neither Brad nor I could find it in us to reply. Finally my father himself broke the silence.

"I'm afraid your Uncle Tom will share your excitement, Jonathan," he said. "Tom hasn't liked the war at all, as you know, but our defeats have cut him sorely."

"He won't be able to do much rejoicing in Aunt Betsy's presence," I said.

"That he won't. In fact, he is worse off than you are. Your mother and I are appalled at any slaughter of human life, but in your Aunt Betsy's case, the situation is personalized because the lives lost now are British lives, and, deep down, Betsy is still a bit of a Tory."

"Well," said Brad, the relief obvious in his voice that the conversation had changed direction, "this news certainly makes Governor Strong, Harrison Gray Otis, and all the other Federalists favoring the Convention, even Stephen Longfellow, Jonathan, look pretty silly."

"All that's needed to cap their embarrassment is news of peace," I said.

"Do you realize," said my father, grasping us both by the arms, "that if we presently hear peace has been signed, that terrible battle at New Orleans need never have been fought?"

The thought was indeed horrifying. The agony that could have been avoided if only our means of communication were swifter! And the rumors of peace were so persistent that it seemed likely my father was right. A victory under such conditions, even if it brought glory to our arms, a radiance to our badly tarnished national honor, and a promising future to an ambitious soldier-politician like Andrew Jackson, was hardly worth the battlefield price at New Orleans. The only consolation was that should word of peace presently arrive, it would save further loss of life. And God grant that our peace commissioners had stood fast against any move to attach eastern Maine permanently to the British Crown. It had been said that even the great Duke of Wellington thought such an acquisition unwise. I dearly hoped that if our commissioners had not persuaded the British government, the Duke's intervention would be decisive.

[ 356 ]

Soberly we approached our house, Brad coming in for hot tea, and scraped the snow from our shoes. Perhaps because ours was the parsonage, the curtains were rarely drawn. To our surprise, however, when we returned, we could not look into our living room. Had my mother drawn the curtains after Father and I had left for fear of what might happen this strange evening?

"Were the curtains closed when you left Mother?" I whispered to Brad.

He shook his head, which left me more mystified than before, so we hurried through our cold hall and into the living room. I heard Brad ahead of me suck in his breath sharply.

Then I entered, in time to see my father bowing to a woman sitting opposite my mother in the chair where I had slept the latter part of the afternoon. As my father stepped aside, my heart thudded into my throat, and I looked into the unforgettable greenish-gray eyes of India Mitchell Bierce.

---

# XXXV

On seeing India, the impulse to shout her name, above all to take her in my arms, was almost overwhelming. Had we been alone, the latter I would surely have done. Now, however, feeling constrained in the presence of my family and Brad, I merely bowed, held her hand briefly, and asked if there was anything I could do to help her.

Though neither she nor my mother had made any explanation, it was plain enough that she was in trouble. She looked distraught despite the smile she gave us, and I had an odd impression that she wanted to keep looking over her shoulder.

"Why don't all of you sit down?" my mother asked before India could reply to my question.

When we had done so, she said, "If India doesn't mind, I will tell you why she is here."

"Please do," India said, flashing my mother a grateful smile.

"Good. Brad had just left the house to find you men when the knocker fell and I went to the door to see India and that colored man, Philip Adair, standing outside. When India asked if they could come in and I said, Yes, of course, they stepped into the hallway and would not move from it until I had drawn the curtains in this room. Then Mr. Adair explained that he had brought India here for her protection. He said that we — and especially you, Jonathan — would know what to do about her."

I stared at India, who seemed engrossed in some pattern of the rug. I certainly did know what to do about her, but she was still Warren Bierce's wife.

"Anyway, Mr. Adair left soon afterward. India told me she and Mr. Bierce had quarreled, he had locked her in her room and, while there, she had heard Mr. Bierce and that man Rudd plotting something dreadful, though she couldn't make out exactly what it was. But when she heard your name mentioned and Jedediah Daniels's, she made up her mind to escape and come here and warn you. So she climbed out of her window and down the vine that grew up alongside the house and would have fallen if Philip Adair had not seen her and helped her.Then he escorted her here."

"Were they plotting murder, India?" Brad asked.

"I honestly don't know," India said. "Jonathan, your name was mentioned several times and Mr. Daniels's many times. There were others, too, though I didn't recognize them. But when I heard Rudd say, 'We'll see that both those bastards get what's coming to them,' and then Warren say, 'Let's not waste any more time,' I decided to come here as quickly as I could."

I went over and kissed her lightly on the lips. "Thank you, India," I said, and took her hand in mine.

I'm sure my father was startled by my act, but he ignored it and said, "What a coincidence that Adair happened to be around just then!"

"No coincidence at all," Brad said. "Jedediah Daniels has had Philip watching Bierce and Rudd for days. He's probably back there right now. Which reminds me, I'd better be getting over to Mr. Daniels's home at once and warn him."

As I saw him to the door, he whispered, "You'd better keep your pistol with you. I'll alert the constables, but they're not likely to be of much help — we don't know what Bierce will do or when he'll do it."

He was gone in a crunch of footsteps in the snow, and I closed the door with some perplexity as to what to do. Had the *Argus* been in port, I'd have spoken with Lester Jordan who would surely have let me have a few of his crew to guard India at our house and Daniels's newspaper office and home. But Lester was somewhere off the coast of Ireland by this time raiding British ships in their own waters.

The hour was getting late, so my mother took India upstairs and put her in a bedroom next to hers and Father's. My own was opposite theirs overlooking the street.

With the women upstairs my father and I locked up very carefully. We spoke casually to each other and bade each other good night as though this were like any other night, but his lips set in a straight line when he wasn't talking, as they often did when he was disturbed. Recalling Uncle Tom Dearborn's having said that when my father was a boy he was the best shot on Cape Elizabeth, I found myself wishing he were not so scrupulous now about using firearms. He hadn't touched one in years, and the weapons in the house were my own: a musket, two pistols, a cutlass, two knives and a tomahawk which I had never used. I kept my little arsenal in my bedroom closet — my mother hated firearms so fiercely she wouldn't even let me hang the musket over the fireplace in my room. Besides it wasn't seemly, she said, that a weapon be visible anywhere in a parsonage. But that night I dragged out the musket, loaded it, and leaned it against the corner of the wall near my bed. I also loaded both pistols, putting one on the night table and the other under a pillow. One of the knives I thrust into my left boot. Then, feeling a little absurd but relieved, I stretched out on my bed and dozed, but kept an ear half alert in the event anything should happen.

And happen it did, though to my shame I never heard the beginning of it. It was already faintly light before dawn when I awoke to a whispering and padding of feet in the hall; a board creaked, which it never did under the weight of anyone in my family except myself. Then a scream tore the silence apart.

Instantly I reached for the pistols and dashed for the door.

The hallway seemed filled with men. In the room opposite, two men with pistols had my mother and father backed against the wall. From India's room came screams and terrible struggling. All this in a glance and a moment. Then men crashed through the doorway into my room. I leaped aside, tripping the lead man, who went sprawling one way and his cutlass another. The second man fired his pistol, and only his poor aim saved me. The ball flashed by my ear like an angry hornet. I fired and he clutched his shoulder.

Then I myself went down as the first man recovered and leaped onto my back.

I am no giant in stature or strength, but there are times when a fierce energy may come to any of us in a desperate situation. I have seen a frantic father lift a log off his son's leg where three strong men had failed. This was one of those times. Rolling and kicking, I managed to shake free of my attacker and scrambled to my feet. As he whipped a knife from his belt, I fired my second pistol at him. With an anguished groan he grabbed his wrist as a fountain of red gushed from it. Then I dashed for the door.

As I appeared in the hall, one of the men in my parents' room leaped to the doorway and fired. Luckily for me, I had seen him raise his arm, so I flattened myself against the wall, and as he burst through the doorway, I brought a pistol butt down across the back of his neck.

It was at that moment that two men appeared, carrying India, bound and gagged, while behind them stood Warren Bierce. The instant he saw me he fired, but his aim was so hurried that the bullet went wide. My instinctive response was to hurl the empty pistol at him. The weapon hit him in the forehead, and he collapsed like an empty flour sack.

My next move was to throw myself at the two men with India. All of us went down in a heap. Luckily, though bound, India managed to squirm out of the pile-up, for it turned into the most savage hand-to-hand struggle I had ever been in — one of fist, foot, knife, and pistol-butt. Never had I fought as during those terrible minutes. The semidarkness in the hallway aided me, I think, but the realization that my own family and India were being subjected to such treatment gave me a strength and a wiliness I had never known before.

My whole body ached, my clothes were in ribbons, and my face and arms ran with blood, yet I actually clobbered one man into insensibility and had the second cowering from my knife when I heard a terrible scream. Turning around, I saw my mother throw herself at the man who had remained guarding them. He had come into the hallway and had his pistol pointed at me when Mother's body struck him.

"Bitch!" he yelled as she knocked him off balance.

Then he raised his pistol again. This time it was my father who knocked his arm up and the ball buried itself in the ceiling. For a moment the two men struggled — but only a moment for Father was of slight build. With a violent heave the man threw Father off and dashed at me with his cutlass.

Glancing at the sailor who had momentarily cowered from my knife, I suddenly spun and threw the knife as Uncle Tom had taught me when I was a boy. The blade pierced my attacker's chest, his cutlass clattering to the floor. As he grabbed the knife handle and backed away, I reached for the cutlass and turned toward the cowering sailor.

At that moment the house shook as men thundered into the front door and up the stairs.

"Thank God!" I thought. "It's Brad and Philip Adair and men they've collected," and I turned to greet our deliverers.

But I looked instead into the hard, froglike face of Jake Rudd, first man up the stairs.

He fired the instant I raised the cutlass, and I felt the ball break my arm, which seemed suddenly to burst with anguish. This time it was I who let the weapon fall from my hand.

His bullet spun me half around. As I reached for the wall with my left hand to steady myself, I stared at the cold eyes of Warren Bierce, whose forehead was bloody from where my pistol had struck him. Then flame spurted from the pistol in his hand, and hot agony rocked my head. I felt myself falling, endlessly falling, as if I would never touch the floor.

But touch it I did, in time to see the look of horror in India's eyes. Then as I struggled to get up, two men held me fast.

"Tie him up!" Bierce said.

"I'll do it myself," Rudd growled, "just to make sure this son of a bitch stays put."

Though I gave him no easy job despite my arm, he had me triced and knotted in an embarrassingly short time. Then he pulled out his handkerchief and, making me open my mouth by holding my nose and thereby shutting off my breathing, he stuffed it so far back I nearly retched.

"Let's get moving," Bierce said.

Two men slung me on their shoulders and two others took India. Then with their injured tagging along as best they could the raiders hurried through the streets toward the waterfront.

But if they expected an unopposed passage, they were mistaken. Attracted by the sounds of fighting in the parsonage, a crowd quickly gathered. Though it fell back before the cutlasses of the raiders, some of the men and boys darted back into the houses for weapons. Word of the attack had evidently spread, for a small body of men blocked the route to Fore Street. Instantly the raiders fell upon them with cutlasses. Though these men also retreated, a few fired at the raiders.

"If you shoot again, we'll kill Dearborn and the girl!" Rudd bellowed.

Grudgingly the citizens withdrew, though they followed even to the wharf. Then as reinforcements arrived from the *Ghost*, which was partly shrouded by a light fog, India and I were quickly carried aboard the schooner and dumped onto the deck of one of the cabins.

Overhead the maindeck of the *Ghost* thrummed with activity as the crew cast off her lines and raised the great fore-and-aft sails. Soon I could hear the unmistakable creaking of a ship under way, and turned in despair to India. Both of us could communicate only through our eyes and facial expressions, and, believe me, there is no substitute for speech.

I still had one point of hope, and that was that the batteries at Fort Preble might challenge us. But presently I realized that no boat could possibly get to the fort in time to warn the garrison. There seemed little doubt that eventually Rudd would work his way through the harbor to the open sea.

Then a door opened, and Warren Bierce stood over us, the blood caked on his forehead. For a moment he stood staring down at us before he said with an air of triumph, "Well, we are clear of Fort Preble, Dearborn. We raised the American flag so they all could see it, even if there is a little fog. Now we're flying British colors. You're quite a fighter, Dearborn, I must concede that to you —" he continued harshly, "I ought to have taken you more seriously right along."

"As for you, my dear," he said, turning to India, "you ran out on me. Oh, I know what you'd say in defense, but the fact is, a wife is loyal whatever her husband is or does. Traitor? Murderer? You've called me that before, and I deny that I'm either. All's fair in war, you know. But all that's past history, and I shall soon have to decide what to do with you."

He sat down, staring at us and evidently relishing our helplessness, even our inability to reply.

"I had had hopes," he went on, "that America might come to her senses long ago and submit. Peace may now have been concluded, but news of it will arrive too late to help you or myself. I might have been able to live out a life of respectability in this town if it hadn't been for you, Dearborn, and your friends."

His voice was so bitter and regretful that I could almost feel sorry for him. But when I thought of the condition in which India and I found ourselves, when I thought further of what he had done to Captain Vail, I felt no pity but a wild, consuming anger that I fought to keep from showing. Now, if ever, was a time to keep a clear head — though as I considered how I was tied up and gagged with a filthy handkerchief, I wondered if I'd ever have another chance to use my head. Then he started to speak again in his incredible monologue.

"If Daniels and his crowd had ever had me in court, Dearborn, you may be sure they could not have proved a case of treason against me. They could never have procured evidence from London that I had suggested the British should occupy Castine. The British might have occupied it anyway — after all, they had held it during the Revolution — but what I said may have impressed them with the urgency of taking the town. Would Whitehall have revealed that to Daniels? Nonsense! As for trading with Castine, look at the New Englanders who are doing that very thing right now. Did I betray Vail to the British? Of course I did, but prove it! Rumors are cheap, and the lawyers would have had nothing but rumors."

He got up and stood over us again. "The trouble was," he said, "a jury is emotional and I might well have lost had the case come to trial. Even if I had won, people would have remembered the slanders and I could not have remained in Maine. So now I am going elsewhere, perhaps somewhere in this country but probably to a British possession. And you two —"

He paused, his face expressionless, "You two," he went on, "will likely not be around to trouble yourselves further about me, though I must confess that I am not as sure about what to do with you as I was a few hours ago."

With that he went on deck, and India and I could only stare at each other in helpless wonder.

I tried to work at my bonds, but the rope was too tight and the effort caused me so much pain in my chest and my broken arm I soon lay still. Then I listened intently. Bierce had said the *Ghost* was at sea, but either the sea was very calm or we hadn't picked up the Atlantic swell as yet — if this last was so, we were not far beyond Portland Head. There must still be a little fog and Rudd couldn't be more than inching along. I thought I could hear the leadsman calling out the fathoms, but it may have been my imagination. At any rate, it was what I'd have ordered had I been Rudd. One thing I could hear, and it was no trick of the imagination, and that was a soft thunder of breakers somewhere off to starboard. The Cape Elizabeth coast is cruel with reefs and rocks, and even in calm weather the shores are a smother of surf and foam. Rudd probably had lookouts posted along his decks and aloft, his leadsman at work, his helmsman steering small, and men standing ready at the braces. Eyes would be straining to see through the fog, and apprehension would be growing by the minute. The raid of Bierce and Rudd on our house, added to whatever else they had done in Portland, must surely have inspired some kind of pursuit. Though a schooner or a sloop or even several would be up against the same handicaps of weather that confronted the *Ghost*, heavily manned whaleboats might catch up with her, and powerful as the *Ghost* was, she could have her troubles with a determined boat attack in the fog if the attack was pressed home with skill and determination.

But even as my hopes began to rise as I considered this possibility, my reason told me that it would take so much time to muster boats and qualified men and find the *Ghost* that Rudd really had little to fear. There was more to fear from the breakers, though actually not much at that because of Rudd's knowledge of the coast and the currents and his skill as a seaman. Besides, even if a rescue was attempted, I doubted that Bierce would permit either India or me to survive it. The very fact that he refused to remove our gags, let alone untie us, seemed evidence of his resolution or desperation. A woman's scream has a penetrating quality even from within the confines of a ship's cabin and might just be fatal where silence is necessary to conceal one from pursuit.

Try as I did, I could think of no satisfactory way of breaking loose. Whether it was my injuries or the rage and frustration that was responsible for my feeling feverish I don't know. But I definitely became light-headed and ranged from the fringe of unconsciousness to an almost preternatural sense of awareness. It was during one of these latter moments that I felt the *Ghost* surge forward, heel slightly, then settle down to a steady rise-and-fall motion. Shouts broke out overhead and the deck echoed with the sound of rushing feet. Instantly the schooner began a long rhythmic creaking. All these were the sounds of a ship beginning to run before a light but steady breeze. This meant, too, the fog was breaking. Now indeed the *Ghost* would soon be at sea, and the very thought filled me with despair and anger.

Then out of nowhere came the shattering crash of guns followed by a sudden lurching of the schooner. By the way the *Ghost* was trembling under an unending succession of heavy blows, and by the shrieks and shouting overhead, it was clear that Rudd had run into some kind of trouble.

Then as I stared into India's frightened eyes, the door burst open and Philip Adair, his jacket in tatters and drenched with blood, bounded into the cabin with a dripping cutlass and bolted the door behind him. Before I could ask a question he knelt, removed our gags, and slit the ropes that bound India and me.

"Now, listen," he said, and his usually soft voice was hard and peremptory, "the *Vulcan*'s out there. I cut down the British flag and raised our own, so she thinks we're American and Rudd and Bierce can't make her think differently. You follow me on deck, understand? We're maybe five hundred yards offshore and you'll have to swim for it."

"He'll never make it!" India cried out. "His right arm is broken!"

Without a word he hauled me to my feet, my body a thousand points of agony as the blood flowed through cramped muscles. I saw India stagger to her feet, then tumble against a bulkhead as the schooner lurched again. Only Philip's strong hold and wide stance kept me from falling.

Quickly now he cut a length of rope from our severed bonds and bound my arm to my chest.

"That will have to do until you get to shore," he said. "You won't have to swim far. There are boats out there that'll pick you up. You can swim?" he anxiously asked India.

"Yes." Learning to swim had been one of the earliest of India's protests against conventions for young girls. There had even been rumors that India hadn't been above going swimming in the nude at night up along the Stroudwater River, but no one could ever trace the source of these rumors. It was always "someone saw" or "someone said."

He merely grunted and thrust his knife into my hand. Then, nodding to us, he led us to the deck.

I hardly knew what to expect when we reached the deck, but I certainly never anticipated what I saw. To larboard, half obscured by the smoke of her own guns and the remaining streamers of fog, towered a King's frigate. Powerful privateer though she was, the *Ghost* was no match for the *Vulcan* at any time. But what amazed me was the destruction aboard the *Ghost*. Boarding nettings were torn to shreds and guns were knocked off their trunnions. The deck was a clutter of fallen spars and strewn with broken men, while forward a fire was leaping out of control. Thanks to Adair, Rudd had evidently been completely surprised by the British, and the *Ghost* had made matters worse by returning the frigate's fire. Four men near the helm, however, had died by cutlass wounds, proof of Philip's determination to keep the flag flying long enough to deceive the British.

"Jump!" Adair yelled to us.

"Where's Bierce?" I asked.

The Negro pointed forward. There, not fifteen feet from where we were standing, Bierce sat with his back against the railing. No cutlass stroke but a cannon ball from his beloved British had struck near, and a gigantic splinter, like a two-by-four, had passed through the man's chest. He was bowed over in a pool of blood.

"Oh, Warren!" India cried out in horror and pity, and quickly knelt beside him.

"He's dead! Jump!" Adair shouted.

"Let's go, India," I said, taking her arm gently. "There's nothing we can do."

"Oh you fools, you damn fools!" And Adair threw himself over us.

Even as we were flattened to the deck I felt the *Ghost* tremble under the British broadside and heel sharply as the foremast toppled over. Fragments of wood rained on the deck, and Adair refused to move until the deadly shower had subsided. Then he got up and said, "Go now. Jump while you have time!"

"Rudd?" I asked.

"I've half taken care of him," he said. "Now I'll finish the job."

"You will like hell!"

Even as we stared in horrified surprise Philip leaped aside like a cat, and the cutlass that would have split his head open whistled vainly through the air. Rudd had crept up behind Philip without any of us seeing him, and, but for Rudd's own remark that warned him, Philip, and then likely we ourselves, would have died.

But Philip was at him in an instant, and it was cutlass to cutlass in the hands of two desperate men. Rudd, like Philip, had already been badly cut up. Evidently Philip had fought him before, knocked him unconscious, and dashed below to get us. Why he hadn't killed Rudd outright at that time I could only guess; and the guess was that he had reserved the murderer of his wife for an even more dreadful fate.

What the fate was only gradually became clear. The men swung, slashed, closed, and leaped apart. Once Philip slipped down in a pool of blood, and Rudd's cutlass cut deeply into his side. At this, Philip went berserk. As Rudd with a shout raised his cutlass for a finishing stroke, Philip swung his own weapon at the man's legs, and Rudd fell with his right leg nearly severed below the knee. Adair then deliberately slashed Rudd's cutlass arm off at the wrist, and the cutlass, still gripped in Rudd's hand, went flying across the deck.

As Philip lifted his cutlass again, India's shriek of protest cut through his rage. Quickly he glanced at us, and the look on his face was utterly wild and menacing — and absorbed. Then he turned back to his task, and this time when the weapon fell, Rudd broke into an inhuman screaming.

"Jump, India!" I shouted.

Without a word she ripped her dress and petticoat over her head and plunged into the sea, wearing only a pair of lace pantalets that came to her knees and some sort of underbodice.

I followed at once but not without a backward glance. Crying "Seba! Seba!," the name of his wife whom Rudd had thrown to the sharks, Adair held the bleeding, moaning mass that was now Rudd and stumbled forward toward the blazing part of the *Ghost*.

The water was so icy I could hardly get my breath, but there was no doubt about it, it cleared my head, though I don't recommend the Atlantic off Cape Elizabeth in February as a cure. I could hear India gasping beside me. Then we settled down to some pretty determined swimming, India remaining close to me.

How far we had gone I didn't know, not far enough, anyway, when I realized I couldn't make it.

"Jonathan!" India screamed.

I must have gone under a moment, for I choked and threw up the sea water I had swallowed. I felt her holding me up while she trod water.

"Go on in, India!" I begged her. "No sense in both of us drowning."

"That's a crazy thing to say, Jonathan Dearborn!" she said angrily.

I struck out again with my good arm, but it was an agonizing effort. Time and again I felt her supporting me. When I thought again that I could go no farther, I heard her scream, "There's a boat coming toward us, Jonathan!"

Somehow, with her help, I held on until the boat came alongside. Soon I was being lifted gently aboard. I saw India helped in, too, and two men quickly wrap her in their coats. She looked almost literally blue with cold. Someone gave her a cup of rum, and as he turned, I saw that it was Brad.

Even as I looked up at him the sky flashed a bright orange-white light and the *Ghost* seemed to leap out of the water. A moment later she disintegrated in a whirling mass of smoke and blazing fragments.

"Jesus!" someone gasped.

"Down everyone!" Brad called out.

The men bent low as the sea around us hissed and boiled with the shower of debris. Before it was over I heard Brad say, "Let's get them over to Captain Tom Dearborn's house." Then I lost consciousness.

"Well, he seems to be coming around at last," I dimly heard someone rumble.

"There never was any doubt about it!"

I forced open an eyelid at the clear, ringing tone and saw my Aunt Betsy looking down at me, her blue eyes bright with triumph.

"See, Tom, he's awake."

"How are you, boy?" My uncle's voice was gruff, as it so often was when he meant to be kind.

"I think I'll live," I whispered, and tried to smile, though my face felt wooden.

"You'd better," he growled.

"Is India all right?"

"Course she's all right. What the hell d'you suppose I meant?"

"Now leave Jonathan alone," my aunt said crisply.

"He's been alone long enough," my uncle said. "Three whole days."

"Three days!" I said. I started to raise myself up, but found it almost impossible. I was so completely swathed in bandages I felt as if I were in a suit of armor. As I struggled, Aunt Betsy pressed me back on the pillow.

"Lie still, Jonathan!"

When my aunt spoke like that, there was nothing to do but obey her.

"How are Mother and Father?" I asked.

"They're fine except for a bruise or two and a great worry over you," she said. "Your uncle went to them yesterday to tell them about you. He said your parents are suddenly enjoying more popularity than they've ever had. The parsonage was filled with people. Some were just curious, but most were genuinely sympathetic. Isn't that so, Tom?"

He nodded, then asked, "What did you try to do, take on a whole ship's crew?"

"I tried not to kill anyone in the parsonage," I said.

"Guess you didn't at that, but you sure spilled a lot of blood around the walls and over the floors."

Just then the door opened, and Brad and Eliza came to the bedside. Liza kissed me, while Brad just stood there and smiled in his superior way and looked happy. Evidently the question he had intended to ask me the night we had heard of Captain Vail's death he had answered himself.

"Thanks for coming in time," I whispered.

"It was a close thing," he admitted.

"Is India all right?"

"She was about done in when we reached you, Jonathan — you probably realize she saved your life."

"But is she all right?" I persisted.

"Yes, yes, India's fine," my aunt said. "Goodness, you're much too curious for a man with broken ribs, a smashed arm, and more cuts and slashes than I've ever seen on a human being who lived! Now, no more questions."

"Just one more, Aunt Betsy," I said. "What happened to Jedediah Daniels?"

"Rudd wrecked the press, Jonathan," Brad said, "and in the process Daniels was knocked unconscious and one of his printers was killed. Incidentally, Rudd also killed Captain Black at the tavern where he was staying. I suppose Bierce and Rudd thought Black might have talked about the Bordeaux affair. Then Rudd came to help Bierce at the parsonage."

"Where was Philip Adair while all this was happening?"

Brad's brow wrinkled. "From all I can tell, he must have been surprised while he was watching Bierce's house. There was plenty of evidence of a fight — broken bushes, trampled snow, bloodstains, and the imprint of a man's body. He didn't show up at the parsonage or at the newspaper. By the time Rudd had reached your house after destroying the newspaper, we had enough citizens together to force him back to the *Ghost* faster than he intended. But as you know, he threatened to kill India and you if we attacked. When we reached the head of the wharf, the *Ghost* was already casting off her lines. It's my guess that when Philip came to, he went straight for the *Ghost* and boarded her in the dark before Bierce and Rudd came aboard. Remember, Philip had his own scores to pay off before he ever knew you or Jedediah Daniels. What he did aboard the *Ghost* India has already told us — or at least what she knew."

"She knew about as much as I did."

"Well, Bierce and Rudd are dead, and unfortunately Philip, too. It was Bierce's bad luck that the *Vulcan* was on blockading station off Portland. He and Rudd planned on raising English colors once they had cleared the cape, but Philip was too smart for them. If the *Vulcan* hadn't come up when she did, we'd have attacked in boats — we had six closing in, Jonathan."

I turned to Aunt Betsy. "Is India here?"

"No, India insisted on returning to Portland when Tom went to your parents' yesterday."

She paused, and I saw everyone looking at her. I did, too, of course, and longed to ask, yet dared not, if India had left any message for me. Evidently Aunt Betsy sensed my unasked question, for she turned to the bureau, opened a drawer, and laid a square of white silk on my pillow.

"India sent this back by your uncle, Jonathan. She said that you would know what it meant and that you and she could discuss it sometime in the future, maybe in a year or so. None of us knows what it's about unless it's Brad, but Eliza and I have a pretty good idea, don't we dear?"

"Brad will tell you," I said.

"And I'm telling you, young man," said my aunt, sternness suddenly replacing the amusement in her voice, "you must rest again, and when you wake up, we'll see about giving you some nourishment."

I was glad to close my eyes, if too excited, and even too weary to sleep. I could see India Mitchell standing on the deck of the *Ghost* as she left for France, could see the white scarf blown from her hand and myself leaping high to catch it. Though I had eventually returned it to her, it had come back to me again, a symbol of hope of a distant but possible fulfillment.

But like a shadow over my joy hung memories I could not dispel: of an arrogant, greedy merchant trafficking in treachery and betrayal; of a frog-faced killer who was his willing tool; of a redoubtable, soft-voiced Negro committed to a terrible revenge; of a stout-hearted privateer captain threading his way through waters thick with enemy cruisers, hazarding his ship against heavy odds to warn of invasion, chancing death rather then rot in an enemy prison; of raw militia scattered in humiliating flight by British redcoats; of a distinguished group of dissident citizens protesting administration policy and being watched by their own military lest they contrive treason. Though such memories would likely be with me for a long time to come, I could now face a personal future without hatred.

Thanks, too, to the Lake Champlain victory of Commodore Macdonough and especially to General Jackson's triumph at New Orleans there was some measure of national honor to be salvaged from this wretched war. And, with peace on the way, our country could find some kind of acceptable balance between central authority and the liberty of the states, mend its divisions, and rediscover its destiny.

# Historical Notes

THE political situation in New England at the time of this story was by no means simple, and any brief explanation may distort the truth. In general, however, the Federalists followed the principles of the deceased Alexander Hamilton while the Republicans, who were sometimes alluded to as the Democratic-Republicans, accepted those of Thomas Jefferson. The Federalists were strongly mercantile and financial in their interests; the Republicans, agrarian; but neither party was exclusively one or the other. Though the Federalists had at times stressed the necessity of a strong central government and the Republicans had upheld the authority of the states, the 1812 era found the relative positions reversed.

Only by a feat of tortuous reasoning could one equate the Republican Party of the 1812 era with the Democratic Party of today or the Federalist Party with the present Republican Party, though there is a line of descent in each case. It is more to the point, perhaps, that Democrats of the current era look to Jefferson as a patron saint, while Republicans of today assume a somewhat similar, if less exalted view of Hamilton.

Four recent sources I have found especially useful on the political aspect are: David Hackett Fischer, *The Revolution of American Conservatism: The Federal Party in the Era of Jeffersonian Democracy* (1965); Shaw Livermore, *The Twilight of Federalism* (1962); Noble Cunningham, *The Jeffersonians in Power* (1963); and Paul Goodman, *The Democratic-Republicans of Massachusetts* (1964).

The Hartford Convention was an illustration of how far even

moderate Federalists could go in expressing their disapproval of the government in Washington. By far the best accounts of the Convention are its history by Theodore Dwight, secretary of the Convention, the analysis in Henry Adams's great *History of the United States,* and, above all, the superb biography of Harrison Gray Otis by Samuel Eliot Morison.

Although Jedediah Daniels and his newspaper, the *Eastern Courier,* are fictional, they are molded, at least roughly, on the courageous Francis Douglass and his Republican paper, the *Eastern Argus* of Portland, Maine.

The cruise of the privateer *Argus* to Europe, including the storm en route, and Jonathan Dearborn's adventures in France and Spain are partially based on the experiences of a crack American privateersman, George Coggeshall (as related in his *History of American Privateers*), whose ship was finally captured by the kindly Captain W. S. Wise, RN. Jonathan followed Coggeshall's escape route from Gibraltar.

The town meeting held after Jonathan arrived in Boston from Europe was actually conducted in September rather than August, 1814, but was essentially as described.

The British seizure of Castine, Captain Charles Morris's efforts to save the *John Adams,* and the battle of Hampden follow fairly closely the actual events. One point, however, should be noted: the *Adams* actually entered the Penobscot several days before she makes her appearance there in the novel. Otherwise the time element in the invasion and the subsequent events is preserved.

The great fight of Captain Vail and the *Argus* off Isle au Haut is based upon several actual engagements, particularly John Ordronaux's defense of the *Prince of Neufchatel* off Nantucket against the boats of the British frigate *Endymion* in 1814 and Samuel Reid's gallant but less successful fight to save the *General Armstrong* when attacked by the boats of a British squadron in the neutral Azores harbor of Fayal, also in 1814.

The escape of Captain Vail and Jonathan from Fort George in Castine is patterned to a considerable extent after the escape from the same fort in 1780, and under fairly similar circumstances, by General Peleg Wadsworth and Major Benjamin Burton.

Rumors of peace were persistent through the fall months of 1814. In fact, American peace commissioners had sailed for Europe as early as the spring of 1813, but the onrush of events in connection with the downfall of Napoleon and innumerable delays, for which the Americans were not primarily responsible, prevented negotiations from opening until August 8, 1814. The American commissioners at Ghent were John Quincy Adams, James A. Bayard, Henry Clay, Albert Gallatin, and Jonathan Russell — a far more brilliant company than their British counterparts: Admiral Lord Gambier, Henry Goulburn, an MP and an undersecretary in the Colonial Office, and William Adams, a jurist. After vigorous, at times acrimonious discussions, the treaty was finally signed on Christmas Eve. Though it dealt with boundaries and Indians and the slave trade, ironically it contained nothing about the war cry of 1812: "Free Trade and Sailors' Rights!" After a wild Atlantic crossing the treaty arrived in New York on February 11, 1815, more than a month following Jackson's great victory at New Orleans. The treaty was sent to the Senate by the President on February 15 and agreed to without a dissenting vote on the sixteenth.

News of the peace reached Camden, Maine, on the fourteenth at midnight when the stagecoach from the "West'ard" lumbered into town, the driver blasting the stillness with his posthorn. Soon candles appeared in the windows and bonfires in the streets, while all the next day from dawn to dusk the heavy guns on Mount Battie roared the good news to the Bay towns. Castine, however, had to wait for more than two months before its celebration, which marked two events: the peace and the long-delayed British evacuation.

The customs receipts at Castine during the British occupation from September 1, 1814 to April 28, 1815 were so substantial that the duties on goods for American individuals or firms amounted to £13,000. This "Castine Fund," as it was called, was used by the British to help establish Dalhousie University in Halifax, Nova Scotia.

Owing in good part to the war and to a feeling that Governor Strong and the General Court had ignored its need for defense, Maine soon pressed for separation from Massachusetts. This movement was strongly advocated by Republicans and their newspapers, and won approval in Castine, Camden, and other Penobscot towns.

Portland voted for it 637 to 188, whereas in 1807 Portland had voted it down 392 to 73. The separation was effected in 1820, and though many Federalists voted for it, Republicans regarded it as their special achievement.

The young boy, Henry Longfellow, mentioned here and there throughout the book, will undoubtedly have been identified by readers as the future poet, who spoke of Portland with affection in his poem "My Lost Youth," and who remembered vividly the fight between the *Boxer* and the *Enterprise*. Less clearly recognized will be the American merchant of Cadiz, Richard Meade, appearing briefly in Chapter Twelve. Encountered by Jonathan (and in reality by the privateersman George Coggeshall), he was soon to become the father of a future commander of the Army of the Potomac and Lee's great opponent at Gettysburg, General George Meade.